I0653500

Book One
Primordial Inheritance

Ashli T Silver

Colaborators:
Trisha Rogers: Editor, Cover Design, Production
Proof Read by Anna Nazario

DEDICATED TO
Harrison Paul Fidler
06.19.94 – 12.31.09

TIGGER WARNINGS
Your mental health matters

Death by Vampire

Death of a child

Death of a parent

Attempted murder

Serial Murder

Physical abuse

Sexual abuse

Dubious consent

Mild restraints

Burnt flesh

Burnt books

Blood (drinking and bleeding wounds)

Alcohol consumption

Car accident (not due to alcohol)

Detached eyeballs

Stabbing and general bodily harm by others

Self-righteous misogyny

These violent delights have violent ends
And in their triumph die, like fire and powder,
Which, as they kiss, consume.

ROMEO AND JULIET ACT II.VI

PROLOGUE

1634, England

Tap tap tap.

The parish was located down the hill from the small country church. The crumbling building of brick and stone was a sacred place where the aging priest held mass and took confession. The holy man was determined to atone for the demons he knew roamed the earth, one Hail Mary at a time.

Tap tap.

Even though it was the middle of the night, the aging clergyman shuffled to the door. One of his parishioners could need his guidance. His candle flickered as he walked, shifting in the stale air around him.

"Yes?" he asked as he pulled the door open.

"May I come inside, Father Laurence?" The voice was vaguely familiar, but the priest couldn't quite place it. Like it was from a dream that his mind couldn't hold onto in the waking hours. The figure was cloaked and stood in the darkened doorway, his face hidden in shadow and wool.

"Yes, yes. Of course." The old man shifted aside, unknowingly granting access to a demon, like the ones who plagued his nightmares.

The visitor almost glided into the small human home. Father Laurence saw a flash of pale white skin. The demon pulled the hood from his shock of red hair and spoke as the door was shut behind him. "You're looking quite rough, old friend." The visitor turned to face the priest.

He grabbed his chest, clutching it through, what he assumed was a hallucination sent by the devil. "Nicholas. It's not possible."

"Although highly improbable, I assure you the possibility

is proven with my existence in your..." he sucked his teeth, "home."

"B... but you're dead," Father Laurence stuttered.

"Yes," the one called Nicholas replied. "For decades now." His shrug of nonchalance was followed by a too graceful plop into the priest's rickety kitchen chair.

With a shaking frame, the priest rushed to the cupboard he kept near the door. Inside were relics of his faith that he hoped could save him from this hellish ghost.

"Down to the depths of hell, creature of darkness!" The priest cried, thrusting an ornate cross in front of the visitor's face.

The patronizing chuckle that burst from the demon almost reminded him of the boys they had been together.

"I cast you out, demon!" He emptied a bottle full of holy water on the monster, splattering him across the face.

"Now that was just rude." The visitor wiped his face with the back of his shirt's sleeve.

"You should be dead," the priest's voice wobbled along with his ability to remain standing.

"I think we already established, old friend, I am dead."

The priest's mind struggled, as if struck down with unbelief and fear, "You died and she...she's dead..."

"She's not supposed to be." The visitor moved with an incomprehensible speed. Before Father Laurence could even shriek in terror the demon's hand gripped his throat, shoving the old man into the wall. "You were supposed to protect her." The creature said through the fangs that slid from their sheaths inside his mouth. "But you didn't. You let her die in that fire with no one to save her."

"Nicholas..." the priest grunted out. "She..." he choked.

"And now, there's no one to save you."

The priest would have screamed if he'd had the airflow to do so. The vampire buried his fangs deep into the old man's carotid artery.

The moment Nicholas's fangs pierced Laurence's skin

the memories invaded his mind. Monotonous amounts of penance. Nicholas rolled his eyes while he drank. Self-righteous prick, even in his own mind. Laurence's memories gave themselves over to the vampire draining his life force.

Flashes of memory began to reveal the priest's darkest secrets. The evidence that he had spent his life coercing widows and manipulating altar boys to serve his own perverse, sexual pleasures. This pestilence to society had already marked himself for death through his own misdeeds. Upon his arrival, Nicholas had determined this man's fate for not doing his sworn duty and protecting *her*. His death was originally desired to satiate Nicholas's need for revenge, but now he claimed the life in vengeance for all those abused by this holy man.

Nicholas tugged at the memories, digging deeper. Doing so could tip a human into madness. But that was no matter, Laurence wouldn't live to see ten minutes from now, let alone tomorrow.

He saw them as boys, with her trailing behind them. Her smile matched his in every way as he ran from her. He saw her grieve over his death and almost pulled back, but wouldn't stop now. He saw a moment of love and then right as the heartbeats slowed, near the end of its ability to fight, Nicholas saw what he had not been searching for. A strong and fearful feeling of hatred as Laurence looked upon one who was supposed to have died. He had looked upon her living dead, immortal face with disdain.

Nicholas retracted his fangs and let the body hit the worn wooden floorboards. That couldn't be right. The proof was overwhelming. She was dead. He must have seen the old monster's nightmares. Nicholas didn't look back as he walked out the door and into the night.

CHAPTER ONE

Welcome to Aboit, Maine

Almost 400 Years Later, United States of America

Juliana Bristow raced through the darkened streets. Speed was her ally, the moonlight her friend. To the human eye, a blur of red and white. Still, she stuck to the shadows. The sleepy seaside town was slowly tucking itself in for late evening meals and prime time television. Jules had chosen Aboit, Maine for its quintessential quiet. It was peaceful and safe. Or so it was thought. In Aboit, supernatural creatures, immortals, roamed the streets in the dark.

Jules's run was fierce, rounding corners like a cheetah on the heels of its prey. Deducing a quicker route to her destination than the current path, Jules launched herself onto a nearby rooftop. Supernatural speed and agility making the distance easy. One, to the next, and then the next. Her feet moved soundlessly over the humans' heads. Each and every one none the wiser.

Perching atop the first restaurant rooftop, Jules took in the view. The marina was bustling with unsuspecting humans. The cry of seagulls pierced the air. A large bell clanged, ringing through the salty atmosphere. Taking in a deep, unnecessary breath, peace washed over her like the waves lapping against the distant pier.

Jules was jolted from her reverie as her supernatural hearing focused in on a disturbance, and a familiar voice. Searching near the gallery where they were supposed to meet, she located him. He looked to be in a standoff with another large man, not human either. A snarl was carried to her on the wind. Knowing the altercation could turn physical and easily become a bloodbath, she chose to intervene as soon as possible.

Assessing her choices, Jules peered into the darkened alley beneath. Vacant of human life, it was as good a way down as any. Landing in a puddle with a splash, Jules swore. Water covered the legs of her jeans and had drenched her white sneakers.

"What was that?" someone near the end of the alley asked.

Jules flattened herself against the stone wall.

"Probably nothing," said another.

Once they passed by, she left the alley, moving toward the busy downtown area lining the coast. At least what locals considered busy. This seaside haven was sparsely populated in the off season. Compared to the last city Jules had taken up residence in, Aboit was minuscule.

The sounds of the altercation increased. Jules moved toward it as fast as possible while still remaining inconspicuous. The light blue sweatshirt she wore concealed most of her pale, lightly freckled skin. She pulled her blue hood up over her radiant auburn hair for good measure. People still stopped to stare.

It seemed, no matter the attempts to blend into this human world, being dead made her stand out. A human friend told her once that humans looked for magic in their lives and a vampire's unearthly beauty made them feel like magic. Jules thought it was because humans craved danger, and there was nothing more dangerous than a predator who hungered for your blood.

"Excuse me," she said after bumping into an elderly woman while hurriedly weaving through the crowd.

Approaching behind Gabriel and Eileen, her coven and friends, she took in the scene. Eileen was trembling several feet behind her husband as he faced-off with a rather ginormous werewolf.

One, two, three. Seven werewolves hovering near their

beastly companion, but not one intervened or surrounded Gabriel.

The big one snarled loudly. Jules shrugged. It was no matter. They'd be dead if she wanted them to be. Gabriel retaliated in kind. What she didn't want, was the scene unfolding before her in the middle of the busiest spot in Aboit.

The werewolf charged. Gabriel met the challenge. The two crashed into one another with supernatural force. Jules rolled her eyes. Like it or not, this mess was hers to defuse or end.

Jules paused for the briefest moment next to Eileen and squeezed her hand. Eileen let out a little sigh of relief. Since the other wolves had yet to join the fray, Gabriel had likely managed to get into a brawl with the Alpha himself. The werewolf threw a full-fisted punch at Gabriel, who avoided it by using his smaller stature and sidestepping ever so slightly.

Jules took advantage of the moment and leapt directly between the two fighting men. "Enough." Her tone was stern but not loud, as she pulled the hood from her hair. Her sudden appearance caused both to pause in surprise.

Fearlessly, she stood between the two men, who towered over her tiny frame. Jules turned her full attention on Gabriel, ignoring the danger at her back for just a second. "Stand down," Jules commanded with a hiss. Her silver eyes bore into his that still held the slightest blue ring around the edges.

"Jules, move..." Gabriel said.

Jules silenced him with a glare. "Stand down." She nodded towards his wife a few steps behind him. "Go to Eileen." Gabriel didn't move but Eileen did. Gripping Gabriel's hand, she tugged him back.

Jules heard the Alpha snigger behind her. With a half-smile she turned to confront him.

"Vampire scum," the Alpha spat.

Jules raised her eyebrows. Astonished he was stupid enough to say that out loud. By now, the incident had drawn quite a crowd of spectators.

"Move, or you'll be the one to die." This time it was only

loud enough for Jules's vampire hearing to catch.

The only indication she gave that she'd heard him was a raise of one eyebrow again. "You are the Alpha, yes? According to the rules of proper engagement, you must deal with me now."

"You lead this coven?" the Alpha asked, aghast.

"I do," Jules stated evenly, stepping into a stance that exuded the position and power of her years. Resisting the urge to reach for what wasn't there, Jules's hands rested on her hips. Feeling phantom fighting knives, she no longer carried. They'd graced her hips for centuries.

Out of the corner of her eye, Jules saw the other pack members begin to encourage the crowd to disperse. Internally, she breathed a sigh of relief. Externally, no emotional shift was visible. Fewer humans meant less risk of exposure. Dealing with that on top of this inconvenient confrontation would have been truly irritating.

"You?" the Alpha mocked. "A girl...what about that male of yours?" He gestured toward Gabriel.

"Go ahead, underestimate me, it'll be fun." Her light-hearted tone was mocking. She could rip this beast apart and not think twice, but it wouldn't come to that. One bite and the venom in her fangs would kill him almost instantly.

"You're a child," he said, growling at her a bit as he said it.

"For an immortal being you seem to be unaware of how immortality works." Jules heard two of the pack member's chuckle. The Alpha's face grew red.

"Carson, it's not worth it," one of the wolves behind him said. Probably the Beta, to have spoken so freely.

The Alpha shot a glare over his shoulder. Jules followed his gaze to the one who had spoken.

He was stunning, very tall, and lean. His forest green eyes locked with hers. The moon glinted off bronzed skin. Ignoring his Alpha's glare, he ran a hand through his dark curls and chuckled once. He seemed to be appraising her as well. Her lips parted momentarily. He had features reminiscent of someone

Jules had known long ago.

"And you deal with me," the Alpha snapped, pulling her gaze free of the Beta's.

She licked her lips and refocused on the task at hand. "But he's so much prettier than you are."

"Do you want to die, bitch?" The Alpha growled.

"There you go with those pointless threats again." She sighed theatrically.

He growled in response, again.

"My coven should never have engaged you. And for that, I offer my apologies." Her tone was flat.

"Your apologies mean nothing to me," the Alpha spat. But his expression had turned smug, rather than murderous. He obviously felt like he'd won something.

"I'm sure they don't." Jules rolled her eyes. "But this altercation is over. We've coexisted in this town for years. Why stop now?"

"This town is under my protection. Your kind will never be welcome."

"Oh, so you didn't know we were already here? How embarrassing for you, as the town's protector and all."

His face reddened even farther. She knew she was exacerbating the situation. But bullying bullies was so much fun.

"You will all leave." He pointed his beefy finger at her face. "Tonight."

"No. We shall not. You see, I know that we can live in peace. I've been alive much longer than this feud has had fire to fuel it. Some of the greatest Alphas of your species advocated for peace. Like Stephen Cain. Surely, you want to follow his example."

This seemed to only anger the Alpha. "How dare you speak his name. You have no..."

"I have every right." She cut him off. Her anger the only bit of emotion she'd allow. "We were friends long before your great, great, grandparents were even conceptualized."

"Your kind assassinated him." He snapped his jaws at her like the beast he was.

"It wasn't me," she said easily, making sure any sadness was concealed well. The Alpha shook with anger.

He took another step toward her, closing the rest of the distance between them.

She craned her neck to look up at him. "Be my guest." Her tone took on a breathy air. "Expose yourself right here. Right now. Wolf or man, this is not a fight you will win." Jules prepared to strike if need be.

He growled audibly.

"Carson, enough!" The Beta called.

She glanced around the Alpha and looked the wolf all the way up and down, from his floppy hair to his Converse sneakers. *The resemblance.*

"Stay out of this, Luca," the Alpha, Carson, snarled. His face bent at an awkward angle to glare at Jules.

Jules waited, silent but very deadly.

"We've already been too exposed," Luca added, seemingly undaunted by the orders of his leader.

"Don't you see how old she is? Look at her eyes," another werewolf added.

The Alpha's eyes met hers. Solid, pure, silver. With a vampire's age came increasing strength and skill. He baulked. Fidgeting, his body language betrayed his false bravado. He was losing confidence in his ability to win against her one-on-one. As he should. "As I said, our species have coexisted in peace for years."

Long moments stretched out between the immortal creatures.

In a show of good faith Jules raised her hands palms out and took one step back, but she did not remove her stare or threat from the Alpha until he mirrored the action.

"This is not over," Carson said under his breath as he turned to walk back toward his pack.

"I didn't think it was," Jules said under hers as she took a few more steps backward, still unwilling to turn her back on the Alpha.

Her gaze caught on the Beta, Luca, one last time. He seemed to be peering into the deepest depths of time and age through the windows of her eyes. She nodded at him and he at her, neither looking away for a long moment. Then they did, going their separate ways.

Jules returned to Eileen and Gabriel, who had hovered nearby during the confrontation. "So, shall we enjoy this art show?" Jules asked, gesturing toward the art gallery down the block. Gabriel looked at her in disbelief, while Eileen was staring at her in wide-eyed wonder.

"Oh, relax, both of you."

Luca Cain looked away from the strange and beautiful creature. He'd never seen a vampire before, heard of them yes, but had never come into contact with one personally. She wasn't like the rumors suggested. Not a walking corpse at all. Although technically dead, she was definitely full of strong and fiery life.

"Luca let's go!" his best friend Kyle called.

Luca turned. It wasn't until then that he realized the pack had moved on toward the parking garage while he still stood outside the building she'd entered. He stared through the glass doors of the art gallery, watching the red-haired vampire as she chatted with the other female.

"Luca!" Kyle called again.

"Coming," Luca called back and made to follow the rest of the pack.

"So, she was hot, you know, for a dead person," Kyle said when Luca joined him. Kyle was a thirty-seven-year-old werewolf who had stopped aging in his late twenties. He was tall and lean, but shorter than Luca by a few inches. His dark hair hung to his shoulders when it wasn't pulled back.

"Have you ever seen one before?" Luca asked him as they

walked a few paces behind the rest. Luca was in his eighties, yet he looked to be a few years younger than Kyle.

"A couple of them," Kyle said, "but none as hot as that."

"You two need to cut that out before Carson hears you," Ben said, falling back to reprimand them. Ben was yet another member of Carson's inner circle. He looked to be in his early thirties, but Luca didn't know how old he really was. *Old, like really old.* "Vampires may look enticing boys, but remember they are soulless, immoral beings. Trust me, I've known the worst of them in my years."

Kyle shrugged, and Luca nodded. Ben had a lot more life experience than either of them. He probably knew what he was talking about. Ben patted Luca on the shoulder and then moved back toward the front of the group.

"Cover for me?" Kyle asked when they'd reached the side-by-side parking spots that contained Kyle's sleek motorcycle and Luca's soft-top Jeep.

"Don't I always?" Luca asked rhetorically.

"Yep. I don't know why you put up with me," Kyle commented playfully.

Luca laughed.

With a wink Kyle hopped on his motorcycle, leaving to go see his biggest secret.

Luca unclipped and pushed the top back on the Jeep as the other pack members started to pull out of the lot themselves. He always preferred the top-down drive when the weather was favorable. His route took him straight through the town's center. The smell of the sea surrounded him as his drive paralleled the coast. The balmy air blowing his hair wildly.

Luca loved this town. But he was seeing none of that this time. Luca's mind was racing as he processed the events that had transpired. Or rather, as he thought about the fiery, petite, stunning, dead, vampire coven leader. There was something about her. Something he'd felt. He was curious about her, and he couldn't figure out why.

Once Luca got back to the place he tentatively called home,

he pulled past the cars belonging to various Den members and parked his Jeep on the side of the house, under his bedroom window. The Den was a six-bedroom, three-bathroom, two-story crap pile on the far side of town. In which, Carson crammed the six members of his inner circle. Luca and Kyle included.

Luca looked up at his closed, second-story window forlornly. Sometimes, he preferred to jump directly into his room, rather than deal with the chaos that was life at the Den. Luca sighed and walked through the yard to the front door. On his way, he passed one of the two shutters remaining on the front of the house and ran a finger along the chipped, white paint. As he entered, the front screen door squeaked and banged shut behind him.

"Luca," Carson called as he walked quickly past the family room.

Luca backed up a few steps without turning around.

"Where's Kyle?"

"He went for a run," Luca lied easily.

"Are you sure?" Carson asked, one eyebrow raised.

"Yep." Luca nodded and then moved down the hall before Carson could ask him any more questions.

Kyle flew through town toward her home, the wind roaring all around him. He came to a speedy stop in front of the old apartment building, just in time to see the love of his life walk from her family's apartment. Her older brother, Adam, followed closely behind.

"Dad doesn't always know what's best Adam!" she shouted when he grabbed her arm, spinning her around.

"Neither do you!" He shouted back.

Kyle turned off the ignition and dismounted but kept his distance. Relaxing against his motorcycle, content to wait for the fight to fizzle out.

"Why is he here?" Adam questioned, catching sight of

Kyle.

"Kyle's a part of my life, Adam. Deal with it." Hayley pulled her arm free and turned away from her brother.

"Dad's not going to like this!" Adam shouted after her, shoving his hands into his pockets and storming back inside the apartment.

Hayley ignored him as she reached the motorcycle.

"Do you two ever get along?" Kyle asked, wrapping her in his arms and pulling her into him.

"We have our moments." She smiled at Kyle in a way that suggested her brother and their quarrel were no longer on her mind.

"Hello, wife." He smiled and ran one hand through her long, brown, sun kissed, hair.

"Hi, husband."

He bent down slightly and met her in a kiss. Hayley was all tone curves, full breasts, and rare beauty.

A few weeks back, Kyle had done something that, when discovered, would not be easily forgiven. Kyle had whisked Hayley Reynolds, now Hayley Reynolds-Cooper, off to Las Vegas and married her. The marriage was legal by the United States standards, of course. However, pack laws were quite different. When the Alpha of your pack had his eye on a mate, marrying her was severely looked down upon. A little over a month ago, Carson had demanded that Hayley's father grant him his daughter's hand in marriage. Mr. Reynolds had not immediately complied, but Kyle would not take the risk that he would relent; damn the consequences.

Their kiss deepened, Hayley fisted his hair, while his hands slid from her waist to her muscled ass.

"Get a room," another one of Hayley's brothers, younger and still attending Aboit High, commented as he walked past them.

"Good to see you too Landon!" Kyle called after him.

He waved once but didn't turn around.

"Let's go somewhere we can be alone," Hayley whispered.

"I had an idea about that," he whispered back, rubbing his nose softly against hers.

Carson growled and resumed his pacing. Having Luca as his Beta was truly a pain in the ass, but it was Luca's birthright. Not only had he been in line to inherit his father's pack before they were massacred, but he was a descendant of Stephen Cain's family line. Those facts alone gave Carson no choice as to who his Beta had to be. The fact that he couldn't entirely trust Luca was an annoyance that had to be swallowed.

As Carson paced, his anger only grew. Of course, Carson knew that there were a few vampires in Aboit. But until now, they had seemed to understand that this was his town. They had certainly never challenged him before.

Defiance could not be tolerated; humiliation even less. The little vampire bitch had damaged his reputation with his pack. How could the pack trust him if they saw this weakness in him? Something needed to be done to repair the damage that tiny, dead girl had inflicted. The vampires needed to be dealt with.

"I am not fond of vampires," Ben complained as he joined Carson in the common room.

Ben was one of the only pack members that didn't make it a point of avoiding him when he was angry. Carson saw value in that. "Yes Ben, something must be done," Carson said, with fury in his voice and conviction in his heart.

CHAPTER TWO

Phantoms of Past and Death

Jules slowed to a walk as she approached a quiet street directly next to the sea. Four houses down sat her own little home. Parked in the driveway was the small, silver, car that had been neglected in favor of running to the art gallery. A cobblestone path led toward green siding, white trim, rounded storybook windows, and stone arch over the door. Over the four centuries of her existence, Jules had lived in a lot of places she'd called home. This one was one of her favorites.

Her first hundred years as a vampire had been spent in extravagance and indulgence. She'd lived on an English estate, in a grand manor, which housed the oldest coven in existence. In the century that followed, she roamed and killed aimlessly, until Gabriel. With him, came an existence of family, one as strong as her human one had been, though they'd remained platonic throughout. It had only been in the last few decades, since Eileen's arrival, that Jules had finally understood the beauty and solitude of living alone.

The porch step creaked under her feet, adding to its character. The darkened house greeted her gently. Neglecting to turn on any lights she walked past her living spaces and into her bedroom near the back.

Walking to the far side of the room, she opened the French doors, stripped off her sweatshirt and jeans, pushed back her covers, and dropped gracefully onto her mattress. Memory foam was a brilliant invention.

Flicking on the Tiffany lamp on the bedside table, Jules picked up her current smutty fantasy novel she kept next to the bed, and started to read. Many a night passed this way in recent years. Just a few more hours before she had to resume her current life as a modern-day American.

The sound of the waves crashing and the words of escapism had her shifting, shaking her head a little as she felt herself drifting sleepily. Setting down the book, she pulled her soft feather blanket up and slipped into sleep.

Jules tossed, unprepared for her past to haunt her dreams this night, and yet he returned with a vengeance like he always did. Waves of familiarity crashed into her as she stood at the entrance to an opulent ballroom. Inside, candle light and haunting music set the mood as couples moved across the dance floor. They were all iridescent ghosts floating around the ballroom. Beings she once loved floated amongst the dancers. Gwendolyn, a primordial vampire, one of the first of their kind, dressed as a ghostly bride, a long veil covering her delicate features. Stephen, her werewolf husband, a gaping hole in his chest, blood draining out over his white, linen shirt. "Help me, Juliana." His voice was tinny, not fully recognizable.

"Hello, my pet," a familiar voice crooned as he slipped a hand around her throat from behind.

Jules thrashed in her sleep. *Not this.*

He turned her as his grip tightened. His other hand threaded in her hair and yanked, forcing her to look up into his malice filled eyes. His face was the one she dreaded most. The monster of her own nightmares. The hand around her throat squeezed even tighter. Her body recoiled on the mattress like she could feel the physical pain he caused. He was not faded, a memory bathed in time, but a fully corporeal nightmare. Every cruelty, every feature as vivid as if he were standing before her. An accustomed, cold, smile shown on his primordial lips. "You are mine, Juliana."

"No," the dream version of her said.

"You will always be mine."

Hector's hand connected with her face yet again as the dream shifted. The back of her head slammed into the wall as he threw her.

Crumpled on the ground, her eyes opened to the bloodied and lifeless body of her friend lying on the riverbank in front of her. "Juliana, help me," called the distorted and rotting corpse of Stephen Cain.

Startled awake, Jules sat up in bed. She wiped her matted hair from her face and took a few deep breaths. A human reaction to steady the nerves, but still relatively effective. Jules swallowed, her throat dry.

Attempting to shake free of the nightmare, Jules pushed back the covers and walked to her sparsely stocked kitchen. In this area of the home, her own need was extremely specific. Pulling one of her few glasses from the cupboard, she squinted as she opened the refrigerator to retrieve a bag of blood with the hospital's tag still on it. Only a few were stored here from her last raid on the local blood bank. Gabriel kept most of the stock at his home to protect it from Jules's addiction to the consumption of it.

Ripping the bag open with her teeth, she poured its contents into the glass. The empty bag was discarded in the sink, and then she walked to her tiny living room. Jules settled into her favorite floral and filigreed chair that was in fact from times past. The room was cluttered, but only with books that no longer fit on one of her six over stuffed bookshelves. The furniture was outdated in the best way. A large television hung across from the blue velvet, claw-foot couch. Picking up the remote she put on some news channel for mindless chatter as she sipped from her glass.

For a moment, Jules thought of nothing but the liquid seeping into her tissues as she drank. Everything inside her was consumed by the quenching of her thirst. She drained the rest of the blood in a few gulps. The ecstasy and rejuvenation that blood brought to her erased the pain of her nightmare. But not the lingering sting of his presence.

Her now crimson-colored eyes blinked as she regained her composure. Jules set the blood-stained glass down on her wooden coffee table and sunk back into her chair. Dreams of him had been dormant for so long, it unsettled her that they'd surfaced once more. Seeing the Beta may have caused it, he did resemble Stephen Cain, although his stature was off.

Her thoughts drifted to her life before the English coven had taken her in. It was a time when humans greatly feared but believed in such superstitions as vampires. They were considered demons on earth, and she had just become one of them.

Once the physical pain of her death had receded, her heart stopped beating. The change from human to demon complete. Desperately seeking solace, she'd run faster than she'd ever thought possible to her fiancé, Laurence; ever her rock and protection. After being invited into his home, she'd told him what had happened. Hoping he would try to see past her demon face and into her heart. Instead, he'd cursed her and cast her out.

She'd run from Laurence's cottage, straight into the arms of her primordial abuser. He had taken her to his home, to his coven at Pelmoore Manor. His sister, Gwendolyn, was as sweet as she was mad. The werewolf Gwendolyn had loved against all odds. Stephen had saved Jules's life in more ways than one.

Hector had broken her down to nothing. To worthlessness. It was only with Stephen's death that she'd escaped him. Jules could feel the bitterness overtaking her. That night still haunted her, the one down by the river. The night of Stephen's death.

If only he hadn't been walking alone. Out of jealousy and greed Hector had ended Stephen's life that night, but he hadn't stopped there. He'd torn him apart bit by bit and sent the pieces to the neighboring werewolf packs. Instead of disheartening the werewolves as Hector had intended, this whipped the packs into a frenzy. They retaliated. Both sides lost many lives. Hector wanted war, and he'd gotten it.

Jules felt a single, thick, blood-tear escape her right eye and slide down her cheek. Shaking herself free of her thoughts yet again, she wiped under her eye. The back of her hand came away smeared with blood.

The Manor and all those within were no longer a part of her existence. They hadn't been for centuries. Jules tried to focus on what the late-night newscaster was ranting about; some string of murders in Fort Miles, a large city not far from Aboit.

Nicholas's lack of self-control was his greatest weakness. The Phantom Killer is what they were calling him now, and this alone proved it was true. He should move on from this city and become a new city's nightmare. And yet, something told him to stay.

He didn't set out to murder people, he never did. There were hundreds of humans around him every night who lived to see another day. The unfortunate few that didn't were the inevitable sacrifice made to satisfy his thirst for blood.

He was a vampire, and lived in a way that being a vampire suggested. Vampires who didn't give in to the hunt, who refused themselves the ecstasy that only came from draining warm, fresh, pulsing human blood did exist. He, however, couldn't comprehend the reasoning behind this choice. Not to kill humans he supposed. Many could drink from the source without killing the host. Once in a while, he wished that level of self-control wasn't beyond him. But the thought was always a fleeting one. He was only vampire, after all.

As Nick walked the city streets, on his way to the home of a lover he'd taken to fill the night hours, a couple of drunken college kids fell from a bar and stumbled down the sidewalk in front of him. He moved past them without contemplating it further. A mother and her young child waited on a bus. He left them there. A gentleman late into his allotted years bumped into him. He righted the man and walked on.

Almost to his destination he smelled it. The unmistakable scent of fresh, human blood. Like a shark in an ocean of people, he stalked toward it. His throat began to dry. His nose began to burn. Closer and closer to the source he closed in. The distinct dripping pounded in his ears. It wasn't far now. Unable to continue at his slow pace, he closed the distance between him and the dripping blood in moments.

In a blur, he was in the alley. There, just past a big angry-looking man, was his prey. The large man who had obviously let the blood out of its human vessel fell at his feet, his neck broken, bloody knife clattering to the pavement. Nick didn't register the face of his prey, all he saw was the trail of blood running down her neck and into her cleavage. She whimpered only once more before his fangs were in her throat. He drank. One last scream faded across the open alley as she fell into her killer's arms. With each passing second, the thirst inside him was satiated. The intoxicating smell of fresh blood diminished as he consumed it.

"Let go of the girl!" a low voice said from behind him.

When the body was empty of every last ounce of blood, he pulled his fangs out of her cold, dead neck and licked the last drop off his bottom lip.

"Get your hands in the air, vampire," the voice growled.

Releasing the now empty vessel, the body fell to the alley floor with another thud. Raising his arms, he turned toward the interrupting voice. It only took a moment more to grasp the reality of the situation. "Really?" he said. "A gun, wolfficer? What is a gun going to do to me exactly?" he asked the werewolf officer of the law.

The brawny man flinched, realizing his fatal mistake.

"Too slow." Nick rushed forward with vampire speed. In less than a second, he'd overpowered the officer, hand buried deep in the werewolf's chest. The officer strained to look back at his cop-mobile.

"Run!" the werewolf shouted at the same time that his heart was ripped from his chest. The body fell just as the passenger door of the car opened, and a teenage boy ran for his life.

Luca woke abruptly as a door slammed and someone yelled, "Get the hell out of this house!" Carson was roaring in anger about something or another, again. Luca rolled over and closed his eyes, content to ignore this rather regular occurrence.

"She was never yours, you bigoted brute," Kyle shouted back, apparently finding a shred of defiance deep inside himself and acting on it.

Luca's eyes opened sluggishly.

There was a sound that meant one of them had gotten punched. Luca assumed that the soon to be bruised one was Kyle.

Sitting up, Luca tried to shake himself awake and untangle himself from the twisted bedsheets. He wobbled as he stood, kicking at the sweat drenched fabric still clinging to him. Once free of his linen confines Luca pulled on shorts and moved to the door. He met Kyle on his way up the stairs. As expected, Kyle's lip was bleeding.

"Did you know about this?" Carson shouted, upon seeing Luca at the top of the stairs.

"Nope," Luca lied and followed Kyle to his room.

Kyle started haphazardly shoving his belongings in one of three large duffle bags he pulled from his closet. Luca stopped at the door and watched.

"Hayley's brother told him," Kyle explained, without turning around.

"Which one?" Luca asked referencing Hayley's many brothers.

"How should I know?" Kyle snapped as he continued.

"Probably Adam," Luca said.

"Probably."

"Where will you go?" Luca leaned against the doorframe and yawned.

"I've got a place," Kyle said, then smiled mischievously.

"You didn't think I was gonna stay in this frat house forever, did you? I'm a married man."

Luca shrugged. He'd moved into the Den around ten years ago, Kyle had been here before that. Kyle leaving after he and Hayley had tied the knot hadn't really occurred to him.

"Come by the apartment later," Kyle said, picking up bag after bag, slinging each one over his shoulders. He looked like an overstuffed pack-mule as he walked toward the door. "It's on the floor above Hayley's parents."

"I bet they'll love that," Luca joked.

"We're married now," Kyle said. "They'll get over it."

"You're sure?" Luca asked, rubbing his eyes, still feeling a bit groggy.

"Ehhh," Kyle waved his hand in a swiveling motion to indicate that the real answer was maybe. "Can I borrow the Jeep?" Kyle asked, looking down at his belongings.

The image of Kyle trying to get himself and three large bags balanced on a motorcycle came to mind. Luca chuckled.

Kyle shifted until he could dig the keys to his motorcycle out of his pocket.

"I'll bring it by Hayley's later." Luca caught the keys when they came flying toward him.

"It's my place too," Kyle chided.

Luca made a face.

"You're right, it's Hayley's." Kyle conceded. Despite being thrown out of the house he'd lived in for over a decade, Kyle was in good spirits. Of course, he was generally in good spirits. It was just in his nature. "Throw down the Jeep keys," Kyle requested as he thudded down the stairs.

Luca walked back to his room. His bedroom was the largest room in the house, the master suite. It was a fair bribe for someone with Luca's lineage to become Carson's Beta, instead of putting forth the challenge for Alpha. At first, Luca had laughed it off, but now he was thankful for the space to escape.

Shutting the door behind him, he searched through clean and dirty clothes and clutter until he found where the keys had been dropped the night before. Housekeeping wasn't Luca's strong suit. Luca opened the window and tossed the Jeep keys into Kyle's outstretched hand.

"Be careful with my Jeep."

"Don't crash my baby," Kyle called back, looking forlornly toward the driveway and his motorcycle.

Luca laughed and pulled his window back down, turning to prepare for the day.

Jules was unable to resume sleeping after the night's dreams. She had read a few more chapters and then dressed for work early. Deciding to take a stroll down her street before sunrise.

She'd chosen this street for its ambiance. The cottages that lined the rocky coast were homey and individualized, but often vacant this time of year. Jules struggled to understand the vacation home mentality, seeing the waves crashing on the rocks from her back porch was her favorite part. It always felt like she was chasing a peace she would never find, like the waves chasing the shore.

As the time for her to leave for work approached, she walked back to her own house and started her car. It was still dark out during the few minutes' drive to the coffee shop she frequented. Not because the dead drank coffee, but because her best, human friend worked the early shift most days.

Per-usual, the coffee house was relatively empty inside while the drive-through was a mass of honking cars and impatient drivers. Jules saw Monica handing the same old man his coffee order. "Is there anything else I can get you, Mr. Boyer?"

"What do you think?" he snapped grumpily.

Monica smiled regardless and wished him a good day. Jules approached the counter as Mr. Boyer made his way back to his usual little table.

"Does he ever go home?" Jules whispered to Monica once

she was close enough to keep from being overheard.

"Yes, between ten and noon," Monica said and they both giggled.

Monica was several inches taller than Jules, with caramel skin, and brown, curly hair that she let grow down past her shoulders. Monica had graduated the year previous, before Jules started working at the school, and was in the middle of a gap year, which she'd promised her parents would be used to think about her future. Jules suspected it had more to do with the fact that her boyfriend, Tai, was taking classes at the local community college so he could save money and continue helping his parents with their family restaurant.

Jules knew that Monica planned on going to college but wanted to wait for Tai to finish his first couple of years, so they could take on the adventure of moving across the country together. Monica had her whole life planned out, down to the year and moment she wanted Tai to propose. Always put together, looking immaculate even serving coffee. If life worked out for anyone, it would be Monica. Life rarely worked out how one planned, but she hoped in Monica's case it would.

Monica picked up the forty-ounce tumbler she always carried and walked out from behind the counter. "I'm taking ten," she called to her co-worker, who was in the back.

"Okay!" they shouted in return.

"Are you still coming over tonight?" Monica asked.

Jules nodded as they sat down at their usual table.

"Good. How was your night? Mine was fine. Tai and I just hung out with my family. I got into a fight with Ethan because he didn't knock first, and Tai and I were making out. Thank God that's all he saw. So, what about you? Anything eventful happen last night?"

Jules smiled. The number of words Monica could get out in one breath was almost inhuman. "Actually, yes." Jules lowered her voice. "Gabriel, Eileen, and I had a run-in with a pack of wolves."

"Did anything dramatic happen? I mean, to be honest, we

both knew that was going to happen eventually. But what do you mean 'a run in'? How many were there?" Monica waved her white and silver sparkle acrylic nails for emphasis.

Jules just smiled and waited for Monica to take a breath. Monica had a familiar comfort about her. They possessed the ease of interaction that naturally developed out of a deep and honest friendship. Jules had had a few human friends over the years, but Monica Martin was different. She knew what Jules and her coven were. To Jules's surprise, she'd guessed about a year after they'd become friends. Jules couldn't understand Monica's acceptance of vampirism and everything that came with it. She was relieved that she showed no signs of wanting to be turned into one. Monica's life plan required that she keep her heart beating.

"How'd Mr. Prentiss take it?"

Jules simply made a face at her.

"That bad, huh?" Monica asked. Gabriel had been Monica's English teacher sophomore year. She knew him personally now, through Jules, but couldn't seem to stop calling him 'Mr. Prentiss'. Even after she'd graduated high school.

"He, umm, got into a fistfight with the Alpha," Jules said.

Monica looked at Jules, shock on her face.

Before Monica could ask, Jules said, "don't worry. I took care of it."

"Wow. I mean, I'm glad it wasn't worse, I guess," Monica replied. "With what happened to Eileen, I'd have guessed he would've bitten one of them, right then and there."

Just then, Monica's phone beeped. She pulled it from her pocket to check the text. A happy smile appeared on her face as she returned it. Jules thought it was likely from Tai. "Oh, I have to get back," Monica said standing.

"See you after work," Jules said, standing too.

"Jules, I almost forgot," Monica stopped and spun toward her again. "You know how Saturday is Tai and my two-year anniversary, right?"

Monica had mentioned it on more than a few occasions, so

yes, Jules knew. She nodded.

"Well, Tai kind of forgot. He made plans with a friend."

"Anyone I know?" Jules asked.

"Probably not, he works at the restaurant. Anyway, Tai was wondering what you were doing on Saturday night."

"Monica. No," Jules said, taken aback. She knew what Monica was asking. She also knew that it was a very bad idea. "Can't Tai just change his plans to another night?" Jules didn't like the idea of any form of romantic connection with a human. Not even a blind date. Not even once.

"I asked that, and he suggested that you should come with us instead."

"Monica, you know I don't get involved with humans." Jules looked at her friend seriously.

"You don't get involved with anyone."

Jules made a face.

"Of course I know why you avoid involvement with humans. But Tai doesn't. I couldn't exactly say 'yeah, she can't. She might drain him before dessert', could I?"

Jules chose not to respond to that one.

"Come on, Jules. You're my best friend. Please don't make me lie to Tai any more than I already am," Monica begged, sticking out her lower lip.

Jules contemplated this. She would only have Monica for as long as one lifetime allowed. So, she offered up a long, aggravated sigh and relented. She could handle one night of small talk with a human boy.

"Thanks. You're the best!" Monica grinned widely. "It'll be fun."

"It had better not be," Jules retorted as she left the small coffee shop.

Kyle parked the Jeep in front of the two-story apartment building, grabbed two of his three bags, and headed toward the shabby structure. Some of Hayley's younger siblings were out front. They were all piling into the family vehicle, heading across town for school.

"Hayley inside?" he asked Landon, who was climbing into the driver's seat.

"Not that I know of," he replied, without making eye contact with Kyle.

Kyle shrugged and hauled both his bags inside the building.

"Seriously dude." Adam stopped Kyle just outside his parents' doorway.

Kyle couldn't resist. He dropped both bags with a loud thud and punched Adam square on the jaw.

"What the hell was that for!" Adam shouted.

Kyle ignored him, picked up his bags again, and walked up the stairs toward his new home. The apartment door was standing open.

"Honey, I'm home," Kyle called as he walked into the new living room. It was furnished with hand-me-downs and thrift shop finds. He'd spent the last week acquiring the furnishings as a surprise for Hayley. It was already feeling more like home than the Den ever had.

"Yes, you are," Hayley said, walking from the bedroom. Kyle dropped both bags on the floor and opened his arms for her. She ran at him. Long legs wrapped around his waist as he lifted her off her feet and kissed her. Hayley Reynolds-Cooper was average height, shapely, strong, opinionated, and adventurous. Everything he'd ever wanted in a spouse. Yes, she was young, in her early twenties, but being raised with so many siblings had caused her to mature quickly.

"Just adorable."

Still holding Hayley off the ground, Kyle turned toward the person who'd commented on their couple-cuteness.

Hayley's little sister, Amy, continued, "I'm done organizing the bathroom."

A horn honked outside.

"I think your ride is leaving," Kyle told her.

Amy swore and ran out the door and down the stairs.

"Alone at last," Kyle commented, looking down at Hayley and pecking her on the lips. "Are you ready to start our life together Mrs. Reynolds-Cooper?"

"Yes," she said as he put her back on her feet. "As soon as you put all that crap where it belongs. As in, not on the living room floor." She pointed at the bags he'd dropped.

Kyle rolled his eyes.

"Is there more?" she asked, tapping him on the chest.

"Yeah, downstairs in Luca's Jeep."

"I'll get it. You unpack." Smiling, Hayley pulled the keys from his back pocket, smacked his backside, and walked from the room to bring up his last bag. Kyle watched her go. He was finally home.

Jules reached Aboit High and pulled in to a parking spot marked for staff. The sun had risen fully during the short drive. She put on her dark sunglasses and grabbed her large black umbrella from under the passenger seat of her car. Cracking the door open she stuck the umbrella out of the top, like someone desperately trying not to get rained on. Quickly, she jogged toward the building, trying to slip inside without being spotted. Once through the glass double doors, she stowed both in her tote bag. The guards against the sun did their job well. Between the umbrella, sunglasses, long jacket, and tall boots, she had barely begun to sizzle. Her knees were a little worse for wear, but her quick healing had her back in perfect shape in just a few seconds.

Jules walked down the darkened hall, greeting her co-workers as she went. When she reached Gabriel's classroom, she pushed the door open without knocking.

Ever the safety-first type, he'd of course arrived early and had all of the blinds tightly closed. He sat hunched over his desk, blonde hair falling in his eyes.

"Lunch today, my office?" she asked.

"If I get these papers graded, sure," he replied, sifting through the tall stack in front of him.

"Do you want me to grade some for you?"

"No!"

"Just thought I'd ask," she teased, letting the door close behind her and heading to her own work area.

Reaching the far side of the quiet building she walked through the darkened library to her small office in the back corner. After pulling her hair back in a tight bun and reaching into her bag for her prescription-less glasses, her transformation was complete. This, along with a cardigan, pleated skirt, and a change into kitten heels, was all part of the act. Like Clark Kent, she was a master at hiding what she truly was.

Although, instead of concealing superpowers from another planet, she was pretending that she hadn't died at seventeen, and didn't have the natural desire to drink the student's blood.

CHAPTER THREE

The Librarian Drinks Blood

J ules's transformation complete, she moved into the library itself and flipped on the light. Slowly walking through the stacks of books, straightening as she went. At the far end was the computer area. One by one she pushed the power button on the machines, each one humming to life in canon. She'd only had this job this past school year. Gabriel loved his job as a teacher at this school so much that Jules had decided to try her hand at joining the community as well.

As the students began arriving for the day, voices rose and lockers started to slam out in the hall. The clock on the wall ticked closer and closer to the first morning bell. Her Monday morning, student-aid would be arriving any moment. Just as she moved behind her rounded desk in the middle of the small library, he did so.

"Good morning, Ethan," she greeted as Monica's fourteen-year-old brother walked through the door. He was one of the shorter boys in the freshman class, but Jules figured he'd be tall someday soon. His whole family was. Ethan's features were nearly identical to that of his sister, save for the light blue eyes he'd gotten from his father.

"You're dressed like my mother," he said in response and tossed his backpack onto her desk. Then he plopped into one of the nearby study chairs, his head dropping onto the round table in front of him.

"Not true," Jules said. "Your mother dresses way better than I do."

Ethan rolled his eyes. "I got to level twenty-six last night," he said, yawning.

"You wouldn't be so sleepy if you didn't stay up all night with a gaming controller in your hands." She flicked on her computer screen and started browsing her work emails.

"Hey, sometimes I do sleep… with a gaming controller in my hand."

She smiled over at the boy who had become like a little brother to her in recent years. She'd spent a fair amount of time with Monica's family, and had gotten to know them all accordingly.

Ethan yawned again, his blue eyes droopy from lack of sleep.

"You shouldn't stay up so late."

"Thanks, mom."

She chuckled.

"Miss Bristow."

Jules looked up from her computer to see a young girl standing in front of her.

"Can you help me find…" she looked down at a paper in her hand. "Something on the suffragette movement?"

Jules chuckled at the inaccuracy. "Let me look." She typed in variations on the desired subject matter to find what books they currently had available. Satisfied with what was found, she pulled a piece of scrap paper from the pile and jotted down some numbers and titles. Pausing, she blinked at the paper. The section these books were in, *of course*, was the one spot in the small library Jules couldn't get to during a sunny day. Even looking at it burned her eyes. It gave her a bad headache, if she looked at the rays on the carpet long enough it would blind her.

Jules handed the scrap paper to the student. "Ethan can walk you over."

"Oh, come on!" Ethan exclaimed.

"You volunteered to work here, didn't you?" she asked as he reluctantly stood up.

"Yeah, because I thought I wouldn't have to do anything for the first hour of school." He took the paper from his classmate and studied the numbers on it.

"You're not that special." Jules winked at him, and he scowled.

"You sure you don't want to just look this up online?" he asked the girl standing in front of him.

"One paper source." Her tone was as whiny as his had been moments ago.

"You have Mr. Prentiss too, don't you?"

"Yup."

Luca had just gotten out of the shower when the banging on his door began. "Carson wants everyone downstairs."

Luca didn't respond to the demand. He could guess what this was going to be about.

"There's coffee in it for you!" yelled Ben.

"Okay!" Luca shouted back through the closed door. Annoyed, he grabbed some clothes off his closet floor and pulled them over his dripping body.

Down stairs he was immediately cornered by Carson. "You knew about Kyle's betrayal, didn't you?" Carson's tone didn't really have a question in it.

"No," Luca said flatly and walked past him into the Den's musty family room. Grateful for his status, it made the lie an easy one. He plopped onto the couch beside Ben, who handed him a steaming cup of coffee.

"Thanks," he said, taking a long drink of the hot liquid.

"Caffeine makes the world go 'round," Ben commented, drinking from his own mug.

Luca nodded.

"Anyone seen Kip this morning?" Carson growled angrily. Kip was the tallest, brawniest wolf that Luca had ever met. He was also notorious for charming women; werewolves and humans alike.

"Kip's not here," Max told him as he entered the room. Max was a Den member that looked to be just out of high school but was actually close to forty. "He had a date last night."

"Typical," Carson snapped and turned to address the Den members who were present and accounted for.

Jules retreated to her office at her normal break time. Shutting the door behind her and pulling the blind down over the glass window that looked out into the library. Reaching into the mug that was repurposed as a pen holder on her desk, her fingers dug around until they gripped the key to the lock fastened over her mini refrigerator door. When asked about the strange practice she'd told the principle it was due to an unfortunate paranoia concerning the things she ate. This was just another lie necessary to conceal what she really was.

Checking over her shoulder to ensure the door had been properly locked, she pulled out one of the blood bags, grabbed an opaque tumbler off her desk, and filled it with the red liquid. The sound of footsteps froze her in place.

"It's me," Gabriel called from the other side of the door. Jules grabbed a second blood bag and walked over to let Gabriel in. Behind him, several sniggering girls huddled close to her current student-aid.

"I swear they think we're having an affair," Gabriel said, chuckling as he shut the door behind him. He pulled out his own travel mug and filled it with the contents of the bag Jules had retrieved for him.

"Teenagers have wild imaginations," Jules said as she slid back into her desk chair. Gabriel gracefully sat in the chair opposite her.

"And we are lucky they do. Those imaginations tend to create much more interesting explanations for our abnormalities than we could ever concoct ourselves."

"Yes, like me... in a relationship," Jules said with a snicker. After her last disaster of a relationship, she'd never opened herself up to another. Three hundred years of romantic avoidance and going strong.

Finally, Jules placed the tumbler straw against her lips and drank, sipping it at first and then taking several long gulps. Her eyes closed as blood flowed into her very being, awakening her; giving her unnatural strength and unending life. The blood coursed through her like a drug. She craved it. Needed it. One more big gulp and a slurp and it was gone.

Dropping her tumbler to her desk Jules looked over at Gabriel, who had continued to sip from his cup slowly, little by little. His eyes, as red as hers, were still calm and steady as he always was. During the civil war she'd plucked the new vampire fresh off the battle field and taken him under her wing. She taught him about what he was and he'd taught her control. He'd been her tether, her rock ever since.

Gabriel tapped his finger to his mouth, indicating that she had a little something left on her lips.

"Thanks," Jules said, licking her plump bottom lip. A spark of envy surged through her as he took another small sip. She was never able to master that level of control over her baser need for human blood.

Gabriel philosophized that by denying himself the experience of the kill from the beginning of his vampire life, he was able to maintain complete control. Jules suspected that, like humans, some vampires naturally possessed more control over their addictions than others.

"By the way," Jules began when she could think of something other than the blood again, "I can't come with you Saturday night. I told Monica I'd go on a double date. Her and Tai and a friend of his…"

"A human friend? Really Jules?"

"It's for Monica," Jules explained.

"But you just said yourself that you don't do romantic relationships." Gabriel looked incredulous, if not judgmental.

"It's not my romantic relationship I'm celebrating, it's Monica's. Besides, it's just one blind date."

"I don't know Jules."

"I am aware that it's not the best idea. But it's important to Monica, so I'm going."

"I don't think it's a good idea."

"Well, I don't think fighting with a werewolf Alpha in the middle of the town is a good idea, but that didn't stop you," she retorted.

He looked sheepish. "Sorry about that."

Luca arrived at Kyle's apartment around mid-day. The front door was open and there was shouting coming from inside. *They've been married, what, a week,* he thought to himself. "Knock, knock," he said aloud.

"Luca. Come in," Hayley said, spinning toward the door. "Please tell him he's an idiot." She turned back to scowl at her new husband.

Luca complied.

"Ha ha ha," Kyle grumbled, but his mood seemed to be lightening already. He wasn't one to hold onto an argument. "Preserve tonight?" Kyle asked as Luca sat in an armchair while Hayley plopped onto the couch next to her husband. She took his hand, all remnants of the fight seemingly forgotten.

"I can't tonight," Luca said. "I'm working. Keys please." He held Kyle's motorcycle keys out toward him.

"On the hook by the door." Hayley pointed.

Luca stood to retrieve them, hanging Kyle's keys where his had been.

"Are *you* at least gonna go running with me tonight?" Kyle asked Hayley, while he played with a strand of her hair.

"Nope." Hayley made a face. "I promised my parents I'd babysit."

"Come on people," Kyle began, "first I get thrown out of the Den and now you two are abandoning me?" Kyle scowled.

Luca shrugged and took to looking around the small living room while the two of them conversed. It was charming, in a somewhat shabby way that worked for the couple well. Luca even recognized his old desk chair in the corner, the one he'd replaced because it wobbled whenever he sat.

"You could help me with my siblings," Hayley suggested.

"Your Dad won't throw me out?"

"Eh. If he doesn't, Adam and Landon probably will," Hayley said, smiling playfully. "Nice going, punching Adam when Landon's the one who reported us. Now they're both mad at you."

Kyle shrugged. "What can I say? I don't burn bridges babe." Kyle smiled back. "I load them with dynamite and get the hell out of there."

"Yes, you do," Hayley said, leaning toward him like she was going to kiss him and then backed up quickly.

"Hey!" Kyle complained.

"What? I'm late getting downstairs already," she teased. She then jumped off the couch and headed for the door. "Great to see you, Luca. You're welcome anytime," she said before disappearing through it.

"Almost anytime," Kyle amended matter-of-factly.

Nick kissed his place-holder of a lover on the mouth and then left his place of residence. He was thirsty. Yes, Chad was human, but Nick didn't drink from his lovers. Having their memories clogging up his brain was far too messy. Besides, they were always madly in love with him, and he didn't have space for that. Love was across the sea somewhere, not in this backwater city in Maine.

Tonight, anyone was fair game. Well not everyone. The blood of the elderly ran too slow and was often full of too much regret. *Too young.* He thought to himself, spotting a human who'd not yet reached maturity. "Too smelly," he said after taking a whiff of a passerby. Nick swallowed, his throat scratchy.

He spotted a stunning college age girl. Beautiful brown skin and luscious curls of hair he could twine his fingers in. She walked alone and had headphones in her ears. She'd never even notice him coming. He sped up a little and directed himself onto a collision course.

He crashed into her, knocking her phone to the pavement below. He mumbled a sorry and continued on his way. He'd chosen his prey, she smelled of jasmine and honey.

Doubling back, he locked onto her and followed. Waiting for her to duck too close to a side street or turn a convenient corner.

He saw his moment when she went down a small alley, a short-cut to the public parking lot on the other side. She lifted a hand, pressed her thumb to the key fob, and distantly, her parked car beeped, preparing to drive her away.

It was almost a pity she wouldn't make it to the end of the alley. With a speed closer to light than human he attacked. He had her around the throat and pinned against the wall in only moments.

She didn't scream, but swung out an arm he didn't brace for and stabbed her car key at his neck. It was a good move. "Nice try." If he'd been human, she may have stunned him enough to have gotten away.

He didn't look her in the eyes, he never could. But he did listen to her heart beat like thunder in her chest. Inviting him to take and take and take.

His hand found her mouth and his fangs found her neck, sinking deep into her frantic memories as he took his first sip. He drank through her early life. Drank through her first heart break. Drank through the pain of a lost loved one.

Her strength waned and he took on more of her weight.

When he got to her greatest joy he paused. Fresh after birth and crying, she held a tiny baby in her arms.

"What's her name?" someone asked.

"Nylah," she replied beaming. A man kissed her. Her daughter's name escaped her lips in a breath right next to his ear. He pulled back then. Yanking on his own mind, his own lack of control. The little girl's face was the only bright spot behind his red eyes.

Jules ducked out at the last bell, retreating to her darkened house, to change and wait out the rest of peak sun hours. Heavy drapes covered all outside access points. Although being in direct sunlight did kill vampires, it was not as instantaneous as some stories suggested. Non-direct sunlight drained her energy, weakened her, and gave her a pretty much continuous headache.

Towards evening, once the sun had slipped under some clouds for the day, Jules drove to Monica's house. She honked. Monica came bounding out of the house and settled into Jules's passenger seat, chatting in that happy Monica way. Multitasking, Monica also changed the music to something on her phone and cranked it way up. Jules rolled her eyes at the choice of music. Monica rolled down the windows, letting in the chilly night air. They both began to sing loudly while Monica bounced in her seat.

At the first red light, Jules stopped singing and glanced over toward the car on their left. Jules's hands tightened around the steering wheel. She moved her eyes to stare pointedly out the windshield but stayed attuned to the occupants of the car beside them.

"Jules? What is it?" Monica said. When Jules didn't respond, she repeated the question and turned down the music.

"Werewolves," Jules said, remaining calm but on guard. Normally, Jules wouldn't give this coincidence another thought, but she wasn't sure what the repercussions of last night's interaction might be. Also, having Monica with her if something was going to happen wasn't a factor Jules was overly fond of.

Monica followed her next glance at the three men, who were illuminated by the streetlights. They were all intently watching her.

"Yikes," Monica said. "They look... mean."

"Those wolves were with the Alpha Gabriel had his unfortunate confrontation with last night," Jules told her. "Since their Alpha is not with them, they may not follow," she calculated out loud.

Monica stayed silent but began to roll the heavily-tinted windows back up. Blocking them from the werewolf's direct view. As the stoplight turned green, Jules sped forward.

"Are they following us?" Jules asked, focused on weaving through traffic carefully.

"Yes," Monica said, sounding a little shaken now.

Jules glanced in the rearview mirror as the driver of the other car cut across traffic, almost hitting an oncoming vehicle. Monica sucked in a breath, and Jules heard her heart begin to race.

"It's going to be okay, Monica," Jules said softly. Jules made another daring driving maneuver and hissed a curse when they matched her move. "We're taking a detour," Jules said. They turned and again were followed. "If I tell you to do something, don't hesitate," she instructed.

"You make that sound so easy," Monica said with a strained smile. The rate of her heartbeat was tempting Jules, begging her to relish in the adrenaline flowing from the human beside her.

Jules shook herself, slamming the door shut on her temptations. *This is Monica.* Two more turns were made and duplicated. Jules slammed on the breaks. They were nearing downtown. *This can't go on any longer.*

Monica let out a scream as Jules abruptly parallel parked. In one swift movement, she was in the space and the engine was off.

"Get out and head into the tea shop," Jules instructed.

Monica did as she was told without hesitation and Jules entered the shop close behind her. The Alice in Wonderland themed shop was jam-packed with patrons, just as Jules had hoped.

"They won't do anything here, it's too busy. But if they

follow us in, I need you to take my car and go." Jules placed her car keys in Monica's palm, wrapping her fingers around them. "Home, to the mall, I don't care. Just go."

"I can't leave without you?" Monica protested. Her heart was still racing, and her breath was coming in quick spurts.

"Monica, I need you out of this equation. Don't worry about me. I can run faster than they can." Jules gave her a reassuring smile. "I'll be fine." Jules's attention shifted when the door opened again. All three men stormed in but hesitated. Their presence felt contradictory to the frilly surroundings. "They will follow me. Take the car," Jules instructed.

"Jules, I don't like this..." Monica shook her head in protest.

"Here." She shoved her phone into Monica's hand. "Switch phones with me. Call Gabriel. And get out of here." Jules squeezed Monica's shoulder.

Without looking back, Jules rushed through the shop and out the back door. She was right. All three men came rushing after her.

CHAPTER FOUR

The Beta's Prerogative

L uca entered his current place of employment just in time to clock in. Panda Plate, the Chinese restaurant, was a small, family-owned, buffet, with a dining room that sat less than fifty customers. The back door automatically swung shut behind him as he entered.

"On time today then," Mr. Yang said as Luca joined him in the kitchen.

"It appears so," Luca joked as he pulled on an apron and took over what Mr. Yang was preparing.

"Hey," Tai Yang greeted as he entered the kitchen from the front of the restaurant.

Luca nodded at him and continued to stir the contents of his pot.

Tai turned to his father and said something in Mandarin Luca couldn't comprehend and then returned his attention to his friend.

"Thanks for agreeing to do that double date thing," Tai said as he lounged against one of the stainless-steel counters. "According to Monica, I really messed up." Tai cringed.

"No worries, I'm happy to help," Luca said as the contents of his pot came to a boil.

"Two years is a long time. It's important to celebrate such a day," Tai's dad added while dumping ingredients into yet another pan. "Monica's not the only one who thinks my son messed up."

"Yeah, yeah Dad," Tai mumbled. "You and Mom have both made yourselves clear on that one."

Luca smiled as he watched father and son.

"Sometimes I think they like Monica more than me."

"Sometimes we do," Mr. Yang commented, although his son was no longer speaking to him directly.

Luca remembered interacting with his father with the same level of familial banter and ease. It was part of why he liked working here, in this family atmosphere. It reminded him what a family really was and made him remember his own.

The phone began to ring. Luca finished dumping the chicken in another pan, set it on the warmer, and walked over to answer the call. Scribbling down the order, he walked it back and stuck it to the metal bar over Mister Yang's head.

"Speaking of that favor," Luca said as he walked back to his own workstation. "Tell me, who is this girl I've agreed to go out with?"

"Well..." Tai joined him at the counter near the warmer. Luca began working on another entre as Tai spoke. "She's around your age. I think. It's kinda weird since she works at my school, but whatever. And don't tell Monica that I said it but, she's super sexy but also, like, cute..." Tai paused, presumably thinking.

Luca laughed. "I meant her name."

"Oh," Tai looked a little embarrassed. "It's..."

"Boys," Mr. Yang called. "Work." He pointed to the warmer where the chicken was waiting to be taken out to the buffet.

"Okay, I'm going." Tai rolled his eyes, picked up the pan and walked into the dining room.

Jules turned the corner and headed away from the town's center. The wolves were still on her tail. The sound of labored breathing far too close for comfort. *Come on! Give up!* One of the pursuers howled. *If he turns now...* Her train of thought was interrupted by a hard smack on the back of her head. She spun, opened her mouth, and let out a threatening snarl.

The wolves stopped in their tracks. The one who had

thrown the brick took one step back. They were in an abandoned alley now, she could attack. But chose to run into a more open area instead. Past a deserted bus stop, toward a highly populated restaurant. Once inside, she hurried past the hostess, toward the restroom in the back. The wolves entered just as Jules passed through the swinging door.

Once inside the restroom, she looked around. There were three stalls and a small window at the far end. Going for the window, she jumped through it into the back alley. Leaping onto the roof of the neighboring shop, she waited. Finally, with the sound of the restaurant door slamming, followed by angry voices, the wolves emerged one by one. *I may have lost them.* She couldn't count on it though. Just then, Monica's phone vibrated.

"Where are you, Jules?" Gabriel's voice was rushed, anxious.

"On top of the office building next to Seaside Soda Shop," she told him.

"I'm six blocks away. Head east," he instructed calculatingly.

The wolves had headed north-east so if she swayed just slightly to the south, she would probably avoid them. Walking to the far side of the building, away from the restaurant, she jumped off the roof. Landing soundlessly on the pavement below, she bolted in Gabriel's direction.

Within moments Gabriel's car skidded next to her. She didn't slow and he didn't stop as she yanked the door open and slid into the car next to him.

"Hi there." Her tone was light, despite the circumstances.

"I can't believe those animals actually chased you," Gabriel spat.

Jules shrugged her shoulders as if to say, it's no big deal. "Gabriel, I'm fine." She lifted her head to smile at him reassuringly.

"No, you're not. Your head is bleeding all over my seat. What happened?"

Jules lifted her hand to the back of her head and flinched when she felt the gaping wound there. "I'm fine. It's already healing."

"How are you fine?" he asked, glaring at her.

"Gabriel," Eileen chided from the back seat. "She says she's fine. Trust her."

"There is a strong sense of relief that comes when one is no longer being chased," Jules teased as she fiddled with her hair, attempting to mask the blood in it.

"Jules, these beasts..." Gabriel began to argue.

"I'm sure they were following orders," Jules interrupted.

"So that makes it alright!"

"I didn't say that, but..." Jules began.

Eileen cut her off, "Gabriel is right. We can't just pretend we don't have a problem." Eileen leaned forward to be more a part of the conversation.

"We don't know that we do," Jules said. "Obviously, they chased me and that's not promising..."

Gabriel started to say something, but Jules continued, cutting him off.

"It's not a great sign, but I won't do anything to escalate this. It might just fizzle out if we don't feed into it, and we are going to give it that chance," Jules said, looking back at Eileen and then at Gabriel to ensure compliance.

Gabriel nodded. He was obviously not happy with this course of action. However, she was his coven leader, and he would respect her wishes.

"Now take me home," Jules said, frowning slightly. "I should wash this blood out of my hair before I meet up with Monica."

A few minutes later they were in front of Jules's little green house. Her car was parked to one side of the driveway.

"Monica must have come here," Jules commented.

Gabriel still looked uneasy, but she smiled at him brightly anyway. Monica often came to Jules's after a fight with her parents or Tai. It was one place Monica felt safe. *Ironically.*

"May I?" Jules asked Eileen, holding up a hat she'd found on the passenger floor.

"Of course," Eileen replied.

"Thanks." Jules pulled on the hat. She didn't want to scare Monica unnecessarily. "See you later." She held up her hand to stop the protestations before he could voice them. "Everything will be fine."

She waved him off as she approached her front door. As expected, it was unlocked.

"Monica?" Jules walked into her living room and found Monica sitting on the couch, curled up, knees to her chest, wrapped in a blanket. She was staring silently at Jules's cell phone.

"Monica," Jules said again, getting the girl's attention.

Monica looked up, shock and concern written on her face.

"Monica, it's okay. I told you I'd be fine," she comforted, sitting down beside her and wrapping her small arms around her friend.

Monica began to cry softly.

"You said you took care of it. So why did they chase us?" Monica whimpered, but then sat up and tried to compose herself, wiping the tears out of her eyes.

"I may have humiliated their Alpha yesterday." Jules smiled sheepishly.

"What does that mean?" Monica asked, her tone a mix of confusion, anxiety, and interest. But Jules could tell by listening to her heartbeat that she was starting to calm down.

"I just might have stepped on his pride a bit." Jules leaned into the couch and pulled her feet up, making herself more comfortable.

"So, what you mean is that you kicked it, stomped on it, and then lit it on fire."

Jules made a non-committal sound and then chuckled.

"Jules!"

"He had it coming. He called me a child."

"Too be fair you were a minor when you died. Hundreds

and hundreds and hundreds of years ago of course."

"Yes, I know. I'm a long dead corpse," Jules said.

"But a very sexy one," Monica added.

Both girls laughed.

Luca was exhausted and smelling like spices and soy sauce, as he always did after a shift. Parking under the bedroom window, he grumbled seeing it was once again closed. Begrudgingly, he walked around the house to go in the front.

"Luca!" Carson's voice called as the screen door slammed shut behind him. Luca scowled and turned in the direction of the family room. Upon entering, he realized the rest of the residents of the Den were already gathered. Apparently, Carson had called some sort of emergency meeting. Kyle, of course, was no longer among them. However, a sixth man, that Luca had seen before but never officially met, was leaning against a far window. The lanky wolf wore glasses and was constantly fidgeting from one foot to the other and then back again.

"Luca," Carson addressed his Beta.

Luca's attention shifted to his Alpha, who was pacing menacingly in the center of the room. "I've asked Jed here," he motioned toward the man Luca didn't know, "to move into that vacant room."

Vacant. Luca thought, *Kyle has only been gone for like twelve hours.*

All Luca wanted to do was go upstairs, shower, and fall into bed. Despite this, Max stood, creating a space on the couch for their Beta. Luca had no choice but to collapse beside Ben and wait for Carson's rant to be over. With a thump, he let his head flop against the back of the couch. *No telling how long this will take.*

"As I was saying, the vampire problem must be dealt with. Jed may be a bumbling fool but he's the best tracker in this pack."

Luca looked over at the poor man, who was being subjected

to Carson's insults. Jed's cheeks turned crimson, but he remained silent.

"Why are we bothering with these vamps anyway?" Kip asked from where he sat on the floor by the wall, legs stretched out in front of him. "It's not like there have been killings every night, or any night for that matter. Why bother?" The question granted him a glare from Carson that was so powerful that Kip shrunk away from it.

"Why bother!" Carson repeated. "We bother because vampires are disgusting, soulless creatures who don't deserve to walk this earth," Carson's voice raised, and he shook slightly.

Luca's fists clenched. Exhausted and a little annoyed Carson's tirade was more granting than usual. "It's a fair question," Luca said, standing. Only he had the power to oppose their Alpha. "Why start something with the vampires when we don't have to? They, at least their coven leader, didn't seem to want to start anything." Luca thought momentarily of the small, red-haired vampire who had captivated and intrigued him. It wasn't the first time his thoughts had drifted toward her since last night. He shook her from his mind and continued. "If they kill, they don't do it in Aboit."

Carson snarled, undoubtedly angered by Luca's defiance. His instincts told him to flinch under the Alpha's powerful command and yet Luca resisted.

"They all kill." Ben's voice was soft and controlled like it always was. "They hunt and they feed. It's in their nature."

Luca looked down at the old werewolf. Ben was leaning forward, elbows on his knees, eyebrows pulled together, looking a little stressed.

"Instinct or not. I say we do nothing until we know more," Luca suggested.

Kip looked like he might agree with Luca but said nothing. Carson looked as if he might explode at any moment, but still Luca pressed on. "We do nothing until we have proof that they are a danger to the people of Aboit."

"It... is... not..." Carson took a strained breath between

each word. "Your place... to oppose me."

Luca resisted the urge to clench his own teeth. "It is my right to present other courses of action, even if those ideas are different from yours." Luca sighed. "I've said what needed to be said. Take my opinion into consideration or don't. That's up to you." With that, Luca walked from the room, retreating up the stairs to his bedroom.

Nick lay on his back in a bed that wasn't his, in a tiny apartment that left something to be desired aesthetically. To be fair, he hadn't had a bed, or a home to call his own, in several years now. The room was cramped, barely big enough to fit a bed inside. It smelled of sex and potato chips. The first, he was fond of. The second just made the place he'd currently decided to lay his head smell rancid.

Place-holder Chad's limp frame lay on his chest. Boneless and snoring softly, but not bloodless. How the human didn't notice that his heart didn't beat, he would never understand.

Chad's body was warm on his. Too warm. Wrapping a blond curl around one finger Nick lamented. The hair wasn't right either. It was too coarse, the curls too tight. Not like the feel forever imprinted on his fingertips. Nick shook free of the thought. They'd split ways many times. Their differences irreconcilable. Not Chad. He was a timely convenience and nothing more. A bit dim, and a bit short, but Chad was handsome enough. He was a warm mouth to fill the daylight hours. Who conveniently worked nights in tech security. Or maybe he was a security guard, Nick couldn't remember. In a few years he wouldn't even remember this man's name.

He should move on from the city. Things were getting messy. The werewolf teenager, the officer's son he guessed, had gotten away. Nick had chased and searched for him halfheartedly. Letting him live was a liability. Still, he was kind of glad he hadn't found him. His morals were gray at best, but he did have a very strict line about killing kids.

Werewolf, human, or some species not yet to be encountered, it didn't matter. Even with that hard line he had a serial killer nickname now. The Fort Miles Phantom. Catchy yes, but also problematic. Remaining in Fort Miles could be dangerous but something inside him demanded he stay. And it definitely wasn't Chad.

Luca tripped up a stair on the way up to Hayley's apartment the next day, Kyle and himself holding a large television between them.

"Don't break that thing before we get it up the stairs," Hayley said as she squeezed past her husband and Luca to go open the door to the couple's apartment.

"It was just a little stumble," Kyle chided.

"Oh I know. I was talking to you, my love."

Kyle rolled his eyes at his wife and took another step up the stairs. Luca stepped up and Kyle mirrored him. They were making their way quickly with the light but cumbersome box.

"Hayley door!" Kyle shouted after his wife swung the door shut behind her.

"Just kidding," she said, smiled, and held it open for them. "You know I could have helped you with that."

"Yes, My Queen. I know, you can do whatever I can do, but why should you have to when Luca is around to do it for you?" Kyle asked, teasingly.

"Fair point." She shrugged then disappeared into the bedroom. Kyle smiled after her as he and Luca freed the electronic entertainment device from its packaging and placed it on a rickety, old table.

"Can I ask you something?" Luca said as he plopped down onto Kyle's new-to-the-apartment, old couch and sighed.

"That's a bad idea," Kyle replied.

"How do you feel about Carson's whole vampire vendetta?" When Kyle didn't immediately respond Luca continued, "I just think we should have proof of wrongdoing before we start an all-out supernatural war in Aboit." He had been very distracted all morning by the meeting that Carson had called the previous night. Something just didn't feel right to him. There was too much hate without an obvious purpose behind it.

It was Kyle's turn to sigh. "Okay, honestly, I think blood-suckers need to drink human blood to survive. This does make them dangerous to our town. However, I do see your point about wanting more information before we start a war over it. From what little I actually know about supernatural history; these types of wars can be messy, and a lot of our kind generally end up dying. However, everyone also knows that Carson always does what Carson wants and everyone around him had better do what Carson wants as well, or things might also get out of hand. So, like, pick the lesser of two possibly shit-storm outcomes I guess."

"I know you're right," Luca said. "The question is then; is following Carson's orders really more important than murdering potentially innocent beings, of any kind?"

"Potentially is the key word there, Luca," Kyle said as he began to stretch cords from the television to the wall. "It's my understanding as well that all vampire's kill. Even if they aren't killing here, they're probably killing somewhere else. You've heard of the uptick in homicides in Fort Miles recently, haven't you?"

"True," Luca said, sighing.

"It does sound like Carson has a solid argument," Hayley added as she walked back into the room and sat beside Luca. "Murder is wrong, and murders should be dealt with accordingly."

Luca flinched.

"Hayley," Kyle cautioned. He knew why Luca had flinched, but Hayley probably didn't. "She means non-remorseful murderers."

"Kyle," Luca used the same tone on him that he'd used on Hayley.

"Why do you care about the vampires so much anyway?" Hayley asked, returning to a safer subject.

Kyle connected the last cord and picked up the remote to assess his work. He then joined Luca and Hayley where they sat. "Because he thinks the little one is cute," Kyle said jokingly.

CHAPTER FIVE

Date with the Enemy

Jules's shoes squeaked on the marble entryway floor of the Martin family residence. Normally, human residences were impossible for Jules to enter. This white pillared, three floored, ocean front, house was the exception. At the Martins' Jules had a standing invitation.

"We're home!" Monica shouted.

"Hello girls," Monica's mother, Sherri, said as she entered from the direction of the kitchen. She was as stunning and tall as her daughter. A lawyer with a reputation as formidable. Her white suit contrasted with her dark skin in the best way.

"Hi," they said in unison.

"Are you staying for dinner, Jules, dear?" Sherri asked, spectacles perched on her nose and an important looking file in her hand.

"Yes..." Monica started.

"Um... no," Jules cut her off. "I'd better not."

"You're staying." Monica rolled her eyes. "We need to pick out dresses for our date tomorrow," Monica told her mother.

"Oh, in that case, I'll let Dad know to pick up food for one more for dinner. You better get started." Sherri smiled at them both. "With your indecisiveness, you never know how long that will take," she said, teasing her daughter.

Jules laughed with her while Monica scowled. "Oh, come on." Monica took Jules by the arm and pulled her up the marble stairs, complete with antique rug runner up the center, to her bedroom.

"I'm glad you're here Jules, dear, we've missed you." Sherri shouted after them. Jules replied in kind while allowing herself to be led past the balcony to Monica's room.

"So, do you know where Tai is taking us?" Jules asked, perching on the end of Monica's four poster bed.

"No." Monica walked to her closet and started pulling out designer dress after designer dress, throwing them down beside Jules. "But he told me to dress up." She plucked a dress off the top of the stack, walked to the gilded mirror, held it in front of her, and then discarded it on the floor. "I told him not to waste a bunch of money on something fancy, I doubt he listened."

Jules stood and walked to Monica's walk-in closet, rifling through the clothing hanging there.

"By the way, don't be a pain about it but," Monica hesitated, "your date is paying." Monica picked up another dress and turned to smile at Jules.

Jules rolled her eyes. Monica knew her too well. "It's not a date. It's a favor," Jules replied. "Why should he pay?"

Between ancient investments, centuries of financial success, and holding onto belongings for hundreds of years, most vampires were generally pretty well off. In fact, Jules had some first edition novels in her home that were worth a small fortune on their own.

"Yes, you are his date as a favor to me, but just because you won't date a human, doesn't mean he knows that." Monica continued to sort through the pile of dresses, carefully assessing each option. "Besides, you could wear an orange jumpsuit with a stamped cell block on the back and he'd still become completely obsessed with you. You are that stunning."

At this, Jules grumbled.

"I did say don't be a pain about it didn't I?" Monica discarded yet another dress onto the floor.

"Fine." Jules's fingers touched velvet. She reached into the closet and pulled a long, formfitting, black dress from the back to examine it.

Monica dropped the dress she was examining to the side and stared at Jules.

"What?"

"Oh, you should definitely wear that!"

Jules looked back at the dress. "I don't know."

"Try it on. If you don't like it, don't wear it. But it suits you."

Jules had just managed to pull up the zipper when Monica called, "Hey Toad, come in here!" After a few moments, Ethan moseyed to the door and pushed it open. "What do you think of this?" Monica asked him about the dress she had tried on.

"I don't know." He shrugged, lounging against the door frame.

"You're almost a guy. What do you think?" Monica had on a short, red, strapless dress that showed off her dainty shoulders beautifully.

"It's fine, I guess," he said, and then looked over at Jules. "Now that's a dress!"

Jules was about to respond but before she could, he blushed and walked to his own room down the hall, swinging the door shut behind him a little too forcefully.

They both laughed.

Jules's breath caught when she smelled it. Blood. Fresh, dripping, human blood.

"Jules, what is it?" Monica asked. Jules stood statue still, fists clenched, lips pressed together tightly and had stopped breathing. These were the precautions that kept her from bolting toward the source of her bloodlust. Monica knew the signs.

"Downstairs," Jules managed to mumble.

"Stay here. I'll take care of it," Monica said, walking around Jules and closing the door behind her.

Jules dropped to the bedroom floor, clamped her hands over her mouth, and whimpered. She knew she couldn't do what every instinct in her was screaming for her to do. Jules knew that if she gave in, by just a fraction of a thought, she would kill whoever was leaking out their life-source. It was likely she would kill everyone in the house once the initial bloodlust was satisfied. And these people were like family to her.

"Monica. Jules," the doorknob to Monica's bedroom began to twist. *No. No. No!* This couldn't be happening. Ethan was coming too close. She couldn't kill him. She couldn't. But if he opened that door, could she stop herself. He was a child. He was family. But he was also a human. Blood, pure rushing blood lay just beneath the skin. Pumping, pumping through his body. Adrenaline.

Jules began to rock. Trying to soothe the pain in her throat and lock onto something other than Ethan's blood.

"Ethan!" Monica's shout was too far away. Still down stairs. "Stay out of my room!"

"But Jules..." He began.

"Is naked!" Monica shouted back.

"Oh. Wow." Ethan took his hand off the doorknob. "Sorry Jules." He shouted through it and his footsteps receded. Blood tears slid from her eyes and down her face, staining the white carpet near her knees. The relief she felt at having resisted threatened to tear her in two. She shouldn't be here. In this house. With these people. Demons and humans were not meant to coexist.

After a few minutes, which felt like hours, the smell of fresh blood disappeared. Its memory still burned into Jules's mind. She took a few, steadying breaths.

"Mom got a nasty paper cut," Monica said, returning and closing the door. "You should see the sensitive legal document, it's..." Monica's voice trailed off.

Jules nodded but didn't speak.

"Oh Jules, it's okay." Monica grabbed a box of tissues off her desk and sat down on the floor in front of her. One hand pulled a tissue free and stretched out toward Jules, the other took Jules's hand and grasped it tightly.

Jules focused on Monica's touch. The human she cared about most, sitting in front of her, anchoring her back in the living world. "It's over Jules. You didn't hurt anyone. It's over,"

Monica continued softly.

Jules wiped at her eyes with the soft bit of paper, it came away red. More composed, Jules looked up at Monica.

"Yeah, that's still gross."

"What?" Jules asked, taken aback.

"You got a bit of..." Monica pointed beside her own eye to indicate the blood she'd missed.

"Oh," Jules wiped at it again while both girls chuckled softly.

Monica gagged.

"You let a blood sucking murderer into your home and blood tears are what get you?" Jules asked.

"It leaks from your eyeballs."

"Tear ducts," Jules corrected.

Monica's nose was still scrunched in disgust. "At least you didn't cry on your dress."

Jules laughed and Monica joined her.

Carson had gathered those closely ranking beneath him to announce his decision regarding the vampire situation. He had taken enough time indulging Luca with the idea that he would consider his Beta's plea. Vampires did not deserve, nor would they ever receive, any mercy from him. A vampire was a demented killer, and that was that.

All his Den member subordinates were watching him intently, as his impassioned speech came to an end. Well, all but one. Carson scowled down at his Beta. "Do you have somewhere to be?" Carson snapped, as Luca checked his phone for the fifth time.

"I do," Luca said, offering no further explanation.

Having this entitled whelp as a ceremonial second was becoming more and more bothersome by the day. If only Luca's lineage wasn't... Carson halted that train of thought and returned to the task before him. "That said," Carson began again. "If any of you come in contact with one of these bloodsuckers, or any vampire for that matter, you are to report their position immediately. A proper offensive will be formulated, and I assure you, the threat will be promptly dealt with. If you can, follow them to their dwelling, that would be ideal…" Carson stopped as Luca looked down at his phone yet again. Ben reached over and tapped Luca's leg to get his attention.

"Going to be late?" Carson snarled.

"I am now," Luca said, standing and making to leave the room.

"Luca Cain," Carson called. Luca's audacity was boarding on insubordination.

Luca's Beta status did allow him to be somewhat legitimately adversarial. Carson had to accept that. Thus, this behavior was simply a consequence of the position Luca held within the pack. So, in favor of not escalating this irritation any further, Carson swallowed his rage and said, "if you see a vampire…"

"I know what to do." Luca sighed and left the house, the screen door slamming behind him.

Carson continued, speaking more freely now that the thorn in his side was out of earshot.

Jules was woken up around midday the next day by a frantic Monica with clothes and makeup in tow. Jules sighed. It was going to be a very long day.

While preparing for the night's events, Monica did Jules's hair twice. Jules had watched as Monica took her own hair down and put it back up four times. Now, she sat in front of her travel mirror with a pencil to her eye. Jules watched as she drew a perfectly angled line on her top eyelid. "Give me five more minutes, then it's your turn," Monica said.

"Oh, no. You don't have to do that," Jules began. "I'm fine going like this." Jules waved her hand over her own face.

"Come on, Jules. It's not like you can see to put it on yourself. I only want to do a little bit. I don't even need to use foundation. I mean, for being dead, your skin is perfect. Please, let me do your eyes at least," Monica begged as she finished applying eyeliner to her second eye.

Jules never did anything to enhance her appearance, humans were drawn to her regardless, no need to help them see her in the crowd when all she wanted was to blend in. The pleading look in Monica's eyes broke her resolve.

"Just this once."

"Yay!" Monica shrieked. She held up the mirror, inspecting herself closer. "That is so weird," she commented aloud.

"What is?"

"I know you're back there. I can see your t-shirt hanging in mid-air, but you just aren't there." She pointed to the mirror in front of her.

Jules shrugged, it'd been centuries since she'd seen her own reflection. "Punishment for being a walking nightmare, I guess," Jules replied.

"You take that back right now!" Monica chided. "You are not a nightmare. You are awesome! Say it."

"I... am... awesome," Jules repeated, to appease Monica, but her face crumpled distastefully on the last word.

"Good but not great, now come sit so I can put some eyeliner on those iridescent, silver eyes of yours."

Jules did as instructed, a giggle slipping out as the blush brush hit her face. It was a weird sensation, being tickled by soft bristles. Monica did her makeup and then her hair, curling it into soft red waves.

Jules had just managed the zipper on the black dress when the doorbell rang.

"They're here," Monica shrieked, almost dropping the mascara tube she was holding. Jules had been expecting Tai to walk in unannounced like always, but it seemed he was taking this anniversary as seriously as Monica was.

"Go answer it, Jules," Monica pleaded. "I want to make an entrance."

Jules smiled, resisting the urge to roll her eyes, and walked from her bedroom to the front door. She could hear hushed voices on the other side of the door as she reached forward to open it.

She smelled it before she saw him. "Hi Jules," Tai greeted. "Monica inside?"

Jules didn't respond but stood frozen in the doorway.

"Jules?" Tai questioned.

She nodded but didn't take her eyes off the man who was supposed to be her date.

"Have you two met?" Tai was looking from Jules to her date and back again.

"Not officially," he said. "I'm Luca." He held out a hand toward her.

Jules looked down at it, not sure whether to shake it or break it.

"Jules, Luca. Luca, Jules. Now you have," Tai said when Jules made no move to take Luca's outstretched hand. Tai shrugged and then stepped around Jules to enter the house and find his girlfriend.

After a few more long seconds, Luca pulled his hand back and dropped it to his side.

Jules watched as Luca's eyebrows drew together. He looked down at her with a concerned expression. She was surprised not to see the hatred of his pack reflected in his face. "Are you alright?" he asked cautiously.

"Not..." Jules found her voice. "Not really."

He reached a hand out like he may try to comfort her.

One step back, her eyes narrowed, appraising him. This wolf was truly as beautiful as she remembered. Perfectly muscled, warm bronzed skin, and very tall. He probably had twelve or fourteen inches on her petite stature. But more importantly, he now knew exactly where she lived, and Jules had no way of knowing what he might do with that information.

Luca's breath caught. The vampire was just as alluring as he remembered. Even if her expression told him she wasn't sure whether to kill him or not. Although, that was kind of hot too. He couldn't help it. His gaze followed the lines of her. All the way up, from her black heels. Up that velvet dress that hugged every curve, even the ones she had hidden under her hoodie the first time he'd seen her. Up to her slender neck, to plump lips he would die to have on him. Two captivating and ancient eyes, all the way to her curled auburn hair. He was having trouble breathing. She wasn't breathing either, but he guessed it was for other reasons.

"Shall we go?" Tai said as he reappeared near the door with one arm draped around Monica's waist.

"Monica I…" Jules began to say.

Luca cut her off, "of course," he said. There was no way she was getting away that easily. Smiling, Luca gestured for Jules to accompany him to Tai's mother's car.

The stunning vampire's eyes widened momentarily and then settled in a scowl and a glare that could kill if it wanted.

If this vampire turned out to be just a gorgeous, soulless murderer, then he'd follow Carson's orders and report her. If not, and he was right about her, the possibilities were endless. Luca rolled that thought over in his mind and smiled to himself.

Monica and Tai walked a few steps ahead of them to the vehicle. Luca walked her to her door and pulled it open for her. She looked up at him. Her eyes wary and body stiff. He smiled again and leaned over to be closer to her ear. "If looks could kill, little corpse, then I'd already be dead."

This earned him another death glare.

He held out his hand for her. "Will you get in the car?"

"For Monica." She ignored his outstretched hand and stepped into the car. "Touch me and die."

"I have no doubts that you mean that," he said, shutting

the door and walking around to the other side.

They rode in silence, but Luca continued to steal glances at the icy figure sitting as far from him as possible. Which was difficult seeing as his legs didn't really fit in the back seat. His knees were spread wide and still jammed against the seat in front of him. When the car jostled his knee bumped her thigh but her posture didn't change. Head held high, she stared straight ahead.

"Dang it," Tai said from the front seat. This pulled Luca's attention away from his date. "Sorry, everyone. We need to make a pit stop."

As Tai got out to fill the car with gas, Monica rambled. "It's so great of you guys to do this for us. Luca, do you know where we're going?" But before Luca could tell her that he wasn't telling, she moved on. "See Jules, I told you that it wouldn't be so bad…"

Just then, Tai stuck his head back inside the car. "Stupid thing is telling me I have to see the cashier. I'll be right back," he said and then unexpectedly leaned across the car and kissed Monica on the lips.

Monica kissed him back, giggling and blushing simultaneously.

Luca thought he saw a smile flash across the vampire's face, but he couldn't be sure. It happened too fast.

Monica looked down and gasped, "oh! Tai may need his wallet." She grabbed it off the seat. "I'll be right back."

"Monica, no…" Jules started to say, but she was already gone.

"So, was all that 'peace and love' bullshit or what?" Luca asked as soon as the door shut behind the human girl.

"Excuse me?" she turned an angry glare on him.

"You said…" he trailed off. "Look that doesn't matter right now. Before they come back, I need to say something," Luca said. He watched as Tai shifted from one foot to the other while standing in line and Monica clung to his arm happily. "We're both here for our friends, correct?"

The vampire didn't justify his question with an answer.

"I don't know about your human friend, but Tai doesn't know about me. I would really like to keep it that way."

"Monica knows about me," Jules said coolly.

"Really?" Luca asked, stunned. Monica couldn't really understand how dangerous Jules was and still be comfortable around her, could she?

Jules nodded.

"Wow," Luca said. If Jules was a cold-blooded killer surely, she wouldn't tell a helpless human her secret and let them go on living. He studied her face as she studied his.

After a few moments Jules broke the eye contact. "If you don't try to kill me tonight, I won't tell them about you."

"That's an easy deal to make. I have no intention of killing you." With his secret safe, his ease returned. He stretched his arms up over his head. Leaning his head back on his palms he took up even more space in the back seat. "I could think of some other fun things to do with you but..." he smirked over at her.

"Touch me and die, dog man."

Jules resisted the smile that threatened to escape at the sound of the werewolf's laughter. *Brazen, confident, beast...* Jules's thought was cut short and her head jolted up when the front car doors opened; Monica and Tai reappearing.

"At least you two are becoming friends," Monica said.

"That's a stretch," Jules mumbled.

"She hasn't killed me yet though," he added.

Monica and Tai laughed.

"I knew you two would be a good fit," Tai said.

"You meddlesome busybody," Monica chided and laughed at the same time as the car's engine sputtered to life.

Luca's leg bumped her again as he sat forward to add something to the story Tai was telling Monica about work. She took the moment to glance at him. He was massive. Tall, tan, and muscled. His arms and legs straining against the jeans and suit jacket he wore. But his facial features were soft. He seemed to radiate light like the sun she could no longer soak in. His smile was sunshine incarnate.

He confused her. Considering the game of cat and mouse she had played with his pack mates earlier in the week, she assumed he had orders from his Alpha. But he hadn't made any moves to pick up his phone to report her whereabouts or home location since he and Tai had arrived. As the ride stretched on, it looked like he didn't have any intention to. At least not immediately. Jules remained stiff and silent at his side.

They had left Aboit and were heading for Fort Miles, the nearest large city. The car pulled up in front of an elite Italian restaurant. "Tai, no," Monica began.

"You love this place," Tai said.

"When my dad buys," she snapped.

"Come on," Tai said. "I've got reservations and everything."

Monica sighed. "I love you."

"Happy anniversary," Tai replied while exiting the car. Luca followed suit. While Monica waited patiently for Tai to get her door. Jules waited until the right moment to open her own door. With perfect timing she whacked the werewolf with the door and stepped out.

"Ouch," Luca said. "Was that really…"

"Yes, it was absolutely necessary," Jules cut him off and finished the statement for him, once again ignoring the hand he'd outstretched toward her.

"Aren't you a violent little corpse?" His whisper was low, meant only for her ears.

"You have no idea," she said under her breath as well.

"No," he admitted. "But I'm starting to think it will be fun to find out."

"For me, maybe," she smirked, stopping and looking up at him through her eyelashes. He studied her lips, so she bit the lower one ever so slightly.

"Oh, I think I'd enjoy it too," Luca said, motioning for her to move towards the door but not brushing her skin in any way.

Jules went ahead of him as he held the door open for them all. She didn't like having the massive wolf at her back, but it couldn't really be helped.

"Do we have a reservation tonight?" The hostess asked, glancing over the party with a pasted on smile. She got to Luca and her fake smile turned flirtatious. "Sir?" She added as an afterthought.

Jules had the ridiculously possessive impulse to reach forward and take Luca's arm, but it was a preposterous thought, so she ignored it.

"Cain, four," Luca said to the hostess.

Jules gasped audibly. The similarities already had her thinking it could be true but having it confirmed made her feel strange.

Luca glanced down at her and gave her an almost imperceptible nod. He was a descendant of Stephen's family line. Jules scowled. There was no killing him now. Luca seemed to read her mind, because he chuckled at her annoyed expression.

The hostess showed the two couples to a table on the balcony overlooking the dance floor. While setting the menus down she brushed Luca's hand, obviously not an accident. Jules picked up her menu, again purposefully ignoring the interaction.

"These reservations are nearly impossible to get." Monica began casually as she perused her own menu. "How did you get it?"

"I know the chef," Luca admitted.

A werewolf chef. Great.

Almost immediately a waitress came to take their orders. "For you miss?" She asked Jules. "Um… I'm not feeling well," Jules said. "I'll just have some water." She had been so busy fighting off baffling thoughts about Luca that she had neglected to think up a reasonable excuse for not eating.

"I'm buying." Luca smirked at her. "So, you're eating." A glint of a smile appeared on his lips.

She would wager that he knew full well she didn't eat human food. "No," she whispered harshly.

"Well, then…" Luca studied the menu for a few seconds. "She'll have the shrimp. You like shrimp, right Honey?" He nudged his menu at Jules, playfully mocking her.

She glowered at him and Luca smiled, then he looked back toward the waitress.

"I'll have the steak and tell the Chef that Luca said he wants his steak the way we like it." He winked at the waitress. "He'll know what I mean," he assured her. "Thank you."

The waitress looked skeptical but smiled at him.

"How do you both like it?" Monica asked as the waitress left a few minutes later.

"Just rare," he replied, shrugging.

"Reminiscent of a fresh kill that way?" Jules said, her voice inaudible to even the closest humans.

Luca's eyes widened. He glanced nervously at Tai, then back again.

"Oops," Jules said quietly, lacking any remorse.

When their meal arrived, Jules stared at her plate. What was she going to do with such a massive amount of smelly little sea creatures? She glared at Luca, wanting to imbed her fangs into his throat.

Throughout the course of the meal, some of the shrimp disappeared as she dropped them one by one into the napkin on her lap. Luckily, Monica, who was sitting beside her, was all too used to the little ways in which Jules disposed of human food. Eating the food in front of her was not an option. She'd tried once long ago and spent the night with her head hung over the chamber pot.

Luca seemed to be studying her carefully from across the table while keeping a steady stream of conversation going with Monica and Tai.

"Are you alright, Jules?" Monica asked, leaning over to speak in Jules's ear.

"I'm fine." Jules tried to smile reassuringly. "I just need to powder my nose."

Monica made a face, reminding her that it was an outdated term.

Jules shrugged. Luca's presence had thrown her completely off her game. This whole situation was very unsettling. As she stood, Jules slid her napkin in front of her and turned to leave the table. She heard Luca chuckle lightly and scowled.

Walking into a stall in the bathroom, she dumped the little creatures into the toilet and flushed them away. Checking that the restroom was still empty, Jules paused in front of the mirror and leaned on the sink. She didn't bother looking up at her reflection-less form.

Her chest rose and fell as she purposely took some deep breaths to help her focus her thoughts. She still hadn't seen Luca reach for his phone. He probably would now that she had walked away but that couldn't be helped. If the rest of the pack did come to his aid, she would have to run. The idea of abandoning Monica and Tai made her very uncomfortable, but Jules believed that Luca wouldn't let either of them get caught in the crossfire. Of that much, she was sure. He seemed to be a good friend to her human companions.

The bathroom door creaked open. She rushed away from the mirror toward the exit.

Lost in thought and gaze on the floor, her eyes caught on a pair of Converse under black jeans. A cozy, earthy scent assaulted her brain. Snapping her face up, her nose bumped into a hard, muscled chest.

CHAPTER SIX

The Dog and the Demon

L uca's instinct was to reach out and steady her. Part of him did take her threat of death at physical contact seriously, so instead he put one hand on the wall far above her head in an attempt to appear nonchalant. Silently looking over her again, his cock strained at the ample amount of cleavage showing in the blessedly slim-fitting dress.

"What?" She almost hissed up at him.

"I'm just admiring how someone so small can house so much animosity," he replied with a lopsided grin.

Her arms crossed, pushing her breasts together even more. He was going to explode if he didn't stop standing over her like this.

"I thought you were supposed to be a friend to werewolves? Or were you lying about knowing my famous ancestor?"

"Stephen wasn't hunting me." Her voice was filled with a venom Luca didn't feel he deserved.

"And I am?" He was puzzled but tried not to show how much.

"Your Alpha is." Jules continued to glare at him. "In my experience, the Alpha's desires are the desires of the pack." Her words were barely audible, kept very low to assure that he was the only one who could hear her.

Luca sighed. There was some truth to her words. He had never felt the Alpha's insatiable desire for control under his father's reign. However, as Carson's Beta, there was a lot of pressure to ensure his actions and opinions aligned with Carson's. Not that they ever did. He alone had the ability to defy him, even if the rest of the pack was compelled to comply in every way. "I suppose," he admitted. "Carson does have the final say on things."

"Your Alpha has already failed to capture or kill me." Her voice was low and sharp as she stepped toward him, not taking her eyes off his as she did. "He will continue to do so." He should have taken a step back for his own self-preservation, but he didn't. Instead, he dropped his arm, utterly baffled.

Luca's body tensed. Carson had already sent wolves to make an attempt on her life. He was frustrated. Not only had Carson made a move without informing him, but he had done so completely disregarding Luca's concerns. "I can guarantee you, I didn't know." He crossed his arms.

"Why should I believe you?"

"Didn't you trust my ancestor?" Luca had never cared much about his famous heritage but if it helped gain her trust, it was worth the name drop.

"The twelve times great grandson of his brother is a little removed to use Stephen as support for your argument."

"Five generations. Werewolves have long lifespans," Luca said, winking smugly. "Carson may want you dead, Little Corpse, but unless you give me a reason too, I won't help him do it."

"Why?" Jules asked. The silver eyes that met his seemed wary.

"Because you intrigue me." It was as honest of an answer as he could give her in the moment. His gaze landed on her full lips. An image of what he wanted her to do with them had his jeans feeling even tighter.

Her eyes locked with his as she studied him for a long moment. Scoffing, her expression shifted, some of the tension receding. Luca froze in place as she stretched a palm up, planting it on his chest. "Move, you mountain of a troll." She shoved. To his utter bemusement the impact moved him enough that he stumbled back. With the way clear, Jules moved around him, walking back in the direction of Tai and

Monica.

He chuckled, low and gravelly. Deep in his chest a warmth began to build. Physical contact or not. He was pretty sure she was going to kill him.

Luca went into the bathroom, leaned over the sink, and splashed cold water on his face. He stared at his reflection as water dripped from it. "Get it together man. She is technically dead," he said aloud to himself. A man exited a bathroom stall, made a concerned face towards him while he washed his hands and then left. Luca chuckled again. "She is going to be the death of me." Giving up on the decidedly unhelpful self-pep talk, Luca dried his face on a soft white towel and went to rejoin the others.

"Where'd they go?" he asked as he approached the table where Jules sat alone.

Without looking away from the balcony she pointed to the dance floor below. He walked to the banister and watched as Tai and Monica moved somewhat clumsily across the floor. When Tai dipped Monica low and nearly dropped her, Jules laughed out loud. "Sometimes I envy them," Jules admitted sadly. She likely hadn't been talking to him, but he took the opportunity anyway. Luca squared his shoulders, came around the table, and offered her his hand.

She scowled at his hand and then her gaze dropped to his Converse. "You look like you have two left feet," she said as she finally met his eyes.

"You'll never know unless you agree to dance with me." Luca waited patiently, his hand outstretched, a soft smile playing on his lips.

"One dance with the devil."

"I'll be the one dancing with the demon," he said while he smiled down at her. "You get the dog."

Jules rolled her eyes but slowly placed her hand in his. Her skin instantly cooled the fire inside his own. The feel of her cool skin on his could easily become an addiction he'd never be freed from. Placing her hand on his arm, he led her down the stairs to the dance floor. She spun away and back to meet him, her fingers never leaving his right hand. With a jolt from further contact he rested his free hand on the bare skin of her back, leading her off into movement. They were transported back to a time when a dance was more than a simple sway. He spun her out and back in, her back sliding flush with his front. Her arms wrapped around herself, her hands in his. Gracefully, she moved under his arm. No need to bend, she slid right beneath it. He grinned at this.

To him, it felt as if no one around them existed. In this moment, nothing else seemed to matter. Not Carson. Not the pack. Not the differences in their species. Not even her diet. Never in all the years of his life would he have imagined himself dancing with a vampire. Let alone one as cute, sexy, and temperamental as this one.

Seemingly lost in the music she began to hum to the gentle tune as their bodies glided across the floor. As the song ended, Luca placed his warm hand on the back of her neck, sending her into a dip. She let him lean her all the way back. As he pulled her up, he saw her lips part slightly. Their eyes met, Luca never wanted to look away again.

Jules gasped audibly at the feel of his werewolf-warm fingers brushing the back of her neck as he raised her back to standing. She should never have touched him. She'd forgotten the feel of the species inner mingling. Forgotten the warm glow of the werewolf skin on vampires'. Forgotten the feeling of being attracted to another being. If Luca had been a hideous beast, Jules doubted she would be quite so flustered. Something ignited inside her, desire.

As the music ended, she pulled her gaze and hand free of his and stepped away. Pushing away the unbidden emotion and coating it in denial.

Monica ran up and threw her arm around Jules. "Well, that was fun." Jules walked with Monica back to the table and for the rest of the meal, did what she could to avoid looking at the werewolf across from her.

Nick's fangs were once again imbedded in the carotid artery of a human. The only difference was this one wasn't an unsuspecting victim he'd stalked. This was a willing participant. Sensing the end of the human's life, Nick clamped down on the man's head with his hand, holding the human to him. Ten heart beats, nine, eight. Nick felt a supernaturally strong hand grasp his shoulder and the grip began to tighten. It was a warning. "Mr. Bristow," A low voice called out to him. Nick ignored it. "Mr. Bristow."

"Nicholas," a familiar feminine voice said.

Reluctantly Nick withdrew his fangs from the human's neck, letting the body and the rest of its blood be removed from his vicinity by the beefy vampire bouncer. He accepted the white handkerchief that appeared in front of his face, offered by a hand with long, talon-like, acrylic nails in shocking shades of yellow, pink, and orange. He followed her six-inch platform heels to full thighs, and rounded hips that were barely covered by black spandex.

"Sorry, Cleo," he said to the establishment's owner. A dark stain of red blood smeared the white cloth when he wiped the sticky, warm trail off his chin.

The ancient vampire stood. Nick's gaze followed her snatched waist up past full breasts pushed up and together at a ridiculous volume and finally landed on her angular face. "I'm surprised to see you in my new city." She moved away from the corded off section of the vampire bar.

This section was lined with long black, leather, couches. A private area set aside for the exchanging of blood between vampires and humans. For the human, the consumption of vampire blood provided a unique high. To his left another vampire pulled away from his meal, blood dripping down his chin. Although, Nick felt no pull to it. Blood laced with vampire venom held no appeal for other vampires.

Nick followed Cleo into the more densely populated area. The atmosphere of Incognito was dark and the music booming. It had an upscale gothic feel that most human bars lacked. "We just relocated a few decades ago."

"I just followed the blood," Nick teased. "And the scent of your stunning self." He picked up one of her hands and kissed the back of it. "My lady." Cleo was not one of the first vampires ever created but she'd lived a lot longer than his four centuries.

"Ever the charmer Nicholas," she said pulling her hand away and running her sharp nails down one cheek. "Where is your other half these days?"

"We're not..." Nick's voice trailed off.

Cleo slipped a hand around his arm and began to guide him across the space. Dancing bodies parted for them as they walked straight through the crowded dance floor towards the crammed long wooden bar. "You will be," she said. "Antonio," she called to the busy bartender.

The gorgeous, copper skinned man didn't pause his drink making but cocked his head, acknowledging his boss.

"Nicholas's whiskey is on me tonight."

The bartender nodded.

"My goddess," Nickolas crooned.

"For your broken heart," she said pulling her hand from his arm. "Don't make any trouble for me." Her voice was gentle but deadly.

"I make no promises," Nick said, kissed her on the cheek and watched her turn. Long, stick-straight black hair brushed against her round backside as she walked through a velvet curtain even he didn't get an invitation past.

"Top shelf, neat," Antonio the vampire bartender said, sliding an overfilled glass with no ice in front of Nick. "Only the best for Cleo's personal guests."

"I'd rather be your personal guest," Nick said, taking a big gulp of the burning liquor. His little chat with Cleo had brought up some things. Someone he preferred not to talk about. Antonio looked him up and down while Nick raised the glass to his lips once more. Antonio nodded to one of his fellow bartenders and then leaned over the bar, close to Nick. He brushed long fingers against Nick's wrist. "Come with me Baby. I've got something that can take that edge off."

Nick shrugged, downed the rest of his whisky in one go, and followed the bartender into a back hallway behind the bar. He was led into a comfortable staff lounge area. Antonio closed the door behind them and before the lock was slid fully into place, Nick's mouth was on his, pressing Antonio up against the wall. Nick went for the vampire's leather pants and then felt long fingers on his, halting him.

"Oh no gorgeous. We're here to fight your demons."

Antonio flipped them, pressing Nick's back to the wall. He kissed Nick's neck while he unbuttoned his pants. He slid down in front of Nick as he exposed his length. Antonio made a pleased sound and Nick stiffened. Long fingers brushed up the underside of his shaft. Mouth and fingers encased him and Nick lost himself. His hands gripped the bartender's hair and pulled. Antonio responded with even more pressure. He stroked and sucked, and Nick knew only the feel of the stunning vampire's mouth on his cock. But it wasn't this vampire. It was a different one entirely. One with eyes plagued by past misdeeds and porcelain skin. Soft waves of hair were gripped in Nick's hands, but they were golden, not black.

His body tensed, on the edge of release. Just before he came, the face he wanted to escape flashed through his mind. He would never be released from this torment. He would never be free.

The bartender sucked every last drop that flowed through his soft lips and swallowed. With one last swipe of his tongue, he licked Nick clean and stood, bringing Nick's jeans with him. Nick's eyes burned with the hunger for more. "My break is over I'm afraid."

Nick made a face.

"Come on ginger Ken Doll, I'll get you some more

whiskey."

Antonio led him back to the bar. Nick waited somewhat impatiently. Antonio slid the whiskey in front of him. Nick drained the glass in one go, winked at the bartender and moved towards the exit. Chad was off in an hour, he could finish up what he had in mind with the human.

He decided to take the short cut through the Rose Garden and get back to the apartment before his heightened libido had him killing someone tonight. He passed an attractive couple in their forties as he hurried down the path. His pace quickened until it came to a very abrupt stop. He sniffed. Blood. Fresh and dripping. His cock would have to wait. Fate had other plans.

Jules walked from the restaurant next to the tall wolf. She expected Tai to hand the ticket to the valet, but instead he took Monica's hand and walked down the side walk. "But the car..." Monica began, trailing behind him

"You didn't think dinner was it, did you?"

Jules cringed, more than ready to return to Aboit and never see the werewolf again. Being around him was unfortunately intoxicating. He reminded her of a time when the only light in her life was the presence of a few werewolves, and one mad vampire queen. He was warmth and kindness as Stephen and his brother had been. Between his lazy calm and consistent snuck glances, Jules had a feeling he was already wrapped around her finger. *I'd like to see what he could do with those fingers...* She cut off the thought, full stop. *What?* That part of her was long dead. Her only desire felt between the pages of her romance novels. There was no way that was coming back now. Towards this werewolf.

"Tai has something planned for Monica." Luca said once again close to Jules's ear. Or as close as his tall stature would allow.

Jules shook free of her surprising previous inner monologue. "You know I can hear you from up there." She didn't bother to angle her face in his direction conversationally but instead continued to stare straight ahead.

"Yes," Luca said, but leaned over again. "But this way I get closer to you without you threatening to kill me."

"You're mistaken." Crossing her arms, she continued to avoid looking up at him. "The threat should remain implied."

"Okay." Luca chuckled lightly. For the briefest of moments, she let herself enjoy the deep, rich sound.

The four of them turned yet another corner, toward the Rose Garden downtown and Tai announced, "we've arrived." He gestured dramatically. Jules's gaze shot up. An elderly man in a top hat rode toward them atop an old-fashioned carriage. The kind Jules knew well, it reminded her of a time that had long passed.

Tai motioned toward the cart, covered in lines of roses. The man's lapel and even the horses' restraints were adorned with them.

"For me?" Monica asked in playful shock.

"Just for you." Tai offered a hand to help Monica up. "It's like that movie you made me watch about a dozen times now."

"Hardy har har," Monica mocked as he climbed up and sat on the seat next to her. Monica motioned for Luca and Jules to join them.

"They're just going to start making out," Luca whispered in her ear. She startled, not having noticed he had moved to stand behind her. His breath brushed her cheek, but no part of him touched her.

"Are you coming or not?" Tai asked.

"No, you two go ahead," Jules answered. Luca wasn't wrong about what was to come for the young human couple. Jules didn't want to spoil their fun.

"You sure?" Monica asked, looking from Jules, to Luca, and back.

"We're sure," Luca answered for them both.

Jules nodded, reassuring her friend.

"Your loss is my gain." Tai shrugged and put an arm

around Monica. She kissed him behind the ear as the carriage pulled away to circle the gardens.

"Good call." Jules chuckled once.

"Walk with me?" Luca motioned toward one of the many pathways and then put both hands in his pockets, like he was resisting touching her. Something stirred inside her at the show of respect for the boundary she'd set.

"Do I have a choice?" Jules glared at him, but there was more playfulness in it this time.

"No." He stated evenly and continued to wait for her. "But, I'm a good time. Trust me."

"That's a lot to ask."

"It doesn't have to be." He smiled softly at her. Jules met his eyes once more. She narrowed her own, decided, and then moved to his side. It could be a trap. If it was, he was the best liar she'd ever known. "See, that wasn't so hard." His long stride slowed to fit her pace.

"You have no idea."

He glanced sideways at her retort. "I don't. But I could." Luca stepped off the path to create space for a young family headed toward them, while still not touching Jules.

"I think no." She fumbled with what to do with her hands. Pockets were a truly wonderful invention.

"Why?" He raised one eyebrow. "Is it because I'm a werewolf?"

Jules remained silent for a moment considering her answer. She chewed on her bottom lip while she considered how truthful to be. "Ironically, no."

"Hmmm... Okay." He didn't press her farther.

They crossed into a deeper section of the garden. Roses lined both sides of the path. Grand rose-covered arches stood over them. Curious, Jules glanced up to see if Luca's head reached the top. "I'm not that tall," he said, smirking down at her.

"Fooled me," she said, surprised to find herself smiling.

"Okay, garden fairy."

She backhanded his stomach. He grunted in surprise. There was no way he was as surprised as she was. She was flirting with this werewolf. There was no point in continuing to tell herself she didn't find him annoyingly attractive.

"So, how old are you really..."

Jules cut off Luca's next question with a hand on his jacket sleeve. This couldn't be happening right now. Jules's body went stiff. Her senses alert. The world around her quieted until all she heard was the sound of sucking and female whimpering. All she smelled was fresh, human, blood. A vampire was draining a human just around the distant corner. Her senses zeroed in on the location. It was close enough. She still had time.

"Jules what's wrong?" Luca asked looking around them, seeing nothing amiss.

"Blood," Jules croaked. "Vampire."

Luca began to say that she was a vampire, but balked as Jules ran away from him. "Jules, stop!" He ran after her. He had to stop her. She would not take a life, unless it was his. He reached for her, but she sped away from him. She was fast, so much faster than he would have guessed. Straining every muscle, he attempted to catch up to her.

Just as she was about to round the corner to another path, he reached her. Threat or no threat he had to stop her or die trying. Luca wrapped both his arms around her, lifting the vampire off her feet. Throwing her body weight against him, she made to kick out. As a counter move, he dropped her feet to the pavement and curved his body over her, around her. Arms and legs thrashed against his grip, but it held firm.

"Get off me," she demanded. Her voice lethal. She clawed at his arms.

"I can't." Luca panted, struggling to hold onto her. "Jules, stop. I can't let you kill anyone."

The fight left her. His grip loosened and she wriggled

free, shoving him away from her. He stumbled back and then crouched, hands raised in a defensive position. An unmovable barrier between her and the corner.

"Kill someone?" A look of incredulity crossed her beautiful face. Trying to dodge him, she ran again, but he cut her off. Pausing, her gaze floated past him. Sighing in defeat, she stood straight up and stilled on the path "I was trying to save someone."

"What?" He straightened, feet stuck to the pavement. His gaze flicked over his shoulder in the direction she had been headed. The smell of fresh blood and vampire stung his nose.

"Now it's too late." Jules motioned in the direction behind him. "Whoever this other vampire is, they're gone, and it's done."

"The human..." Luca began.

"The human is dead. There is no one left to save."

Luca moved toward her slowly, hands out in placation now. Once he was directly in front of her, he reached out to put gentle hands on her arms but then thought better of it. He awkwardly dropped his hands down to his sides. "I'm sorry. Everyone told me you'd be a killer. I just assumed."

Her eyes met his gaze, but there was a vulnerability there he hadn't seen before. It was like her mask had cracked. "I am a killer. But I try not to be one now. It's hard. I slip up. But it's been decades since I...I don't kill at will. Many of us don't."

"I didn't know." His eyes pleaded with her to understand. His fingers twitched, desperate to brush her cheek, her neck. Anything she'd give him access too. He moved one more step into her space, eyes locked on hers. "Forgive me?"

"Fuck it," Jules said under her breath.

"Fuck what...?" Every thought flew out of his brain when she gripped his jacket, pulling his face down to hers. Luca hunched at an almost extreme angle as their lips met. Her hands slid around his waist, under his jacket. His fingers found her hair and the side of her neck. A thumb brushed over her exposed collarbone, causing a shutter to escape her. Her mouth opened for his. Their tongues caressed and searched each other's mouths. His mouth cooled pleasantly as her touch eased the fire inside him.

Jules had gone mad. She was confused, elated, on fire, and alive. More alive than she'd felt in centuries. Something inside her knew that Luca could wake her up in a way she'd never experienced if only she'd let him close enough to try.

The first impulsive decision she'd made, maybe ever, had changed the course of her life. At least she suspected it would, if she chose to give in to him when they came up for air. Well, when he did, she didn't need to breathe.

His hands slid down her shoulders to her back. Her skin burned lightly wherever his fingers trailed. Large, warm hands settled on her hips. He gripped her like he was about to lift her off her feet when his phone buzzed. Hers was in Monica's small clutch, back on the carriage ride.

They pulled back simultaneously as the phone began to ring. "It's probably Tai. He'll just keep calling," Luca said, voice deep and breathless. His forehead rested on her own. Noses almost brushing as they breathed.

"You'd better answer it then." She pulled away. One of them had to. A gasp emitted into the air when he pulled her back into him, wrapping one muscled arm around her as she rested against his torso. With the other hand, he answered his ringing phone. "Yeah. We'll be there in a minute," he said to Tai and then hung up.

Jules shifted enough to look up at him. Studying his flushed face her teeth dug into her bottom lip. A warm thumb brushed over it, releasing the pressure. He hunched again, his lips becoming a gentle whisper against hers.

"Nope." She shoved him back. Unable to keep from smiling, she turned from him, walking back the way they had come. "We're out of time."

"Oh, that's just cruel," he said, jogging a little to get beside her again.

"I never claimed not to be."

"So does this mean you forgive me?" His hands moved back to his pockets while he paced her. "Am I out of the dog house?"

"Maybe," she conceded. "But don't get too excited. You're still chained up in the yard."

A laugh burst from him, joined by a delicate chuckle.

"I'll be sleeping on the couch before you know it," he said with a wink.

"Don't get ahead of yourself, Dog-man."

Luca wasn't ready for the evening to end. He wanted to know everything about and do everything with this creature next to him. He found himself committing fully to the idea. But he sensed hesitation in her. Despite the fact she had initiated the best kiss of his eighty years of life. They had time. Impatiently, he'd wait. However, one thing was certain. He would have that time with her. He would do what he must to keep his pack from hurting her. His new objective was to keep her safe at any cost.

CHAPTER SEVEN

Becoming Star-Crossed

J ules laid frustratingly awake in her bed that night. The book sitting on her bedside table wasn't even an adequate distraction. After reading the same page three times without comprehension, she'd given up. Instead, their perfect kiss replayed over in her mind, yet again. Was he worth it? Was Luca Cain, a werewolf, worth giving up the peace she found in her solitude? Would he add to her life or destroy it? Maybe both, if she was honest.

With an aggravated groan, Jules got up and walked to her living room. Gliding to sit on the plush couch, remote in hand, she turned on some makeover show Monica had been watching. She zoned out, almost immediately. Jules bit her bottom lip, remembering his heat, his taste. Woodsy, earthy, with a hint of spices that couldn't quite be placed. One kiss had gotten her so tied up inside. Nearly three centuries without romantic physical contact of any kind was probably the cause of that.

Due to how the first century of her immortal life had been spent, and with whom, she'd vowed to never trust anyone with her body or her heart again. Romantic attachment was not in the cards for her. However, Stephen Cain and his Beta best friend were two of the kindest and gentlest men she'd known in her life. Luca, it seemed, had followed in their footsteps.

"This is hopeless," Jules said aloud and walked out the French doors in her bedroom and through the grass. She gingerly padded down the path of rocks, worn from years of use that came long before her life there. When grass gave way to sand she started to jog.

With no destination in mind, she kept moving. Slowly enough that if some night owl was watching the water they wouldn't see anything other than a young girl running on the beach. Heaven help anyone who thought to take advantage of that.

Jules ran for miles. Five, maybe ten. Her paced slowed as she happened upon a rocky cove she'd never seen before. The clustering of large rocks and caves jutted into the sky above her. Sitting alone on the highest cliff was a lone figure. The moonlight silhouetted his tall and lean frame. Her heart knew him instantly. Frozen and looking up from beneath him, she considered her next move. Watching as he stared out at the water. Two choices arose, hide in the caves until he left or approach. Move on with her life like he'd never existed or throw all her mantras on love, trust, and life into the ocean to be swept away with the waves.

In a blink of time and space she was standing behind him on the rocks. A metaphorical portal to her past life closing behind her. "Did I just discover your thinking spot?"

Luca twisted at her question. Concern, surprise, and then a glimmer of happiness flashed through his eyes as she walked up and sat on the rock next to him.

"Not my only one," he said, his voice husky and deep. "But it's the closest one to you." He nudged her with his elbow.

She giggled quietly. "Hmmm... I hadn't pegged you as the broody type."

"Oh, I am," Luca claimed, playfully stern. "I brood like it's an Olympic sport."

"Oh okay," Jules said, smiling. "My mistake." For a few moments they sat in companionable silence, looking out at the water and listening to the waves.

"Couldn't sleep either, I take it?" he asked, shifting on the rock next to her and looking down at his hands, planted on the rocks by his thighs.

"You know, I really tried..." Her voice trailed off as she shifted enough to face him. Eyes locked, they sat there searching each other for a long moment. Breaking eye contact, Jules bit into the soft flesh of her bottom lip.

Very tentatively, Luca lifted his hand to the side of her face. Fingers just barely brushing against her skin. When she didn't pull away his thumb caressed her lower lip, releasing the tension there. "What have you done to me?" she asked, leaning across the small space between them. His forehead dropped to rest against her own.

"I suspect," he whispered, his lips gliding closer to hers. Breath kissed her skin like a warm breeze. "It's the same thing you've done to me."

Closing the distance between them, her lips met his. The kiss was a chaste one for only a few moments. As his tongue caressed the seam of her lips his hands gripped her hips, moving her onto his lap. She opened for him, melting into the fire that was his touch. One hand moved from her hip to slip under the thin satin tank top, caressing her bare back. Her icy skin warmed at every touch of his fingers, her body igniting at every point of contact.

Jules lifted her hands to his shoulders and pushed him back slightly. He complied with the distance she had put between them, although somewhat reluctantly. Her eyes found his as she panted. "This is a bad idea."

His eyes darkened. "I don't care."

With shifting hands, she released him. Luca's lips came down harder on hers, more desperate than before. Hands sliding down to her backside, pulling her towards him. Her breath caught, feeling the size and hardness of him between her thighs.

Luca stilled as Jules placed one delicate hand against his chest, just over his pounding heart. He paused at her hesitation, pulling back to look at her. She fidgeted with nervousness and uncertainty, tentative for reasons he had yet to discover. "I…" Her voice trailed off.

"We can go as slow as you want." It pained him to offer it. He wanted her right here, right now. Wanted to taste her and cum inside her. He wanted to claim her body and soul. Wanted, with every fiber of his being for her to be his for the taking. Luca could sense uncertainty in her as she stiffened against his lap.

Luca had been with women here and there, mostly human, and mostly only once or twice as needed. Werewolf women wanted mates, partners for life. Until this moment he'd never even considered the possibility. Until this woman, this vampire, had kissed him in the Rose Garden he'd never entertained the idea of something long term.

"I'm sorry. I'm not..."

He dropped his hands from her body as she shifted back, off his lap. He missed the feel and weight of her on him.

Standing, she started to back away. "It's definitely not you I don't want, I just..." She was rambling. It was impossibly vulnerable, and adorable. He'd seen sexy, strong, confident, untouchable, but this was something new. Something deeper. She turned away. He bounded to his feet before he lost her completely. Luca reached out, spun her gently, and pulled her toward him. His hands came to rest on either side of her neck, thumbs tipping her head up softly until her gaze met his hungry one.

"Don't be sorry." He leaned back to bend enough to touch his lips to her forehead in a soft kiss. "If being immortal taught me anything, it's patience."

"Okay," she said pulling herself closer to him, resting her cool cheek against his abdomen.

A growl escaped low in his throat. "However, if you keep touching me, I'm definitely going to have to take a swim in that very cold ocean, like now."

Jules smiled against him, her body shaking slightly as she chuckled. "Well come on then Dog-Man." She pushed away and jumped from the top of the cove of rocks to the sand below. The drop was long, a human would have broken something on impact, but not her. She landed nearly soundlessly while sand shifted and sprayed around her. He watched in awe as she stood from her crouch, salty wind whipping red tendrils of hair around her. A goddess of something, maybe death. She turned, looked back up at him, and threw her arms wide. "You coming or not?"

He was definitely coming. He'd almost cum in his jeans at the sight of her. With a howl he launched himself off the rocks and chased after Jules who had already almost reached the waves.

Nicholas opened the door to Chad's apartment about an hour before sunrise and promptly tripped over a black duffle bag right inside the door. "Again?" Nick mumbled a string of curses under his breath.

"Hi Baby," Chad called over the cheery music reverberating off the walls around them.

"You left your gym bag in front of the door again," Nick chastised.

"Oh, did I? Silly me." The human's tone of voice was strangely clipped. Off somehow.

Nick's nose crinkled as he moved farther into the small space. Chad left the human concoction that smelled rancid to Nick's vampire senses boiling on the stove, walked over, stood on his sock covered toes, and pecked Nick on the mouth. Nick grasped the back of Chad's neck and deepened the kiss, thinking of the satisfaction to be taken from the human's body. Not blood, he'd had plenty of that earlier tonight. He hadn't actually meant to kill the two humans in the Rose Garden. Unfortunately, the woman had pricked her finger and sealed her fate. The man might still be alive. He'd caught up with him shortly after finishing the woman. But he'd scented werewolf and fled the scene of the crime without looking back. He hadn't taken the time to ensure the man was finished.

Every once in a while, he felt actual remorse about his lack of control. Dwelling on it tended to unsettle him. Tonight was one of those rarities, he wanted nothing more than to get out of his head and into Chad's bed. Nick slid one hand under the man's t-shirt. He was rock solid, very muscled for a man in tech security.

Obviously not on board with that plan, Chad pulled away, tapping Nick on the chest with his palm. "Welcome home. I hope you're hungry." The human, dislodged himself from Nick's grip and returned to the stove.

"I already ate, sorry," Nick replied.

"You never eat my cooking," Chad complained in a whine.

"I only eat when I'm hungry," Nick lied. "And I got hungry before I got back." He added, leaning on the counter with a grin, hoping to change the path this conversation was on.

Chad rolled his eyes as some of the pot's contents plopped into one of the two bowls on the kitchen table. He moved to add noodles to the second bowl until Nick snatched it, replacing it in the kitchen cabinet. "Fine." Chad moved from the small kitchen counter to the two-seater table nearby. "How was your night?"

Unable to think of a way out of a mundane conversation and into immediate sexual depravity, Nick sat in a chair next to Chad. "Not exceptional. How was yours?" Nick asked flatly, his lack of true interest not being properly concealed.

"Were you anywhere near the Rose Garden?" Chad asked instead of responding to the question.

"No." Nick flinched. "Why?" Nick was glad that Chad was likely too dense to notice the action or slight pitch change to his voice.

"Two people were murdered there, I was worried."

"How terrible," Nick said, feeling Chad's eyes studying him in a way that made him curious as to what he was thinking.

"Completely drained of blood. That's five murders this week," Chad added through a mouthful of noodles. "They're calling him the Fort Miles Phantom now."

"How do you know it's a man?" Nick asked, purposefully

relaxing into a position that conveyed complete nonchalance he didn't feel.

"Statistics." Chad chewed again, grating Nick's nerves. "Besides, that cop he killed was massive. Had to be a man. Cut out his heart and everything. Very vampire melodrama TV show vibes if you ask me."

"Yeah, good thing monsters like vampires don't exist," Nick added trying to sound calm while talking through his teeth.

Chad stopped and stared for a moment, fork half way to his mouth. "What if they do though?" Chad's eyes narrowed on him.

This was not a conversation that could lead to anything good. Chad had never shown interest in the news before. He tended to blather on about nothing, people and places Nick didn't actually care about. That suited Nick just fine. "What did you and your buddies snort at work?" Nick stood and took the bowl out from under Chad's fork. Chad protested. Nick ignored him. The bowl clattered into the sink. He was either getting this man into bed or killing him. Whichever made this line of interrogation stop first would have to do.

Shoulders tense, Nick remained facing away from the human. He waited until the sounds of Chad rising and walking over came from behind him. Reaching around Nick, Chad put his fork in the sink next to the discarded bowl and slid his arms around Nick's torso. "Why so tense, Baby?" he kissed Nick's back, through his shirt. "Bad night?"

Nick's hand rested on one of Chad's. "You could say that." He turned in the man's arms and then pulled his shirt over his head. To bed it was then.

Jules walked with Luca back toward her little house. Dawn was minutes away. They were taking a risk, even now, walking down the secluded beach together. But, when he'd asked if she wanted company on her walk back, Jules couldn't bring herself to say no. The entire night behind her felt out of time and place in Jules's life. Today she wasn't just living, she was alive.

The sky lit with pinks and oranges over the water. Jules was cutting it close but hadn't been able to leave him until now. She'd drawn a line in the sand just on the far side of kissing and Luca had respected every boundary. Not once had he pushed her or coerced her into more. It was a foreign feeling, being respected in one's boundaries. With every passing minute, she felt her walls crumbling. In his large hands, she might just feel safe enough to let her guard down.

The left side of her body was pressed against Luca as they walked. Her arm rested comfortably above his hips. His hand stretched down to reach her waist, caressing her slightly over his flannel button down he'd insisted she wore. The shirt dwarfed her, hanging almost to her knees. The arms rolled up four times to stop at her wrists. She hadn't been cold, but he'd asked her to wear it anyway. She suspected it had something to do with the fact that her nipples had been peaked by the cold water, and his physical closeness. She wasn't going to lie, even to herself, about that one.

"Luca, I know you said you don't care, but if we do this, if we spend any time together, it's going to be very dangerous for both of us." She felt him tense beneath her touch, but it needed to be said. Seeing each other was the selfish choice. "For your pack and my coven, we really should just part ways and move on with our lives."

He stopped walking and spun to face her. When her face craned up to look at him, his hands found the sides of her neck, thumbs caressing her jawline gently. "Do you want that?" he asked after a few more silent seconds.

She bit her bottom lip, thinking through multiple scenarios. Finally, her head shook slowly. "No. I don't. I don't want to disrupt your life... or mine. But I don't want to end this... us, without giving it a chance, either."

"Please, blow mine up." Luca laughed a little. "Let little pieces rain down around me." He wrapped both arms around her, pulling her into him. "I feel more, right here with you, than I have in a long time."

His words mirrored how she felt perfectly. She didn't know how it happened, but in the matter of one night, she went from being completely closed off to the idea of letting someone in, to this. For the first time in centuries, she had hope for the future of her heart.

"I've lived too long to turn away something, or someone, who can make me feel like you do."

"How's that?" he asked

"Alive."

"Yeah," he said with a quiet sigh.

He leaned down to kiss her again, but one pale finger rose to rest against his lips, stopping him. His lips pressed against her finger instead. He smiled. She dropped her hand and smiled despite herself. Tapping his torso her expression hardened into seriousness. "If we are going to do this, Luca, no one can know. Not now. Not until the tension between your pack and my coven has settled."

"Secrets are kinda sexy," he said as his hands slid down her arms and onto her waist. With his large hands he lifted her, her legs bending at the knees to rest on either side of his torso.

"Oh, really."

"One-hundred percent, really."

Face to face, their mouths found each other. Her hands tangled in his hair while his held her to him. Tongues searching once again. Their kiss deepened, melting what was left of Jules's frigid heart. A warming sensation began to tingle across one side of Jules's body. Jules's skin began to heat as she finally pulled back enough to feel the danger.

"Sunrise," she said, breathlessly.

Noticing the impending danger they'd put her in, Luca set her on the sand and turned their bodies so his was blocking hers from the direct rays. "Run," he commanded. Covered in his shadow she ran for her open back door. He stayed close behind her.

Once inside her bedroom she threw the blackout curtains across the open window, plunging them into darkness.

Luca froze in place. He was in Jules's bedroom. Not good. "Um..." he stumbled for what to say once she flipped on the bedside lamp. "I'm going to go." Luca started backing away, towards the door he'd entered through.

Jules studied him. That damned bottom lip being bitten again. That particular action alone was literally going to destroy him. "Or you could..." she hesitated, "stay."

Luca walked toward her, his hands finding the sides of her neck again, fitting like they belonged there. "I would love nothing more than to stay. But I can sense that you're not sure. So, I'm going to go."

"I..." she let her voice go quiet, giving him confirmation that she wasn't ready to open that door entirely.

He tipped her face up again. Her eyes were closed.

"When I get to have you. I want you to be without doubt that it's what you want. I can wait." Luca bent and brushed his lips to her forehead. "I'll see you soon, Little Corpse." Before she even opened her eyes, he slipped out the back curtain, careful to let in as little light as possible.

Jules missed him before she opened her eyes. But she respected the fact that he'd walked away in that moment. That choice cracked her heart open just a little more than it had been moments before. She was falling for this werewolf and was starting to believe she no longer had a choice in the matter.

Jules showered and then crawled into bed to sleep the sunniest of Sundays away. Blankets pulled up over her shoulders, wet hair fanned out behind her, she hoped to dream of a tall, overtly sexy, werewolf rather than the demon who usually haunted her nights.

Luca had dealt with his sexual frustrations by running

back to the cove to retrieve his Jeep. He had taken the long way. He pulled the keys from his pocket and jumped inside, shot Tai a text, and then drove to the nearest gas station before his E-level gas tank left him stranded. He jumped out and jammed his card into the reader when a feminine voice called his name.

Luca spun at Hayley's call. She was seated on Kyle's motorcycle while he pumped gas into its tank.

"Hey," he called back, trotting over to join them at their gas pump.

"What are you doing out here?" Hayley asked.

Luca opened his mouth to answer and then closed it again, knowing he couldn't be honest in his answer. He had always trusted the couple before, but he wouldn't trust either of them with Jules's life.

"Hiding from Carson. That's what he's always up to." Kyle's comment was the first indication that he even knew Luca was standing there talking to his wife.

"It's necessary from time to time," Luca replied, letting the assumption stand.

"Especially when you're his most hated golden boy," Kyle continued.

"Hated?" Hayley asked skeptically.

"Well not by anybody but Carson," Luca responded for Kyle. "At least, I don't think I am."

"It's a safe bet that you're well-liked," Hayley said. "You are a Cain, after all."

"And no one will let me forget it either." Kyle's whiney impression was a little over-dramatized, but not that off from the way Luca had said this to him many times before. Somehow, he felt different about living in that legacy now. Maybe it was that Jules had said the famous ancestor whom he was known for was, in fact, deserving of his reputation. Or the fact that being a Cain connected him to Jules in ways he'd never have imagined, he didn't know.

"Where are you two headed?" Luca asked, noting that they were on a side of town that they didn't usually frequent.

"Beach day with my babe," Kyle said, winking at his wife.

"Little chilly for a day at the beach," Luca commented. The sun was out, yes, but the spring air still had a bite to it.

"That's what I told him," Hayley said.

"Oh, pipe down both of you! It'll be fun."

"Do you want to join us?" Hayley asked.

"No, that's okay. I think I have to stop hiding."

"Suit yourself," Kyle shrugged.

Luca waved to the couple while returning to the Jeep. It was time to find out how much Carson knew about Jules and what he had to do to keep her safe. In eighty years of life Luca had had girlfriends and flings, but what he felt with Jules was different. He would do what it took to keep her safe and away from his Alpha's brutality.

Kyle lay sprawled on the sand, music in his ears. The chilled sun was beating down on his skin as he dozed. Hayley tapped Kyle on the shoulder with her foot. Kyle stirred, pulled one earbud out, and looked over to where she sat. She looked so beautiful, looking down at him, the watery horizon framing her outline. The perfect view. She'd stolen his jacket long ago and had her long dress tucked down around her feet, but she looked happy. Or she had the last time he'd looked at her. Now, she looked confused.

"What's up?" he asked.

"Did Luca seem off to you?"

"Off how?"

"Like he was hiding something," she explained.

"Not really," Kyle said. "Same old Luca to me." He hadn't really thought about it, if he was being honest.

"I wonder how his date went last night," she said conversationally while scrolling through something on her phone.

"What date?" Kyle asked. Wondering how or why Hayley would retain such information.

"You told me about it!" she almost scolded, her phone forgotten beside her.

"I mentioned it," Kyle clarified, "in passing. Haven't thought of it since."

"You're such a great friend," she said sarcastically.

"I am actually. Luca doesn't like when people pry."

"I wouldn't call this prying. I'd call it being interested."

"Oh, you're interested in Luca are you."

"Inescapably," she said, teasing him now. Her smile was irresistible. Without warning, Kyle pulled her toward him.

She laughed and let her body drop onto his carelessly. The wind was knocked out of him when her elbow struck him in the stomach. He groaned.

"Serves you right, now my feet are cold," she said. She then tucked them between his legs and the sand.

"All better?" he asked, playing with a strand of her hair as she looked down at him, her face expressing the same amount of love he felt.

"Everything's perfect now," she said, then kissed him softly.

CHAPTER EIGHT

Howling at the Moon

Luca was stopped just as he was approaching the front door of the Den. "Where have you been?" Ben demanded in a hushed tone.

"Around. My phone died." Which was true in a sense. Its battery had died sitting on the seat of his Jeep.

Just then, the screen door opened, nearly hitting Ben in the side of the face. "Be forewarned, Carson's very unhappy with you," Kip whispered, poking his head through the open doorway.

"What else is new?" Luca asked, rolling his eyes.

"Luca!" Ben scolded. "It's that lack of respect that has you on such rocky ground."

"I think it's a difference of opinion that has me in our Alpha's crosshairs. The attitude is just a byproduct," Luca half-teased.

Ben looked at him sternly. Apparently, he was in no mood for jokes, but he didn't say anymore.

"You worry too much." Luca clapped Ben on the shoulder and entered the Den.

Carson cornered him the second he walked through the front door. "You are my Beta. Being unable to reach you is unacceptable."

"Dead phone. No charger." He held it up as if to prove that it was in fact dead.

Carson stormed toward him, his face inches from Luca's. "Next time, buy one," Carson snarled between gritted teeth.

Luca didn't back down. "What did I miss that was so important?" Luca asked, keeping his voice flat, unaffected by

Carson's threat.

Carson stared daggers at him, but still, Luca didn't submit. The call to submit to the Alpha was difficult to resist, but not impossible for the Beta, like it would have been for any other wolf under Carson's command.

Carson sniffed in Luca's direction. "You smell like dead things and the ocean." Carson backed up with a grimace. A clear cover to look like he'd won the standoff. He squared his shoulders and said, "now that you're here, maybe we can start the meeting I called before noon."

"Five minutes and I'm all yours." Luca shrugged. "Like you said, I smell."

Carson growled audibly.

"Thanks for the understanding," Luca said with a smirk and then took the stairs two at a time, laughing to himself as he went.

Luca headed for his bathroom. In six minutes he was showered, dressed, and was walking back out of his bedroom door. When he arrived downstairs once again, the pack had congregated in the family room. Carson was pacing menacingly. "Well, now that the Beta has finally graced us with his presence, we can start," Carson snapped as Luca took a seat on the dilapidated couch.

"Who has good news?" He looked momentarily, manically gleeful.

No one spoke.

"Are you telling me that no one has any information on the vampire problem?"

Luca looked away. Luckily, some of the others did too, out of guilt at being unsuccessful no doubt. Luca looked at the floor, hoping that his expressive face wouldn't give him away.

"No one has found their location?" Carson asked, glowering at the group. "That is unacceptable. This leader of theirs has evaded us once already. That will not happen again." Carson's tone confirmed that orders were going to be to kill Jules when they did catch her. Fierce, fiery, and sexy as hell,

Jules. His Jules. If he could call her that. He nearly smiled but caught himself. Luca's jaw clenched tightly.

Jed finally spoke up. "I've been unsuccessful at finding the coven's location."

Luca tried not to sigh due to the relief he felt.

"But I have ascertained that the red-headed female lives somewhere near the coast. Also, I believe she lives separately from the others," Jed continued, turning Luca's emotions upside down. They were too close to her.

"But I'll keep looking."

"See that you do!" Carson snapped.

Max sniggered.

Luca scowled over at him. There was no need for Carson's temper to be indulged.

As the lack-of-progress reports continued, Luca had to bite his tongue. He wouldn't let them harm her. He would do whatever he had to. To keep from giving himself away, however, he planted his feet on the floor and tried to keep the finger tapping to a minimum.   After what felt like hours of Carson's subjugation and the pack's pandering to their over bearing Alpha, Luca was convinced that, other than Jed's information, no one had learned anything else he needed to know to keep Jules safe. Carson's rant, however, was dragging on.

"Now, who's with me?" Carson shouted.

This got a rise out of everyone except Luca.

"We don't have enough cause to attack. We have no proof that they've killed. We are rushing to uninformed conclusions," Luca stated evenly.

His point was met with utter silence.

"They may not kill here in Aboit. But there were two more vampire murders in Fort Miles last night. That's six this week alone." Ben said in his ever soft tone. "They likely use the city as their feeding grounds."

Carson motioned towards Ben, like the matter was settled.

"But we have to prove it's them," Luca countered, his voice

strong and commanding.

"It's enough proof if I say it is," Carson growled.

"You are not judge, jury, or God," Luca snapped back, standing to his feet. Carson's considerable height still unable to diminish Luca's ancestral presence.

"No, I'm better," Carson growled low in his throat. "I'm the Alpha."

"You're an Alpha," Luca growled in response. "I've followed better." Then he took a step back for his own self-preservation. He could take the pack. His father's line gave him that right. But Carson's death was still the only way to do it.

Carson's glare was murderous.

"Killing them without clear evidence is wrong." Luca turned his back on his Alpha and pack, walking from the room.

He strode furiously out the front door heading for his Jeep until he realized that he'd left the Jeep keys upstairs. So, he paced angrily in the side yard instead. He desperately wanted to storm back in and defend her. To tell them all that he knew she didn't kill humans, didn't even feed from them. To convince them that they were wrong about her, but that desire was utterly illogical. What he was doing with Jules was a betrayal the pack would never forgive. In fact, Luca thought that if Carson knew the extent of his betrayal, he would kill Jules just for spite. But that didn't really matter, because Luca was pretty sure Carson intended to kill Jules no matter what. It was clear that their relationship had to remain a secret. Revealing his feelings for her to anyone endangered them both.

"Luca. Luca! What was that about?" Ben asked, running up beside him.

Luca ran his tongue over his teeth, deciding how much he could say without throwing Jules, and likely himself, under the bus. "I don't know." Luca shrugged. "This vampire. She didn't attack us. She's the one who stopped the fight." He spoke very carefully. "And we don't have proof that she's hurt anyone. Why is Carson so intent on killing her?"

"Killing?" Ben raised one eyebrow. "She's already dead. You understand that, right?"

"You know what I mean."

"We can't risk letting those monsters roam around innocent humans," Ben said.

"What if she doesn't kill?" Luca asked.

"They all kill," Ben stated bluntly. "Luca, you're a young wolf. You haven't seen the terrors that I have. The tyranny they've enforced over our race throughout the years is unacceptable. Every being on earth will be better off with one, or three, less of those things in existence. You get that don't you?" Ben asked, jabbing Luca in the ribs. He guessed Ben was trying to lighten the mood.

Luca faked a chuckle. "I know, but…"

Ben took him by the shoulder and steered him back toward the Den. "Luca, you're young. I know you don't understand fully. Be assured that they are the enemy. And that they are dead, soulless beings. To destroy them would be to put them out of their misery."

"How?" Luca stopped walking and looked at Ben.

"Only one thing is as deadly to them as silver is to us. The sun," he stated simply.

Luca offered a fake, lighthearted, eye roll. "I know that. But how else do you destroy them?" He was treading on thin ice, but if there was another way, he needed to know.

"Yes, Luca, everyone knows that sunlight kills vampires. But just as…"

Luca waited patiently. Ben's explanations sometimes took a while, but his knowledge was vast.

"…silver has to circulate in our bloodstreams to kill us," Ben continued, "vampires have to be in direct sunlight for prolonged periods of time for the sunlight to be fatal. Vampires are quite strong, so this can be hard to accomplish. Our ancestors devised another way. Years ago, we used to bury them alive. It is likely that many are still buried deep in the ground. Their locations forgotten forever," Ben's voice trailed off like he was remembering something.

"We bury them?" That doesn't sound so bad, Luca thought.

But Ben continued, "not in this age. Today's technology makes killing them much simpler."

Luca waited, impatiently now, for his real question to be answered.

"Now, we have sun emulating lightbulbs we can carry to weaken them for the kill. Then, removing their heads works quite nicely."

Protecting Jules from this fate was now Luca's number one priority.

Jules tapped snooze on her alarm, feeling like only moments had passed. She woke from a dreamy haze with images of Luca and memories of his touch coaxing her gently awake. As she hit snooze for the third time, she noticed a bunch of waiting messages. Five were from Gabriel asking where she was and telling her to be more careful in five different ways. One from Monica wishing her a happy sun-induced hibernation day. And the last three were from an unknown number. She read the first one. *Hi, it's me. Tai gave me your number. Don't be mad at him.* And the second. *I assume you know who me is.* And the last. *They are closing in on you. I know you can take care of yourself, but please, be cautious.* She smiled, saved the number under the contact name L.C., and punched in a quick response to each of them and then rose to get ready for the work day.

She didn't know if it was wise to stop at the coffee shop. She wasn't sure that she could keep a secret like this from Monica. After a short amount of consideration, she decided to stop in anyway.

When she walked through the door, Monica beamed at her. "I know something good," she teased.

"Don't tell me." Jules knew it probably had something to

do with Saturday night, and that would send her straight into an immersive Luca Cain spiral.

"Okay. Then, spill. Why didn't you answer my text yesterday? You did promise me you'd explain everything." Monica wore a faux scolding expression.

Jules had contemplated how much to say on the drive over. She didn't like the idea of creating a wedge between herself and the human who knew her best. "I really can't tell you," Jules said and smiled sheepishly.

"Jules!" Monica came around the counter, neglecting the customer waiting to order. "What do you mean you can't tell me?"

Jules pointed toward the waiting woman.

"I'm taking ten," she shouted to the back. No one responded. Monica rolled her eyes. "Don't go anywhere." She pointed an accusatory finger at Jules.

Jules walked a couple paces away and stared aimlessly at the television over her head. "The Fort Miles Phantom has struck again. Two more civilians fell victim to this madman in the Rose Garden Saturday evening. The civilians' identities are being kept confidential until the families can be notified. The Harrison family is still unavailable for comment on the murder of Officer Micha Harrison, however the official statement from the department will be released later today."

Jules looked over as the door dinged, announcing the now very angry customer's departure.

"Come on." Monica walked past Jules, motioning for her to follow her outside. Monica rushed over to one of the metal tables set up for customers who preferred the open atmosphere and sat quickly. Jules slid into a chair opposite her. She glanced up, it was going to be a blessedly foggy day.

"Now can you tell me?"

Jules sighed. "It's not that eventful really. I went for a run Saturday night and slept all day Sunday" Jules hesitated, "by myself."

"And your phone was?"

"On silent."

"Jules, I know you. You're hiding something."

"Maybe." Jules's face scrunched into a supremely guilty expression.

"See, the last time you looked at me like that, you were trying to friend-dump me for my own good. Now look at us, we're better friends than we ever were before I knew your crumby secret."

Jules sighed.

"What? Is it Luca?"

Monica smiled giddily when Jules failed to respond. "He likes you. I could totally tell that he likes you." She was seeping excitement.

"Yeah," Jules said. "I caught that too." She pressed her lips together, unable to say more.

"So, then what's the problem? Mrs. Prentiss was human once, right?"

"She was." This was irrelevant to Jules and Luca, but she ran with the excuse anyway. "And Gabriel had to turn her into a vampire."

"And is she unhappy?" Monica asked.

"No," Jules answered honestly. Jules didn't like this. She wanted to be honest with Monica. She wanted to tell her everything that had happened since the anniversary double date had come to an end. She desperately wanted to tell her how accepting the idea of being with Luca had changed things inside her. How she felt more hopeful and alive. However, the secret had to be kept, for her safety and for Luca's.

"But you do like him, don't you?"

"I don't... not like him."

"So, what? Because you're..." Monica didn't say undead, but Jules knew she was thinking it. "It means you can't ever find love?"

Jules's phone beeped. It was a message from Luca. Jules couldn't help but smile.

"You're smiling. Who was that?" Monica asked.

"No one. I have to get to work." Jules stood.

"Jules! There is still something you're not telling me."

Jules hesitated and then spoke. "Yes," Jules admitted, "and I promise to tell you what it is when I can."

"Well, that is very frustrating." Monica scowled.

"I know. I'm sorry, please trust me."

"Fine. But this conversation is not over." Monica stood, taking a few steps closer to the coffee shop.

"Agreed." Jules smiled at the annoyed look on Monica's face. They'd be alright. And as soon as she could, Jules would tell her everything.

Nick was dreaming. Glowing around the edges like always, was the object of his most prominent affection. Hair curled and golden. Body strong and agile. His love's mortal life had ended before his twenty-second year of life. Long before even Nick's grandparents had been conceived. Eyes, of the most unique color, stared up at him as a body glided down his own. Nick felt... feelings from his still heart as he desperately hung onto sleep.

Tingling touches slid down his abdomen as soft, full lips took his cock deep, to the back of the throat. Blood tears were forming in his eyes. Nick didn't want them to escape.

Nick woke with a start as his body reacted to the real time blow job he was currently receiving. He'd spent all of Sunday locked inside Incognito, the vampire bar, due to the sun. It had to be the next morning by now. Nick pulled on sexy bartender Antonio's curls, yanking the man off his stiff cock. Antonio's grin was almost manic. "Come on, Baby. Don't get shy on me now."

"Did I ask you to put my dick in your mouth?" Nick asked, incredulous.

Antonio shook his head coyly.

"Then I don't want to be touched." Nick sat up, turned off by the uninvited contact. And the fact that the mouth in his dreams was a thousand miles away and not currently speaking to him. If he hadn't messed things up again, he would be home right now. Wherever the one he loved was. The fight that ended them this time had been ugly. He'd been drifting through his undead, life drinking and killing his little heart out. Fucking and faking it ever since. This time felt final and for the first time in his immortal existence, Nick felt truly dead.

He stood from the black leather couch, forcing Antonio to move aside as well. Pulled up his black ripped jeans and stepped away to find his boots. He swore when he tripped over a nearly empty whiskey glass, dumping the rest of its contents onto the floor by accident. He pulled on one boot, leaving the laces loose, while the glass rolled away under a piece of furniture.

"You didn't mind yesterday," Antonio whined.

"And now I do." He looked under the staff lounge table and found his other boot. He pulled it on. Picking his phone up off the side table he checked the time, saw a missed call from Chad, and strode for the door. He'd sent his place-holder a message letting him know he'd be gone all day and all night. What could the man possibly want? And why hadn't he thrown him out yet?

"When will I see you again?" Antonio asked, still sitting on the couch where Nick had left him.

"Don't know," Nick replied and walked from the room, back to the main bar area. Incognito was nearly empty for the day, just one Vampire drinking from the source and the bouncer watching over them. Nick nodded at the bouncer and had almost made it to the door when he heard Cleo call out to him. "Stop."

He did so.

"Come here," she ordered.

Nick's shoulder's dropped. Feeling like a scolded child he did as he was told. The stunning specimen of a Vampire looked deep into his eyes before she spoke. "I do not mind harboring you here, darling boy, but you're haunted." She rose her long painted fingernails to his face, caressing it gently. "I see it in those eyes. They carry such mirth, normally. You're lost, Baby."

"Yeah," Nick's voice was clipped. Fighting back emotions he didn't want to feel. "I lost my anchor. I'm adrift. I can't find my way back."

Her hand slid down his arm. Both her hands settled where his arms crossed over his chest. "You can be your own anchor."

Nick shook his head but couldn't speak.

"You can. You will."

Nick wanted to believe her but didn't know how. Without saying a word, he kissed her on the cheek and walked from the bar. Just in time to wipe a stray blood tear off his face with the back of his sleeve.

Nick shook himself free, boxing up the emotion once more, and the Fort Miles Phantom roamed the streets for another day.

Jules walked into the school at her normal time. The day being a rather foggy one. "Jules!" Gabriel shouted as she passed his classroom door on the way to the library.

She stopped in her tracks but took a moment too long to turn around to face him.

"Gabriel, I was fine. I am fine. You need to stop worrying so much."

"It's my right to worry about you," he said with a smile that didn't reach his eyes. "I thought the..." He hesitated and lowered his voice. They were a stone's throw away from a student in every direction. "Wolves may have found you."

Jules sighed, she'd been doing this over protective song and dance for too many years now. Jules had thought that bringing Eileen into the coven would have mellowed him out in that respect but, if anything, his need to know everything had amplified. "I'm sorry Gabriel. You'll just have to trust that I can take care of myself."

"Why are you being like this?" Gabriel asked, but it sounded like an accusation.

It grated Jules's nerves more than it had the right too. "You set them on this path Gabriel. But the consequences are ours to bare."

"I didn't realize my caring about your wellbeing was such a burden," Gabriel snapped.

Jules tried not to roll her eyes. She knew his intentions were pure but if she was going to keep Luca a secret she needed him to back off and let her breathe, metaphorically of course.

"We should have moved when we discovered a pack resided here, like I wanted to, years ago," Gabriel said, crossing his arms.

"I'm not having this fight again." Jules was so tired of this merry-go-round of the same fight repeating every couple of months. "And we can't talk about this now anyway. You know that." Jules's tone was harsh, authoritative.

"We can't just not talk about it either," he said, under his breath. Their body language must have been giving off the signals of their argument, because kids were skirting around them and beginning to stare.

Gabriel sighed audibly. "Fine. I have to run study hall today. Come to our place tonight, we can talk about it then."

"I don't know. Maybe." She turned and began walking toward the library once more.

"What do you mean maybe? What else do you have to do tonight?" he shouted after her, making more than one student gasp and giggle.

Jules ignored this outburst and continued on her way to her destination.

Luca had been in relatively constant contact with Jules throughout the day. He now knew that she worked at the school library. And that she very much enjoyed her current job. That Monica had questions and suspicions, which was probably his fault. He hadn't been very subtle when asking Tai for Jules's number. And he now knew that the male vampire in her coven was being weirdly overprotective. Luca thought he was being more possessive than protective but didn't say this to Jules. He read her latest message before he started the Jeep.

I have to go over to Gabriel's tonight or he will keep pushing me. I probably won't respond for a while. I get a dopey smile on my face every time I read a message you send. He's bound to notice.

Luca laughed out loud, then punched in a reply. *Perfect timing. I'll be away from my phone for the next few hours. Apex full moon.* And then as an afterthought he added another message. *That dopey smile. I have it too.*

The Jeep's engine roared to life as the key turned. He was not looking forward to all the inquiries concerning his behavior of late. However, if he was late this time, Carson may actually have his head. Still, it was comforting to know that Jules was safe for the night. All the wolves would be preoccupied.

Luca's phone beeped.

Do you, Boo. Go howl at that moon.

Yet another burst of laughter escaped him. At the next stoplight, he replied. *Very funny.* Luca glanced up through the windshield. The moon was already on the rise.

The next message he received winked at him with the addition of, *I think it was funny. Have a good hunt.*

I will. Have a good night.

Luca put his phone down, in the center console. He had arrived. He pulled up to the fence at the local preserve, which was already lined with cars. This was the night of the full moon, tonight the animal would take over. Werewolves could, of course, turn at will. But during the apex of each full moon cycle, the animal inside was forcibly, wonderfully, released.

The patch of gravel next to Carson's vehicle was left open for the pack's Beta. Luca parked the Jeep there and climbed out. With a running leap, he launched himself over the chain-link fence, landing with a thump on the other side. Luca wasn't sure how Carson managed this, but every full moon, the pack that Carson called his own, gathered to pay their respects to their Alpha and run as one.

A few young wolves howled as Luca approached one of several groupings of werewolves. "Hi Luca," said a female wolf, batting her eyelashes at him.

He smiled cordially but moved farther into their midst. Some wolves bowed slightly toward him when he passed. Luca saw many familiar faces, some of which he did not expect to see tonight.

Kyle playfully barked in his direction. Hayley, standing next to him, smacked him on the back of the head. Luca joined them near the center of the gathering pack.

"I'm surprised you're here," Luca commented.

"I am too," Kyle admitted. "However, our almighty Alpha informed me that I was to be here, or else."

"What do you suppose that means?" Hayley asked. A look of barely restrained panic on her face. She took Kyle's hand and made a face at Adam, who had scowled at her.

Luca shrugged. He didn't want to worry Hayley, but, he figured it probably had something to do with whatever punishment Carson had decided Kyle deserved for his insubordination.

Kyle ran his hand down Hayley's long, silky hair, kissing her on the side of the head. "It'll be fine."

Watching them together made him think of Jules. Of his new-found passion for her. Of his need to protect her. Everything seemed to bring his mind back to Jules.

Carson's howl pierced the darkening night sky. It was met with more howls. Luca, Hayley, and Kyle did not join them.

"Once again, it is pleasing to see you all," Carson began.

Some wolves continued to stand in their human form. Some of the more feral wolves crept from the woods in their wolf form. Luca, Kyle, and some others began to sit on the grass, knowing Carson's speeches tended to run long.

"Looking at all of you shows me the inspiring strength I

have behind me..."

"Here we go," Kyle muttered.

Hayley kicked him lightly.

Luca suppressed a snicker.

"A lot has progressed since the last Moon Hunt, but first and foremost I must announce a cause for celebration."

Kyle looked at Luca, who was silently hoping Carson hadn't had Jules killed in the last three minutes since he'd left his phone.

"A wedding has taken place," Carson continued.

Hayley nervously took a step closer to her husband, who instinctively wrapped a hand around the back of her calf.

"Kyle Cooper, Mrs. Cooper, please join me."

The couple looked at each other, apprehension in their eyes.

"Go." Joe Reynolds nudged his hesitant daughter. Hayley reached both hands out to Kyle, who took them, pulling himself off the ground.

Kyle spun his wife into him and kissed her full on the lips, dipping her. Chuckles, cheers, and wolf whistles followed the display. The motivation being one of falsified joy to sway the crowd to their cause.

Hand in hand the newlyweds approached their Alpha. Luca watched, attempting to conceal his worry with a smile.

"We all know these two. We've grown up with them, raised them. The Reynolds are an esteemed family, who have resided in Aboit for generations. Kyle Cooper has been like a son and a constant asset to me, time and time again. With all this in mind and with my full blessing, they have been joined together as one in marriage."

Hate, frustration, and annoyance showed through the façade to those who knew the Alpha well enough. Luca clapped loudly, praising his Alpha's choice, even though it was a lie. Kyle, still smiling, tucked Hayley even closer to his side.

Carson had recently declared his intention to talk to Hayley's father, to claim the rare jewel she was, for himself.

Luca had informed her actual boyfriend, setting the couple's elopement into motion. Smiling and agreeing that Carson had given his blessing was the best course of action to help keep his friends alive.

"After tonight's hunt has concluded, a celebration will be held at my home, the home of your Alpha. All are welcome." At this, he gave a sweeping gesture, but the statement was untrue. If you were not one of Carson's favorites, you were not actually invited. This was a common understanding amongst the pack. The suggested inclusion was just for show.

Luca suppressed an eye roll as he half-listened to Carson prattle on. His mind began to wander after Kyle and Hayley had safely rejoined him in the grass. He listened for the word vampire to pull him back to what Carson was saying, but it never came. Carson didn't say a word about the current threat to Aboit, or the pack. Luca found this odd but was relieved all the same.

As Carson's voice continued to wreck the peace of the evening, Luca spied a pair of late arrivals over Carson's shoulder. Being late to the Moon Hunt was not a normal practice and often had less than desirable consequences. It was a woman Luca had never seen before and a teenage boy. The woman was tall, curvy, and beautiful. Her dark skin gleaming in the moonlight. The boy's hair was braided tight to his head. He wore tight, ripped jeans, a dark colored hoodie, and a scuffed-up pair of Jordan ones. His facial expression looked like he pretty much permanently had something better to do with his time.

Once it must have become apparent that the majority of his pack was seeing something he wasn't, Carson turned to look behind him. Luca prepared himself, this kind of disrespect was generally considered a punishable crime. But Carson made no move against them.

The woman spoke without waiting to be addressed. "Micah is dead. Carson, we need your help."

"Demetria Harrison," Carson said invitingly, which was

odd.

A few of the wolves near Carson, who had been hanging on his every word, jeered at the audacity of interrupting their Alpha's speech.

Carson rose his bulky arm to silence them. "This woman has come back home, we will welcome her," Carson instructed. "Ben, Luca," he said, then motioned for them to join him by the woman's side.

Max bounded up beside them, but Carson held out his hand, sending the over-eager wolf away.

"Tell me what happened, Demetria," Carson instructed, almost softly.

"I didn't see it happen, but my son Ricky did." Demetria motioned toward the teenager.

Ricky glared back.

"Tell our Alpha what happened, baby," Demetria instructed the boy sweetly.

Ricky rolled his eyes and paused. "It was a vampire," Ricky said finally.

Carson's eyes grew brighter, hungrier.

"How do you know? What did it look like?" Ben asked.

"I didn't get a great look, but...fangs, pale skin, red hair..."

"Female?" Carson nearly shrieked.

"No, it was definitely a dude."

Carson's face fell.

"When did this happen?" Luca asked.

"A few days ago." Ricky didn't say more.

Luca flinched. *Poor kid.*

"We've been living in Fort Miles," Demetria said. "Micah was looking into the string of murders there. They were vampire killings, he was sure of it. He must have closed in on the demon. When it attacked, it overpowered him, but he fought hard. His sacrifice gave our son a chance to run," Demetria's voice cracked as she spoke. She reached out for her son's hand. He yanked it away before she could take it.

Carson rested a hand on her lower back. The gesture was a

bizarrely intimate one.

"Demetria, I'm so sorry. Where are you staying now?" Ben asked.

Luca was starting to put things together. This woman must have been part of this pack's past. A past that took place before he had come to Aboit.

"Nowhere yet. We grabbed the important things and came straight here. I didn't want to take the risk that that monster would come back to finish the job."

"I understand," Carson said. "You and the boy can stay with me. At least until you get back on your feet. I must say, it will be nice to have you back with us."

"I'm truly grateful, Carson." Demetria smiled at Carson like he had just rescued her from certain death.

"It's not a problem in the slightest," he assured her, putting one hand on her shoulder, close to her neck. "It's my job as Alpha now, to take care of you. Do you have a car?"

"We do."

"Let's go now, so you can get settled before the pack arrives," Carson decided.

"Are you sure? The full moon..." Demetria looked around at the many pack members hovering nearby, pretending they couldn't hear the conversation being had. Luca couldn't believe she had blatantly questioned him.

"Of course, I'm sure. We can be back to the Den by the moon's apex, and my Beta can lead the hunt tonight," Carson said smoothly, motioning dismissively toward Luca.

Luca's fingers twitched, it was a lot of power to hold, leading the Moon Hunt.

"Your troubles are over, dear one." Carson brushed Demetria's cheek with one finger. "You are no longer alone; you have me now."

Demetria nodded her thanks.

Ricky rolled his eyes but said nothing.

"Wolves!" Carson demanded the pack's attention. "Your Alpha must take his leave. Your Beta, Luca Cain, has command."

Demetria's eyes grew wide at the announcement of his surname. Several wolves muttered their approval. The boy, Ricky, Luca noted looked mildly interested, but only for a moment.

Carson began to propel Demetria in the direction of the preserve's entrance.

"I want to run with the pack," Ricky announced, not following his mother.

"I don't know Sweetie. I..." Demetria began, turning to face him.

"Demetria, dear, let him. After what he's been through, the hunt may be just what he needs. Besides, this way you and I can catch up." Carson instructed, but Luca seriously doubted there was any concern for the boy in Carson's motives.

"He can catch a ride back with me," Luca offered.

Demetria looked from Luca to her son and back, then she conceded. "I'd like that," she said to Carson. She was now looking up at Carson like he'd hung the moon.

With that, Carson and Demetria walked towards the entrance to the preserve. Luca turned away from their receding forms.

"Find me after the hunt," Luca told Ricky, then moved to address the pack. It was obvious that he held the position of power now, all faces turned obediently toward him.

During the following minutes, Luca allowed the pack to prepare for the change. Some wolves began to remove their clothing, some simply their outerwear. Some of the teenage girls tucked their phones in their bra's. Whatever a wolf changed with stayed with them, became part of them. So, how one chose to run was seen as a highly personal decision. Luca always found that the less you had tying yourself to your humanity the more freeing the run, the more animalistic his werewolf nature became. This is how he preferred it. This is how he let the wolf fully take over, to leave everything behind.

After only a few more minutes, Luca knew the time was

right. The moon had risen high in the night sky. But most importantly, Luca could feel the pull of the animal inside him intensify. "With the moon, with the hunt, with our pack, let's do this!" Luca shouted, building their anticipation with his own. The need to run as one was taking over his senses.

Kip, Ben, and Kyle appeared at his side. Ben glared at Kyle. "You lucky dog," Kip whispered to Kyle while glancing over at Hayley, who stood next to her family, prepared for the change from woman to wolf.

Luca's insides twisted, the moon's power pulling the change from inside him. Normally, when Luca shifted into wolf form, he was still himself inside. Even as a wolf, he was in full control of his thoughts and actions. Tonight, things were different. Tonight, like all other full moons, Luca would lose the part of him that made him human. Tonight, the wolf would run free.

Luca's shoulders bent forward, his body curling in on itself. It was time. He turned his back to the pack and let out a great howl, which started a chorus of responses. Luca focused what was left of his concentration, he bounced on his heels a moment longer and then bolted, in human form, farther into the forest.

He could hear the footfalls of the pack taking off behind him. Once his adrenaline was pumping, his mind was clear, and his pack was paces behind him, he launched himself into the air. In a flash of light, he turned from man to beast. His swift paws landed soundlessly on the forest floor. The man he was, now fully buried inside the animal.

Luca was lost in the hunt, fueled by heightened senses, and gathering strength from those who ran with him. He sniffed, the scent of deer came to his nose. He turned, leading the pack in a new direction. The wolf ran as fast as he could, his heart pounded in rhythm with his pace. He was liberated from his conflict with Carson, from his concerns for Jules, all of it. For this moment, he was consumed by the freedom of the pack. He howled as he closed in on his prey, the moonlight glistening off

his silver coat.

CHAPTER NINE

Living with the Dead

J ules pulled into Gabriel's driveway. His front door opened before she could knock. Eileen stood in the entryway, smiling widely. "How is he?" Jules asked. Eileen was dressed in a long skirt, black hair braided down her back, and scarred face smiling.

"A bit grouchy to be honest," Eileen replied, none too quietly. Eileen turned back into the house, her many bracelets clanking as her arm swung. Jules followed behind her.

"He's fine," Gabriel said from where he sat on the sofa, his nose in a history book he'd probably read a hundred times.

"He says that and yet he's being grouchily defensive," Eileen teased, carefree as always. "Come, get something to drink."

Jules followed Eileen to the kitchen where she pulled a pre-poured glass from the refrigerator and handed it to Jules. Jules felt an overwhelming need at the smell of it. She took the glass and drank. The red liquid surged through her, soothing the thirst. She closed her eyes, soaking in the immediate calm. All her troubles seemed so far away. Nothing mattered, just the ecstasy of the blood.

"Jules, what's wrong? You seem a little off." Gabriel's voice came from just behind her left shoulder. His question pulled her out of her blood-induced trance. "What happened Saturday?"

"Not yet." Jules heaved a breath of air, then another, and wiped her mouth after drinking the last drop. Now, she felt ready for almost anything. The pair returned to the living room. With a relaxed sigh, Jules dropped onto the green couch, curled her feet underneath her, and stretched her neck back and forth.

Eileen stayed in the kitchen, most likely cleaning the glass Jules had just emptied.

"Are you ready to tell me now?" Gabriel asked, a tinge of annoyance in his tone.

"Stop badgering her Gabriel," Eileen commanded as she rejoined them, sitting on Gabriel's lap in the armchair. "She can have secrets, you know."

"Do you have secrets from me?" he asked, almost playful.

"Not at the moment, but who knows, maybe I will someday. And, if that day comes, I expect you to honor my right to have them." Eileen's voice was unwavering. Gabriel hugged her waist tighter, seemingly appreciative of her opinion rather than angered by it. Eileen was laid back, but also unwavering when it came to her boundaries and beliefs. Jules had always liked that about her.

Eileen and Gabriel were born a century apart. They shared no cultural similarities, the people of Eileen's birth being native to this land. And yet, the idea that a woman would speak to her husband that way had come directly from her matriarchal tribe.

Jules was glad Gabriel had adjusted to Eileen's ideals, rather than the other way around. Jules's homicidal ex preferred a firm hand to an open mind.

"My wife is right, of course. And normally you are allowed to have secrets, but right now it's too dangerous."

Jules offered a sigh of exasperation. "Gabriel, you may be one of my dearest friends, but my existence is my own."

"But that doesn't explain why you weren't returning my calls," he said. "At least tell me that you weren't in any danger."

"I wasn't. I'm not in any danger. I'm perfectly fine. Okay?" Of course, this was not at all true. Especially if the Alpha ever found out about her and Luca. "I silenced my phone for the day. I just needed some space. Is that so hard to believe?" Jules felt angry and guilty all at the same time. Angry at him for making her lie to him, and guilty because she had never lied to him before. But Luca's safety was worth this lie.

"If that's all, why didn't you just tell me that? Or better yet, let me know ahead of time."

"It wasn't a plan, it just kind of happened. But everything is fine, so can we just drop it?" she said, keeping her voice calm but feeling quite irritated.

Gabriel did not look overly pleased, but he nodded in agreement, backing down.

"Now that that ridiculousness is over, anyone up for a movie?" Eileen asked. "I saw this great one the other day!"

"You two go ahead. I'm going to get some reading in," Gabriel said, picking up the book he'd discarded. He tapped his phone several times and classical music began to play throughout the house's surround sound.

"Unbelievable!" Eileen flung herself off his lap and onto the couch, head coming to rest on Jules's legs.

"Romantic Comedy in the guest room?" She asked Jules, looking at her upside down.

"Actually," Jules pulled a book out of her bag. "I'm almost on the last chapter," she said with a sheepish smile.

"Fine. Be boring, both of you. I'll be in the guest room with Kristen Bell."

Jules giggled as she watched her go. Eileen slammed the door a little harder than necessary. Jules and Gabriel smiled down at their respective pages. They sat in comfortable silence, the disagreement between them forgotten. The soft tones of classical music fostered the peaceful atmosphere.

Many nights had passed like this, in the joint calm and comfort of a book. But tonight, Jules sat there pretending to turn page after page. When, in reality, her ability to retain a single word was escaping her. Everywhere she looked today, something or someone had reminded her of Luca. The amount of time spent thinking about him made her slightly annoyed with herself. A man with his stature entered the coffee shop as she left. One of the students who came into the library had hair like his. Another was wearing sneakers like the ones he wore the first time they'd seen each other. The persistent wish was to turn around and see him right now, in this and every moment.

Jules glanced up from her page, looking at the top of Gabriel's blond head. His sharp nose just barely stuck out over the top of his book. He had been her rock for centuries. She couldn't bear the thought of betraying him now. Gabriel was a brother to her. The only one she had now. Still, falling for Luca wasn't a plan. It seemed more like an inevitability. Once Gabriel discovered her secret, he would feel betrayed. She could only hope it wouldn't separate them entirely. Smiling at Gabriel, she pushed Luca from her mind, wanting to be in this moment with her dearest friend.

Nick opened Chad's apartment door around dusk. He'd been in no mood to return to the human's home after leaving Incognito. He'd spent the day roaming the city. Surprisingly, kill free. He'd thought about a pick-me-up drink a couple times, but in the end decided against it. Nick paused on the apartment's threshold. He could hear Chad talking on the phone in hushed tones; like he didn't want to be over heard, even though he was in the apartment alone.

"No. I'm not losing him," Chad said angrily. "Things are still going to plan."

Nick's eyebrows raised in curiosity.

"No, not yet. But I believe he trusts me." Chad continued. Completely unaware of Nick's presence. "He'll give something away soon."

Now Nick's face scrunched in confusion.

"No, don't let them pull me." He sounded panicked. "I can still do this."

Nick was beginning to think something odd was going on with his dense bed buddy. This intrigued him more than it should have. Was he a target of something? *How curious.*

Nick accidentally on purpose kicked the doorjamb to announce his presence. "Honey, I'm home." Nick said cheerily. Listening for Chad's reaction to this.

"He's back. I gotta go." Chad hastily ended the call and turned around. He smiled widely but the only emotion in his eyes was fear.

"You didn't have to end your call on my account." Nick waved toward Chad's phone, now discarded on the counter.

"That's okay." Chad approached him, wrapping his arms around Nick and planting a kiss on his mouth. "It was just my brother."

"You have a brother?" Nick asked, looking down at the man.

"A twin," he confirmed.

"How did I not know this?" Nick thought of his own twin. He'd searched for her after seeing her in her ex-best friend's blood memories. But he'd never found a trace of her, as he had expected. Nick knew she died in the fire. Laurence's muddled brain made it up because of the fear he had carried of the creatures of the night. All Nick saw was the old bastard's nightmares.

"We haven't exactly done the family breakdown or body count list." Chad released Nick. Moving around the counter he discarded his dinner dishes in the over full sink and pocketed his phone.

"Yeah." Nick watched Chad carefully. "I guess we haven't." Nick found it very odd that he wasn't at least being berated for disappearing for about thirty-six hours. It seemed, things were not what they seemed with place-holder Chad.

"So, tell me about your exes," Chad said retrieving a bottle of beer he'd obviously been nursing before Nick had returned.

Chad was obviously fishing for some kind of information. He'd bite. Just to see where Chad went with this line of questions. Nick's sexual body count was probably higher than his kill list, no harm in divulging a few random names. "Well..." Nick plopped down on the dilapidated couch, in front of Chad's large TV and entertainment system with the broken cabinet door. "There was Michael. George. Chris and Chris; at the same time. They were great. Jaylan. Greg. Ralf and Katherine: Great couple. Helena. Miles..."

Chad cut him off. "You've dated women? I didn't know you were bi."

"I'm only a little bi." He opened his mouth to continue.

"Oh," Chad tapped his fingers on the arm of the couch. Nick took notice of the anxious tick. "Well, was there someone who like really meant something to you? Someone you've gone back to more than once?"

Nick's suspicions grew. There was only one past relationship that mattered. He'd never speak the name to anyone. Especially someone who seemed to be searching for specific information about the beings in Nick's past. "Nope. I'm a one and done kinda guy. Maybe twice."

Chad looked back and forth between them with a questioning look.

"Must mean you're special," Nick lied. "What about you?" Nick shot the question back at him conversationally.

Chad's phone dinged. "That's my alarm. I have to leave for work," Chad announced standing. "Table this conversation?" Chad leaned forward and put the now empty beer bottle on the coffee table next to a few others.

"Sure." Nick's red flag alarm was flashing all over his brain.

"Will you be here when I get back?" Chad asked before pulling on his shoes and grabbing his black duffel bag.

"Probably."

Chad leaned over Nick pecking him once on the lips. "See you in the morning."

"Sure." Nick knew he wasn't disappearing again. He needed answers.

Nick waited only a couple moments before leaving the apartment after Chad. He tracked the man to a side street, where he was picked up by a black Sudan with severely tinted windows. Losing him was not an option. Nick frantically looked around for inspiration. He found an easy to climb building, knocking someone over in the process of running to it. Making his way to the rooftop, he scanned the cars on the street. Desperately searching for the bland black vehicle. He found the Sudan two streets over pulling up in front of a nondescript motel. It was the type of establishment that looked like it housed people's dirtiest secrets. *So very curious.*

Luca's humanity regained control a few hours before sunrise. He brought the hunt to a close, hours earlier than normal. Some of them had a surprise wedding reception to attend. The rest of the pack followed his example reluctantly. Some of them, very reluctantly. It took him several minutes to locate the wolf-form of the teenage boy he'd offered a ride to. Luca suspected that Ricky was in no hurry to start his new and abrupt life crammed into a place called the Den. Not that Luca could blame the boy for wanting to leave the wolf in control of his mind. He'd seen his father murdered; Luca knew what he was going through. It took the Beta's command for him to relinquish the animal inside.

After a few minutes of awkward silence and Ricky fiddling with the Bluetooth, Luca decided to voice something that had been nagging at his mind. "I'm sure your mother has asked you this, but, are you okay?"

Ricky's hand fell from the dashboard. He froze, staring forward. "She hasn't actually. She went into panic mode when she found out Dad was dead and hasn't stopped since."

"I'm sorry," Luca said honestly. "Seeing a parent murdered is a hard thing to bear."

"What would you know about it? You're a Cain. I'm sure everywhere you go people worship the ground you walk on!" Ricky's anger was understandable so Luca didn't take offense.

"I am a Cain, you are not wrong." Luca sighed. "I also saw my father murdered when I was sixteen. He and the rest of my family were killed on the same night." It was a harsh reality and, to this day, hard to admit aloud. However, Luca felt that if someone had confided that they too had experienced his pain, it would have helped him process his grief sooner.

Luca glanced over. Ricky was staring at him. "Oh." Ricky blushed scarlet; clearly embarrassed by his misplaced anger. "That sucks."

Luca's phone beeped. He ignored it as he continued. "It really does. It still haunts me. But, if you ever want to talk about what happened to you, now you know I'll understand."

"Yeah, I guess so." Ricky chewed on his lip. "Who's Juliet?"

Luca glanced over and saw that Ricky had picked his phone up off the center console.

"Nobody. Put that down," Luca instructed.

Ricky rolled his eyes but did as he was told.

"This is where you're taking me?" Ricky almost laughed as Luca pulled onto the grass beside the Den.

"This is home," Luca said, "for now."

"Wow." Ricky's tone suggested that this was not said in wonder but in disdainful disbelief.

"Come on then," Luca prodded. The sounds of revelry were already coming from behind the privacy fence's chipping paint.

Ricky followed steps behind Luca as he entered through the front screen door. Luca spied Hayley through the back screen door, leading to the back porch. She was in the yard talking to her mother. She had somehow acquired a short white dress between the run and this backyard barbeque celebration.

"My girl looks great, doesn't she?" Kyle asked while throwing an arm across Luca's shoulders as he and Ricky entered the backyard. She did, of course, her hair fell in soft waves to one side, and she wore the smile of real love.

"Do you really need me to answer that?" Luca retorted.

"Nah, my opinion matters more anyway," Kyle shot back.

Ricky snorted.

Luca had momentarily forgotten he was there. "Ricky, this

is Kyle, the groom." Luca pointed at Kyle and then Hayley.

"Awesome, another of the Alpha's flying monkeys." Ricky rolled his eyes.

"Well, you're a bucket of cheerfulness, aren't you?" Kyle quipped.

Ricky glared in Luca's direction.

"Actually, I am neither flying nor a monkey if you must know," Kyle added with a smile, tossing his hair.

Ricky narrowed his eyes.

"I'm just lucky my wife is celebrating a wedding tonight instead of preparing for my funeral."

"Really," Ricky said. It wasn't a question.

"Our Alpha is kind of an overbearing control freak that may be losing his mind at this very moment..."

"Kyle!" Luca silenced him, motioning with his eyes toward Ben who had just walked through the back door.

"Anyway. This guy is our Beta and he's a thumping good one." Kyle whacked Luca on the shoulder. "Get it, 'thumping?'" he asked playfully.

"Shut up," Luca replied, but he was teasing.

Ricky may have cracked a smile, whether with Kyle or at Kyle, Luca couldn't be sure.

Just then, Ricky's mother approached them, jogging up the four wooden steps to the back porch. "Did you behave yourself tonight?" she asked, moving to ruffle Ricky's hair.

Ricky yanked his head away and glared at her, blushing. "I'm tired. Where am I sleeping?"

"Carson has made up beds for us..." Demetria began.

"Where?"

"My apologies Beta." She nodded, a sign of respect.

Luca shrugged.

"This way." Demetria led her son into the house.

Luca didn't watch them go. Instead, he was distracted by a tugging on his hand. The girl who had greeted him at the preserve was pulling him toward the makeshift dance floor, as music boomed from a large stereo. "Not tonight," he said, pulling his hand back.

"But you've danced with me before," she whined.

"Not tonight."

"Your rejection is to my advantage, thanks dude," Kip whispered to Luca as he passed him.

The woman giggled as Kip scooped her into his arms.

Luca walked over to sit on the picnic table bench. He glanced up. The sunrise was a smearing of vibrant colors painted across the sky.

"He looks happy, doesn't he?"

"Huh?" Luca asked, focusing on Hayley, who had sat down next to him.

"Luca, are you alright? You seem..." Hayley started.

"Distracted. I know. It's nothing," Luca replied staring past the partying pack.

Hayley patted his arm.

There were many times over the years when Luca wished this pack had never found him. He needed a pack, all wolves did, but he sometimes wished he wasn't under Carson's thumb. His obsessive, controlling personality was a lot to live with. But that was the price he paid, and it was well worth the cost of having Kyle and Hayley in his life.

Carson scowled as he watched the Reynolds girl walk over and introduce herself to Demetria. A young and beautiful prize she would have been. A radiant, white, wolf for a queen and bedfellow. This was extremely rare and, in fact, why he'd chosen to enter into talks with her father for her in the first place. The whelp he'd helped raise had scorned him. Carson would not easily forgive Kyle's audacity. However, his long forgotten ex-girlfriend was a good distraction for his rage. *Even if she does have a brat child with her.*

Max bounded up next to Carson, delivering the beer he'd instructed him to retrieve ages ago. He grabbed it from him and dismissed the hyperactive spaz with a wave of his hand.

Carson's scowl deepened as Kyle wrapped his arms around the beautiful young wolf and whispered in her ear. She giggled and the pair headed to the dance floor.

Carson had decided to stay Kyle's punishment because he felt Luca's loyalty waning. He couldn't afford to lose such a reputable Beta. Even if he was the freak who'd lost his family in a fire, he was a Cain, that meant something in pack life. He would allow this marriage to stand and grant the traitor mercy, solely to regain Luca's obedience. "Such a waste," he said aloud, still looking the Reynolds girl up and down.

"You did a good thing," Ben said, approaching Carson from his right. This man should be his Beta. He was loyal. However, he was also mysterious. He refused to talk about his past. All Carson had gathered is that he was old and that he hated vampires, which was enough for him.

"Did I?" Carson sneered as Kyle kissed the woman he'd had no right to claim. He'd taken her from him. It stung, but his pride would never allow this fact to become public knowledge. Kyle's punishment would come one day. This slight could not go unanswered forever. However, before he could enact justice, he'd have to see Luca's friendship with the traitor come to an end. Luca needed to fall back in line. *Now*.

Ricky shifted off of a loose spring on the couch after only a few hours of sleep. The cot that had been made up for his mother had not been slept in, even though the noises of last night's party had died down hours ago. He yanked the headphones out of his ears as the alarm on his phone continued to blare. Blinking, Ricky looked at the time. *6:00 A.M.* He hadn't remembered setting his phone alarm last night. In fact, he distinctly remembered turning off his school alarm since he obviously wouldn't be going to Fort Miles Preparatory Academy anymore.

Hopeless that he would be able to get any more sleep, Ricky stood and began aimlessly walking through the house.

He opened the front door and looked out. Most of the vehicles were gone. Just four remained. He bypassed the stairs where the bedrooms, undoubtedly, were when he heard his mother's voice coming from the kitchen.

His mom was standing in front of the stove and the stupid Alpha's massive arms were wrapped around her. He said something in her ear, and she giggled. One beefy hand pulling at the waist band of her yoga pants.

Ricky made a noise that showed his disgust.

Upon seeing him his mom cleared her throat, pulled the Alpha's hand away, and turned to retrieve something from the refrigerator.

"Breakfast is almost ready sweetie," she said, being way to cheery considering the circumstances.

"You know Dad died less than a week ago, right?" he asked, glaring from his mother to Carson and back.

"You'd better get dressed or you'll be late for your new school," his mother responded, completely ignoring that she ever had a husband apparently.

Ricky's anger spiked. In a matter of moments, his life had been completely obliterated. His father was dead, and his mom was acting insane. Did he really have to change schools too? He liked Fort Miles Prep, he had friends that knew him for what he was. There, he knew where he fit in the scheme of things, and he liked it that way.

"Carson made a call to the superintendent of Aboit High this morning, you're all good to go."

"You are unbelievable," Ricky commented flatly.

"Don't speak to your mother that way," Carson said. Ricky thought that Carson was attempting to appear calm, but he also thought he saw something strange in the look in his eyes. Something unsettling.

"Who the hell do you think you are..." Ricky snapped.

Carson took one threatening step forward. Ricky thought Carson might just haul-off and hit him. But Demetria held up her hand and Carson chose to stay by her side.

"Ricky, enough," Demetria commanded. "This is our life now. You have to go to school here, in Aboit."

"Fine." Ricky turned and walked back to the family room. He heard his mother apologizing for her son's behavior. Ricky couldn't stand it in this dump anyway. So, he found her purse, dug out her keys, picked up his phone and charger, and walked out the noisy front door. As he was digging through their mess of belongings, Demetria joined him on the driveway.

"That was uncalled for, young man. This is our home now, and we owe this Alpha our loyalty and respect."

Seriously, he thought but didn't say aloud. Instead, he threw her a glare and continued digging through what was left of his old life. He found his skateboard and schoolbag buried deep in the trunk and yanked them both free.

"Do you want me to walk you? The school's only a few blocks east of here."

"Yes, because I'm in kindergarten," he snapped, slammed the trunk shut, hopped on the skateboard, and pushed off.

"Check in at the front desk when you get there!" she shouted after him. "Have a good day, sweetheart!"

He raised his hand but didn't make the effort to wave.

Rolling along the sidewalk, wind blowing through his dyed black hair, he trick-flipped his board a few times. Once he had to stomp on the back end to grab it and carry it over a broken stretch of sidewalk.

Ricky hadn't intended to actually find the school building, but he did. Students were pouring in from the sidewalks and parking lot as he stood before the large, brick building. FM Prep, commonly known to its students as FML prep, was a fancy private school. Ricky was basically the one and only fashionably rebellious student, but he'd known those kids all his life. Here he had no idea what to expect. At least he had taken the precaution of wearing street clothes.

"Hi, you're new here, aren't you?" A voice said from right beside him.

His eyes grew wide when he turned. Beside him stood an

attractive, edgily-dressed human girl, who looked to be about his age. She was wearing a short skirt, which Ricky quite admired, and a black, faux leather jacket. The only shred of real color she wore was coming from the rainbow of colors in her hair.

Ricky nodded, a little stunned. There were no girls like this at his old school.

"I'm Tasha," she said, offering her black, nail polished, fingers toward him.

"Ricky."

"Come on. I'll walk you to the office."

Ricky wasn't sure why, but he followed Tasha up the stone steps and into the school building. "I saw you boarding earlier," she continued.

Ricky sort of smiled but didn't say anything.

"Here." Tasha motioned to an office on their right. "Oh, and I don't know if you're interested, but a bunch of us are working the carnival after school if you want to join."

"Thanks, I'll think about it."

"Okay, I'll hold you to that then," she responded as a smile spread across her face. Then she turned and almost trotted down the hall, leaving him to walk into the office alone.

Girls! Ricky thought as he shook his head a little and smiled to himself.

He then contemplated running back out of the school, but where would he go if he did. He'd just have to make it through the school day like he had at FML Prep; by making sarcastic comments to his teachers and thinking about how ridiculous the whole school thing really was for a werewolf.

He squared his shoulders and walked through the open door. Stopping in front of a cluttered desk, he cleared his throat and waited.

"Oh hello," a round, dark-skinned woman in glasses greeted.

"I'm Ricky Harrison. I think you are expecting me."

"Right," she said and then looked at all the sticky notes

attached to her workspace. "I did hear something about that."

Ricky waited.

"Tell you what. We aren't actually ready for you at this moment. Why don't I walk you down to the library? I'm sure Miss Bristow could put you to work for a few hours."

"Whatever," Ricky replied.

Jules crouched at the back of the library shelving a pile of books some juniors had left in a stack on the floor.

"Jules?" Belinda, the office assistant, called.

"Back here!" Jules peaked her head around the shelf. "Be there in a second!" Jules shoved the last book into its place on the shelf, stood, and walked toward the front of the library.

"There's a vampire in your library," said the boy standing next to Belinda.

"You have quite an imagination young man. But in this school, our students treat our staff with respect," Belinda scolded.

"But..."

"Sit." She pointed to one of the tables nearby.

The boy scowled but walked over to the area she was pointing at and sat with a thud.

Jules walked behind her desk, eternally grateful that Belinda had reacted as she had. "I'm sorry about this, Jules," Belinda began, walking behind Jules's desk as well. "The superintendent called this morning, demanding that we find a place for this kid. We don't have things worked out yet. Can you keep him here for a while? Get his books together maybe. I'll email you his class list once I get him enrolled."

"Bee, breathe." She patted the woman on the shoulder. "Yes. We'll be fine."

"You're sure?" The middle-aged woman looked skeptical. Jules looked over at the werewolf boy. He looked more annoyed and prickly than scared.

"Positive."

"Then, I should really get back." Belinda pointed over her shoulder.

"Go. I've got this," Jules assured her, yet again.

"You're a miracle worker," she called back as she left in a rush.

Jules gave her a few minutes to disappear back down the hall before approaching the teenager.

"Are you going to kill me?" he asked without looking at her, his hands clamped over the edge of the table.

"I wasn't planning to. Nor would I," Jules said honestly. She continued to stand several feet back from the seemingly skittish youth.

"How about we don't do anything this morning Jules," Ethan blathered as he came through the door. "Did you replace me?" he asked, noticing the other person his age sitting where he usually plopped down in the mornings.

"For today," she said, her concerned expression softened as she looked at Monica's little brother.

"Works for me. See ya J!" He waved once as he walked back through the door.

"Go to study hall!" she shouted after Ethan.

He turned and shrugged, smiling mischievously at her through the glass.

"So, you just... work here." Ricky spoke again. "At a school. Like a human?"

Jules glanced out the glass door before responding. The students were already tucked into their homerooms, leaving the halls pretty much vacant. "I do. I've been here for three years now." Jules tentatively sat across from the boy.

"And the students don't die off mysteriously or anything?" He sounded skeptical.

"I don't feed off humans. Or werewolves for that matter."

He looked up at her for the first time since he'd sat down. He searched her eyes. Looking for what? She wasn't sure.

"Juliana Bristow. Or Jules, as it were." She smiled as unthreateningly as possible.

"I'm Ricky Harrison," he said but didn't offer his hand.

"What brings you here, Ricky?"

Ricky just looked at her, baffled.

"You're obviously new here for some reason."

"My father was murdered. By a vampire."

Empathetically, Jules wanted to comfort the boy. And yet, if his story was true, he was probably feeling very scared, insecure, and sad right now. "You have nothing to fear from me."

"Awesome," he said sarcastically.

She searched for something else to say and then remembered that she was playing the part of a school librarian. "How about you help me out. Can you shelve some books for me?"

Ricky yawned involuntarily, pulled his phone out of his bag, put his earbuds in his ears, and music started to blare.

"Or we can do that later," Jules said to no one, since Ricky was obviously no longer listening. Just then, Jules's in-house messenger dinged from her computer. She took the excuse to leave the boy alone and walked back to her desk to pull up her staff messenger. She had a message from Belinda waiting for her. *So, this kid's transcripts just came in from his last school. He was at the top of his class. Go figure. I've attached his class schedule and book list. He can start tomorrow. Hope you're doing okay with him.*

Jules looked over at Ricky, who was typing out a message of his own. This was going to be a long day.

Luca was sleeping late due to the previous night's celebration. If dreams were a choice, he would have chosen to dream of Jules. Instead, his subconscious haunted him with his greatest shame. Forcing him to relive his greatest pain, over and over again. Luca dreamt of a picturesque little cabin, secluded from prying eyes. It lay in the Canadian forest of Ontario. A loving family lived there; it was his family, this had been his home.

A woman stood in the cabin doorway waving at him. Jenna Cain, Luca's mother, looked as radiant as she had on that day. His father, Bill, a strong and wise leader, clapped him on the shoulder. In the dream, Luca jumped at the unexpected contact. He looked over and saw blood pooling on his father's forehead. Bill seemed unconcerned. Luca looked again, the blood was gone.

The dream shifted, and Luca saw a face, one he'd never been able to forget. The face of the human girl Luca had fallen in love with. Luca and Rosemary fell in love young, and they loved each other recklessly. He lived for the look she got in her eyes when they were together. That look he saw now in his sleep. For the briefest of moments her face became another's, her hair wasn't blonde but red, her eyes lightened, her features softened. *Jules.*

"Rosemary, I have to tell you something," the teenage version of him said. The face turned back into the tall blonde. He didn't want to have secrets from Rosemary, not even this one. "There is something about me you don't know."

"Really?" she asked coyly.

In his dream, adult Luca was screaming at his younger self to stay quiet. The course of events that followed this act of trust would destroy everything Luca loved.

"You're a liar, Luca Cain," Rosemary screamed. "Never speak to me again!"

"Wait, Rosie, I can prove it to you!" he called after her.

"How?"

Then he did the one thing he'd promised his father he never would. He showed Rosemary the truth. He turned into a wolf before her eyes.

Rosemary screamed and fell into hysterics. "You're a monster! I'll destroy you if you ever come near me again!" And then she ran.

Luca had ignored her threats but had tried to keep his distance. He had wanted to believe that once the shock wore off, she would come around.

He had been very wrong.

Rosemary had told her father Luca's secret. He, in turn, had rallied the townsmen to hunt the wolves down. In a bold attempt to destroy what they didn't understand; the unruly mob had armed themselves and had stormed Luca's family's home.

Luca and his father had been out in the forest. "It'll be your responsibility someday," Bill had said.

The angry mob had broken into Luca's home that night. They'd murdered everyone he loved. Not only did they shoot his mother, ten-year-old brother, older sister and her husband, but they also murdered Luca's two young nieces.

Luca and his father had rushed toward the house, but Bill never made it inside. An athlete Luca went to school with had shot Bill between the eyes before he could save his dying family.

Luca woke when the gunshots rang in his mind. He was drenched in sweat, tangled in his sheets, and trembling from the dream. Shaking himself from the nightmare, he tried not to relive what had happened next.

Enraged, Luca had lunged at his father's killer. In one swift movement, he killed the boy. *His first murder.*

As Luca had run into the cottage, he'd heard terrified screams coming from his nieces' room. He'd made it just in time to see five-year-old Elena transform into a wolf for the first time. Rosemary's older brother had shot little Elena out of mid-air. She'd died instantly, her sister already gone. Luca's rage had consumed him. He'd torn the boy apart. *His last murder.*

When the mob found the dead boy outside, they'd taken the body and fled. In a daze, he'd tried to wake his sister and then his mother, but nothing could be done. His entire family was gone in those few terrible moments.

Luca had dragged his father's body inside the house to lay with the rest of his family. With a mighty howl, he'd lit his family home on fire. Guilt-ridden, heartbroken, and afraid he wouldn't be able to stop himself from exacting his revenge on all the humans involved, including Rosemary, he'd fled Canada immediately following the start of the blaze. He lived inside the wolf for many months following these horrific events.

Luca shook the memories from his mind. He didn't know why this dream had chosen to haunt him once again. He suspected it had something to do with telling Ricky that he understood his pain.

Luca stretched noisily and dropped one hand over the side of the bed. He shifted things around the floor until he found his phone lying under the shirt he'd worn the day before. The screen blinked to life. He'd missed one message from his Juliet. *Hope I don't wake you, but I have a very angry werewolf boy here today. Any ideas on convincing him not to out me?*

The message was only a few minutes old. Luca held his phone above him as he typed. *Is his name Ricky Harrison?* He dropped the phone on his bed and started detangling himself from his sheets.

Jules's response came back almost immediately. *That's the one.*

Jules had told him that she worked at the local high school. He thought it odd that Carson seemed not to know this. Especially since werewolf kids did regularly attend Aboit High. But they were also kept out of most pack drama. The majority of them probably didn't even realize that their school librarian was a four-hundred-year-old vampire.

I'm on my way, he sent back and then got up to shower and dress.

CHAPTER TEN

Beta at Aboit High

J ules responded to Luca. That's probably a bad idea. Then
set her phone down on the desk. It'd been half an hour
and Ricky still hadn't moved. His head stayed bent over his
phone while he did whatever he was doing to pass the time.
Jules had tried to start a conversation once, but his hearing was
either obscured by his music or he was just very selective with
what he chose to hear.

A group of students came into the library on assignment.
Jules kept one eye on Ricky as she helped them. She saw an
older werewolf boy named Landon Reynolds approach Ricky.
She eavesdropped on their conversation, it remained fairly
neutral.

Jules's attention was pulled away momentarily by her
vibrating phone. *Probably so, but I'm outside.*

Wait there, she sent back.

Jules typed out a quick message to Belinda.

After the next bell rang, pulling the current group of
students into their next class, she told Luca to go to the office.
A few minutes later, Belinda returned with Luca two steps
behind her. "This is very odd Jules," she commented as she
showed him into the library.

"Is it?" Luca asked.

"We don't usually allow attractive uncles such as yourself
into our school, but Jules has vouched for you," Belinda told
him.

"Did she?" Luca chuckled.

Jules tried to suppress the utter joy she felt upon seeing
him, but one smile slipped through the façade. "Thank you,

Bee," she said while pointing Luca in the direction of Ricky's turned back.

As Belinda left, Luca raised his eyebrows and pressed his lips together. Jules assumed this was his own version of being discrete. Ricky didn't look up from his phone until Luca sat down across from him and tapped his hand on the table to get his attention. Ricky slowly pulled his headphones out of his ears. "What are you doing here?"

"A friend called," Luca replied.

Jules's phone vibrated again but she ignored it. Whatever it was it could wait.

Ricky looked from Luca to Jules and then back again. "This vampire is your friend?" Ricky asked skeptically.

Luca nodded. "She is."

Jules wasn't sure she would have gone with that approach, but Ricky was Luca's pack member. How he handled this was his call.

"Okay, but what are you really doing here?" Ricky asked, clearly not buying the 'you can trust her because she's my friend' angle.

Luca sighed. "I need to know if you are going to tell Carson or anyone else that she works here. Doing that would put her in danger, and I don't want that."

"So, order me not to," suggested Ricky sarcastically. "Only Carson could demand the information from me then."

Luca leaned forward across the table. "I don't want to do that. Forced control is not my style. I would rather just decide that I can trust you." Jules watched him closer. She'd never heard a man that she loved utter such a thing in her life. Yes, it was not directed at her but... Jules realized in that moment that it was true. *I could fall for him.*

"Jules?"

Luca's voice pulled her back to the present. She'd been, not so discreetly, staring at him.

"I'm fine," she said and then looked anywhere but at the werewolves.

Luca rolled his eyes playfully. "Perfectly fine in every way, huh?" He kind of loved that he'd caught her staring at him.

"She's Juliet." Ricky's comment took Luca by surprise.

"No, she isn't," Luca said, but doubted that he'd recovered enough to sound convincing.

"My name is Juliana," Jules said.

"I know," Luca replied, continuing to look at Ricky.

"Yes, she is." Ricky stood, knocking into the table as he did. "You've been making goo-goo eyes at each other since you walked in here. You have this crazy forbidden love thing going on and you don't want me to tell the pack your secret."

"I don't make goo-goo eyes," Luca said, trying to remain calm and stretching his feet out in front of him.

"Have you seen your face?" Ricky asked rhetorically.

"Not recently," Luca admitted a bit sarcastically. "Sit." Luca used a little more of his Beta power than he would have liked to get Ricky to do so. However, he couldn't take the chance that Ricky would run.

"Well, it's not hiding what you want it to," Ricky said while he slumped back in his chair.

"I'm going to go talk to my..." Luca pointed toward Jules, "friend. Stay," he ordered.

"Woof Woof," Ricky snapped back angrily.

Luca walked over to Jules's desk and leaned across it. With his elbows resting in the middle of the desk his shoulders were of equal height to Jules's.

"What do we do now?" Jules asked, her voice below a whisper.

Luca shrugged a little. He didn't have an answer. Not a good one anyway. "He is right. I could order him to keep quiet, but I don't want to do it. I really hate taking away someone's free will. It's not right."

A look that Luca hadn't seen before crept across Jules's face. She smiled back and then picked up a pen, scribbling something down onto a pad of sticky notes. After she was done, she peeled the one she had written on free and stuck it onto the desk right between Luca's arms. It read, *I really like that about you.*

Luca chuckled.

"You two really think you can fool people?" Ricky asked. Luca had honestly momentarily forgotten he was there.

"I told you coming here was a bad idea," she whispered.

If Luca was being honest with himself, he'd known that she was right even before he had left the Den. Even so, he had wanted to see her, and this was as good of an excuse as any. So, as a response, he simply shrugged minutely and offered her a playfully-guilty looking expression.

She lifted one eyebrow, but then a soft smile appeared on her lips and she chuckled lightly. He took this to mean that she found him somewhat silly and maybe a bit sweet. This was, of course, true.

But what to do about Ricky? It hurt Luca to even consider ordering Ricky not to speak of Jules. However, if he couldn't get through to the boy, it was very likely the only way to protect her and keep their secret safe.

Luca let out a long breath, his head hanging low for a moment. "Okay," he finally said.

"Luca." Jules's hand clasped down on his arm.

"What?" He looked back up at her. He saw worry in her eyes.

"Hide."

Luca looked over his shoulder. Through the glass, he saw Gabriel heading in the direction of the library. Luca ran back into the stacks, crouching by one of the book-filled shelves that would obscure him from the view of the front door.

"Gabriel, hi." Jules's cheerfulness sounded forced. "Don't you have class right now?" This was said a little more naturally.

A class? He works here too. Luca thought.

"You haven't been answering my messages again," the male

vampire's angry voice said a few seconds later. Luca thought that perhaps he could've asked her if everything was okay, rather than coming at her so accusatorily.

"I've been a little busy today." Luca could hear some annoyance in Jules's response.

"Too busy to respond to a text message?"

Jules didn't speak.

Luca was distracted from the conversation by the sound of tentative footsteps walking across the library. He waited for Jules to call out to warn him. The sound grew closer. What was he supposed to do if Gabriel discovered him?

Luca's gaze shot sideways when Ricky appeared. He'd backed across the library, evidently less comfortable in Gabriel's presence than in Jules's.

Gabriel's voice raised.

"There is a werewolf in here, Jules. One I don't recognize." He spoke low enough that a human would have been unable to hear him.

"Yes, Gabriel, there is," Luca heard Jules say, and wondered for a moment if she was going to tell Gabriel about him. But then she continued, "he's a new student. And if I had to guess, you are scaring him. You do know you teach quite a few of them."

Luca thought that this would shut the male vampire up. But instead, he said, "and the one sitting outside in his car. What about that one? Is he just a new student too?"

Luca and Ricky exchanged confused looks.

"What are you talking about? Who's outside?" Jules asked, voicing Luca's confusion.

"I don't know. Some beast. Scrawny, glasses, overactive camera."

"Jed," Luca said under his breath.

"Why is he here if not for us?" Gabriel continued.

Luca was horror-stricken. Jed must have tracked one of them here. *How long has he been out there?* Had he seen Luca enter the school building? Had he spotted the Jeep in the parking lot? Luca's mind was spinning as he caught sight of Ricky watching him. The kid was looking at him kind of strangely like he was trying to decide something. Then, suddenly, Ricky cleared his throat, drawing all attention in his direction, stepped away from Luca's hiding spot and said, "He's here for me."

Luca's astonishment made him sway in his crouched position.

"My mom's dating the Alpha now. I don't think he trusts me," Ricky added.

Luca didn't know how or why he was coming up with this lie, but he was eternally grateful that he was.

"See, Gabriel," said Jules. "You may, in fact, be overreacting."

"Don't start with me, Jules," Gabriel spat back. Tension filled the seconds that passed. Luca held his breath. All at once, he heard footsteps recede.

"He's pleasant," Ricky said flatly.

Luca looked up when Jules rounded the corner, looking down at him.

"That was close," she said.

"Too close." Luca took the hand that she offered to help him stand. He should let go of her hand, but he didn't.

"Why did you do that?" Luca asked the boy who was now standing a few feet away.

Ricky contemplated his answer before speaking. "I've decided that you can trust me."

Luca glanced at Jules.

"Both of you," Ricky added. "I don't really know why, but I think I'm like on your side or whatever."

At this, Luca smiled mischievously and tugged on the hand of Jules's that he was still grasping. She fell into him gracefully, one hand coming to rest on his abdomen as he simply gazed down at her.

"I guess we've got a friend," Jules said, looking up at him and then over at Ricky.

Ricky shrugged and blushed all at the same time.

Carson had taken Demetria back to bed once the house had emptied out for the day. Laying naked and snuggled against him, she felt familiar by his side. Softer now, having birthed another man's child. But he liked the larger curves, they suited him. Fifteen years was no time at all to a werewolf. It was true, those years she had married, made a family with, and fucked the man she'd chosen over him, but he was dead now. And Carson had become the Alpha of this pack, despite her and Micah's betrayal.

Carson saw silent tears escape from her eyes as he stroked her hair. However, he chose not to speak to her about the reason she was crying. His mind was on other things.

Jed had texted to say that he'd discovered where the vampires worked. Carson couldn't believe that the pack's children had been in danger for years and he had not known. This oversight was a mistake that he'd carry with him. Every day they went to school, they were at risk of not returning home to their parents.

Of course, he had no intention of telling the parents this. *Why worry them?*

However, this vampire problem would need to be dealt with as soon as possible. Another thing that troubled him greatly was that his Beta had been seen entering that same school, and had not yet reported the vampire's location. He would have to do whatever needed to be done to find out where his Beta's loyalties truly stood.

Deep in thought, Carson picked the knife he always carried up off his bedside table. He caressed the silver blade, making sure not to slice himself with it.

Demetria sniffled beside him. "Why do you keep that? It's dangerous."

"This?" he asked holding up the knife.

She nodded. Shifting her ample breast against his side and

chest.

"To hold something so deadly in my hand, to control if it kills, is the essence of power." Like the gift granted to him over his subjects, the weapon could only do what it was meant to do with strength behind it.

"Oh," Demetria said quietly. He squeezed her round backside and kissed her forehead. She didn't have the temperament to comprehend such things. She did, however, understand how to fuck. Rolling over, he gripped her throat and plunged his tongue back into her mouth. His other hand kneaded one ample breast. He pinched her nipple hard, enjoying the accompanying gasp into his mouth. His half-hard length grinded against her soft center. He growled when her acrylic red fingernails made more scratches down his back.

"You'll pay for that."

At her soft whimper he was done waiting. He sat up on his knees, lifting her by the throat as he went. Red nails scratched at his cock and he growled, squeezing her throat a little tighter still.

"Woman, you'll be the death of me," he said, his voice husky with lust.

She shook her head, trying to speak. "I would never," she said as he released her throat just enough to allow it.

"I would never..." his voice trailed off in question.

"My Alpha," she added with doe-eyed fright.

He growled and pumped his own length to her simpering tone. "Good girl."

Hard again, he flipped her onto all fours. His hand clamped into her curly hair and pushed her face and shoulders down into the pillows. She gave an enticing little squeak when he raised her hips up farther, jamming a knee between her soft thighs to spread them wider. Meeting a little more resistance than strictly necessary he leaned back. Assessing. "Don't move," he instructed as he stood. Reaching to the floor he retrieved his jeans, yanking the leather belt free. He slid the hard fabric between his fingers and then against the tip of his cock, covering it in pre-cum. Holding the belt by the buckle and end, without warning, he swung his arm forward, whacking her displayed cunt and ass.

"Carson, please d..." she began to beg.

He loosed the belt again, leaving two beautiful, red marks across her luscious skin. "Lashes for scratches, my little whore."

Mounting the bed behind her once more he reached over her and pulled her arms from the sheets beside her breasts. Bending them behind her back. Her face fell back into the pillow as he looped the belt around both wrists and pulled tight. He twisted one hand back into her hair, yanking her head back while the other guided his cock to her entrance. She panted with exhilaration or fear, probably both. He pushed her head back down and with one swift thrust, seated himself fully inside her. She let out a muffled cry that was so delicious he could devour her whole.

Nick had struck out at the front desk of the hotel. Chad was there most of the night, as was Nick, who had been perched on the building across the street watching. At sunrise he'd left and returned to the apartment to wait for Chad's arrival. Nick was beginning to think he should be more careful who he jumped into bed with.

But that hadn't stopped him from fucking Chad's brains out when he'd gotten back. Nick began to slide out from under Chad's arm, but stilled when Chad shifted around him, wrapping his arm and leg around Nick's torso. Nick groaned, clamping his lips together when Chad emitted a particularly loud snore. "Clingy bastard," Nick muttered.

"Hmmm?" Chad said, or snored.

"Nothing. Go back to sleep." Nick slumped back against the pillow to wait.

Moments later an atrocious train horn sounded in Nick's ear signaling that Chad had fallen back into the world of dreams. Carefully, little by little Nick lifted his leg and picked up Chad's arm, stopping every time Chad made a noise or twitched.

After several minutes, Nick wriggled free successfully. Soundlessly, he left the bedroom and padded barefoot across the apartment on his toes toward the gym bag that Chad always dropped directly in front of the front door. With a quiet buzz, the zipper slid across the bag. Nick gagged at the smell coming from inside as he pulled the flaps apart. Sliding two fingers inside he began to route around the smelly chamber, unsure of what he was searching for. He guessed he'd know it when he found it. His nose scrunched as he sifted through old socks and sweats. Picking up a pair of used underwear with his thumb and one finger, Nick's face scrunched with even more utter disgust as he flung them to the linoleum beneath his feet.

He was about to give up on the bag when he felt another zipper running along the bottom of the duffel. *A false bottom.* "You're not a stupid as you look, are you sweetheart?" Nick said aloud to himself as he pulled the rest of the clothes out, unceremoniously tossing them on to the floor. He pealed back the layer, eyes bugging at what he saw.

Before him was a strange array of tech and weapons. Guns, tasers, even a couple of daggers and a collapsible crossbow. "Who the hell are you? G.I. Joker?" He asked the air in front of him.

Replacing all the items in the bag he zipped it and pushed it quietly back into the place he'd moved it from. Standing, he went back into the bedroom to Chad's nightstand. Carefully and quietly, he picked up Chad's phone. It blinked to life but was obviously locked. He leaned over the sleeping human to hold the device out in front of Chad's sleeping face.

Shifting his stance, he lost his balance. Almost dropping the device and waking the moron. Nick flailed his arms and one leg until his body convinced itself it wasn't going to fall. With one glance over at the still snoring human, he padded to the kitchen. Plopping onto a kitchen chair he glanced at mundane socials. Random contacts. Bank accounts. Again unsure of what he was actually looking for. A hint as to why this human had a secret cache of weapons and seemed to be treating Nick like his undead target or something.

His search history revealed a sexual kink or two Nick had been unaware of but nothing that fulfilled Nick's desires at the moment. Abandoning that. He pulled up old downloaded files and noticed one with a name so obvious Chad was seriously incompetent. Target #1. In it, was one AI rendering of the one being Nick would sacrifice his undead life to protect.

Luca was again leaning across Jules's desk while he and Jules whispered in low tones. Ricky seemed to have completely relaxed and retreated back into the confines of his cell phone screen.

"You should go," Jules told him for the third time.

Their fingers had somehow become entwined as they spoke. It was becoming instinctual to need to be closer to her, to touch her. He could easily become addicted to the light in her eyes when she looked at him. She was so much more than he had ever known before. "I know," Luca replied yet again.

"It's nearly my lunch hour, and I have another class coming in after."

"Alright," Luca conceded.

He rolled his eyes playfully and bopped her nose lightly with his curled pointer finger. He glanced out into the empty hallway and then over his shoulder at Ricky. Facing her again, without warning, he closed the distance between them and kissed her. A giggle escaped her lips through the kiss, and her hands rose to his neck. This perfect kiss lasted for only one fleeting moment.

"I'll see you tonight," he said, backing away slowly. It almost hurt to pull back from her; everything in him was screaming for more.

"Go straight to the end of the hall and then turn left," Jules instructed. "It's the long way back to the front door but you'll avoid Gabriel's room."

"I can do that." He looked at her a moment longer and then turned away.

Luca tapped Ricky on the shoulder. The boy jumped, obviously not expecting the physical contact. "I'm leaving," Luca told him. "Will you be okay?"

Ricky looked over at Jules and then back at Luca. "I'm good."

"Thanks, Ricky," Luca said again. They both owed him, and they both knew it.

"It's whatever," Ricky said, but there was no venom behind it.

"It's not."

"I thought you were leaving," Jules said with a small laugh.

Luca looked over at her again. "I am." With that, he left the library.

The long way back wasn't that long, but it was strange being inside a high school again. Things had been slightly different in the nineteen-fifties.

Once he was on the outside of the school building, Luca scanned the lot until he saw Jed. He was sitting in his beater car, looking down, taking a bite of a sandwich. Jed looked up between bites. When he saw Luca, his food slipped through his fingers making a mess of the driver's seat. Luca headed toward the Jeep, chuckling.

Luca weaved through the lines of cars until he reached his Jeep on the far end of the lot. Once inside, he pulled out his phone. He had no new messages, which was a good sign. He hesitated only a fraction of a second before he found the contact name and hit the phone emblem. The call was answered after just one ring. "Carson," Luca began, "I've found her."

CHAPTER ELEVEN

Hall of Mirrors

J ules went straight to the local fairgrounds after work. She'd volunteered to help set up for Aboit High's biggest fundraiser of the year. That was, however, before the tension within her coven had crept in. Tonight, she would be overseeing the carnival games with Gabriel which, for the moment, required stretching up on her toes and holding the end of the banner off the ground as he stood on a tall ladder, tacking it high above their heads.

"Give me a little more slack," Gabriel said, tugging on his end.

Jules let a few more inches of banner slip through her fingers.

"Where has your mind wandered off to this time?" Gabriel teased as he tugged on the banner again and smiled down at her.

"It's gone on vacation. Someplace nice though. Maybe Tahiti," Jules replied with a wide smile of her own.

It was nice to feel less tension between them. They'd talked things through a bit during their lunch break. Since then, he seemed to be much more relaxed. Apparently, Ricky's lie had done the trick. He'd told her that he wasn't comfortable with Ricky knowing what he and Jules were, but since there hadn't been any more altercations with the Alpha, he would try to put the whole werewolf thing to rest. Jules appreciated the effort this must have taken on his part. Gabriel had just reason to lack trust in werewolves. Eileen's scared face was reason enough not to trust them. Jules simply couldn't judge the whole species for an act that only a few had committed.

Once, a few decades ago, she'd said this to Gabriel. However, he was convinced that it was werewolves' very nature that made them dangerous. Jules had tried to argue that all vampires must then be judged by their species' nature, and Gabriel hadn't spoken to her for a week. He was wrong on this, and she believed they both knew it. But Eileen had lost her human life because of a werewolf attack and Gabriel simply hadn't been able to find forgiveness inside himself yet. He did say this afternoon that he would try to let it go. This gave Jules hope that Gabriel would, one day, find peace.

Just then, Gabriel finished his side of the banner, jumped down, and moved the ladder to the other end. Jules regained her focus and followed suit, keeping the banner out of the dirt below.

The pre-carnival atmosphere made Jules's senses throb. The music had begun to emanate from the rides on the midway, which were set up starting one street over. The rising smells of the food vendors were wafting from near the entrance to the grounds. Excited teenagers were chattering and horsing around while they waited for their families and townspeople to arrive. All these things reminded Jules of a day long gone, when she and Gabriel had visited the first circus together.

"Alright, gather around," Gabriel shouted as he jumped off the ladder again. Jules watched as several girls swooned. Slowly, all the students assigned to the carnival games meandered over.

Jules picked a clipboard up off the nearest table and handed it to Gabriel. Gabriel began taking a shrewd form of attendance and giving each student their individual assignment.

"Missy Thomas, Asher Danforth, Terry Pope, with me at the ring toss." Several students' faces dropped at not being able to work with their favorite teacher.

"Tasha Anderson and Ethan Martin with Ms. Bristow at the balloon pop." Both students nodded. Ethan and Tasha glanced a little awkwardly at one another. Their families lived next to each other, but they didn't have much in common. Normally, Ethan would have made some crack about not working at all, but Gabriel moved quickly down the list.

"Kara Willis and Amy Reynolds with Landon Reynolds and Mason Smith at the water shooter."

"All of you freshmen and sophomores will listen to your upperclassman. Seniors, any questions see Ms. Bristow or myself."

Amy scowled, possibly at having to work under her older brother. Mason and Landon high-fived, enjoying being in charge for once. Amy smiled at the girl, one year younger than herself. Landon winked at Kara, who giggled.

Nodding and muttering erupted all around, some students happy with their assigned group and some disappointed.

"I don't have an assignment?" Ricky said quietly. He was standing a few feet behind Jules. Apparently, he was more comfortable with a vampire he barely knew than a whole bunch of peers he didn't know at all.

"That's okay. You can work with me." She smiled softly at him.

He looked grateful at not being left out completely, not that he was the type to admit such things.

"Alright gang, the carnival opens in twenty minutes. Go prepare your booths." With this, the groupings went their separate ways. Jules and her unlikely trio took up position between Gabriel's booth and the one being run by Mason and Landon.

When Jules entered her booth, Tasha was sitting on the front table and swinging her legs while Ethan lounged against a stack of heavy crates.

"Okay," Jules began. But she changed directions when she saw that Ricky continued to stand awkwardly at her side. First things first. "Have either of you met Ricky?" Jules asked them.

"Nope," Ethan said, "other than the fact that he gave me an extra hour to hide under the bleachers and make out with Kara Willis this morning, that is."

"Ethan!" Jules said, aghast. "I told you to go to study hall."

"Yeah. I didn't do that."

Ricky raised his eyebrows while watching the exchange between Ethan and Jules.

"Thanks, dude." Ethan gave Ricky a wide smile.

Jules made an exasperated, older sister sound.

"I thought we respected teachers in this school?" Ricky commented to Jules, doing a nasally impression of Belinda.

Jules was about to respond when Ethan spoke again. "For the most part I do, but you see, Jules practically lives at my house."

This time Tasha joined Ricky in the eyebrow raise.

"She's my sister's best friend. So basically, she's like another bossy big sister I don't have to listen to," he clarified.

"Oh," Tasha added as she and Ricky nodded.

"Does he...?" Ricky began to ask.

"No, he doesn't." Jules cut him off before he could say anything that Ethan didn't need to know. "Tasha, have you..." Jules began.

"What don't I?" Ethan asked at the same moment Tasha responded to Jules's first question.

"Ricky and I met this morning," she said, looking over at Jules and then turned, smiling at Ricky.

"Good," Jules said, ignoring Ethan completely. "Ricky and Tasha, why don't you two work with the darts and re-tacking balloons, and Ethan you can fill more balloons."

"Why do I get the sucky job?" Ethan asked.

"Trust me, you don't," Ricky said.

"What will you be doing then?" Ethan asked.

"Helping." Jules crossed her arms and looked down at Ethan, who had dropped onto the dirt and gathered up the air hose to start filling more balloons. The first balloon Ethan filled, burst with a bang.

Ricky was regretting his choice to work the carnival once

the gate was opened and people began to fill in. But he'd wanted to go back to the dilapidated dump and watch the Alpha grope his mother even less.

Many people went straight to the food or the midway, others meander toward the games. "You don't strike me as a particularly social person," Tasha said observantly. In fact, Ricky hated massive amounts of social interaction. When there were too many people around, he generally started to feel overwhelmed. "So why don't I take the front office?" She motioned toward the front of the booth.

Ricky shrugged. But, in reality, he was relieved by the thought of not having to converse with hundreds of strangers throughout the evening.

In the first couple of minutes, Ricky could see why Tasha had offered to be the one who talked to the carnival goers. She thrived amidst the chaos. Talking to anyone and everyone seemed like a completely natural occurrence. Ricky was genuinely surprised that her personality was as openly vibrant as her hair colors. At first sight, he'd thought she was introverted like him, but now he could see that they were actually opposites. This intrigued him all the more.

He pulled the darts that had just been thrown from the board and handed them back to Tasha. "Better luck next time Mike," Tasha said, waving off the customer who failed to hit his mark.

"Ethan behave," Ricky heard Jules say.

Ricky rolled his eyes, he had tuned out Ethan Martin's banter with the vampire long ago. He was amazed that the teenager seemed so comfortable around Jules. Still, he didn't think Ethan knew what she was. So, he didn't know that he should fear her.

The next person missed the board completely and Ricky picked the darts up off the ground, brushed them off on his shirt, and handed them back to Tasha for the next person to use. "Cheer up, Ricky Harrison," Tasha said, taking the darts from him. "It's for charity."

"Charity?" Ricky repeated skeptically.

"Well not technically, it's for the school. But it feels like charity on my part," Tasha joked. It feels like slow, arduous torture to me, Ricky thought but didn't say aloud. This was going to be a long night.

A little under an hour after the gates opened, a pair of bi-racial couples arrived at their booth. One set, obviously the parents of the stunning caramel skinned young woman walking hand in hand with a man just a little taller than her. "Monica, Tai." Jules waved the couples over.

"Hey bud," the man from the older of the two couples addressed Ethan, who was sitting on the ground filling balloon after balloon.

Ethan didn't respond.

Jules tapped his leg with the toe of her shoe.

"Huh!" Ethan shouted, looking over at Jules, who pointed. "Oh, hi dad." Ethan turned off the air compressor.

"Jules has got you doing the hard work I see." Mr. Martin winked at Jules.

Jules left her spot near the front of the booth and walked to the corner closest to the middle-aged couple. "Oh yes." Jules smiled. "He's my least favorite student, you see."

"I am not!" Ethan said, most likely not as offended as he sounded.

"How is it going sweetie?" the woman asked, but she wasn't talking to her son. She was addressing Jules. This had to be Ethan's, clearly human, family that Jules, the vampire, practically lived with.

"Pretty good," Jules replied.

"Are you behaving?" Ethan's mother asked her son, who had walked up next to Jules's shoulder.

"Yes," he said.

His mother looked at him skeptically.

"That's half true," Jules told her.

"Traitor," Ethan grumbled.

Ricky heard a pop which indicated that someone had hit

their intended target. He turned and watched a girl hit two more in a row.

"Great job!" Tasha praised.

Without comment, Ricky walked over, returned the darts, and stapled three more balloons over the empty rubber carcasses of the last. As he did so, he continued to watch Jules and the humans from the corner of his eye.

"You should probably know that I'm coming over tonight," the pretty woman, Ethan's sister he guessed, said to Jules. "I feel like I haven't seen you in forever. I mean, I see you in the mornings, but I haven't actually spent time with you since..."

"Monica, really," her father chided.

"What?" Monica shrugged.

"Inviting yourself over to other people's homes whenever you want. Where did we go wrong?" The man asked his wife, but it sounded like a joke.

"It's Jules," Monica said as if this was an obvious exception to propriety.

Ricky was watching this family's interaction sadly. Last week, that was him. Happy family, loving parents, snarky teenager who they loved and adored. It was very different now. His mother wasn't the same person she'd been last week. He assumed she was upset about his father's murder somewhere deep inside, not that she had shown that to him. But it was his dad, not his mom, who had always been the one to let Ricky in on the inner workings of his mind and emotions.

"You okay, Ricky?"

Ricky turned, expecting it to be Tasha who'd inquired, but she was making some grand gesture, calling people over to the booth to take their chances. It was Jules who had momentarily turned away from the human family and spoken to him.

Ricky scrubbed a tear from his cheek that he hadn't realized he had shed. Instead of answering her question directly, he said, "so, does she know what you are?".

"Who? Monica?"

Ricky nodded.

Jules hesitated for a moment as if deciding how much to say. "She does."

"And she's okay with it?" he asked, astonished.

Jules looked him dead in the eyes as she spoke. "I don't hurt people."

"I believe you." Ricky turned at another set of multiple popping sounds.

"That's the best round so far!" Tasha said, congratulating the man standing in front of her. "For that, you get a bunny." Ricky handed Tasha a blue, stuffed rabbit, who passed it to the victorious customer.

"Luca!"

Ricky's attention was jerked to the next booth over. Luca, along with the couple whose wedding reception he'd skipped out on last night, approached the booth next to theirs. Between the hunt and the reception, Ricky had put together that Amy, Landon, and the newly-wed wife were siblings.

"Kyle, I didn't know you knew Hayley Reynolds," Tai said, looking from one werewolf to the other.

"That's Hayley Reynolds-Cooper to you," Kyle said, putting an arm over Hayley's shoulders.

"You're married?" Tai asked astonished.

Ricky saw a scowl cross Landon's face from the next booth over, but he remained silent.

"Look who it is," Monica whispered to Jules. "I know you like him."

"Don't," Jules said.

"Luc..." Monica began to shout in his direction.

Jules grabbed her waving arm. They exchanged a weird glance and then Jules shook her head minutely. But it was too late, Luca had already turned in their direction. His eyes met Jules's for the briefest of moments and then he turned his back, stepping between Jules and the other werewolves.

"I'll explain later," Jules whispered so lowly to Monica that Ricky almost missed it, even with wolf hearing.

Monica nodded and stepped away from the balloon

pop booth. "Mom, Dad. This is Tai's friend Luca Cain," Monica introduced, drawing all nearby attention. "And Hayley Reynolds, she was on cheer squad with me a couple years ago and, I'm sorry, I don't know your name?" she said to Kyle.

While the newly-arrived werewolves were distracted, Ricky saw Jules discreetly take a few steps farther into the booth.

Ricky decided belatedly to be helpful and stepped in front of Jules, obscuring her from the view of the others.

There was another pop.

"That's a turtle," Tasha said. Ricky didn't move to hand her the prize. Tasha looked around confused, but Ricky pretended not to notice. Tasha rolled her eyes and walked over to retrieve the small turtle shaped bag of beans herself.

Ricky looked behind him. To his surprise, Jules was gone.

Jules walked from her booth to the back entrance of Gabriel's. There could not be an altercation here, so preemptively warning Gabriel seemed like the preemptive choice.

He spun at her call and then turned back to his three students. Of course, Gabriel had picked three with the most behavioral issues. He could always see the best in humans others overlooked. "Missy, you're in charge until I get back," he said to the only girl in his booth. The boys groaned. He ignored them and joined Jules on the other side of the tent flap. "What is it? You look startled."

"Werewolves. I'm fine," Jules whispered, peaking around the edge of the tent. "You'll leave them alone, right?"

"You think I'm going to make a scene in front of my students?" He seemed more than a little offended by her question. He had severely overreacted at the Promenade and had been on constant edge about it since. She felt it was a fair question.

"No, of course not. But..." She back peddled, not wanting to start yet another fight.

"I'll be sure to avoid them and, no, I won't make a scene," Gabriel interrupted. "I would never risk the safety of my students that way."

"Okay. Fine." She felt foolish for being concerned, but she wasn't sure why.

He sighed, exasperatedly. "Thank you for warning me, Jules." Gabriel squeezed her arm.

They exchanged a smile and then he left her, returning to the inside of his booth. "Terry, give that back right now!" Gabriel said sternly. "You have customers."

Jules was about to walk back to her own booth when Gabriel's head appeared through the tent flaps once more.

She turned toward him at his call.

"Can you check in with the other booths? Leaving these three doesn't appear to be possible."

"Sure," Jules replied. "My kids will be fine for a little while."

"Yeah, you got some easy ones."

"You totally did that," Jules pointed toward his booth, "to yourself."

"What can I say? These are the ones who need me," he said with a shrug and a smile. Just then, more shouting came from Gabriel's booth. "What now?" he muttered, then disappeared once more.

Jules was moving to step back through the flap in the back of her booth when she discovered that the entrance was being blocked. *What on earth?* But as she peered in the small opening she could see Ricky standing in the entrance, holding the flaps of heavy plastic together discreetly. "Bye Mom, bye Carson!" he shouted a little louder than was necessary and stuck his hand through the flap, palm out. Probably signaling that she should wait there. After a few more moments, Ricky stepped aside.

"Sorry about that," Ricky said quietly.

"Thanks, you didn't have to do that," she said. Understanding that he'd just put himself between her and the Alpha.

Ricky shrugged.

"Dude, your stepfather is a beast," Tasha said once both Jules and Ricky had joined her closer to the front of the booth. "He popped like eight balloons in a row."

"He's not my stepfather," Ricky said flatly.

"But he is a beast."

"You have no idea." Ricky said this under his breath, but Jules heard it clearly.

"Was that really your mom?" Ethan asked.

Jules cut him off. "Listen up guys…"

Tasha rolled her eyes and groaned.

"And girl," Jules added. "I need to make a run to the other booths. Tasha's in charge until I get back."

Tasha smiled widely at this.

"Why is she in charge?" Ethan asked incredulously.

"Because she's the girl," Jules teased, raising her eyebrows at Ethan. "If you need anything, Mr. Prentiss is right over there," she told Tasha.

Tasha nodded.

Jules left them to their own devices and walked by Landon's booth. Silently, she asked the question of 'how's it going' by moving her thumb sideways and up.

Landon gave her a thumbs-up and she moved on down the long row of booths. She was just about to check in with the fourth booth when her phone beeped in her pocket. She stopped in the middle of the humans meandering the strip and retrieved it. The message was from Luca. It read, *meet me at the funhouse.*

She knew that she shouldn't go but hesitated only a moment before replying and changing directions, heading toward the midway.

This section of the carnival was far busier than her own. The humans were more crammed together and much louder. She passed the ticket booth, which was being overseen by the administration staff. Then dodged around the Ferris Wheel, and approached a small, colorful building that was adorned with a creepy-looking clown.

She looked around for Luca but didn't see him standing outside or anywhere near the funhouse. Shrugging, Jules entered through the clown's open mouth to see if he was somewhere inside.

Up a moving staircase, across a bridge jerking this way and that, down a twisting slide, Jules walked into yet another room. This one contained a springy rope obstacle course. The family in front of Jules was giggling wildly. Jules supposed something like this would be fun with loved ones to share it with. For her, it was frustrating and unamusing. The family ahead of her skipped into the next room gleefully. Jules stopped short. She couldn't enter. The room in front of her was a maze of mirrors. She couldn't see the expression on her face, she never again would. As they bounded away, the family's reflections were warping into many different shapes, sizes, and contortions.

Jules looked behind her, she couldn't go back but she couldn't go forward. The family successfully made it to the other side just as another group entered the rope room. It was now or not at all. Jules sped through the maze, her lack of reflection accosting her from every side. She hit a dead end, spun, and tried another angle. The next group was catching up to her. She heard them enter the mirror maze just as she ran into the next room.

The world around her went dark. The music was wild. Lights were flashing, obscuring her sight. It was enough to make her dizzy and disoriented, which Jules guessed was the point. She was just about to rush from the room as well, when she felt herself being pulled across it. For a moment, she thought it was part of the funhouse until she realized it was strong arms moving her into position against the wall. A tall body pressed against hers.

The whites of his eyes were glowing down at her.

"Hi," Jules said, looking up at Luca.

"Hi." He greeted, putting his hands around the back of

her thighs and lifting her. Her legs wrapped around his hips, locking her ankles to hold herself. He pressed her back against the wall. She should feel trapped but instead felt secure. Their eyes locked. She bit her bottom lip. He groaned. Bending his neck toward her, his teeth trapped her bottom lip and pulled it free. She gave a tiny gasp in surprise at the small amount of pain. His body leaned into her even more and her mouth opened for him. Her body ignited at each point of contact.

After a minute or two that could have been hours or seconds, Luca pulled back. Resting his forehead on her own, breathing heavily, he spoke softly. "Thanks for meeting me."

"I wanted to see you," she said, her hands coming to rest over his white tee-shirt.

"To see you there and not be able to touch you. To kiss you. Torture." He admitted.

"I thought secrets were sexy."

"Oh, they are." He leaned in and kissed her again.

Carson meandered back through the games as the carnival started to die down. The music from the midway started to fade into the background, and the smells of the food vendors grew closer. Carson had come to this event to support his town and the local high school. He had encouraged his entire pack to do the same. As the leader of so many, it was Carson's duty to enrich the community in which the majority of his wolves lived.

He had elected to come without the Den members. There was a lot of tension in the Den at the moment, between Kyle's betrayal and Luca's rebellious words. Luca, at least, seemed to be coming around. He had told him that the red-haired vampire was the school's librarian.

Carson's arm was draped lazily around Demetria's shoulders, brushing her right breast whenever the opportunity presented itself. She was tall and strong, with breasts he could barely fit in his hand and ass for days.

He'd originally wanted someone younger to be his queen. Joe Reynolds's oldest daughter was an exceptional beauty both in and out of wolf form. White wolves were a rare jewel. However, his first love, the one that should have been his all along, seemed like a deal he couldn't easily pass up. At least for now. He still lusted after the tight young pussy of the Reynolds girl. If that traitor, Cooper, happened to find himself dead in a ditch, all bets were off.

Demetria squeezed his hand, pulling his attention back to the woman at his side. "Let me go see if Ricky is ready to leave," she said, sliding out from under the weight of his arm.

"Do you have to?" Carson asked with a playful whine. He slipped both arms around her hips pressing her ass against his half-hard cock.

Wriggling free and turning back toward him, she said, "he's my son." Her breasts pressed against him. Squeezing her ass, he yanked her closer, plunging his tongue into her mouth. She pushed back with her palm on his chest, and he freed her from his hold. "So yes, I have to."

"Be quick." He demanded, smacking her ass before she could walk away.

He watched as she walked across the dirt, hips swaying. That's when he saw what he'd really come for, proof of Luca's intel. The ancient red-headed vampire was inside the booth with Demetria's son. *It* chatted lightly with Demetria for a few moments while Carson watched.

It was smaller than he remembered and young looking, despite the fact that it was supposedly on staff at the high school. At first glance, the little vampire looked harmless, and yet, he knew it was a monster, more deadly and grotesque than all others.

Carson desperately wanted to run across the way and rip its head off where it stood. The world would be better off if he did but he resisted. There was a time and a place for such executions. He had tasked Jed with tracking its movements. The time would come. There was already a plan in motion that would ensure the vampire's demise. Soon enough, Aboit and the wolves under his care would be rid of this threat forever.

CHAPTER TWELVE

Burnt Pages

Jules arrived home late that night, Monica was already there waiting on her. "I know, I'm sorry. Work ran late," Jules said as she entered the lighted house.

"It's fine." Monica was stretched out across the velvet sofa, an empty pizza box, dirty napkins, and two glasses littered the coffee table. "Tai just left. So, it's seriously fine." Monica winked.

Jules made an exasperated-sounding sigh as she passed through the living room on her way to her bedroom. She wanted to change out of her work clothes. Monica bounced off the sofa and followed her. Jules slipped out of the slacks and cardigan and into a pair of shorts and a tank top as Monica plopped down on her bed. "So, spill," Monica demanded.

"Spill what?" Jules asked, feigning innocence. Secretly, she'd been hoping Monica would forget about the odd moment earlier concerning Luca.

"Don't play dumb. It won't work."

"Monica," Jules began.

"Don't Monica me!" she nearly shouted as she sat up into a cross-legged position. "Why won't you just tell me what you're hiding?"

"It's not my secret to tell," Jules told her. "Not all of it anyway," she added, sprawling across her bed beside Monica.

"Then tell me the part that is yours."

Jules threw her hands over her face and groaned. She could do it. She could trust Monica completely, no doubt about that. Still, hesitation prevailed. Telling Monica meant that it was no longer just a secret she and Luca alone shared.

"Juliana Bristow," Monica said sternly, "am I your best friend or not?"

"Fine." Jules dropped her hands back onto the bed and rolled over on her elbow, facing Monica. "I've been seeing Luca."

Monica shrieked. "I knew it. You had so much chemistry that night. I can't wait to tell Tai."

"No." Jules sat up, a little startled. "Monica, you can't tell anyone. Not your parents, not Tai... especially not Tai. It has to be our secret."

"But why?" Monica almost whined. "It's just Tai."

Jules slid into a sitting position. "That's the part that I can't tell you," Jules admitted. "I'm sorry Monica, but please, no one can know."

Monica pressed her lips together, considering for a moment. "Alright," she said finally. "The best friend over boyfriend code will be honored," Monica said with a teasing tone. "But you have to at least tell me one thing." The look on Monica's face was mischievous at first, but then turned genuine. "Are you happy?"

Jules thought about the changes that had happened to her since Luca's arrival in her life. The years before she'd been content, confidant, comfortable.

Since Luca, she'd felt things that she'd never expected to. Excited, elated, and yes, happy. She was happy in a way that she'd believed was never meant for her. The kind of happiness she'd only read about.

Jules sighed, but then a ridiculously wide smile spread across her face. "So very happy," Jules almost gushed. "I think I could love him."

"What?" Monica shrieked.

Jules slapped her hand over her mouth. "I can't believe I said that. This is the first time I've had any kind of romantic feelings in..."

"About three-hundred years." Monica finished her statement for her. "You do know that you've known him for less than a week?"

"That's crazy right?" Jules asked. "I think I'm going completely insane."

"You could do with a little crazy now and then."

Jules covered her face again. Knowing she must sound like a love-sick fool, but Luca was worth it.

Monica laughed and crawled closer. She put her arms around Jules in a hug. Jules accepted for a moment until her mouth got too close to Monica's neck. The vein pulsing under the warm caramel skin drew her attention. *Warm, flowing...* Jules wrenched herself free of Monica and was on the far side of the room in an instant. Pressing her palms against the wall to ground herself, then sliding down it. "I'm so sorry." She whimpered.

"How long has it been?" Monica asked, sounding a little shaken, but not nearly as shaken as she should.

"Too long." Jules's head dropped between her knees. Holding the breaths she didn't really need anyway. "Gabriel and I worked on carnival prep through lunch."

"Hang on," Monica got off the bed and left the room. Jules knew where she was going. Grateful Monica knew what to do in these situations and hating it too.

Jules's head shot up when Monica reappeared.

"You're out of blood." Monica stopped in the doorway, leaving space between them.

Jules stared, wide-eyed at Monica. And then she remembered it was true. She'd drank her entire home supply after her all day sleep on Sunday. The blood she'd consumed after waking up this morning should have lasted her another three weeks. Anxious and jittery to see Gabriel after all their arguing, she had over indulged. Gabriel had some at home and there was some in her office at school. She'd meant to bring some home with her.

It couldn't wait until morning, and she couldn't stay here. If she stayed, Monica could end up dead. Drinking from Monica was the last thing she'd ever want to do. Not trusting her ability to stop feeding before every last drop had slid down her throat. Without delay or explanation, Jules bolted past Monica and out her front door. Leaving her car in the driveway, she opted for the faster option. With every ounce of vampire strength and concentration, she ran.

Luca woke abruptly to the sounds of shouts and slamming doors. *I need a new place to live*, he thought to himself. He then pulled himself into a sitting position and shook his head just as his bedroom door burst open, slamming against the wall behind it.

"Luca, let's go!" Ben instructed from the doorway. "Now!" he added when Luca didn't immediately hop out of bed.

"Okay, okay," Luca griped but began to do as instructed. "Couldn't whatever this is have waited until morning?" Luca muttered to himself grumpily as he stood. He stretched noisily and headed toward the commotion.

"What's all this about?" he asked Kip, who he met at the top of the stairway.

"Something big, I gather," he said, springing down the stairs ahead of Luca.

Luca yawned, following at his own drowsy pace.

The pack had gathered on the back porch. This was unusual, but Luca figured it was due to the houseguests, now unavoidably awake in the living room.

Swinging the screen door open, he joined the others. To his surprise, Kyle was among them. "What are you doing here?" he whispered to his friend.

"I was once again summoned, so here I am?" Kyle said quietly, but with a subtle amount of annoyance in his voice.

Luca yawned.

Neither of them were concentrating on Carson's intense, hushed tones until Luca heard something that yanked his focus to his Alpha's overly excited speech.

"What did he just say?" Luca asked Kyle, who shrugged.

"This means that thanks to Jed's stake-out, we know where the vampire is at this exact moment. So now, the time has come," Carson said, balling his hands into fists. "Tonight, we end the demon for good!"

Jules hadn't slowed her pace until she'd gotten far enough away from Monica, and all other human life, to be safe. Running across the school's parking lot, she noted a few abandoned cars but had given them little attention. It was assumed carpooling students would retrieve them in the morning. Patting down her clothing, Jules swore. She'd forgotten her badge for the entry pad. Changing her mind and going to Gabriel's to get some blood was the smart option. Explaining to him that lack of forethought had caused her to run out, felt like a less desirable option to breaking and entering into her place of employment. Besides, if she changed course now, there would be no choice but to go back through town. It was too much of a risk.

Chuckling at her own recklessness, Jules ran at full speed toward the building. With a running leap, she launched herself up the side of the building, grabbed onto the ledge, and pulled herself over.

The roof was littered with years of old beer bottles and half-smoked cigarettes. Ignoring this, Jules walked to the small skylight over the cafeteria and loosened its bolts. "Ouch!" The last bolt left a nice little slice in her index finger. She sucked on the cut momentarily and then lifted the Plexiglas window off. Slowly lowering herself over the edge feet first, she dropped onto one of the long tables below. Her feet making no sound, but the screech of the shifting table reverberated around the cavernous room.

Familiar with the darkened passages Jules chose a route that avoided the security cameras, slipping through the teacher's lounge and the back side of the gym. After a few long minutes, she reached the far side of the school, and the library.

Once inside, Jules rushed through the stacks to her office. Not bothering with the key to the padlock in the refrigerator, Jules yanked it off the small, white door and opened it. Bypassing the glass she ripped the bag open with her teeth. With every gulp, the desire to kill her best human friend dissipated. Back in control, relief flooded her. Only after the entire bag was drained dry did she realize she was being watched.

A pair of dark eyes stared at her through the outside window, and he was snarling. Jules recognized the Alpha of Luca's pack instantly. Unsure of what his next move would be, she waited.

He raised his face to the sky and let out a long, deafening howl. It was a call to battle.

Jules spun, preparing to run, but found the door to her office blocked by two other members of Luca's pack. They stood panting and snarling at her. "Your time is over, Demon," the shorter of the two said. He twitched, betraying his nerves.

A threatening hiss pulsed through her throat and the twitching wolf ran at her, bouncing wildly as he did so. Jules evaded his attack easily. Spinning, she grabbed him, throwing him as hard as she could. With a loud crash, her desk broke under his weight. He lay, unmoving, on the office floor. She turned on the taller wolf, who had been lounging against the door frame looking more at ease than his companion. He was the largest wolf she'd ever seen. Near Luca's height, but much bulkier.

Jules's confidence waned. Defeating him would not be as easy. Going for a round kick, but not making contact with his large frame. He was surprisingly fast and even stronger than Jules had anticipated. He took her second kick square in the stomach, then grabbed ahold of her foot. The wolf swung her hand against the wall. So hard that it cracked under the impact. She dropped to the ground but rolled to standing, barely feeling the impact's effects.

As she got to her feet he came at her again. This time, she was able to bolt a few feet out of his path. With any luck his speed would cause him to hit the wall hard, but for a man of his size, he was quite graceful in his movements. Not lumbering as Jules had expected. *Which is unfortunate,* she thought to herself. He navigated a turn easily and they were now facing off once again.

Just then, a groan sounded from the wolf still on the floor. Instinctively, Jules glanced sideways at him but only for a fraction of a second. It was long enough. The wolf was still satisfactorily incapacitated.

"Sorry about your friend," Jules commented, trying to buy herself time to come up with a plan.

"Not really a friend," the big wolf said with a shrug.

Jules took the moment that his response time allowed and picked up one of her file cabinets. Launching it across the office, she hit the wolf in the face, knocking him backward. Both the cabinet and the wolf landed simultaneously against the wall with a crash, and she bolted toward the office door. But the wolf recovered too quickly. He stood and caught her arm as she passed him. Their eyes met for a fraction of a second. His eyes began to glow wolf yellow, and his huge hand clamped down tight on her neck. He sneered at her and lifted her off her feet by the throat. After a few long seconds, her body went flying backward.

The impact reverberated through her body. The glass of her large internal office window shattered as she flew through it and hit the bookshelf just outside the office. Landing on the floor with a thud, glass shards dug into her back and books rained down on her head.

Jules laid there, stunned, for a fraction of a second. Everlasting death would be too real a possibility if she didn't get moving. Glass embedded itself deeper into her back as she shifted to stand. Causing her to cry out and involuntarily drop back to her knees.

Nose wrinkling, Jules took in the smell of gasoline. The friend that Luca had been with at the carnival was dumping it around the perimeter of the room and on all of the books. *Why didn't Luca warn me?* This was a completely irrational time to be thinking about him, but still, the question grabbed hold of her mind as she again tried to stand. Another failed attempt had her collapsing to the glass ridden floor.

A pair of large boots stopped in front of her and the Alpha crouched next to her, his face coming into focus. "You're going to die tonight." It didn't sound like a threat, but a promise. Then one of his large hands came to rest on the back of her head. He caressed it for a moment. Instead of delivering a fatal blow, however, Carson grabbed Jules harshly. The glass in her back twisted inside her skin as he and the big wolf, who had apparently just joined them, made her stand. "Nice job, Kip," the Alpha congratulated the big wolf who had defeated her.

"The job's not done yet," Jules spat. The Alpha had made his first mistake. If he wanted her dead, he should have killed her while she was still on the floor. Jules lashed out, nails creating long scratches across the Alpha's snarl. In the fleeting moments the Alpha was distracted, Jules turned to run but was grabbed by Kip, who held her against him. His beefy arms clamped tightly around her. Jules got a small amount of satisfaction when the wolf groaned as the glass still embedded in her back cut into the flesh of his abdomen.

As she struggled against the tight hold, the Alpha's hand connected with her jaw. The blow would have knocked her back to the floor if she hadn't been trapped between Kip's arms. Jules turned back to face him and spat blood in Carson's face. The Alpha's fist connected with her ribcage. More than one rib cracked under the impact.

"Carson," a wolf called. The Alpha walked a few paces away to meet the newcomer.

Jules struggled to free herself. If she didn't get away now, this might actually be how her long existence would end. "Why are you doing this?"

"Orders," Kip replied blankly. Before she could manage to wriggle free, the newly arrived wolf joined Kip in restraining her.

"Were you able to erase the security footage?" Carson asked the new wolf as he approached them.

"Just like the alarms, it wasn't a problem," he responded calmly.

"Excellent." Carson lifted the object the new wolf handed him and turned the switch to on. The bright light flicked on and the scalding rays stung her eyes.

So that was his plan. He was going to burn her alive. Without whimpering, Jules struggled against the two men who were holding her in place, knowing what came next. Jules wanted to beg for her life but never would. She'd live, or she would not. However, there was no doubt her immortal life would not be spared by begging for it.

"You should have left town when I told you to," Carson growled, waving the light back and forth in front of her face.

"Do it!" Jules shouted. Taunting having gone on long enough.

With a growl Carson placed the bulb on Jules's chest and pressed down slightly. She cried out involuntarily as her flesh started to burn. The pain was like nothing Jules had experienced before. No physical pain was its equal. Just as the skin directly under the light began to melt away, Carson pulled the light back. Unable to stop it, Jules visibly trembled. Carson looked down at the angry red burn, undoubtedly an open wound now.

"That's disgusting," Kip said from behind her.

"Why torture her?" Luca's friend said as he approached. Apparently pouring gasoline on every inch of the library was sufficient. "Why not just kill her?" This wolf sounded different from the others, less jovial.

"Where is the fun in that?" Carson said, a dark desire in his yellowed eyes.

"Kyle's right Carson, protecting Aboit doesn't mean we have to torture people, even if they are already dead," Kip said from behind Jules, still restraining her. "And the whole, melting her skin off thing is just gross," he added, sounding a little like he might be trying to lighten the mood.

How absurd, Jules thought but said, "I agree with the big one." Jules found that with this short reprieve she was regaining some of her determination, despite the pain.

"Kyle, where is Luca?" The other wolf that was holding her in place inquired.

Jules didn't catch his reply, for Carson had touched the bulb to her skin again, in the middle of her forehead this time. She screamed as he began to drag it slowly down one side of her face. The searing pain made Jules weak on her feet. The large wolf took her weight. The smell of burnt flesh made Carson wrinkle his nose as he laughed maniacally. Jules knew that he was enjoying watching her suffer.

"Seriously Carson, you don't have to do this," Kyle said, standing tall.

Carson growled. "Kyle, that will be quite enough, get back to your post," he ordered.

The wolf strained under the order in defiance, but after all to brief a moment, did as he was told.

Weak, but not weak enough to give up the fight, Jules used this distraction to elbow the big wolf in the ribcage. She kicked the other in the back of the knee and he went down hard. This would have been her best chance to escape if the first wolf she'd knocked out hadn't regained consciousness. As the others' hold faltered, he grabbed her around the neck and slammed her into the wall. The glass in her back penetrated farther. The pressure on her neck was harsh, but he couldn't exactly choke her, she didn't have to breathe. Her hands came to his wrists. She squeezed hard, probably breaking at least one of them.

"You idiot," Carson shouted. He shoved the energetic wolf out of the way and kicked Jules in the leg. She dropped to both knees, pain shooting up and down the left side of her body. He was about to kick her again when someone shouted.

"Everybody get out!"

The shout made Jules look toward the door of the library. A wolf stood in the entrance holding up a lighter, flame blazing.

"Luca," Jules said under her breath, astonished.

He didn't meet her gaze. He refused to look at her at all. *He did know about this.* He was a part of this pack and this attack. Her heart broke. He'd been using her and she had trusted him. She'd opened her heart again, that was her choice, this pain was on her.

"Luca don't..." Carson began to shout but it was too late. Luca tossed the lighter down onto the gasoline-soaked floor. The room around them erupted into flames. The pages of the books blackened and curled, feeding the fire. As the smoke built, the wolves released her and rushed from the library. Luca slammed the door behind them, locking her inside the inferno.

When the wolves had let her go and ran for safety, Jules was left kneeling on the floor. The pain of Luca's betrayal felt equal to the cuts and burnt flesh.

Sitting there, next to her office, Jules could hear the Alpha snicker as he watched the blaze close in on her. Everything was burning. The flames were rising higher by the second. If she stayed much longer, she would most certainly die. All at once, the snickering stopped and a great howl ripped through the air. More howls followed.

This would not be her end. Not while she still had the smallest chance of escaping. With every last ounce of strength she could muster, Jules pulled herself to her feet. Her hand gripped the broken window frame, glass cutting into it as she stood. A quick glance back toward the werewolves showed all were still congregated around the doorway. One step toward the far wall and then another. One moment to calculate the distance.

"Wait!" Carson shouted. "This can't happen!" Luca and Kyle grabbed onto Carson, keeping him from entering the fire-filled room.

Jules didn't wait for the Alpha to over-rule them. This was her only chance. Jules ran through the fire and launched herself through the wall of glass opposite them. Cuts from this glass were added to her chest and face. Oxygen wafting into the burning room caused an explosion. Jules escaped in the chaos. Smoke from the library followed her path.

Completely exposed in the empty hallways, she ran. They followed. There was little hope of escaping them, but she wasn't ready to give up.

Jules could hear several four-legged beings pursuing her now. They were much faster in this form and her pace was much slower than normal. Jules pulled one of the trophy cases away from the wall. It shattered, obscuring their path. A wolf yelped.

Jules didn't slow her pace. She ran down two more hallways and burst through the doors at the top of the auditorium. Hit the lights, blackening the room, she slid the lock in place on the door. Running towards the stage, she skipped several steps. Panic seized her halfway down the aisle. A set of yellow, wolf eyes glowed from the right side of the stage. She took one step backward, intent on leaving the auditorium until several sets of pattering paws on the other side of the double doors gave her pause.

Taking her chances with the one on the stage, she continued up the aisle. Watching wearily as it crept backwards into the shadows and disappeared. Facing one was better than facing them all together. Jules sprinted the rest of the way to the stage and jumped up onto it with a grunt. She fumbled on her most injured leg but, kept the cry of pain silent. With more effort than strength, she ran for the left of the stage where there was a back door to the school.

Before she could reach it, large hands grabbed her. A muscled arm wrapped around her waist pulling her off her feet, while his other hand clamped over her mouth.

Jules fought against his hold on her.

"Jules stop," Luca whispered in her ear. "It's me."

For a moment, she considered biting the hand clamped over her mouth, but didn't. It didn't matter how betrayed and used she felt. It didn't matter if he handed her over to his Alpha now. She wouldn't kill him. She did, however, kick him in the shin. Forcing him to release her. Spinning and shoving him hard in the stomach made him stumble backward. *Run!* Her mind told her. She needed to run and keep running, and yet, there was so little strength left.

Jules stumbled backward. Luca reached out as if to steady her. "Don't touch me." She spat the words, having had enough of werewolves tonight.

"Jules?" Luca looked down at her questioningly.

"You tried to burn me alive." Her tone was harsh but not loud. There was no sense in helping the rest of the wolves find them sooner.

"I had to..." Luca's explanation was cut short at the sound of the doors to the auditorium being broken open. Luca's eyes began to glow the soft yellow of a werewolf about to transform.

Before she could protest, Luca had grabbed her again and pulled both of them behind a long curtain. His grip was looser this time. It was gentle. He didn't release her. His arm came to rest around the front of her neck, on top of her shoulders. Footsteps and sniffing confirmed that at least one wolf had entered the auditorium.

Jules leaned forward, peaking around their velvet hiding place. The wolf had stopped as he reached the stage. Nose in the air, he was sniffing around him. Luca pulled her back and his grip tightened a little. If they ran, they'd be heard. If they stayed, they'd be found.

A wolf on four paws stepped around the curtain. He zeroed in on Jules, lowered his head, and growled quietly.

"Kyle!" Luca's whisper was nearly silent, pleading.

The wolf's gaze shifted from Jules to his Beta. In one swift movement, Luca swung Jules behind him, putting himself between her and his friend. Jules grabbed his waist to steady herself and keep from hitting the wall next to them. "Please, don't."

Kyle looked at them a moment longer and then lifted his snout and howled. Another howl answered it and Kyle bolted away.

For the next several moments, neither of them moved. Then, before she knew what was happening Jules was enveloped in Luca's arms, shoulders, and chest. She hurt everywhere but didn't resist the affection. Jules felt her consciousness slipping. Dying from her injuries was not likely, but still a possibility. She clung to Luca, trying to anchor herself to the living. Focusing on the sound of his pounding heartbeat, the tickle of his hot breath on her hair, the feel of his body covering hers. "They'll stop looking," he whispered. "Give them a minute."

After several more long moments, Luca moved first, looking over his shoulder as the sounds of the aggravated wolf pack began to be more distant. Luca let out a quiet sigh. Releasing her, he walked to the edge of their hiding place. "They're gone," he said in a hushed tone.

Jules began panting quietly. She was out of breath. She hadn't been out of breath in four hundred years. Jules knew it was her mind playing tricks on her; telling her that her adrenaline was dropping. She tried to speak, but couldn't make her voice audible. Shock, her body was going in to shock.

Luca walked back over to her and placed one finger under her chin. Jules lifted her head, her hair dropping away from her face. He sucked air in through his teeth, cringing. "I'm sorry."

His pack had done this to her. As their eyes met, there was guilt in his. Jules did not respond verbally but pulled closer to him, hugging him around the waist. His hand rested on her hair softly, the other touched her back and she cried out accidentally.

"I'm so sorry," he said again. "Can you walk?" Luca asked. "We should get you out of here." Luca stepped back, offering her his hand. She took it and attempted to take a few steps forward. Pain ripped through every part of her. What little awareness she had left in her fled and she fell. Luca's strong arms caught her, lifting her back off her feet. Glass dug into her back and his arm where he held her, but she couldn't cry out and he didn't. Her consciousness waned.

"Jules!" Luca said quietly, shaking her a little.

"Luc..." she mumbled and then her head fell against him.

CHAPTER THIRTEEN

Blood Heals all Wounds

Luca shook her gently. "Jules, wake up," he pleaded. She stirred, but barely. Luca's mind searched frantically for what to do. He didn't know much about saving a vampire's life. He didn't know where the rest of her coven lived. There was only one thing he did know; she needed human blood. And there was only one place that might have some readily available. "Hold on Jules. Please. Just hold on. I'm taking you home."

Luca shifted her weight, cradling her more tightly against him. He took a back door out of the school. Which should have set off an alarm, but he knew Ben had disable the system before this whole, abhorrent thing had started.

Luca avoided the street where the pack had left their vehicles. He took the darkest alleys he could find, cut through as few yards as possible, and worked his way across the sleeping streets as silently as his running footsteps would allow.

Luca moved to open Jules's front door. Luckily, it wasn't locked. *That's strange.*

Luca maneuvered through the doorway, still holding the barely conscious vampire in his arms.

"What happened!" he heard someone cry from the living room as he passed by it.

Jules stirred again, mumbling something incoherent.

"She was attacked," Luca explained to Tai's girlfriend as she followed them into the bedroom and he set Jules carefully on the bed.

"You probably shouldn't be here right now Monica," he

said. "It's not safe."

"I'm going to pretend you did not just say that," Monica said, sounding almost offended. "I'm only going to ask once more, Luca. What the hell happened!"

"Werewolves. They attacked her at the school. I tried to warn her, but she didn't answer the phone. I tried to...,"

"She didn't have it on her when she left. I heard it go off from the other room. I should have answered it. I'm so sorry. You did what you could. You got her home," Monica replied, walking to Jules's other side and sucking in a breath. "Now we need to figure out what to do with her. She has cuts and burns all over her," she said more quietly. "Why aren't they healing?"

"I think she needs blood." Luca sat gently on the bed next to Jules. Her eyelids fluttered but didn't open.

"She doesn't have any here, but..." To Luca's amazement, Monica bent over the vampire and started feeling around on the bed for something. Monica knew what Jules was, how dangerous she could be, and yet, she trusted her completely. "Found it." Monica pulled a phone out from under Jules's shoulder. Her hand came away bloody. Somehow ignoring this, Monica stood and scrolled through the phone for a moment and then pressed it against her ear.

"Mr. Prentiss, it's Monica. Jules needs help. She's been attacked. We're at her house. No, a friend brought her here." Monica sounded impressively strong, but her voice was shaking a little.

Jules's eyelids fluttered again. This time they opened. "Jules." Luca leaned over her. Her eyes focused on him.

"Don't let me hurt Monica," Jules managed to mumble.

Luca looked between Jules and the pacing young adult.

"I won't," he said. That was the least he could do. Since he'd obviously failed to protect her.

Monica ended the call. "You're not going to hurt me," she told Jules. "Gabriel is on his way."

Jules offered him what he thought was supposed to be a smile. Then he watched as she turned over slowly, obscuring the cuts and burns on her face, but exposing her shredded back.

"Gabriel. Jules's coven?" Luca asked, tentatively.

Monica looked at him wide-eyed and then looked back at Jules, who nodded at Monica.

"I'm going to pretend that I haven't guessed the rest of this massive secret you two have, but assuming I am right, you'd better leave," Monica said in a rush.

Luca did not confirm or deny Monica's assumption. "How long will Gabriel take to get here?" Luca asked instead, looking down at Jules again. He was reluctant to let her out of his sight.

"He'll be here any second," Monica assured.

"I'll have to be gone."

"You're a werewolf."

Luca said nothing. He didn't want to leave Jules's side, but he doubted that the angry, blond-haired, male would ask questions before killing him. "We both need to go." He looked up at Monica.

Monica fumbled over this new information but said, "I am not leaving her."

"I made a promise to Jules. If you won't come with me, you at least have to wait outside. I can't leave you here, it's too dangerous."

Monica said nothing, but nodded.

Luca began to stand.

"Luca..." Jules's soft voice was barely audible.

"Jules?" Luca paused, leaning over her.

She turned to face him. "Thank you." She mouthed the words, but no sound came out.

Instead of responding verbally, he bent down and brushed his lips lightly against her shoulder. She smiled a small and broken smile. "Anytime, My Little Corpse." He squeezed her hand once before ushering Monica out the front door.

He knew he didn't have much time. So, he sprinted a few blocks and then slowed his pace. He wasn't going anywhere in particular, just away. He certainly wasn't in a hurry to face whatever would be waiting for him back at the Den.

As he looked down and noticed that his tee-shirt was covered in Jules's blood, he was hit hard from the side. He rolled to a stop. His eyes glowed yellow and his nails became lethal claws. Standing only feet away was the vampire who was supposedly on his way to help Jules. Luca glanced in the direction of Jules's house, which he could no longer see.

"Fight me, beast!" the vampire male shouted.

Luca looked around them. All was quiet. This vampire was important to Jules. If they fought, one of them was very likely going to die. Luca could refuse to fight but would that stop the vampire from spilling Luca's blood all over the sidewalk?

With a speed hard to comprehend, the vampire came at him. Luca dodged the attack, sending his assailant into a barrel roll. The vampire hissed, extending his fangs but Luca resisted the urge to embrace his animal side. If he lost control of the situation they would likely fight to the death.

The vampire leapt again, this time, slamming his fist into Luca's stomach. "Fight back!" the vampire shouted as Luca hit the sidewalk beneath them.

"No!" he growled.

"Fight back!" the vampire shouted. It appeared he wanted a fair fight. Luca would not give it to him.

In a flash of light, Luca the man, was gone and only the wolf remained.

"That's more like it." The vampire lowered his fighting stance to accommodate the change in his opponent's shape.

Luca wanted to charge him. This asinine male was supposed to be helping Jules. She was dying, or fading, or whatever vampires did when they died for the final time. Yet, here he was, caring more about a fight than his injured coven leader. Taking himself out of the equation entirely, Luca turned and ran back towards town, leaving the angry vampire shaking with rage behind him.

"That's right beast! Run away. Next time I see you, you're dead."

Yeah, whatever asshole, Luca thought to himself as he left the quiet coastal street behind.

Jules heard a familiar voice shout, "she's over here!" Jules heard shuffling inside her bedroom but couldn't make her eyelids open. She mumbled something, incoherent to even herself.

"Jules!" Another familiar voice called to her. Weight settled on the bed beside her. "It's alright Jules." Gabriel crooned. "I'm here now. It's all going to be okay." There was more shuffling as Jules tried to open her eyes again, unsuccessfully. "Can you give us a moment?"

"Sure," Monica said, the door clicking shut as her footsteps receded.

"Come here, Jules." A hand was placed under her neck and her shoulders were propped against his leg. A zipper unzipping, a nearly silent tearing of plastic, and the scent of blood rushed into Jules's muddled brain. She needed it. She needed it now, but she still couldn't move her own body.

Gabriel tipped her head back and then, the cool, sticky, liquid dropped onto her closed lips. She gasped, her mouth opening. Gabriel squeezed the bag and Jules drank. With the first gulp, she opened her eyes. With the second, feeling came back to her limbs. With gulp number three, she took the bag in her own hands and drank.

Once she'd polished off everything Gabriel had brought with him, she wiped her mouth. "Monica?"

"Here, Jules," Monica said, opening the door and walking back into the bedroom. "Whoa, red eyes, sorry. I knew. I just haven't seen... are you okay?" Monica asked.

Jules nodded. "I will be."

"What happen?" Gabriel asked, looking from Jules to Monica and back.

"She was attacked I guess," Monica replied.

"I'm okay." Jules replied at the same time.

He studied them for a moment.

"I'm getting you out of here."

"No Gabriel. I'm fine." Jules protested.

"Eileen is already on her way. You are not staying here. Please don't fight me on this."

Jules conceded, too tired for this fight.

"Where are you taking her?" Monica asked.

"My house, for now," Gabriel replied. "You should leave too. It's not safe for you here."

Monica nodded and then walked around the bed. She hovered over Jules. Her soft brown eyes searching Jules's red ones. "Are you okay with this?"

Jules nodded. "I still have glass in my back. He's going to have to get it out."

Monica nodded, what would she have done if Jules had said no, she wondered. Taken on a male vampire? Probably.

"Tell..." Jules paused. She knew Gabriel was listening. "Tai's friend thank you. Let him know I'm okay."

Monica glanced skeptically over toward Gabriel and then nodded. "I will."

The moment Jules heard Eileen's car pulling into the driveway, Gabriel walked around the bed to lift her into his arms. "I can walk," Jules said stopping him.

"Jules..." he began to protest.

Monica reached forward, took Jules's hands in her own, and pulled her to a standing position. Jules felt the glass shred her back farther. She grunted in pain, but put a hand out to stop the hovering Gabriel. "You should go home," she told Monica.

She followed Monica's gaze to her bed. Her white sheets, smeared and drenched in blood. "I'm going to throw your sheets into the washer with some bleach. Then I'll go."

"Okay. Thank you."

Monica bent and brushed her lips lightly to Jules's forehead. "I'm glad you're okay."

"Me too." She squeezed Monica's hand.

With this, Jules walked from her room and through her house. Every step hurt. Every small motion tugged at the glass embedded in her back. But she was not broken. Carson had nearly ended her, but ultimately he'd lost. She was still here. She still existed. He may have beaten her this time. But this was a war he wouldn't win.

Ricky had been so tired from being on his feet all evening that he'd collapsed onto the couch after the carnival, not even caring when his mother went upstairs to sleep in Carson's bed. At least working the carnival had paid off. He'd gotten Tasha's phone number.

Regardless of his exhaustion, he'd spent the night sleeping not-so-peacefully until the moment he was no longer sleeping at all.

Ricky sat up groggily after the front door slammed against the wall. In Carson's rage, Ricky heard the wall crack. *Nice guy my mom's screwing. Really stable.* Ricky pulled his headphones out of his bag and connected them to his phone.

"How the hell did she get away!" Carson yelled at a few of the other wolves who had trailed in behind him. Kip's shirt was covered in blood, Max was nursing a bloody scalp, and Ben was limping.

"I don't know," Max said. "We just lost her."

"How do you lose a five-foot-something, blood-sucking demon exactly?" Carson shouted.

The younger wolf whimpered, cowering.

Well, you were there, weren't you? Ricky thought to himself. *How did you lose one then?* Ricky stuck the headphones over his ears and laid down, closing his eyes. However, he did not turn on any music. He was awake, listening intently, he assumed they were talking about Jules.

"Can she even survive all those injuries?" Kip asked.

"Unfortunately, she can," Ben replied.

"How?" Kip asked.

"Blood, you idiot," Carson growled. "She'll only have to kill a human or two to heal herself right up."

But she won't do that, Ricky thought, laying too still. What had they done? Was Jules going to die? Where was Luca? Ricky wasn't sure why he'd decided to get mixed up in the Beta's relationship drama. Maybe because Luca was the only person who'd asked him if he was okay after he watched his own father get murdered. Also, vampire or not, Jules seemed cool. Yes, a vampire killed his father. But after meeting Jules, he'd decided that vampires, like werewolves and humans, weren't as cut and dry evil as he'd always been told. Carson, on the other hand, was pretty much a beast, not the *Beauty and the* kind either.

Someone's phone beeped. Ricky had the auto response to check his own phone, even though his alerts didn't sound like that.

"Kyle found Luca," Ben said, most likely reading a text. "The vampire is gone, but Luca is hurt. Kyle's taking him home so..." Ben's voice trailed off for just a moment and then he continued, "so, Hayley can help babysit his recovery."

"Fine," Carson said, his voice cold. "I'm over that Beta right now. He started that fire too early. He's the reason she escaped. Let him stay where he's out of the way."

"At least he's alright," Ben said, sounding relieved.

"My life would be easier if he wasn't," Carson commented. "Let's get some sleep. We can go over our options tomorrow."

A few of them muttered something Ricky didn't catch, and then he heard several sets of feet clomping up the stairs to where all the bedrooms were. Still, he remained where he was. He could almost feel Carson glaring at him. And then the last set of footsteps ascended to the second story of the house. Ricky looked blankly at his phone. He'd just realized that, although he wanted to contact Luca and Jules, he couldn't. He didn't have their phone numbers and he suspected that neither were big on social media. Luca was what? Ricky's grandfather's age. Or would be, if he had a grandfather.

Nick was now the needy one. Waiting by the phone. anxiously analyzing all of Chad's texts. He was rotating between spinning the rings he wore on his thumb and pointer finger, and checking his phone. His leg began to bounce involuntarily. With a snarl, he tossed his phone onto the couch, stood, and resumed pacing around the apartment. Nick couldn't remember the last time he felt this out of sorts. Or felt anything at all, save for the rush of fresh blood. There was only one being on the planet that could cause him to panic like this. He had to find out what Chad knew and who he was working for. Then he had to get the hell out of dodge and save the one Chad, and his unknown cohorts, were actually after, preferably without being seen. He'd promised to stay away this time.

"Baby," Nick exclaimed, throwing his arms wide when he heard the front door open. "I missed you today!" He added as he walked over to greet the man he'd been sleeping with for weeks, handing him a beer.

"Okay, who are you and what have you done with my situation-ship?" Chad accepted the kiss reluctantly, then took the beer.

"Situation-ship?" Nick faked disappointment.

"We've never had the talk you know." Chad dropped his duffle down in front of the door like always.

"Not directly no. But it's past time, don't you think?" Nick took Chad's hand ushering him to the old couch. He was playing this too strong. His worry was impeding his unshakable ability to charm anyone.

"Are you alright?" Chad asked. His gaze dropped to Nick's hand where he had resumed spinning the ring around his thumb.

"Fine." Nick's fake smile didn't falter. "Okay. Maybe not. You're right. We need to talk and maybe I'm …. I'm nervous."

"Doesn't sound like you." Chad was still eyeing him skeptically.

"With love on the line it might be," Nick blurted.

"Love?" Chad chugged the beer.

"Yeah. Maybe, I love… you." He forced the unnatural words out. There was no way Chad bought that. He didn't even buy it himself.

Chad stared at him for a moment. Either wheels were turning beyond his studying eyes, or the stare was actually blank with surprise. After just one more moment Chad's demeanor changed, and a wide smile spread across his face. "Awe Baby, was that so hard to say?"

That was too easy, Nick thought to himself. *Way too easy.*

Jules had consumed even more of Gabriel's home blood supply. Seven bags in and she was starting to feel stronger. The burns on her face and chest had already become dark scars. Her broken ribs and leg were healing with time, but the glass in her back had to be removed by hand. She sat backwards on an ornate dining chair while Gabriel cut and pulled glass out of her exposed back. "Hang on," he warned before pain shot though her whole body again. "That was a big piece."

"Yep," Gabriel agreed. He pulled another piece free without warning. Jules cried out and clutched the back of the chair a little too hard. She snapped another piece off the top.

Eileen squeaked at the further mutilation of her dining room furniture.

"I'm sorry," Jules said again. Once the obstruction was pulled from the wound, the cut inflicted by it started to heal as well.

Eileen patted Jules's shoulder. "It okay." She handed Jules another glass of blood with a straw. Jules shook her head. Eileen set it on the table in front of her just in case she needed more.

"How many more?" Jules asked, through gritted teeth.

"More than a few," Eileen said, leaning over her husband to inspect Jules's back.

"Do you need to take a break?" Gabriel asked. He pulled the next shard free without warning. Jules just flinched, this one must have been shallow.

"No, keep going," Jules replied. "I just want this over with."

Gabriel tugged on another piece, but it didn't come free.

"Oh, come on," Jules exclaimed, knowing what he would have to do.

"Sorry," Eileen said for him as he picked up the small blade and cut the shard free. The chair back suffered another blow. Jules cringed.

"Jules, can I ask you something?" Gabriel asked from behind Jules.

"Uh huh," Jules mumbled.

"Do you see the danger in staying here now?" His question came out angrier than she'd anticipated. Although she'd known it was coming. "Surely you'll agree to leave town after this. No human relationship, even yours with Monica, is worth the risk."

"Gabriel…" Jules began to say but stopped when he pulled yet another shard free.

"How about we talk about this later?" Eileen said, a false chipper tone in her voice. This time, she patted Gabriel on the shoulder. Jules looked beside her and noticed the 'not right now' face that Eileen was making at Gabriel.

"That's a good plan," Jules replied in a strained tone.

Gabriel paused, obviously fighting with himself. He probably thought that bringing it up now, while Jules was in active pain would incentivize her to see things his way. It wouldn't. "Fine," he agreed. "But we will talk about it."

"Sure Gabriel. We'll talk about it."

Kyle didn't go back to the Den after the attack on Aboit High. Instead, he went home and texted Luca to meet him there. If Carson wanted something more from either of them, he could call and demand it. Besides, he guessed Luca was going to need one massive alibi. Kyle was deeply shaken by the whole experience. It was a dark business, protecting Aboit from the undead, but he'd never seen Carson play with a vampire they'd captured before. This was a whole new kind of darkness, one that Kyle couldn't understand.

"We knew Carson had a brutal side, but this..." Hayley's voice trailed off. She squeezed her husband's hand from where she sat next to him on the couch. "Are you okay?" she asked.

"Yup," Kyle threw his head back against the couch. "It's Luca I'm worried about."

"Luca why?" Hayley asked.

Kyle hadn't gotten to that part yet. He took a long, steadying breath. "He's the reason the vampire got away. He begged me to let her... them go. The way he was holding her Hayles, the way he was protecting her. There's more to it than Carson's brutality. I know there is."

"So, he asked you to cover for him?" Hayley asked, rather than said. "And you did." This she stated.

"Naturally," Kyle admitted with a half-smile.

"What if Carson finds out?" A little bit of panic was edging into her voice now. "You're in enough hot water as it is Kyle. What if..."

"Didn't you know I'm invincible Babe?" He rubbed her hand gently. "It'll take a little more than one angry Alpha to end me," Kyle joked, hoping to loosen her up.

"That's not funny," she snapped, yanking her hand away and crossing her arms.

"It's a little funny," he said just as there was a knock on the apartment door. "I'll get it," Kyle said, standing.

"Good," Hayley said grumpily. "Because I wasn't planning to."

Kyle glared at her playfully and then wrenched the door open. Luca stood in the doorway, covered in vampire blood.

"Luca," Hayley cried, running to the door as well. "Are you alright?"

"It's not mine," he replied, referencing his blood-soaked

shirt.

"That is," Kyle pointed to Luca's arm.

Luca looked down at the cuts littering his arms like he'd just realized they were there. "They'll heal."

"Is your vampire alright?" Kyle asked bluntly.

Luca's head shot up.

"Don't deny it, dude," Kyle demanded.

Hayley pushed Kyle aside so Luca could come into the apartment. Luca sank into an armchair, head hanging between his knees. "I think she'll be okay, this time," Luca replied after several moments.

"It's true then," Hayley said, dropping down onto the floor in front of Luca. "Kyle wasn't exaggerating. There is more to this than mercy."

Luca nodded toward the floor.

Kyle walked over and joined Hayley, slipping an arm around her back. "What's the real story then?" he asked.

Luca waited a full minute before he moved or spoke. He raised his head and there was water in his eyes. "I'm in love with her."

Hayley gasped, but Kyle's reaction was a little less surprised. "Yes, but how exactly did that happen?" he asked.

A small smile brightened Luca's expression. "Because of a blind date."

CHAPTER FOURTEEN

Secrets Out

J ules lay motionless on Gabriel's guest room bed while her
sore body continued to heal. She could hear him and Eileen
arguing in hushed tones and had never wanted to be
back in her own home more. Gabriel had, yet again, brought up
the idea that they should leave Aboit for good. Jules had, once
again, refused and then excused herself from the situation by
claiming a need to sleep and recover. Which was, of course
true, but she also needed time to think. Luca had saved her.
He'd betrayed his pack to do so. She needed to see him or at
least speak with him.

"You can't make this decision for her." Eileen shouted a
little louder now. "You're being a misogynistic ass."

"Misogynistic?" He snapped back. "Because I don't want
her to die!"

"Because you're acting like your solution is the only one!"

Jules may not have gone that far, but he was being quite
pig-headed. Gabriel was protective of those he loved. And he
wasn't completely wrong. It was dangerous to stay, now more
than ever before. However, if the Alpha was determined to see
her dead, she doubted that leaving town would stop him now.
She also had Luca to consider. He'd betrayed his pack. His life
was on the line, same as hers was now. Also, time with Monica
was precious and so limited. A human's life was very short. She
didn't want to give up that time because of a little danger.

Jules stood from the bed, walked to the window, and peeled
back the heavy drapes. A dripping, gray sky greeted her. A
cloudy mid-day.

Jules heard a door slam and then that same door slam shut

again.

Knowing the arguing couple had receded to their bedroom, Jules crept from the guest room, walked to the kitchen, and scribbled a note to let them know that she was fine and would talk to them soon.

As soundlessly as she could, Jules walked to the front door, pulled an extra pair of dark sunglasses from a basket in the entryway, and slipped through the door.

Jules's body was protected by a sweatshirt of Gabriel's she'd borrowed and a pair of Eileen's pants that bunched around her feet and dragged on the ground, making her trip when she walked. She pulled the hood up over her hair as an extra protection and began the trek home. To her relief, the sun was completely obscured by rain clouds. Her skin only stung slightly where the burns were still healing on her face.

Drenched after a minute or two, Jules walked straight through the center of town. She didn't figure that the werewolves would attack in the middle of the public street. However, she wouldn't have guessed that they wanted her badly enough to burn down the high school either. There were days, not so long ago to her standards, that both species resided together in harmony. The fact that this level of hatred still existed to this extent after three-hundred years was devastating. And it all started with *him*.

Jules kept her eyes peeled for signs that she was being tracked, but there were none. When she reached her home, she walked over and pulled the spare key from under a piece of siding beside the front window. All was dark inside. Jules walked to her room and stopped in the doorway. Her duvet was missing. All signs of last night's traumatic experience were wiped clean. Her phone was off and plugged in by the wall. "Monica," Jules said aloud, shaking her head. A human above humans in her opinion.

Jules turned on her phone and swapped out the wet borrowed clothes for her own as it booted up. Her phone chimed. She flinched when she pulled a shirt over the few cuts on her back that were still healing. She'd picked a shirt that sat just under the burn on her chest. More cleavage than strictly necessary, but at least that pain could be avoided.

Her phone beeped several times, obviously receiving the messages she had waiting for her. The first was from Monica. It said simply, *call me when you can*. The others were from Luca. The first read, *I need to know that you're going to be okay*. The next, *please let me know you are okay*. The next, *when you can*. The last, *I'm going crazy. Please call me*.

Jules replied to Luca first. She typed, *I'm okay*. Then she hit the picture of the phone under Monica's name and the ringing began in her ear. Monica picked up after three rings. "Jules!"

"Hi, Monica." Jules walked to her small living room and sat on the sofa.

"You're better already? I'm kind of surprised, to be honest. You were in really bad shape last night. Those animals! What were they thinking?"

Jules's phone vibrated in her ear. She pulled it away to read the message. *Where are you?*

Home, she replied and then placed the phone back to her ear.

"...But you're really doing better?" Monica asked.

"I am. I should be completely healed soon. Wait..." Jules heard the noise of a mixer in the background. "Where are you?"

"I'm at work," Monica told her. "Do you need me to leave? I can come over."

"No. I'm fine." Jules's phone vibrated again. "Hang on."

Jules looked at Luca's reply. *I'm on my way.*

She put the phone back to her ear. "It looks like Luca is coming over actually."

"Speaking of Luca. That secret you were keeping for him. Not a secret now," Monica said.

"Oh," Jules said, surprised. "How did you...?"

"I guessed, and he didn't deny it. Now I expect the whole story. Promise?"

"Yes. If he knows that you know that part, then I can tell

you everything."

"Good. I'll call you after I get off. I'm really and truly glad that you're okay but I've got to go. I'm pretty sure I'm about to get fired."

"We'll talk later," Jules told her and then Monica hung up the phone. Monica was so, very human.

Too sore to feel like moving anymore, Jules began to scroll through the apps on her phone. A news clip caught her attention. "Reports are that, despite this act of arson, Aboit High will open again on Monday. Sorry, Kids," the newscaster said over a video of fire trucks surrounding the school. Ethan's face popped up over the news clip while he reacted dramatically to what the clip was saying. He was one of only a few humans she followed anonymously. She never put her likeness on an app of any kind.

Jules's doorbell rang. She tossed her phone on the sofa and walked out to get the door. "Jules..." Luca's voice trailed off as he took in her appearance.

"Did you expect someone else?" she asked, making light of the situation.

Without speaking, Luca took two steps into the house. Dripping water onto the wood floor of her entryway. One of his hands went to the side of her face, his thumb tracing the edge of the burn still healing there.

She looked up into his face until their eyes locked. "You didn't do this," she said, taking a guess by his expression that he was blaming himself. She ran a hand down his arm, noticing several faded cuts across his skin. Jules suspected that the glass in her back had not left him unscathed as he carried her.

"My Alpha did." he said, guiding her very gently toward him with his free hand. She accepted the contact but cringed when his fingers brushed an open cut on her upper back.

He released her instantly, stepping back. He covered his own face with one big hand and then aggravatedly pulled it through his loose curls.

Jules approached him, running her hands up the soggy shirt covering his torso. His bronze skin shown through the wet, white cotton, captivating her. She traced his abs while one hand found her hip. The fingers of the other tangled in her wet hair, tugging her head back gently. His shoulders tipped forward to meet her height. His whole body arching so she wouldn't have to stretch to reach him. His forehead dropped to hers. Resting there, he took a deep inhale. "Forgive me?"

"Luca, there is nothing to forgive." Her hands wrapped around his neck, pulling him even closer. Soft lips gently met hers, tentative at first. This time it was her tongue that sought his. His mouth opened for her with no protest "Hips?" he mumbled, breathless.

"Unscathed," she answered. Immediately his hands dropped to the body part he could touch without hurting her. "Ass too," she said into his mouth with a small chuckle.

Without breaking the kiss, a feral growl broke from him. His eyes darkened and his large hands slid to her backside. Cupping her there, he lifted her off her feet. Her legs wrapped around him, ankles locking.

Luca squeezed the soft flesh of her ass. She moaned into his mouth in response. He pulled out of the kiss, face dropping to kiss her jawline, neck, and then the exposed top of the uninjured breast. Her back arched lifting the flesh closer to him as he bit down gently, marking her as his own. She realized then that it was true. There was no going back. Her core ignited at the thought. The flimsy shorts she wore were poor concealment for the pleasure building at the apex of her thighs. Her every sense followed the trail of his nose, as he left her breast and slid back up her neck. He nipped at one earlobe and another low, rumbling, growl escaped his lips and reverberated in her ear.

In the back of her mind, in a faraway place, Jules heard her front door open.

"What the fuck Jules?"

The haze of lust caused her brain to stumble over the

familiar voice. Luca set Jules gently on her feet and she immediately put herself between him and a betrayed looking Eileen.

"I can explain," Jules said, hands outstretched toward her angry friend.

Eileen dropped the cooler bag she was holding, bent into a defensive stance, and hissed, staring only at Luca over Jules's shoulder. She felt his heat at her back, his body twitching in an attempt to stay calm.

"Gabriel was right," Eileen snapped. "You've gone mad."

"I didn't know how to tell you," Jules said honestly. "I know you don't have a reason to trust him but..."

"You're right, I don't," Eileen said, pulling her glare from Luca to Jules. "You do remember I was murdered by werewolves, right? My tribe was slaughtered."

"Yes. Of course I remember." Jules took a step forward. "But Luca didn't do that." She motioned behind her, without looking away from the stunned vampire in the doorway.

"No. You're right. He nearly murdered you instead."

"Eileen, please believe me. It wasn't him." In a blink Jules closed the gap between herself and her friend. "He won't hurt me, or you." She gripped the taller woman's arms.

"So, I suppose that it was just his pack that nearly killed you and he had nothing to do with it." Eileen jerked, trying to pull her arms free but Jules's grip only tightened.

She had to explain. She had to make her understand. "Yes," she said sternly. "He's the one who rescued me," she added, softer this time. "He brought me home."

"And that *kiss*..." She spat the word in disgust. "Was just your way of saying thank you, was it?" Eileen's body shook with fury. Fingers twitching, itching for a fight.

Without turning to look at him or releasing Eileen, Jules spoke to Luca, who remained silent and still where she'd left him. "Luca, could you..."

"I'll be outside." Luca opened the back door and stepped out on the patio, closing the door behind him.

Eileen watched him go but visibly relaxed a little once there was a wall of glass between them.

"Jules, what exactly is going on?" Eileen's shoulders dropped. "Is this why you won't leave town?"

"In part," Jules said honestly, moving a step back from Eileen. "But it hasn't been a motivator for very long." Jules walked over, picked up the bag Eileen had dropped, and closed the front door.

"How long?"

Jules sighed. "Since that double date with Monica."

"A week! You've only known him a week?" Eileen was staring out the back window, but she did walk over to sit on one of Jules's kitchen stools. "And you trust him?"

"I can't really explain it but yes, I do," Jules put the bag in the refrigerator and then joined her in sitting at her island counter. "Can you forgive me for keeping it from you?" She risked the physical contact and put a hand on Eileen's arm.

Eileen sat and stared at the point of contact for a long minute. "Well." She began slowly. "I guess I can't hate the whole species. I hate the ones who murdered me of course, and I'm not too keen on this Alpha that obviously has a problem with you, but," Eileen shrugged, "love makes people do strange things."

"Love? Who said anything about love? I didn't say..."

"Jules, you trust no one. Especially men."

Jules's gaze dropped to the counter as she stared blankly.

"If you trust him. You love him as well. Besides, with the way that kiss was going who wouldn't fall in love with his big animal ass?"

A laugh burst unbidden from Jules. *She loved him.* When her eyes met Eileen's, the other woman was chuckling softly. "There it is."

"Whoa..." Jules said, still stunned. "I love him," she whispered.

"Yes," Eileen agreed. "And you have to tell Gabriel," Eileen said abruptly, pulling back. "I'm not doing that."

"Shit."

Luca sat on Jules's lounge chair on the back patio, headphones in his ears. That conversation was not his to hear. If not for the torrential downpour coming from the sky, he would have gone out to the beach. Sunny weather had always been his preference. However, he suspected he'd grow to enjoy it less, considering that sharing sun-filled moments with Jules was out of the question.

The sound of the blaring rock song vibrated his eardrums as he leaned back on the lounge chair and watched the crashing waves of the ocean. The life Jules had carved out for herself here was very peaceful.

His phone beeped in his ear. Swiping his thumb over the screen reveled the message. *Jeeze, you get a girlfriend and blow off all your friends.* Luca smiled at the utter ridiculousness that was Kyle. However, he then noticed the three missed calls that had come in recently, all from Kyle. He hit call back and waited. Kyle picked up on ring two.

"What's up?" Luca asked

"How is... the vampire?" Kyle began, but paused, obviously not remembering Jules by name.

"Jules," Luca clarified.

"Oh."

"She's going to be okay. Healing well. Someone from her coven is here though, which could be problematic. It remains to be seen."

"The guy? Because he seems unreasonable."

"You have no idea," Luca said. "But no, it's his wife. I'm waiting on the porch. You know, in case she decides to try and kill me."

"So, you've been put outside, are you being a good dog?" Kyle asked playfully. The easy rhythm of talking to his best friend proving Kyle did not have the same reaction of betrayal that Jules's vampire friend had.

"Very," Luca replied. "I'm not fucking this one up."

"Well..."

"Don't say it," Luca demanded.

"No fun. But, now that the secret's out, do Hayley and I get to meet this mystery temptress?"

"Let me talk to Jules about it," Luca said as he saw the back door swinging open. "I'll call you later."

"Wait, no..."

Luca ended the call and stowed his headphones back in their proper case as Jules walked out to him. "Carson?" she asked, dropping down to straddle him on the chair.

"Kyle," Luca replied. He put his hands on her hips, pulling her closer and shifting beneath her. "Is your friend..."

"Eileen?" she asked.

He nodded.

"She's fine. And she left."

"Did she now?" Luca asked with a half-smile. Jules leaned toward him, their faces closing the small distance between them.

He lifted one hand to her shoulder to hold her at bay for a moment more.

Jules's face scrunched playfully.

"What did she mean when she said werewolves killed her?"

Jules sighed. Sitting back a little and dropping her weight back down to his thighs. "Gabriel only made her a vampire because she was attacked on a full moon. She was dying."

"Is that the reason for the scars on her face?" he asked, as Jules interlaced their fingers.

She nodded. "Turning her into a vampire saved her, but she'll carry those scars for the rest of her immortal life."

"I can see why they hate us then."

"So can I," Jules said with a sad kind of smile as she turned her face toward him. "She's right though. I do have to tell Gabriel at some point. I can't keep this from him much longer, and it's not fair of me to ask Eileen too either."

"Speaking of telling our friends..." Luca paused to take a

breath. "Kyle and his wife want to meet you."

"We trust them?" Jules asked.

"We do," Luca replied.

"Will you give me some time to think about it?"

He nodded but said nothing as he brushed a strand of hair back from her face.

Abruptly, Jules stood and walked to the edge of her covered patio. "You coming?" She waved him over.

"Coming where? It's pouring," he asked, still seated.

"A little rain never melted anyone." She smiled mischievously at him, turned, and then pulled her shirt over her head, exposing the nearly healed cuts, and the back of a soft lacy bra.

"Neighbors?" Luca asked, looking toward the house next door.

"Only use their house in the summer months." Jules stepped out into the rain and spun to face him. His heart skipped a beat at the vision of her. Skin and hair dripping. Tiny shorts sticking to her skin hugging her hips. He was on his feet instantly and moving toward her. "It's the perfect time for a swim," she said, taking off running toward the sea. He watched her for a moment, completely mesmerized. She spun, smiling at him and called to him again. She was more beautiful, more intoxicating, than he'd ever thought possible. The drug he'd never shake. Possibly the death of him. But none of that mattered now. He followed her out into the rain and down the beach toward the water.

Carson followed the smell of bacon down the stairs and into the kitchen. There he found Demetria cooking breakfast. She was standing in front of the stove, her back turned toward him. "Thank you for breakfast," Kip was saying as he set an empty plate in the sink. It clanked as it hit another plate in the dishwater.

"Anytime," Demetria said, smiling up at the charming wolf.

Kip put a hand on her back as he moved past her.

Crossing his arms, Carson cleared his throat. Both Kip and Demetria turned in his direction. Demetria looked at him guiltily, while Kip bowed under the pressure of his Alpha's displeasure.

"I didn't see you there," Demetria said, breaking through the tension.

"Apparently," Carson growled in reply.

"Excuse me Carson." Kip slid past him and left through the front door as quickly as he could.

Carson nodded his approval of Kip's departure and walked into the kitchen. He smacked Demetria's backside, giving it an aggressive squeeze. He bent over her back and kissed her on the neck.

"Carson." She said his name quietly.

He wished she'd remain silent as he kissed her jaw, his hand reaching underneath her shirt to fondle one plump breast.

"Carson we're not alone," she said, pushing against him. It was then that he noticed her son sitting at the small, round table in the corner. Spoon suspended over his breakfast as he stared at them in disgust.

"Shouldn't you be in school?" Carson snapped, displeased at the interruption.

The boy scoffed. "Some maniacs burnt it down." The boy stood and walked around his mother. Head held high he approached Carson. "Maybe you heard about it." Carson had the urge to punch the little bastard in the mouth for the way he was speaking to his Alpha. Ricky set his plate down on the counter by the sink, smirked once at Carson, and turned away.

Carson took a small step forward but Demetria stepped between them, addressing her son. "What are your plans today, Ricky?"

Carson walked up behind her and placed his arms around her from behind. Fingers inches from her waist band and itching to rip the joggers she wore off her. His cock twitched at the thought. Get rid of the kid and he'd have her on her face, cunt splayed open over the kitchen table, balls deep before she could count to three.

"Like you care," Ricky replied eyeing the pair of them.

"Of course, I care," Demetria said at the same moment that Carson spoke. "Don't talk to your mother that way."

Ricky ignored him but glared at his mother.

"Ricky, your Alpha is speaking to you?"

"So?"

Carson took in the boy. It almost hurt to look at the spawn of his, at one time but now dead, best friend. "Didn't your father teach you how to talk to your betters?"

"My father was ten times the man you are!" Ricky growled.

Carson sneered. He would have moved around the woman to teach the boy some manners himself if Demetria hadn't taken that moment to grind her round ass into his hardening cock. He could take out his frustrations on the lad or he could take the boy's mother hard and fast. The second option sounded more exhilarating.

"Have fun with your Alpha," the boy spat. Before the screen door even slammed Carson had taken ahold of the back of her neck, brought her around to face him, and forced her down to her knees. He was now releasing himself from his straining gray sweatpants.

"Oh, she will," he growled as he moved his hand into her hair and yanked her head into the desired position. She gasped in surprise, her mouth falling open, possibly laced with a twinge of pain. *You will pay for your son's disrespect*, Carson thought as he plunged his cock into her open mouth. Touching the back of her throat caused her to make an encouraging gagging sound. Tears slid down her face. As he felt her head push back against his hand, he allowed the resistance to move her mouth along his cock. Just for a second, before pressing on the back of her head and thrusting to the back of her throat once again.

Jules stood at the edge of the water. The rain subsiding softly. Waves tickling her toes. Werewolf heat pressed against her back, line by hard, muscled, line. He bent over her shoulder, fingers guiding one delicate strap of her bralette down while his mouth met her neck. A soft moan escaped her as she melted back into him even farther. One hand slipped over the lace covering her ribs while the other tangled in her hair, pulling her head gently to the side for better access. She hadn't let anyone touch her like this in a few hundred years. She'd closed that chapter of her life after fleeing England. In this moment though, she reveled in the feel of Luca. His gentle caresses. The strong arms encircling her making her feel safe, as opposed to trapped. He nipped her jaw and she flinched slightly, smiling. "I want to taste you," he whispered in her ear.

She bit her bottom lip, considering. Turning to face him, her neck bent at an extreme angle for her gaze to lock with his. Searching his genuine and lust filled eyes, she found that she wanted him as well. Her hands rose to his chest as she considered. Her body already beginning to tense with desire for this man. With one deep calming breath she nodded. She was sure.

"I need you to say it."

Biting her bottom lip, she made a playful humming sound but didn't speak. Her hands slid his shirt up. Feeling his chiseled body wasn't enough. She wanted to see him. Complying with her unspoken request, the shirt landed on the sand in a heap. She studied him for a moment with her eyes and her hands. She explored the hard lines and large, bronze torso. His chest rose with heavy breaths. Luca was as breathtaking outside as he was gentle on the inside. Jules trailed her fingers down all the way to the top of his jeans. He shivered under her perusing as a wetness began to gather between her thighs. He growled softly. A soft giggle had his eyes shooting to hers.

He glared at her, but there was no anger in it.

"Yes Luca," she said, dropping all playful pretense. She wanted him just as badly as he wanted her. "I want you. All of you."

In a single fluid motion, she was lifted into his arms. Gasping, her breath escaping in a rush. Legs wrapping around him and hands tangling in his soft brown hair. Then his mouth was on hers once more. The kiss gentle.

Pulling back slightly, she smiled against his lips. "Right here. Right now."

One hand cradled her head and the other pinned her body to his as he carefully laid her back against the sand. The waves kissed her toes as his body hovered over hers, denying her the skin to skin contact she'd been bathing in. Lips lightly brushed hers. Then her jaw. Her collarbone. Between her breasts. She shivered at his feather-light touches. Anticipation building with each point of contact.

Registering his hands sliding her bra up, she shifted accordingly to assist him in his goal. Once the lace reached her wrists, his fingers brushed the underside of one breast and his lips clamped down on the other, sucking her nipple into his mouth. Her brain fogged as it was engulfed by sensation. She'd not been touched in this way for centuries and never with this kind of admiration or care. Luca bit gently. She gasped at the stimulation, back bowing into him. He switched his attention to the other breast while one hand glided down her body. Her breath came out in a quick rhythm of building desire, until his fingers slipped over her already soaked center. She gasped, almost surprised her body remembered how to react to the touch.

He thumbed her clit over the barely there fabric, her body igniting as her desire grew. When her breath hitched, he chuckled lightly. Watching the large werewolf kneeling over her, she found that, although nervous, she wanted him. In every way she wanted him. Luca slid the rest of the fabric from her body. Bare before him, she waited as he took her in from the fingertips resting above her head, all the way down to the knees he guided slowly farther apart, displaying her sex completely to him. "Incredible." His husky tone and lust filled gaze warmed her and soothed her simultaneously.

He palmed one of her calves and kissed it. Her hands fisted in the fabric she still held. Nerves growing, she glanced up at the sky. She wasn't just letting this happen, but wanted it too.

"Eyes on me," he said as he moved higher onto her inner thigh. She sucked in a breath, still looking skyward. He nipped her a little when she didn't immediately comply. Giggling once, she looked down her exposed body until her gaze met his, looking up at her through long, curled lashes. "That's it," he growled from deep in his throat.

She shuttered, but didn't move her gaze from him as he broke eye contact to move into position. He nestled his face between her thighs, his hands on either one, as he held them open a little wider.

"You're so wet for me already," he growled.

A breathy gasp escaped Jules as he sucked that bundle of nerves into his mouth. Her hands left the sand to tangle into his hair. She needed to touch him. To feel any part of him she could reach. Luca licked up her center and back to her clit. More wetness gathered in response to his touch. She thought she might spontaneously combust, then and there, from that one lick alone. He repeated the action. His tongue grazed the edge of her entrance, her body tensing more and more with every pass.

Without warning, one long finger slipped inside her, stretching her gently. Her breath rushed from her lungs in surprise. She writhed at the intrusion and welcomed the sensation. Before her body could fully acclimate, another finger joined the first. Her gasp was audible. Her moans coming in consistent increase as he pumped in and then back out. She bit her lip to keep from crying out as he curled his fingers against her inner walls adding pressure right where it was needed. She could feel his eyes on her face but couldn't focus. Not on him. Not on her own thoughts. All she knew was the build of anticipation in her body as he continued this rhythm. He bent his face down, gliding his tongue over her clit again. Her thighs clenched around his head, her body bucking and begging for his tongue to move again and again. He increased his pace slightly when her body coiled tightly, ready to burst free from its restraint. One more hard thrust in. He nipped her clit, and fireworks exploded behind her eyes. She cried out his name as her body gave into his desires and her orgasm crashed over her like the waves still covering her toes. She felt satisfied, thoughtless, and more free than she had in centuries. Luca stayed with her as she came completely undone, lapping at her wetness without abandon.

Luca watched as the orgasm washed over Jules's body. She was incredible. So alive. Whoever thought vampires were dead had never had one panting, boneless in front of them. Luca rose and crawled up the beach. He stopped, hovering over her. "Off." She panted as she reached for the button of his jeans. He chuckled and let her pull them down over his hips, his boxers going with them. His hardened shaft bobbed free and her eyes grew slightly. He wasn't a small man. "Two fingers," she muttered. He knew he'd needed to stretch her.

He hesitated. "I'll be gentle," he said. "If you want."

She reached out. Her finger tips danced up the underside of his shaft, teasing him with sensation. His whole body went taught at the contact. "Jules." He said her name, a whisper in the wind.

She smiled and nodded. He waited for the words. "I want you inside me."

With her consent he kissed his way to her lips. He rested his tip at her entrance, slipping against her wetness as he waited until her gaze had locked with his. He wanted to watch her face as she took him. Reaching down he guided himself closer and slid in just the slightest bit. She bucked beneath him and he grinned. He pulled out and thrust in again, a little deeper this time. Another exquisite moan escaped her as her eyebrows scrunched together momentarily. He groaned as her pussy stretched around him with each controlled thrust. Out and back in. He reached a hand down, his thumb massaging her clit. His self-control was hanging by a thread, but he refused to hurt her. Reflexively, she opened, stretching to accommodate him. He pulled out most of the way and one hand clamped around her neck, squeezing slightly, he thrust in deeper. He groaned, but she froze. And not in a pleasured way. He yanked his hand off her throat as his eyes sought hers. She had looked away, a blood tear running down one side of her face. "Jules? Look at me." After a few too many moments, she did, but her gaze was glassy. He wiped her face clean with one finger.

He knew as small as she was, she could still end his life. But she was frozen, fragile for the first time since he'd laid eyes on her. Someone had hurt her in a time of intimacy. It broke his heart and made him murderess at the same time. "Jules." He said her name again, softly, but a bit stern. "Can you trust me?" His question seemed to bring her back to him. To this moment.

"Luca," she whispered. Her eyes cleared as recognition settled in. "Yes." Her tone had regained its strength. "I trust you." He bent forward and kissed her lips softly.

Once she kissed him back, he gave her control. Without dislodging and in one swift roll he put her on top of him. The surprise of the action seated her fully onto his shaft and she gasped, her back arching for a moment as she acclimated to the full length of him inside her. A smile appeared on her lips as she looked down at him. He grinned. She smirked, and then she began to move.

Her palms braced against his chest as she rode him, nails digging into his sensitive flesh. She looked glorious in control. A goddess on his cock. Tiny and full of an ancient strength that could kill, and she was giving herself to him. Body and soul, she was his as he belonged solely to her. His fingers dug into her hips, moving with her. She reached forward and pulled him to sitting, her hands in his hair. He palmed a breast in one hand and tangled the other in her sandy hair tugging her head back slightly.

She let out a cry but her body responded positively. His lips brushed against her throat. Her hips continuing to move as she straddled him, creating the sweet friction of their joining. His mouth met hers, tongue plunging deep, filling her there. He palmed her ass with both hands, pushing even deeper inside her. She let out a muffled cry as he groaned into her mouth. Flesh slapped against flesh as the ocean coated their legs. His pleasure coiled as he felt her walls flutter around him. Her body bracing for its next release.

A large wave crashed over her back as another orgasm coursed through her body. The feel and sight of her pleasure entranced him. A few thrusts more, a mighty growl, and he followed her into oblivion. Dropping back, he dragged her down on top of him, cradling her against his wet and grainy skin. She giggled softly and he joined her. Pleasure and bliss washed over them. He tugged wet strands of red hair behind her ear. She leaned up to kiss him softly. The waves crashed over them gently as they held each other soaking in the feeling of completeness.

Jules sat up suddenly and beamed down at him. "Let's go for a swim," she said.

"Now?" he asked, still panting.

"Now," she said. "I've got sand in some weird places."

A boisterous laugh escaped him and he stood, pulling her to her feet. She let out a cry of surprise when he threw her over his shoulder, smacked her backside, and ran into the waves.

Jules prepared for a house full of guests as late afternoon arrived. Luca went on a food run and Jules took the opportunity to drain a couple bags of blood that Eileen had brought over. She was finally starting to feel the injuries fade fully. However, she'd have to back off on her blood intake soon, or it'd be much harder to stop consuming such amounts. She cleaned her mouth with the back of her hand, blood smearing up her wrist. She'd just washed it off and pulled on a shirt that covered what remained of her injuries, save for the one on her face, when her doorbell rang.

Jules walked through the house to answer it, suspecting that Luca had returned with the food he'd run off to purchase. However, it wasn't Luca.

"I'm so glad you're okay!" Monica stepped inside and threw her arms around Jules. She spun Jules and lifted the back of her shirt. "Oh wow, I was not expecting those to heal that fast. You look really good compared to last night."

"Thank you," Jules said, stepping farther inside the house and pulling her shirt back down.

"What are friends for?" Monica asked, following Jules inside.

"By the way, why did you ring the doorbell?" Jules asked, knowing that Monica didn't usually bother with such menial things like alerting Jules she'd arrived before walking into the house.

"Oh, you know," Monica replied. "Luca was here and..." Monica stopped midsentence and moved her eyebrows up and down suggestively.

"Good call," Jules said, winking at Monica.

"I knew it! Was he good?" Monica was just about to pounce when the front door opened, and Luca walked through it.

Both women turned to stare at him.

"What?" he asked.

Bursts of laughter rang through the air.

"Yes, Monica," Jules said and then walked over, put her hands on Luca's abdomen, stood on her toes, and kissed his lips. All while taking one hand full of the grocery bags from him.

"That's why I rang the bell," Monica said cheerfully.

Jules chuckled into Luca's mouth.

"I don't want to know," Luca said to Jules. "Hello Monica," he said while both he and Jules walked into the kitchen, setting the bags down.

"Hi Luca," she said, watching him. "So, tell me about this whole werewolf thing," she instructed.

"What do you want to know?"

Before Monica could respond, a riotous stream of notes rang through Jules's house.

"It seems my doorbell is throwing a temper tantrum," Jules commented while pulling items out of the bags and putting them in the refrigerator.

Luca rolled his eyes and went to answer the door.

"Who's that?" Monica asked.

"Some of Luca's friends. You met them at the carnival I think," Jules said.

"Werewolves?"

Jules nodded.

Moments later, Luca returned to the kitchen with the werewolf couple behind him. "Jules." He walked over and reached out a hand toward her. She took it, interlacing their fingers. "These are my friends Hayley and Kyle."

"Hayley?" Monica asked. "Hi."

Hayley turned toward the human, her eyes growing rather wide. "Monica, what are you doing here?"

"Jules is my best friend," Monica answered with a shrug.

"Oh, that makes sense then," Hayley said with a wide smile. "It's good to see you."

"Sorry to interrupt this impromptu high school reunion, but Hayles, meet Jules," Kyle said elbowing her and pointing at Jules.

"You have a lovely home," Hayley said, turning her attention to Jules, but she didn't step farther into the kitchen.

Kyle, on the other hand, said, "we met very briefly," and stuck out his hand for Jules to shake.

She did so, tentatively.

"Sorry about the whole attacking you and burning your

library down thing," Kyle said and then Hayley smacked him and nodded toward Monica standing on the other side of the counter. "Oops."

"It's alright, she knows," Jules told them.

As if on cue, Monica walked around the counter and placed an elbow on Jules's shoulder. "I know everything. Including the fact that ya'll are werewolves."

Kyle and Hayley looked at Luca, seemingly for confirmation. He nodded as Jules looked at Monica fondly.

"Hayley Reynolds is a werewolf." Monica shook her head, disbelievingly. "I mean that's totally cool or whatever, but I went to school with you. We were on the cheer squad together! I've known you practically all my life and I didn't figure it out. I discovered that Jules was a vampire in a matter of months, so that kind of surprises me actually."

"You know about vampires?" Hayley asked, "and us?"

"Yup. When I said I know everything, I meant everything, everything. Except..." Monica clapped her hands together and turned to face Jules and Luca. "It's about time you two told me about this whole forbidden romance situation."

Ricky had been skateboarding around the seaside town all morning. School was canceled so, the streets were teaming with kids from Aboit High. If this crap place could ever be described as 'teaming'. He saw Amy and Landon Reynolds at the mall with very few stores in it. He dodged them. He was in no mood to talk to any pack members. He saw an early movie and then grabbed lunch at some small soda shop on the coast. The whole town was quaint which, to Ricky, meant boring.

He missed the city, the overcrowding, the bustle, making people split on the sidewalk as he zoomed by them on his board. He was just about to surrender to his boredom and go back to the Den when Tasha finally answered his text.

He made it to the picturesque little coastal subdivision and stopped in front of a one-story, brick house on the land side of the road. It was completely dwarfed by the white monstrosity across the street. He checked his text messages again to make sure he'd arrived at the address Tasha had given him. Confirmed to be correct, he picked up his board and trotted up to the front door. Before he could knock, however, Tasha had it open and was smiling at him.

"Hey!" she said happily. She looked virtually the same as she had at the carnival, cute, quirky, and with more than a little sass, her colored hair high on her head in some sort of messy bun.

"Hi," he said back.

"Mom! I'm going out for a bit!" Tasha yelled back into the house but didn't offer to let Ricky come inside. She shut the door behind her.

"So, what are we up to today?" she asked him.

He had no clue. She said come over, so he had. In all honesty, he would have done nearly anything to stay out of the Den today. Not only was Carson determined to be a slime-ball, but Ricky was still worried about what the pack had done to Jules and wasn't sure that he wouldn't let something slip out if he went back.

"Actually," Ricky said, making a choice, "do you by chance know where the school librarian lives?"

"Why?" Tasha asked, eyebrows rising. "You want to egg her house or something?"

"No." Ricky smiled. This, of course, was an idea he would have loved to act on concerning a few of his old teachers, but not this one. "I heard she was in the fire last night. Kinda wanted to check on her. She seems nice." He tried to make this sound as nonchalant as he could.

"Wow! Really?" Tasha's eyes widened as they continued to stand on her driveway. Ricky couldn't tell if she was referring to Jules being caught in the fire or his obvious concern for a teacher. But he chose not to comment on it.

Ricky nodded.

"Well..." Tasha put her hands on her hips and tapped her

foot. She seemed to be thinking. "I don't know where she lives, but if you really want to be a creeper and check on your new favorite teacher, we both know someone who does."

"Who?" Ricky forgot to defend his lack of creeper status at the thought of seeing if Jules had survived the attack.

"Ethan," Tasha said, pointing to the large, white house next door.

"Ethan lives there?" Ricky asked, pointing at the same house.

"Some people are born rich," Tasha said. "Come on."

Ricky followed two steps behind Tasha as she walked through the perfectly mowed lawn of Ethan's home and up the half-circle driveway. Together they ascended the four steps and walked through the round, white porch pillars. Tasha walked up to the door, with large windows on either side and rang the bell. "Oh, get up here." Tasha yanked on Ricky's sleeve, pulling him up beside her to wait.

No sound came from inside.

"Maybe they're not home," Ricky suggested. Ricky was irrationally uncomfortable, standing there waiting. The house shouldn't have been that intimidating. Many of his friends in Fort Miles lived in gated communities just outside the city. Ricky's fall on misfortune had made him think a lot less of the life he lived now.

Tasha rang the bell again.

Ricky took a step back and looked up. A light flicked on. "Someone is in there," he told Tasha.

"Hey!" Tasha shouted. "Ethan open up!" she shouted again and began punching the doorbell again and again.

"Hold on!" came an exasperated shout from the other side. Finally, the door swung open. "What?" Ethan stood in front of them with wet hair and wearing nothing but a towel around his hips. Tasha stopped and looked him over for a second too long.

Ricky elbowed her.

"Ouch," she said, rubbing her arm.

"Do you know where Jules lives?" Ricky asked.

"Miss Bristow," Tasha mumbled.

"Yes," Ethan said, taking his attention off Tasha and focusing on Ricky instead.

"Well, where?" Ricky asked, standing up a little straighter to make himself taller than the half-naked, rich boy.

"Why should I tell you?" Ethan asked, doing the same, defending his own alpha-male status.

Ricky rolled his eyes, who cares who was the best male at the moment. "Because she was in the fire last night and I wanted to check on her," Ricky said honestly.

"What are you talking about?" Ethan dropped his bolstering stance as well.

"The library went up in flames last night. Didn't you even kind of wonder why school was canceled today?" Tasha said, speaking for the first time. Tasha did not give him a chance to reply. "Ricky here says that your sister's best friend might have been there when it happened. We've decided to check on her. What part of this is confusing?"

Ethan looked at Tasha like she was speaking Greek. "The part where someone that I care about could be hurt and my sister didn't tell me," Ethan said defensively.

"Oh," Tasha said, blushing. "Do you want to come with us then?"

Ethan looked at the both of them for a moment. "Yeah," he finally said. "Come in." He stepped aside, allowing them to enter his home. "Give me a minute to get dressed." With this, Ethan turned and ran up the staircase.

"I'll get us an Uber!" Tasha shouted after him.

"Don't bother!" Ethan called back.

"You know you can't legally drive yet!" She shouted after him.

A couple awkward moments later Ethan came bounding back down the stairs. "We'll take the boat." Ethan turned to walk through the massive house, motioning for them to follow him. "She lives like twenty minutes up the coastline."

Tasha yanked on Ricky's arm when he'd stopped, distracted by the grandeur of the house around him. "This was your idea. I'm not getting on his boat without you."

Ricky nodded and followed them both out the far side of the house toward the ocean and a boat dock with two vastly different sized boats docked there.

Nick walked up to Chad's apartment after receiving an SOS text, asking him to come home. Playing house and the dutiful boyfriend was already getting tedious. However, he still hadn't gotten the information he needed so he would play along as long as it took. He opened the door, stepping wide to miss the bag that wasn't sitting there for once. "Chad?" He called. Something felt off. The apartment was too quiet.

"You're the Fort Miles Phantom," Chad said quietly. Nick heard the quiet click of a gun's safety being turned off. He smirked before turning back towards the door where Chad stood. "Don't move." Chad was an idiot. Bullets wouldn't kill him.

"Guilty." Nick said, raising his hands. "How'd you find out?"

"You got sloppy. Now, tell me where the Primordial is or I shoot!" Chad's arms were shaking from adrenaline or fear, or both.

"Not that sloppy," Nick grimaced.

"Where is the Primordial!"

"That's not going to work on me." Nick pointed toward the gun with one finger.

"Where is the Primordial!" Chad shouted again, looking completely unhinged.

"The what?" Nick asked. He knew what. He knew who. He didn't know where. But he'd die before he admitted any of that.

"I won't let them pull me off the case. Tell me!" Chad shouted, losing all sense from what Nick could see.

"Nothing to tell." Nick moved as Chad pulled the trigger. Nick was fast, but not fast enough. The bullet went straight through his side.

"That stings." Nick's fangs became lethal weapons of venom as he made to lunge at the man he had clearly underestimated.

Chad pulled the trigger again. Once, twice, three times. Nick felt rips in his abdomen, right lung, and left leg. "Nice shots." He said before he dropped to the floor of the apartment. Face up, blood pooling beneath him. Nick felt the fight leave him. His consciousness dripping away with the blood of the last humans he'd killed.

"She will end you all," Chad said, hovering over Nick's face. "Sorry to say you won't live to see her get revenge on your true lover."

The breath of a name and glimpse of a face floated through Nick's mind as his consciousness waned.

CHAPTER FIFTEEN

Unmasked Villainy

Jules watched while Luca and Kyle argued over the best way to make a fire pit in the sand, down on the beach in front of Jules's home. Hayley attempted to mediate the argument. Jules leaned against Monica's shoulder when she felt the human wrap her arm around her. "He's pretty special, isn't he?" Monica asked. Jules watched Luca as he snatched the lighter from Kyle who balked. He was magnificent, kneeling in the sand. The fading grey light bouncing off his bronzed skin and strong frame.

"Yeah." Luca looked up, locking eyes with her and smiling as she replied to Monica. "He is." With his distraction Hayley snatched the lighter and started the fire herself. "Never send a man to do a woman's job." Hayley commented. She patted Luca on the shoulder and then walked over to plop in the sand next to Monica.

Monica removed her arm when her phone beeped. "Tai is headed over," Monica announced.

"No, he doesn't know what either of us are and I'd like to keep it that way," Luca said to no one in particular.

"I wish you wouldn't keep it from him," Monica said.

Jules squeezed Monica's shoulder but didn't speak, it was Luca's choice.

"I can't." Luca's expression was remorseful.

"Why not? Tai knows I'm lying to him about something. He even asked me if I was cheating on him last week," Monica said with a little whine.

"You know him better than any of us," Luca said. "Do you really think he'd take it well?"

Monica sighed, disappointed. "You're probably right that he wouldn't," Monica admitted. "Sometimes I think he has the imagination of a bowl of mashed potatoes."

Kyle snorted.

Moments later, Tai appeared at the top of the path and began the walk down to the beach. "Dude," Tai began, zeroing in on Luca. "Wanting to hang out with your new girlfriend is not an adequate reason to call in sick."

"I um..." Luca hesitated obviously caught in a lie.

Monica rose to greet him, tugging on the front of his hoodie to get his attention.

"It's fine," Tai continued, while only looking at Monica. "I covered for you. This time," he added, just before he kissed Monica on the lips and handed her a bag full of leftovers from the restaurant.

"You're the best," she giggled.

"This, I am aware of," he replied.

"Can we eat?" Kyle asked. "I'm starving."

Minutes later, smoke rose from the fire pit. Everyone, save for Jules, gathered around to roast part of their meals over the fire. In the end, the humans' and werewolves' dinner was a hodgepodge of hotdogs, marshmallows, and leftovers from Panda Plate being reheated in foil.

Luca watched his friend while he sat near his girlfriend, but not next to her. There was a distance between them, that hadn't been there before. He felt guilty for the secret he was keeping, but he knew Tai well enough to know that this reality was not one he would be able to accept. Luca knew that he couldn't be responsible for the collapse of Tai's whole worldview, but that didn't cancel out the guilt he felt. Jules was cradled in his arms, leaning against him as close as physically possible, while his secret was the reason for the space between Tai and Monica. One of his arms was wrapped across her chest, hand resting on her shoulder, thumb absently stroking her collarbone. Jules laughed at something, her whole body shaking them both. He couldn't help but smile. Bending, he kissed the back of her head lightly.

"I'll be back in a bit," Tai announced. He stood and walked up to the house. Monica watched him almost forlornly when he didn't reach a hand out for her to accompany him.

Jules shifted out of Luca's arms and walked over, bumping her arm against her friend's as she sat in the sand beside her. Luca lamented the loss of her presence as he watched Hayley get up from her seat beside Kyle and walk over, plopping down on Monica's other side. Both women took Monica's hands and leaned on her shoulders. Luca was amazed by Monica; this human was knowingly and comfortably sitting between two immortal predators like she was in no danger at all.

"So," Kyle began.

"So, what?" Luca asked when he didn't continue.

"I kinda like her," Kyle said as he dropped a carryout box into the fire. It curled in on itself as it blackened.

"Jules?" Luca saw Jules through the flames. She was laughing at something, her smile wide and intoxicating.

"She's pretty cool, for a vampire. I can see why you're smitten." Kyle dropped another wrapper into the fire.

"Smitten?"

"Oh, you are so far gone," Kyle said. "I barely recognize you anymore."

Luca chuckled. However, Kyle's words had merit. He wasn't the same man he'd been before she had walked into his life. He had something to lose again. Which, of course, made him worry more. But he was also happier than he'd been in a very long time. In a matter of days, Jules had changed everything; his future, all that he was and would become. This love was new, yes, but it was a life-altering kind of love. The kind that even immortals dreamed about. *Love,* Luca thought to himself. He loved her. He just needed to find the right time to tell her that.

"Ouch!" Kyle swore as a bit of packaging floated out of the

fire and landed on his arm.

Hayley rolled her eyes. "Well, that's what happens when you do stupid things."

"I heard that!" Kyle shouted from his side of the fire pit.

A playful growl escaped Hayley's lips.

"That too!" he shouted again.

Hayley stood, walked over to him, and dropped to her knees on the sand in front of her husband. Luca watched them. Their love changed their lives. In fact, Kyle could have died for it. Love has always made people do things they normally wouldn't. Kyle pulled Hayley toward him and began kissing her.

Luca stood and walked over to sit next to Jules. "Hey stranger," he said, smiling.

"Hi," she said. She snuggled under his arm and leaned in against his side.

"Apparently you've received an all clear according to the Kyle test," he told her.

"Did I?" she asked.

"Yup, totally," Kyle called from between kisses.

Hayley smacked him while Jules, Luca, and Monica chuckled.

Luca stilled at the distinct sounds of a motor approaching from the ocean. His body tensed.

"What is it?" Jules asked.

"Are you expecting anyone else?" he whispered in her ear.

"Not that I know of," she turned around to face him.

Luca listened carefully as he scanned the darkened sea in front of him.

Ricky looked around in confusion as Ethan pulled the boat up to a dock in front of a home that looked unoccupied. Ethan pointed. To the right was a small, green, beach cottage, lighted and inviting. Ricky followed the sound of laughter. His sharp wolf vision spotting the assortment of species around a fire pit just down the beach.

"You can't just use someone's random dock," Tasha scolded.

"I have permission," Ethan assured as he began tying off the boat. "The daughter is an ex and surf buddy. We went to Hawaii together last year on spring break."

"Of course you did," Tasha says, rolling her eyes.

"I think she's fine," Ricky said, pointing toward the fire. He could make out the vampire, sitting next to Luca. But, knew their human eyes probably could not.

"Who?" Tasha asked.

"Jules," both boys said together.

Ethan offered Tasha a hand out of the small, sleek, speed boat. Ricky scowled at the floor of the boat and then climbed out after them. The three of them began the walk towards the fire pit. Sand flipping up behind him and into his high-top sneakers. Someone laughed loudly and Ethan took off jogging towards the group.

"Ethan," Ricky heard two women say at the same time.

"What are you doing here?" His sister asked as Ricky and Tasha caught up to him. "Ope and neighbor girl Tasha. Awe. You two together remind me of long days babysitting. The pair of you used to torture me endlessly," Monica added in a whimsical voice.

Ricky glanced over at Tasha's beat red cheeks. She looked flushed and adorable, even if it was out of embarrassment.

"Just kidding. It was fun. Ethan who's this?" Ethan's sister pointed to Ricky.

"Ricky?" Luca said questioningly.

"Who the blazes are you?" Ethan asked, glaring at Luca, whose arm was wrapped around Jules. Ethan was making a face that Ricky was interpreting as jealousy. So, Ethan had a crush on his sister's best friend? Ricky found this to be boringly typical. *The rich playboy wants the one girl he can't have. Pathetic!*

"This is Luca, Jules's boyfriend," Ethan's sister said. "I repeat. What are you doing here?"

Ethan turned on his sister. "Were you ever going to tell me Jules was in a fire at the school?" he asked accusatorily.

"No," she replied bluntly.

"But Ricky said..." What Ethan was yelling at his sister faded to the back of Ricky's consciousness.

"Carson," Ricky said, looking only at Luca, trying to convey the need to speak to his Beta.

Luca exchanged a look with Kyle and then stood, offering a hand to Jules, who took it.

"Ethan stop yelling at your sister, I'm fine," Jules said, walking up to Ethan, who threw his arms around the vampire, hugging her. "Too tight," Jules said, sounding squeezed.

"Sorry," Ethan let go of her immediately and patted her on the arm instead. "Since when do you have a boyfriend by the way?" Ethan asked shoving his hands into his pockets.

"It's new," Jules admitted.

"I don't like it," Ethan said, teasing.

"You don't have to," Monica replied for Jules and smacked her brother lightly in the back of the head.

Kyle stood and joined Luca in approaching Ricky.

"Tasha, right?" Kyle's wife asked the forgotten teenage girl.

"The most popular cheer captain in the last decade knows my name?" Tasha said, but it sounded like a joke.

"Hey," Monica chided. "What about me?"

"I'm actually very nice," Hayley said, ignoring Monica and motioning for Tasha to walk over and join them on the sand.

Tasha dropped to the beach with a thunk and a laugh.

"Let's take a walk." Luca stood, motioning for Ricky and Kyle to follow him down toward the water.

"Ricky?" Tasha asked, skeptically.

"It's cool Tash," he said over his shoulder. "I know them."

When he met her eyes and nodded, she relaxed and turned back to her conversation with Hayley.

Ricky heard footsteps approaching from the direction of Jules's house. "Whoa, what's going on here?" Senior, Tai Yang asked.

The voices near the fire began to fade as Ricky walked away with the pack's Beta.

"What about Carson?" Luca asked when they were out of human earshot.

"He's pissed that she got away, that's what," Ricky told them. "He's not too pleased with you either," he said, pointing at Luca.

Nick's eyes fluttered. "Nick wake up." The voice that spoke was one of honey and home. One that wasn't really there. "You have to wake up."

"Rrr..." Nick mumbled. Behind his eyelids he saw the face of the only one that mattered. Blond curls like a halo. Eyes like melted gold. Silver torque neck band gleaming in the glowing light. Thousands of miles away. Safe.

Nick swallowed. He could sense Chad hovering over him. Hear his blood pumping in his veins. He could feel the gun pressed to his temple. Chad was speaking. Gloating maybe. "She says to keep you alive. But I say, even dead you'll still work as bait. Your love is the key to the end she desires."

"Nick!" The beloved, distant, voice in his head shouted. "Wake up or we die."

"You make me sick. Evil serial killing demon. If she didn't want you alive I'd end you right now. I don't know how anyone could love you enough to fall into her trap..." Nick's eyes shot open at the same time his hand wrapped around the wrist holding the gun. He snapped bones without much effort at all. Chad cried out as he dropped the gun.

Chad scrambled back, clutching his arm to his chest.

Nick was on his feet, then on Chad in the blink of an eye. He gripped the man's throat, choking off all air supply. "I'd ask who you're working for." Chad clawed at Nick's grip with his unbroken hand. Blood from Nick's bullet wounds dripped onto Chad's face and torso. Nick licked it off his mouth. No way this mother fucker was becoming a vampire. Chad kicked desperately, but with no purchase and little strength left, he had no hope of dislodging Nick. "But your blood has all the answers I need." Nick bent and plunged his fangs into Chad's neck.

He sifted through childhood memories, family drama. To parents being murdered suspiciously, drained of blood. He saw the face of a woman with long black hair. Saw rooms of soldiers training. Saw a gleaming platinum building. And then the visions went black. Chad had lost consciousness, which meant his stream of information was cut off at the head. *Oh well*, Nick thought to himself. He continued to drink, going until every last drop was gone. Taking his undead life back from the one who would have ended it.

He sat up, still straddling Chad's limp and lifeless body. "So, not in tech security then."

Jules felt the salty air drift over her body in a soft breeze. She lay on her bed, french doors open to the ocean. The moon had risen high in the sky. Their friends had all gone home and there she was, satiated and snuggled up to the werewolf next to her. Her body feeling limp from his attentions. Her mind at ease. Her heart at peace. Luca played with a lock of her hair while she listened to the heart beating in his chest. "I want to see the wolf," she told him.

"Okay. Someday."

"No. Now. Tonight." Jules propped herself up on her elbow, the other hand on his chest while she looked down at him.

He raised one eyebrow at her.

"Please." A goofy grin spread across her face.

Luca sighed, relenting. "Stay here," Luca said as he stood. "And maybe put some clothes on." He kissed her on the forehead and walked out her back door fully nude.

She laughed but did as suggested. Slipping on his large t-shirt and some small shorts. She saw the edges of a flash of light, the one she knew would take Luca from man to wolf.

Stepping out her back door she saw him. A brilliant silver wolf trotting up the sand, back toward her house. Luca wasn't the largest wolf she'd ever seen, but he was the most beautiful. He stopped, still paces away, and lifting his nose toward the moon, he howled. Her breath caught as she listened. His human face flashed through her mind. "Magnificent," she said in a quiet tone.

He bowed his head towards the sand, but she knew he'd be smirking if the wolf could do so. Jules approached him, kneeling on the sand. His eyes had gone from green to moon yellow, as all wolves' did. Reaching one hand out she stroked his soft fur. Luca leaned into the touch. "Hi," she said, smiling. He bumped her hand with his shoulder and made to move toward the ocean. Turning after a few paces to see if she followed.

She would.

The pair raced toward the water, a barefoot vampire with flaming auburn hair pacing a handsome silver wolf. In wolf form, Luca had little trouble keeping up with her. Jules felt the sand give way under her tread as she ran, felt the cold water splashing over her feet and up her legs, felt the wolf beside her losing himself in the adrenaline of the run.

They ran at full speed until she noticed his energy starting to wane. She saw that they were near the cove and came to a stop once they reached the top of the rocks and caves. Jules sat down on the top rock where they'd shared their first kiss, and the wolf joined her there. Luca lay his nose on her legs and looked up at the moon. She stroked his ears and stared up at the peaceful stars as well. They were two creatures bound to the night. Two beings, whose existence was hidden from the world. Two beings with one heartbeat.

Carson jerked. Something had awoken him. A sound. He didn't register what the sound was and rolled over, throwing an arm and leg over Demetria's body, trapping her with his heavy limbs. She mumbled incoherently, but did not wake. Just as Carson was debating thrusting his hardening cock inside her, the soft tapping sound came again. This time Carson registered that someone was knocking tentatively on his bedroom door. He growled and ignored it, positioning himself to take his pleasure from the sleeping woman. The sound came once more. "Someone better be dead." Carson growled aloud as he threw the blankets off himself and Demetria to stand and answer the knock. "What?" he nearly shouted as he pulled the door open. Standing fully naked and looking into the startled face of the stuttering Jed. Jed's eyes wandered into the room. Carson could see the moment the man took in the naked form of the sleeping woman. Her round ass on full display.

"Keep staring and I may choose to kill you," he said, but made no move to close the door or cover his paramour.

"Alpha I... I'm...m... s...sorry... to," Jed began.

Carson raised his eyebrows to insinuate that the man had better pull it together and say what he had to say.

"I...it's your Beta," Jed finally said.

"Luca?" Carson asked, intrigued enough to step from his bedroom and into the hall.

"You ordered me to.... to keep t-tabs on him."

Carson didn't validate this entirely unnecessary statement with a response but impatiently waited for the man to come to his point.

"He's betrayed you, my Alpha. He's a traitor and I have proof." Jed held his phone toward Carson with a shaking hand. Carson snatched it away from the man so he could see what the tracker was here to show him. What he saw on the little screen shocked and angered him. The proof, captured on the phone screen, was irrefutable. There he was, his Beta, sitting on the top of a rock cliff in wolf form, muzzle laying on the legs of one very alive and, likely back to full strength, vampire temptress.

CHAPTER SIXTEEN

Execution Order

J ules walked up the driveway to Gabriel and Eileen's home. As the sun rose on another gloomy day, she and Luca had decided to face their respective consequences. Jules was worried, but at least she knew her consequences wouldn't get her killed. Her hand lifted to knock but she couldn't bring herself to connect her fist with the door. The temptation to turn back to her vehicle and drive away was a very strong one. However, doing so would be unfair to Eileen. She tapped the door lightly.

Moments later, Eileen yanked the door open and smiled at her. "Jules is here," she called back into the house and simultaneously stepped to the side of the threshold, so Jules could enter.

"Are you here to tell me what is going on with you?" Gabriel said in an almost accusatory tone as he appeared in the bedroom doorway. "If you're going to feed me more lies, you can go." He crossed his arms but made no move toward her.

"Gabriel don't be an ass," Eileen said, walking up next to him. She slid her hand down his arm and intertwined their fingers. "Won't you sit down Jules?"

Silently, Jules nodded and sat in the armchair.

Eileen pulled Gabriel behind her and made him sit next to her on the couch.

"I obviously have something I need to tell you," Jules admitted.

"Should I give you some privacy?" Eileen asked. Jules noticed that she seemed to be silently begging to be excused from this conversation, but Jules couldn't let her go. Eileen triggered Gabriel's compassion. He was going to need his wife's emotional support.

"Please stay," Jules said, her voice almost inaudible. She let her eyes shut. Her eyelids felt so heavy. Every part of her felt guilty for keeping this from him for so long. The lie felt worse than the secret's subject. She was happy, she didn't feel ashamed for being with Luca, werewolf or not.

Gabriel sighed, still sounding exasperated. "Jules, what exactly is going on? And why do you look like you murdered someone dear to me?"

"I don't want to hide the truth from you anymore," she said honestly. "I just don't..."

"Just rip off the band-aid," Eileen suggested.

Gabriel glared at his wife, who shrugged back at him and gave his hand a squeeze.

"I'm seeing someone." That information would be shock enough.

"Seeing someone? Who?" He looked taken aback.

"His name is Luca. He's a friend of Tai. He saved me and brought me home the night I was attacked at the school."

"Jules you've buried the lead," Eileen pointed out as Jules stopped to take an unneeded, but steadying, breath.

Jules looked from Gabriel to Eileen.

"Just say it," Eileen suggested.

When Jules looked back at Gabriel, he was no longer looking up at her but staring determinately down at the floor.

"Please tell me he's not a werewolf," Gabriel said, not looking up at Jules until he'd finished his statement.

"He's the Beta," she admitted and then swallowed hard.

"That beast!" Gabriel shouted, standing now.

Eileen stood also, placing her hand on Gabriel's arm. He threw her an accusing look. "How could you not tell me this?" he snapped at Eileen.

"Hey," Jules called, standing too. "Don't yell at her. It wasn't her secret to tell." Jules felt stronger now than she had in centuries. Stronger because she was defending something, someone, whom she cared deeply for.

"How long?" Gabriel asked. "How long have you kept this from me? How long have you put Eileen and myself in danger without my knowledge?"

"You're not in any danger from him," Jules said as calmly as she could manage.

"I think she's right Gabriel," Eileen said, speaking up at last. "When I met him…"

"You met him," Gabriel said. It didn't sound like a question.

"Briefly," she admitted.

"You, of all people, know how dangerous werewolves can be. How could you keep this from me? I'm your husband!"

Eileen was looking at him incredulously.

Before she could defend herself, Gabriel turned on Jules. "And you! How could you put us in danger like this?"

"Luca is not a danger to anyone!" Jules's tone was calm but stern.

"Gabriel calm down. You're being unreasonable," Eileen said.

"Unreasonable!" Gabriel yanked free from Eileen's grasp and began pacing the floor between her and Jules. "The fact that you kept this from me tells me that you are the unreasonable one. I thought I could trust your judgment, but now I'm not so sure," he snapped back at her.

Instead of saying anything, she walked to the bedroom, slamming the door behind her. Jules could understand. Gabriel's anger was obviously displaced and shouldn't be directed at her.

Jules had known that he wasn't going to take it with a smile, but taking his anger out on Eileen wasn't like him. In fact, this whole thing wasn't like him. This was not the kind and caring man that she knew.

Silence stretched between them for a few more painful moments. Gabriel seething with anger. Jules sat, waiting for her friend to regain control of his emotions. Finally, once Gabriel appeared to have calmed down a little, Jules reiterated her previous statement. "Luca is the one who saved me, Gabriel." Jules's voice was low, barely a whisper. She sank back onto the chair as she waited for him to respond.

"You keep saying that. Why? And how did this even happen? Last I checked the werewolf species wanted us dead, you in particular."

"He's that friend of Tai. The blind date I went on for Monica. It was with him."

"So, you couldn't kill him. How does that make you continue to date him?" Gabriel was talking at a more normal volume now, but the tension had not left his voice.

"I don't know how it happened. It just... did."

"He's a werewolf, a mindless beast. How can you want that?"

"He is not a mindless beast at all. He's kind, and caring, and I feel safe with him."

Gabriel said nothing, but gave her a look that suggested disbelief. Whether it was in her or in what she was saying, Jules didn't know. She guessed it was probably a bit of both. So, she continued. She needed him to understand. "If you and Eileen had met later and she had been a werewolf, would you not have loved her anyway?"

The bedroom door cracked open. Eileen peeked her head out and paused there for a few seconds while Gabriel pondered the question. When he didn't answer, she walked out to sit beside him. He took her hand, looking her up and down and then at their intertwined fingers. Jules could understand now what had just passed between them. It was love. Even when the person you love behaves in a way they shouldn't, being in love with someone meant truly loving them, mistakes, faults and all.

Gabriel leaned back against the deep couch, sighed, and answered her, "well considering her death is what caused me to see werewolves' true colors, I don't know," he hesitated but then continued, "but knowing what I do now, the answer is no. I would not have fallen in love with her. I wouldn't have even given her a chance to get close to me."

"But after? After you had spent even a day with her? Could you have still hated her then?" Jules stared into his eyes as he thought.

He sighed. "It would have been a lot harder."

No one spoke for a while. Eileen and Jules were giving Gabriel time to process everything he had just heard.

"Gabriel, I'm sorry I didn't tell you sooner. I don't want to lose you over this, but I couldn't keep lying to you either," Jules finally said, almost under her breath.

Gabriel sighed. "You're never going to lose me. But I don't know how I'm just supposed to accept this."

"If you would just get to know him..." Jules cut herself off. She knew she'd just said the wrong thing.

"No. No! I don't want to get to know him," he said, almost matter-of-factly. "I don't want you knowing him. But I can't stop you." Gabriel's tone had an unwavering finality to it.

"Gabriel, can't you see it? You are judging the man I love because of his species. What you're doing is no different than judging someone because of their skin color. He was born what he is, he had no control over that. And isn't it our choices that determine who we are? Right now, yours are wrong. Hating all werewolves because of the actions of a few is wrong." Jules looked at him imploringly.

"You love him?" He spat at her.

Jules nodded. "I do."

Gabriel met her gaze but said nothing. After a few moments of contemplation, he offered a look full of pain. "I don't know Jules. All I see is danger. I hear what you are saying, but this pack is obviously dangerous and full of their own hate. I can't just live with that. I'm sorry. I just can't see past it." With that, he stood and walked out the door.

Jules just sat there, staring after him. Eileen walked over to her and squeezed her shoulder. "He'll come around. I think with time, he will accept this."

Jules said nothing as a tear of blood ran down her cheek.

"I'm going to go after him," Eileen said. She turned and trotted into the pouring rain as well.

Jules wiped another tear from her cheek, smudging her face with blood. *Well, there is no going back now*, she thought. For better or worse, Gabriel knew her secret. What he chose to do with that information was up to him.

Jules sat for several moments more until her phone buzzed in her pocket. The message was from Luca, it read, *You okay Babe?*

She typed out, *not really*, and hit send.

With this, she stood and walked to the sink to rinse the blood off of her face. She splashed herself with cold water once more than was probably necessary and leaned over the sink, focusing on her breathing.

She looked at Luca's next message upon being alerted by her phone. *I'll be back as soon as I can.*

She typed, *be careful*, and then ran out into the rain to see the one person that could make this fight with Gabriel completely worth it. Worried all over again, but this time not for herself.

Carson lay awake in his empty bed as the rain pelted the tin roof over his head. Demetria was up and gone already, presumably job hunting. Carson had told her she didn't need to work outside the pack, she was his to care for now. But, for some reason she'd insisted, regardless of every thrust he'd slammed inside of her. After the news he'd received, he'd desperately needed to let out some frustration so he could think. He was starting to wonder how he'd done anything without access to Demetria's voluptuous body. She took him better than any bitch ever had. His mind cleared after every fuck.

With that comforting thought he refocused on the problem at hand. He had the proof he needed to rid himself of this Beta once and for all. This thought should have put his mind at ease and yet he was starting to doubt his hold over the pack. First Kyle, the boy he'd practically raised from a pup, and now Luca, whom he'd taken in during the darkest of times. Both should have been irrevocably loyal to him, and yet both had done unforgivable things. Granted, even taking the Reynolds girl from him paled in comparison to consorting with the enemy. Luca had to pay.

By all rights, there should be a pack wide trial. However, sentencing would come down to him, regardless. His sentence for Luca's actions was death. This thought roused Carson and he stood. Now, thinking of who to instruct to carry out the sentencing. Max was loyal and crazy enough; however, he had nowhere near the concentration to carry out the deed. The tracker had the brains, but not the brawn. He would not sully his rightful Beta, Ben, with the task. There was only one logical choice. All brawn and no brain was what Carson needed.

Carson pulled jeans over his muscled thighs and then stomped across the hall. He balled his hand into a fist and was about to knock when he heard moaning from within. He took a moment to scowl and roll his eyes and then pounded on the door.

"Busy!" came the male voice from within.

"Now!" Carson shouted back.

There was a great groan and then moments later the door swung partly open. The male's big frame filling the gap in the doorway. "What can I do for you Alpha?" Kip asked, relatively chipper considering Carson's urgency. Carson put one meaty hand on the door and pushed it open. He looked past his subordinate into the room. The delicate, tanned, human was fumbling with a sheet, trying to cover herself.

"I need you downstairs," he said. Carson couldn't have this conversation standing here in Kip's doorway in front of the human girl.

"Kinda in the middle of something." Kip pointed over his shoulder.

"Yes, and it's a shame," Carson replied. "She's pretty. Get rid of her and get downstairs. You have five minutes." Carson put an urgent emphasis on this, Kip did not have a choice in the matter.

Kip flinched under the weight of the command.

Satisfied that his instruction would be followed, Carson walked away, leaving Kip rushing around inside his room.

The stairs creaked under his weight as he descended them. He turned the corner and saw the boy sleeping on the couch. "Wake up," Carson said loudly.

The boy didn't stir.

"Up!" he shouted louder. If Demetria was going to go out for the day, she could have at least taken her brat with her. "Now!"

The boy sat up quickly, startled and sleepy-eyed.

"I need the room," Carson said, after a few moments of the teenager staring at him blinking.

"Where exactly am I supposed to go?" Ricky asked disrespectfully.

"That is no concern of mine," Carson snapped. "Out." He pointed into the hallway to emphasize his order.

"Whatever," the boy muttered, rolled his eyes, took too long to gather some of his things, and then walked out of the room in his boxer shorts and tee-shirt. Carson heard him running up the stairs but was joined by Kip and his mind was put back on task.

"What was so important?" Kip asked, still looking flushed, the human ran from the house behind him.

"I have an urgent matter," Carson said matter-of-factly.

"I figured that one out for myself, funnily enough," Kip retorted.

Carson glared.

The larger wolf coward, dropping his cheerful expression altogether.

"I need you to handle something for me."

"Okay." Kip was ever the simpleton, but that was helpful in this situation. "What?"

"There is a traitor in the pack and I need you to take care of it," Carson explained.

"A traitor?" Kip asked. "Who? What did they do?"

Carson pulled out his phone. If he was going to ask Kip to carry out sentencing, then he should at least know the grievance. Carson handed him the phone, clearly displaying a picture of Luca with his vampire slut. "Luca Cain."

"How can you tell that's Luca?" Kip asked, examining the photo closely.

"It's him." Carson's anger flared, questions were not Kip's place.

"Alright," Kip said, conceding. "It's Luca. So, it will need to be addressed at the next full moon. What exactly do you want me to do about it? It needs to be brought before the pack." He handed Carson's phone back.

"I will not sully the pack with the grotesqueness of this grievance. No one must know of this repulsive betrayal. I need you to handle it now, personally." Carson put all of the Alpha authority he possessed into his order.

"But you can't just..." Kip began to protest, his shoulders visually slumping under the Alpha's command.

"I am your Alpha. I can do as I see fit." Carson reminded him. "You will do as I instruct, and you will tell no one that I have done so."

Kip's lips rose into a snarl that was stopped short by a stare. Carson's eyes went yellow.

"What... are your... orders... exactly?" Kip's voice was strained, as if he was attempting to reject the order, luckily, he could not.

"I want you to follow Luca Cain and when you get him alone..." Carson paused, waiting for compliance.

Kip nodded, obviously resistant.

"I want you to kill him."

Luca parked the Jeep on the dead grass under his window,

which was, regrettably, shut. He was there to pack up a few things and scope out the vibes. To check in with Ricky and see if Carson was acting suspicious at all. As Luca approached the house, he saw a pretty, tan woman sitting on the rickety front porch steps. She had her phone in her hand and seemed agitated.

He was about to greet her when the front, screen, door slammed open and Kip came barreling out of it almost running the woman over in his haste. Shrieking and cursing Kip's name, she threw herself sideways.

"Hey, slow down!" Luca shouted.

Kip turned on him. His fists clenched and one arm raised like he would strike Luca. Kip opened his mouth like he wanted to speak but didn't. With his body language Kip should have looked furious, but instead his eyes looked anxious. "Seriously?" The woman questioned, sounding annoyed. Kip looked down at her and breathed a sigh, like he was relieved.

"You good bro?" Luca saw some kind of war raging in the wolf's eyes. Kip let out a growl and then looked down at the woman.

"Come on, I'll take you home." He reached his hand down to help her stand. "Sorry about all that," he said as they walked to his lifted, red, pickup truck that was parked at the end of the driveway.

"Okay then," Luca said to himself. "Weird."

The screen door screeched shut behind Luca as he entered the wolves' Den. It was quiet but being a weekday that was unsurprising. Most of the pack had jobs outside of pack life. He knew Kip was a personal trainer and Max was a night janitor at some office building. Thinking of jobs made him wonder if he still had one. He should probably call work at some point.

"And where, pray tell, have you been?" A cool voice asked from the kitchen. Luca could feel the Alpha's displeasure rolling off of him as he veered into the room to face Carson.

"Pray tell?" Luca asked. "I've been celebrating, staying at Kyle and Hayley's."

"Is that so?" Carson asked skeptically as he shoved some oat cereal into his mouth.

"Yep," Luca lied easily. And thanked his lucky stars that he was able to do so. "And I'm going to be late for work." He said looking at his phone screen and turning to walk from the room. "Did you need me for something?" he added as an afterthought, popping his head back into the kitchen.

"No," Carson replied. "Nope. Give the happy couple my best."

"Okay." Luca's tone was questioning. "Will do." With that he escaped up the stairs, taking them two at a time. He flung his door open and stopped short. His bathroom door was creaking open, steam rolling out of it.

"Cheese and fucking rice dude," Ricky yelped, towel draped over one shoulder. "What are you doing here?"

"Um... this is my room," Luca said leaning against the door frame in amusement.

"Oh," Ricky looked around. "My bad." A look of guilt crossed his face. "I didn't think you'd mind. You seemed pretty shacked up."

Luca laughed and then entered the room, closing the door behind him. "I don't. I'm just messing with you." He pulled an old suitcase out of his closet and started tossing some things in it.

"You moving out?" Ricky asked, watching him move around the room.

"More like packing an overnight bag in case my girlfriend will let me spend the night again." His heart gave a little flutter. They hadn't even talked about the label. But Monica had introduced them that way, and neither had objected. Have you heard anything more from Carson about..." Luca's voice trailed off.

"No," Ricky said. "But you'll know if I do. By the way, you should probably shower."

"Why?" Luca went to sniff himself.

"Because you smell like vampire."

Nick left the dead operative lying in his own blood. Under no delusions that the human hadn't passed on his information to whomever he was working for, he didn't bother scrubbing down the apartment or erasing his presence. He would have to find out who these people were and why they wanted *him*. But, first things first, he needed to get out of sight as fast as possible.

Nick stopped in front of Cleo's establishment, intent on seeking out its owner. She would probably provide him sanctuary and may help dispose of the corpse of his surprisingly mysterious, dead, ex-placeholder of a lover.

Nick pounded on the door calling Cleo by name. No answer. He called again, louder this time. "Cleo please!"

"Alright don't drown your scarabs." He heard her voice faintly from within.

"What?" Nick asked as the heavy front door creaked open. His breath left him in a tidal wave once he laid eyes fully on the bronzed beauty, covered only in a short lace robe, slung wide over her full breasts.

"I need your help," he choked out.

"I gathered as much," she sighed, but stepped aside. "I am quite busy at the moment."

"I gathered as much," he stated back to her.

"I would say you could join us, but Tara doesn't swing that way," her tone was teasing.

Nick held his hands up in surrender. "I just need a place to lay low and a conversation."

"You may lay low on the blood couches." She gestured to the empty leather couches where patrons partook in the exchange of blood for oblivion. "Your questions will have to wait until I am less occupied."

"Understood."

With a nod, Cleo walked towards the private area, past the velvet curtain, rounded hips swaying, bare feet slapping gently on the cool tile floor. "Thank you," he called almost as an afterthought.

She peaked back around the curtain for one more moment. "Anything for the true love of one of my oldest friends."

"Have you..." Nick trailed off. "Have you spoken to him?"

She offered him a half smile, but nothing more, before disappearing.

Nick walked to the empty couch, dropping down onto it gracefully. He leaned forward in contemplation, elbows on his knees. Of all the thoughts swirling around in his head, the one he couldn't ignore was the fact that someone wanted *him* dead. Nick didn't care so much about himself. He'd coasted through life for enough years to not particularly value it. But he wouldn't let anyone near the only being he actually loved.

"Can I do anything for you, Sugar?"

Nick continued to spin the ring on his thumb in concentration.

"Nick?" Antonio the bartender asked, sitting down near but not next to Nick.

Nick startled out of his deep thought. "What?" he snapped, finally looking toward the man.

"Can I do anything? Get you anything? Whiskey?" Antonio repeated.

Nick sighed. "Not unless you have a cleanup crew that can get rid of a body and track the people that come looking for it," Nick said hopelessly.

Antonio chewed his lip in thought. After a few moments the bartender spoke. "Consider it done."

"I beg your pardon?" Nick stared up as the man stood.

Antonio reached out and very gently stroked Nick's jaw. "I do more around here than serve drinks and suck good dick, Nicholas."

"Oh," he said as he watched Antonio's retreating back. He really needed to stop underestimating others.

CHAPTER SEVENTEEN

Trials of Love

Luca parked his Jeep down the street from Jules's house. He slammed the door and stepped out just as Jules's little silver car pulled into her driveway. Jules climbed out, shutting her own car door behind her. At first, he thought she might have missed the six-foot-four werewolf jogging toward her in the pouring rain until she was in his arms. He lifted her off her feet and held her tightly as the rain soaked them both.

Her forehead dropped to his. "I'm sorry Gabriel took it badly," he said, lifting his lips to press them gently to her forehead.

Jules studied him a moment. He felt the missing pieces of his soul taking root in her eyes. He'd fallen fast, but he knew that he never wanted to let her go.

His eyes found her lips and darkened with lust. He closed the small space between them. Enveloping his mouth with hers right here on the quiet street in the pouring rain. She gave a soft moan as his tongue filled her mouth, melting in the heat of his kiss.

With a low growl, he yanked her body even closer. She gasped into his mouth but tightened around him. "That's my girl," he said, barely a whisper. She giggled lightly as her hands found the wet waves of his hair. She was so strong, and sexy, stunning in every way. Strong, sexy, stunning and his. Everything about her felt right, and here in his arms was where he wanted her to stay.

Panting, she backed out of the kiss, placing her palm on his chest to stall him, but didn't wriggle free of his hold.

"Hi," he said, finding her eyes searching his.

"Hi," she replied, biting her lower lip and smiling softly. "Luca..." Her voice trailed off.

"What is it?" He sensed she had something she wanted to say but was unsure that she should. Her legs shifted from around him. He set her on her feet, covering her face from the rain with his body the best he could. "Gabriel is an important part of my life," Jules admitted, palms sliding up his abdomen. "But..." she hesitated. He brushed her wet hair back. "Something tells me that you are more significant to my future."

Everything inside him exploded, especially his heart. But he replied with, "Giving everything up for a guy. Sounds reckless."

Jules rolled her eyes. "Yes, and risking your position within a pack and very possibly your life is a wise decision?"

"I guess we'll be impulsive together then," he said, brushing her cheek with his fingers.

"I guess so," she replied, throwing her head back and letting the rain drip down her face for a moment. The smile on her lips was one of peace and pure happiness. He knew this, he was unsure how, but he did.

"Shall we get out of the rain?" Luca asked.

"Yes," Jules replied. "But let's walk."

Luca slipped one arm around her and, in comfortable silence, they strolled back toward her house, her side pressed against his. He slowed his long stride to match hers. "You know that wasn't actually where I was going with that conversation," she commented, staring ahead of them.

"No?" Luca said questioningly.

"Nope. I guess it just wasn't the opportune moment..."

They walked under a large tree and Luca stopped abruptly, spinning her to face him. Hands coming to rest on either side of her neck he looked down at her. "I love you."

"Yeah, that was it," she told him cheekily as she turned away to keep walking. He grasped her hand, pulling her back into him. "Then say it." His tone was low, barely a whisper in her ear. She leaned back against him, magnetized to every part of him. Turning her face to one side, his hand glided up her arm, over her collarbone to cup just under her chin.

"I." she paused with a smirk. "Love." His face lowered to hers. "You," she whispered just as their lips brushed. "Too. You said it first," she quipped as she pushed off of him, continuing toward the house. He jogged to catch up to her, wrapping her in his arms.

"Shoes." Jules pointed to a spot beside the front door as she opened it. Luca slipped off his soaked Converse and left them there. Before she had time to get much farther into the house, he spun her around, lifting her onto her island counter. She laughed, but wrapped her legs around him, pulling him closer. He kissed her again. Content to kiss her for the rest of his immortal life.

Just as she began trying to free him from his wet shirt, her phone began to ring. He groaned, dropping his head onto her shoulder. It was her turn to chuckle. "It might be Gabriel," she said as she retrieved her phone from the counter beside her. "Forgive me?"

"Never," he said quietly as she put the phone to her ear.

"Hey Monica," she greeted. "I thought you were at Tai's today."

Luca kissed her on the clavicle, and then the neck. He was just about to nip at the flesh there when she pushed against him.

"Wait, slow down. What's wrong?" she asked.

Luca stopped and stood straight, putting a little distance between them. He could hear Monica's rushed and shaky voice, but he had no hope of making out what she was saying.

"Alright. I'll be right over." Jules's expression changed into one of instant regret. "After one teeny tiny little stop." Jules ended the call and slipped her arms back around his neck, pulling him closer once more.

"Where are we going?" Luca asked, running his hands up

under the wet material over her back.

"We aren't going anywhere," she said as he began to kiss her neck.

"Oh?" he mumbled in question.

"No time," she pushed him back, but there was a playful smile on her face.

"What's up?" Crestfallen, he brushed wet hair behind her ear.

"Tai broke up with Monica," Jules said.

"I'm sorry to hear that," he replied. "Did she say why?" His hands came to rest on the counter beside her thighs.

"Actually, she did," Jules said. "And I think it's our fault."

Jules released a steadying breath as she stood outside Gabriel's home. She'd been in such a state leaving Gabriel's earlier that she'd forgotten the second reason she'd come. *Blood.* All was silent inside. Everything was dark. She tried the front door, finding it locked. Swiftly, she reached under one of the wicker chairs on the porch, finding the spare house key.

When she walked inside, there were no signs of Gabriel or Eileen. She went to the kitchen, took a glass out of the cupboard above her head, and pulled open the refrigerator door. Five hospital blood bags sat inside. The sight and smell of it both disgusted and revitalized her. Without hesitation, Jules punctured the plastic with her teeth and poured it in the glass.

The luscious liquid steadied her nerves. Only after Jules stopped feeling the blood pulsing down her throat and through her body did she open her eyes. She saw a note tucked under the bags in the refrigerator, scrawled hurriedly in Eileen's handwriting.

Jules,

I am going to do everything I can to get Gabriel to see reason. But he says he needs space and I'm afraid if he doesn't get it, he will do something we are all going to regret. So, we've gone to Fort Miles for a few weeks. I know this is an impossibly bad time. I'm sorry. We both love you, Jules. Remember that.

Eileen

Luca reluctantly, but at Jules's request, walked into the employee entrance of Panda Plate on his day off. He found Tai and his father in the kitchen preparing for the lunch rush.

"Hey there, Luca!" Mr. Yang greeted him while tossing vegetables into a searing pan. Tai muttered a hello but kept his head down.

Luca moved past both father and son to get himself a large paper cup and fill it with Mountain Dew from the soda fountain. Tai's father chuckled. It was customary for employees to help themselves to soda. Luca slipped a straw into his cup and took several swallows.

"So, Luca, what brings you here? Tai told me you've been sick. Or was it lovesick?" said Mr. Yang with a smile on his face. Tai had obviously just told his father the truth. Luca had been too busy with a girl to come to work. And yet Mr. Yang was smiling. So maybe Luca was off the hook.

"Oh. I um…that's the one. Still am. Sick as a Dog actually," Luca replied smiling at Mr. Yang. But then moved his eyes not so subtly towards the back of Tai's head. Mr. Yang saw the gesture and seemed to catch why Luca was really here. The phone rang and without thinking, Luca answered it.

"Well you just let me know when you are ready to be put back on the schedule. I don't want to stand in the way of young love." Mr. Yang said once Luca had hung up the phone and entered an order in the system. "Speaking of young love, Tai why don't you take a break."

"But it's almost lunchtime," Tai protested.

"It's almost ready and it looks like Luca might really be here to talk to you. Maybe he can fix whatever is going on between you and our precious Monica. Since you obviously won't listen to me."

Tai poured the contents of his large skillet into a pan and glared at his father. Mr. Yang continued to mumble under his breath. Luca thought he was pretty obviously on Monica's side.

"Well, come on then," Tai said as he carried the pan into the dining room and placed it on the almost full buffet. He then grabbed a plate and started fixing one for himself. Finally, his reluctance apparent, he joined Luca at a table in the corner of the dining room. For quite a while Tai said nothing and refused to look up from his random assortment of food.

Halfway through Tai's lunch, Luca spoke up. "Are you really going to make me ask?"

"There isn't anything to say."

They sat silently. Luca knew Tai had to have his reasons to break up with Monica. He also knew that if he waited, Tai would eventually say what he needed to.

"Fine."

That didn't take long, Luca thought.

"I just couldn't stand it anymore."

"And *it* is? You love Monica, don't you?"

"Yeah, I do. A lot, but she's always so secretive. It feels like she's always hiding something from me. I just couldn't take it anymore." Tai started speed-talking, a trait he had picked up from Monica. Luca struggled to keep up but managed to catch Tai's gist.

"Did you tell her all this?" Luca asked him.

"Yes! That's when she blew up and started raving about how she couldn't tell me and if I couldn't trust her then maybe we should just break up. The next thing I know, my relationship of two years is just over. I suppose it's my fault, but I..."

Luca felt a pain in his chest as he listened. *Was Jules right? Was this his fault?* Was the secret Monica was keeping the one about the secret supernatural underbelly of the world? The one Luca had insisted she keep. *Can Tai handle the truth?*

"What good is a relationship without trust? And she doesn't trust me, and I can't trust her."

He wanted to tell Tai everything, to insist that Monica had a good reason to lie, but instead, he said, "that sucks, man. I'm sorry."

He sat there with his friend as he finished up his meal, not saying much more. He needed to talk to Jules. Together, they would decide what to do.

Ricky reached out to touch Tasha's thigh. They sat together on her family's old basement couch. After he'd showered, he'd sought refuge in Tasha's home. Little did he know asylum would lead to kisses. She giggled as he leaned forward to kiss her again. She slid her hands onto his shoulders and bit down lightly on the tender part of his lip.

"Tasha!" someone called.

"Who was that?" Ricky asked as they both stopped abruptly.

"My brother," Tasha said. "Ignore him." Her brother was a senior football player at Aboit High.

He called out for her again as Tasha pulled Ricky down on top of her by the t-shirt. Ricky tried to ignore his increasingly aggravated calls as they kissed again.

The basement door burst open and Ricky heard footsteps clomping down the wooden stairs. He pulled himself off her.

"You little creep!" her brother screamed, rushing at Ricky.

Ricky was too fast for the large football player and easily avoided the charge. With one last smile over his shoulder, Ricky rushed out of the house.

As he headed into the woods, he peeled the layers of clothing off and leaped into the air. Tasha's brother shouted angrily from somewhere behind him, but he would never catch Ricky now.

Even if he did, he wouldn't be looking for a black-haired wolf. Ricky turned and trotted away from the voice with a toothy, wolf-like snicker. Once he was well out of range, he stopped to stretch, utterly pleased with himself.

"That was reckless."

Ricky spun. Before him, in a random patch of woods behind Tasha's subdivision, was Jules.

He stared at her with his yellow, wolf eyes, and then turned his head from side to side, unsure what to do now.

"Hang on," Jules said and then bolted in the direction he'd come from, returning moments later with the pants he'd discarded. She tossed them at him and then turned her back.

In a burst of light and laughing easily, Ricky the wolf became Ricky the boy and pulled on his returned piece of clothing. "Okay," he told Jules, who turned around to face him.

"What are you doing out here?" he asked before she took the opportunity to question him. "You know these woods butt up against the preserve this pack runs in."

"I did not," she admitted. "This is the fastest way to Monica's from my... Mr. Prentiss's house."

"You and Mr. Prentiss huh?" he teased.

Jules made a face at him that he interpreted to mean you know what I mean.

"By the way," Jules began, sounding like his teacher for a moment. "What if Neal had seen you?"

"Who?" Ricky hadn't the foggiest idea who she was talking about.

"Tasha's brother." Jules pointed back in the direction of the houses.

Ricky shrugged. "He didn't."

"Teenagers." Jules smiled and scoffed at the same time.

"Don't you have somewhere to be?" Ricky asked, thinking about the fact that Jules had been on her way to her friend's house.

"Yes," Jules said, like she may have forgotten that fact. "And where are you headed?"

Ricky shrugged again. He wouldn't go back to the Den, that he knew. But he didn't exactly have plans beyond this particular moment.

Jules bit her lip for a moment, presumably thinking.

"Listen, if you don't want to go home."

"It's not my home," Ricky interrupted.

"Well, then, if you need somewhere to be, I think Luca is back at my house."

Ricky's eyebrows raised as he waited for Jules to continue.

"Even if he's not, there is a spare key under the planter by the back door. You can't miss it. The plant is dead."

"You're really offering to let me crash at your house?" Ricky asked. "Why?"

"Honestly," Jules began, "because I see something in you that reminds me of someone I once loved. Someone I loved above all others."

"What happened to him?" Ricky asked, catching the context of the past.

"He died long ago," Jules said. "But what you did back there, that recklessness, he would have loved it."

Jules finally made it to Monica's house. As she walked up the drive, Monica's co-worker was just leaving. "How's she doing?" Jules asked.

"She hasn't stopped crying," the girl said. She looked emotionally spent.

"It's my turn. I've got her."

Jules rang the doorbell and Ethan answered.

"Hi," she greeted.

"Hey," he said, "Thank the stars you're here. I can't stand the wailing."

"Very compassionate, Ethan."

Ethan rolled his eyes.

Just then a gut-wrenching cry came from upstairs.

Jules cringed.

Ethan shrugged and gestured in Monica's direction as if to say, "see."

"You want to come and cheer her up with me?" Jules asked as they walked up the stairs side-by-side.

"No way," Ethan stepped back and Jules moved toward Monica's bedroom door. "I'm not going near that with a ten-foot pole."

"Such a great little brother you are," Jules teased.

"Oh, I know I am." He laughed and then walked into his own room, shutting the door behind him.

When Jules pushed open Monica's bedroom door, she was not surprised to find her curled up in her fluffy chair in the corner; tear streaks down her face and a box of tissues on her lap. Her eyes were red and her cheeks were blotchy. She looked so human in this moment, Jules's heart broke for her.

"Oh, Jules."

Monica rushed toward Jules and hugged her. Both girls sunk onto the bed.

"I can't believe this is happening. I mean, I know he feels like I'm hiding something from him. I mean I am hiding something from him, a really, really big something. But..." Monica continued to speak, and Jules let her, rubbing her back and waiting.

"Monica, I'm so sorry. It's all my..." Jules began, once Monica had stopped to take a breath.

"Don't you dare say this is your fault," Monica snapped, fixing Jules with a glare. "He should have trusted me!"

"Still, if you want to tell him you should be able too," Jules said. "I'll talk to Luca. I promise."

"No. Don't bother. It doesn't matter now. If he can't trust me, it's over anyway." With that, tears began to run down Monica's face once again.

"Are you sure about that?" Jules moved her head down, so she could look into Monica's lowered eyes.

"I don't know. But he's the one who broke it off. I won't go crawling back to him," she said with what Jules thought was false conviction.

Jules didn't say anything. Monica was being too negative to receive any real advice right now. So, she held her in her cold arms as she cried. Jules remained quiet as Monica finally moved on to silent sobs.

"We should have a girls' night," Jules suggested once the tears had stopped and Monica had begun to make an effort to compose herself.

"Maybe... I don't know if I'm up to it."

"Think about it. We could hang out. Maybe watch a movie. You could order in. Take your mind off things."

"That doesn't sound so bad," Monica admitted. "We could invite Hayley."

Jules knew that hanging out with a vampire might be asking too much of the werewolf but if Monica wanted to at least invite her, Jules would.

"Please," Monica begged.

So, Jules picked up her phone and scrolled through her contacts until she found Hayley's recently added name. She hit send and waited through the rings.

"Hey, you were supposed to call me," a male voice greeted. "I'm the one who likes to get phone calls from beautiful women."

"Hi, Kyle." Jules laughed.

"Hand it over. She doesn't want to talk to you," Jules heard Hayley say in the background.

"How do you know? She might have called the wrong number," he said but his voice was no longer near the phone.

Jules chuckled. After what sounded like a chase around the living room, Jules heard the sound of a hand smacking bare skin. "Ouch!"

"Jules. Hi, I'm so sorry about that. He's an idiot."

"Don't be." Jules tried to stifle her chuckling.

"What's up?" Hayley asked.

"Monica needs a girls' night; Tai broke up with her."

"Jerk!" Hayley said. "They were perfect together."

"Are you up for an evening in? With us?" Jules added to clarify that she, the vampire, would be in attendance as well.

"Absolutely! That sounds really great, actually," Hayley said. "Honey," she called away from the phone. "I need you to run an errand for me."

"What for?" Kyle's distant voice asked.

"A boatload of wine. We are having a girl's night in," Hayley said happily.

"Wait! I'm not a girl," Kyle exclaimed. "What about me?"

Jules could almost see the face he would be making at his wife.

"Sometimes you are just not that important," she said away from the phone.

He groaned.

"I'm back," Hayley said. "See you at your place in two hours." With that, Hayley ended the call and Jules set down her phone.

"Party at my place," Jules told Monica.

She raised her eyebrows.

"Don't worry," Jules said putting her hand on Monica's. "It will be girls only." *Once I get rid of the boys,* she added to herself.

Nick had been waiting in all his old murder spots for hours with no luck. After much planning and strategizing, it was decided that Nick would be the bait to catch the people looking for him. Also, a discrete team had been sent to the apartment to watch, with no luck. They still waited to hear back from the two that went to the dank motel Nick had followed Chad to. It seemed the people Chad worked for didn't have any intention of checking on their missing but very dead employee.

"Hi there," Nick greeted an attractive, dark-skinned, young man he had in his sights.

The man gave him a sideways look but didn't respond. Instead, he kept walking in the direction he had been headed when he had been stopped by the vampire.

"Alright then," Nick said aloud, to no one in particular.

He startled when he felt a hand on his arm, and then a frail body bump into his side unsteadily. "Hello?" Nick questioned, looking down at the small woman.

"Hi," said a drunk, and probably drugged, boney human. Nick recognized her as a regular at Incognito. "I know what you are," she mumbled.

"Do you?" he asked looking around for Antonio or one of the other vampires that had accompanied him to the stake out.

"Yep, you can drink from me if you want," she said, sticking out her wrist toward his mouth.

Nick licked his lips in anticipation. He hadn't been looking for a drink, he was on a mission. But when one so readily presented its self, who was he to turn it down?

"You have no idea what you're offering," he told her but walked with her toward a secluded side of the fountain.

"Yes, I do!" she slurred incredulously. "Don't you want to?" she asked, swaying on her feet and dropping onto the edge of the fountain with a thud.

He glided to sit beside her, putting one hand on the back of her neck to steady it. His chuckle was low and breathless. He watched the pulse under her skin, the vein exposed. She was offering herself for a moment of relief from this mortal coil. How could he resist? His fangs slipped free of their sheaths. She lifted her arm towards him again and he shoved it aside. He lunged instead for her neck. Piercing the skin there, he began to drink.

She gave a little shriek and then sank into him. He pushed aside the memories that flooded his mind. Images of a sad and lonely life. Of rejections and endless isolations.

He focused instead on the pulse beneath his lips. It began to slow, and he knew it was time to stop if she was to live. A part of him wanted to, for some reason he couldn't identify. However, he'd inherited his addictive personality from his drunken father. His grip tightened around his prey, holding the source of his addiction to his lips as he continued to drink every last drop.

Hearing the distinct clearing of a throat, Nick pulled his fangs from the dead woman's neck. "Oops," he whispered to the bar staff hiding in the bushes to help him ambush the people Chad worked for, whom they hadn't seen hide nor hair from. He laid the woman against the edge of the fountain on the cobble stones and spoke normally. "I say this one is a wash anyway boys. We should go."

He heard the hidden vampires stalking away nearly silently and was about to follow when he caught sight of a stranger. A blonde, male vampire was watching him. Stock still and furious looking. Nick looked from the vampire, down to his fresh kill, made a kissy gesture accompanied with a nod at the vampire he didn't know, and left to follow the others to his next trap attempt.

CHAPTER EIGHTEEN

Murder Without Malicious Intent

Kyle plopped on the couch with a beer, preparing to sit around and veg the female-less evening away with some form of visual entertainment. He was flipping through his options when there was a knock on his door.

With his face scrunched in an expression of displeasure, he then stood to answer the door. He expected to see one of Hayley's siblings looking for their sister. There were a lot of them, and they all stopped over unannounced from time to time. "Hayley's not here," he said as he pulled the door open.

"I know," Luca said. "We've been cast out." He and the new kid stood in the doorway.

"Women," Kyle chuckled.

"You want to go for a run?" Luca asked.

"How about pizza?" Kyle never passed up an opportunity to let the wolf out to play, but his stomach wanted food.

"Run, then pizza?" Luca suggested.

"Let's do it," Kyle said, stepping back inside to grab his phone and keys. He locked the door and the three of them headed back down the stairs. "Are we dropping the minor off at the Den or..."

The teenager opened his mouth to speak but Luca answered instead. "Nope. He's going with us."

"Great," Kyle said but added, "since when do we willingly babysit?"

"I don't need a babysitter," Ricky said.

At the same moment, Luca responded, "Kyle!" He said this in Hayley's favorite tone of voice.

"You watch out," Ricky continued. "I may just run you into

the ground old man."

All three of them chuckled at this as they climbed into Luca's Jeep.

In just a few minutes, Luca pulled up to the rusty gates and the woods in which they freely ran. Luca and Kyle took a running start and launched themselves over the fence in wide leaps. When they landed on the other side they turned back toward the teenager, who was standing, staring at them.

"Well, you coming?" Kyle asked, panting a little.

Ricky rolled his eyes and walked several feet to the gate. He pushed it open slowly, but deliberately, as if to make the point that launching oneself over a fence ceremonially when one could use the obviously provided entrance was simply ridiculous.

Once the boy had joined them, they walked into the cover of the woods together. Each one of them began to strip off their clothes to their own desired degree.

"Ready?" Luca asked.

"I was born ready," Ricky said with a wicked smile.

With a howl provided by Kyle, the three of them took off at top speed. After only a few strides, they shifted simultaneously. Luca turned into a majestic silver wolf, Ricky a solid black one, and Kyle the standard gray. Kyle tripped on the landing, his muzzle connecting with the mud under his paws. He stood on all fours and shook off his fumble. Luca howled playfully, and the wolves ran further into the woods, escaping the human world and all that was happening in it.

Jules was worried that she would soon be cleaning both human and werewolf vomit off of her carpet. Monica and Hayley were both three glasses of wine in. Monica had gone from perpetually depressed and crying, to her happier self by glass one and a half.

"So, what are we watching after this?" Hayley asked, her head lolled back on the sofa, utterly relaxed.

"I'm up for anything, as long as it's not a romance," Monica answered.

"Of course not," Hayley exclaimed dramatically, sounding a bit like her husband. "A nice action movie where there is a lot of running, screaming, and explosions is much more appropriate at a time like this."

"Maybe one where the guy dies," Monica said, sounding playfully sulky.

Monica smiled and they both laughed just as Jules's phone rang.

"Your man beckons," Hayley said as she picked up Jules's phone and handed it to her.

"Sorry Monica," she said after smiling down at the screen of her phone for a second too long.

Monica shrugged as if to say, 'it's fine' and said, "I'm going to find us a movie." She stood and plopped onto the floor closer to the television, using the remote to flip through her list.

"By the way," Hayley put her hand on Jules's before she could answer Luca's call. "I've known Luca for a while now and I have never seen him this happy. Be good to him Jules the vampire."

"Okay," she said laughing a little and finally answering the call. "Hi," she greeted him, leaving off any endearing terms for Monica's sake.

"Are you near a TV?"

"Yes. Why?"

"Just turn to channel nine." His voice sounded rushed and was hard to hear. She guessed he was at a loud restaurant or something.

"Okay. Monica switch to channel nine for a second."

"The news?" Monica groaned but did so.

Once the appropriate channel had been found, Jules saw a newscaster talking about the string of murders that continued to occur all over Fort Miles. Cause of death was blood drained through two small holes on each body. "What is this? Some psychotic, practical joke? And who is this man caught fleeing the scene?" the newsman's voice asked.

Jules cursed outright. The screen had flashed a security camera capture of Gabriel.

"What is it?" Hayley asked, looking up from her phone.

"Is Mr. Prentiss a killer?" Monica asked Jules.

"No. Of course not." Jules was panic-stricken. *It couldn't be true.*

"Then why do they think he is?" Monica said, pointing toward the television.

"I have to find out. Stay here, both of you. I'll get you rides home."

"I am not that drunk," Hayley said, pointing to herself.

"Hayley." Jules pointed at the inebriated werewolf girl. "Stay," she commanded.

"Woof," Hayley said, and both Hayley and Monica were swept away in a fit of giggles.

Without another word, Jules grabbed her keys and walked out the front door. She reached the driveway, jumped into her car, and backed out quickly. Weaving through traffic, all she could think about was getting to Gabriel and uncovering the truth. The sound of her phone ringing pulled her out of her mind's confusion.

"You hung up on me. What are you going to do?" It was Luca.

"I have to get to Gabriel. I have to get to the bottom of this."

"I'm coming with you."

"No. I need you to take Hayley and Monica home."

"You can't go alone," he said loudly.

"Yes, I can. If Gabriel really is doing this... even though I refuse to believe that... do you think he would hesitate before killing you?"

"Jules, but you..."

"Luca, I'm sorry but I'm not waiting. I love you," she said before hanging up on him.

She punched the buttons on her steering wheel and told the system to call Gabriel. No answer. She tried Eileen. "It's

Jules. Of course I'm going to answer. We need her help." Jules heard through the Bluetooth as Eileen answered.

"No we don't." Jules heard Gabriel's voice in the background.

"I'm on my way."

"I witnessed a vampire draining a human." He sounded shaken, though he was trying to be steady. "I couldn't save her." His voice was strained as he got to the last word. "I can handle this myself."

"No you can't," Eileen protested.

"Yes. I can!"

"Gabriel, they think you're the Fort Miles Phantom," Jules spat into the empty car.

"What?" This time it was Eileen who shouted.

"I don't need you," Gabriel spat back. "Don't come here."

"You are being ridiculous," Eileen began. "She fell in love. There really is nothing to be mad about." Eileen's defense of Jules made her heart swell for her friend. She'd kept the woman at arm's length for a long time, refusing to need anyone. This may have been a mistake.

"There is more than enough to be mad about Eileen," he said, his voice lethal. "Not only did she let herself fall in love with a *werewolf*, but she also lied about it." The hurt and anger in his voice stung. "How can you forgive her?"

"Guys, hello?" Jules must have said to her empty car, for all the good it did.

"Because I fell in love with you!" The anger in Eileen's voice rose as well. Jules felt like she was intruding, and that they'd both forgotten she could hear them. "You are allowing hate to dictate your actions!"

"This conversation is over!" Gabriel snapped.

"Go fuck yourself," Eileen shouted even louder.

Jules heard Gabriel's footsteps getting farther away, a door slam, and then the sound of breaking wood. Jules guessed that Eileen had thrown something after Gabriel and hit the hotel room door.

Eileen's anguished cry ripped Jules in two. "Jules?" Eileen questioned through tears.

"I'm here," she said softly.

"I'll send you the hotel details." With that, Eileen hung up. Jules pushed the peddle to the floor and sped towards Fort Miles as fast as she could.

Nick was walking aimlessly around the city. Chad's co-workers still hadn't come out to play. The motel room had been scrubbed down leaving no trail to follow. Antonio had even had a techy friend go through Chad's phone with no results. Nick was at square one and the staff of Incognito had all gone back to prepare for the evening's influx of clientele.

Maybe it was time to ditch the quiet city. Maybe if he could trick *his* location out of Cleo he would magically appear in proximity. For now, he wandered the busy streets of Fort Miles. Halfway to anywhere, he sensed her before he saw her, almost feeling her panic. She was a young one. That was for sure. She was untrained in the ways of the world. He could sense it. Standing in place on the sidewalk, humans skirted by him on either side. Searching, he spotted her. Taller than average for a woman and strikingly beautiful. The scars on her cheek only adding to her vampiric allure. Dark haired, with the copper skin belonging to natives of this land, but it had not yet paled with extensive years out of the sun. She pushed and shoved through the throng, seeming desperate to get away from the skin-covered blood temptations.

He paced her from across the busy night street until the opportunity to get through the speeding cars arose. One second cars were nearly missing him. The next he was standing in front of her, his hands on either side of her arms. "Come with me," he instructed the overwhelmed and flustered vampire.

She said nothing as he took her hand and pulled her off her current path. He found a secluded alley and stopped them inside the cover of its darkness. "You can breathe," he told her, his hands resting again on either side of her arms.

She took in a long breath.

"Now you let it out," he instructed.

She met his eyes for the first time. Her eyes were still predominantly their original color. She was very young, but not a brand-new vampire like he'd originally assumed. She let a long stream of air out of her lungs.

"Better?" he asked.

She nodded, but was still silently staring up at him. It happened with the young ones sometimes. He wasn't a primordial vampire, but he was several centuries old.

"Yes, thank you," she said. "There were just so many of them out there."

"Several billion in the world I'd imagine," he said, smiling.

"Something's familiar about you," she commented, looking up at him once again, her eyes narrowed in concentration. "But I know we've never met before."

"Considering I was made a vampire hundreds of years before your human life began, and considering I'm not someone you just forget, I'm guessing we haven't." He batted his eyelashes for effect.

She raised her eyebrows at him skeptically.

"I'm Nick, Nicholas as it were," he said, dropping his hands and stretching one out toward her.

"Eileen," she replied.

"So, tell me Eileen," Nick began, "how is it that you have been a vampire for what forty, fifty years and still get thrown off by large quantities of humans that are not currently bleeding?"

"My coven doesn't feed on humans," she said.

Nick scowled. So, *she is part of one of those new era, 'humans are friends not food' community.* He was about to respond when a loud laugh pulled Eileen's attention back to the entrance of the alley.

She made for the human-heavy sidewalk, but he grabbed

her around the shoulders, keeping her concealed in the alley.

"Let me go." She fought against his hold.

"Can't do that, sorry," he said, strengthening his hold against her resistance.

"But I'm so hungry."

He empathized with the desperation in her voice. "Don't worry," Nick said. "We can fix that."

Carson glared down at the stuttering imbecile of a tracker. "Why, exactly have you requested to meet in the yard?" He normally would not allow himself to be summoned by anyone, and yet the man had said that the information he brought was sensitive. So here he was, standing in the front yard, waiting on this moron to spit out what he had to say.

"Th-the... there is a-another traitor, sir," he finally said.

"Kyle Cooper?" Carson asked, almost excitedly. He would love to have proof of his fall along with that of Luca Cain.

Jed looked back toward the house as if checking to make sure no one was nearby. Carson's impatience was growing. However, every time Carson was about to dismiss the stuttering fool the man proved smarter and more valuable than expected.

"No... it... it's the woman's s-son."

Carson stilled. "What did you just say?"

Jed once again handed his phone to his Alpha. "I picked up the vam... vampire at a house n-near the school. This was taken on the way t-to a human home."

Carson studied the picture. Jed was not mistaken. He was holding proof of the boy's treachery. The picture showed the boy standing at ease, conversing with one very bothersome, tiny, dead girl.

Carson felt like shouting. How deep did this anarchy run? Not only was Luca a traitor to the pack, but he had dragged Demetria's son down that path with him. He needed to eliminate these problems, and he needed to do it now. Carson's hand tightened around the phone.

"I…" The tracker began to object.

"Have you mentioned this to anyone else?" Carson asked through a clenched jaw.

"Of… of course n-not," Jed replied, reaching for his property.

"Good." Carson handed the man back his broken phone. "Keep it that way," Carson ordered and then waved his hand in dismissal.

"Ye-yes, sir." Jed nodded and rushed away, seeming eager to be gone from this situation.

Carson's mind was spinning. Luca was like a cancer spreading throughout the pack. It must be stopped. He had to ensure the safety of those loyal to him. This he must do, no matter the cost. The hard choices were his to make and make them he would.

As if on cue, Kip pulled into the drive and climbed out of his lifted, red, pickup truck. Carson took long strides over to him. "Is it done?" Carson asked.

"Um… no Alpha. I wasn't able to locate Luca," Kip said, looking downright mortified. He should be.

"Did you try?" Carson asked angrily.

"I drove around all day. I even went all the way to Fort Miles looking for him."

"Idiot. The vampire is here. Why exactly would he be in the city?" Carson was outraged. Was this wolf just that simple or was Kip more clever than he'd ever given him credit for, finding a way to avoid his duty, while technically following orders? Was he a traitor as well?

Carson pulled forth every ounce of control he had as the Alpha of this pack and spoke after a long moment. "No more delays. Find him. I do not care who gets in your way," Carson snarled.

Kip paled. Everything in him seemed to be fighting against this instruction. This angered Carson greatly. His orders had to be obeyed. Carson backhanded the taller man across the face.

The wolf stumbled back against his vehicle. "Do it tonight or you will suffer the same fate."

Luca, Kyle, and Ricky had eaten their fill of pizza. He'd dropped Ricky off at the Den. Then he and Kyle made their way to Jules's house to pick up Monica and Hayley, upon Jules's request.

When they arrived, both girls were fast asleep on the blue, velvet, sofa, a movie continuing to play with no one watching. Kyle stopped Luca with his arm and then he himself crept into the room, looking down at his sleeping wife for a few seconds too long. He seemed enchanted by the delicate drape of her hair and the way her chest rose and fell slowly. Then Monica snorted in her sleep. Luca and Kyle laughed in unison and both girls sat up, startled.

"Don't scare me like that," Hayley grumbled, smacking Kyle's leg with a soft thwap.

Monica threw herself back down onto the sofa, head resting on her arm. She looked toward Luca.

"You ready to go home?" he asked, raising his eyebrows at her.

She nodded and yawned at the same time in response.

"Come on then." Kyle reached both hands out toward Hayley, who took them and allowed herself to be pulled from the sofa.

Monica sat up and looked around. "Let me clean up before we go." This sounded more like a question than an instruction. She started to stand and then dropped back down. Luca was by her side in an instant.

"I'll do it. You sit." Luca walked around the sofa and started to clean up the mess the girls had made.

"Keys Hayles?" Kyle asked.

"Kitchen counter." Hayley pointed.

Kyle nodded. "You want help?" He motioned around them.

Luca looked around the room and then shook his head.

"No, you guys go. I'll finish up and take Monica home." He gathered up discarded carryout boxes, paper plates, and drinking glasses.

"Are you coming back to the apartment after?" Hayley slurred a little as she spoke.

"I should probably show my face at the Den," Luca replied.

Hayley nodded with sharp, concentrated movements.

"Good luck," Kyle commented as he caught a swaying Hayley. "Hang on, baby." With a small grunt he lifted her over his shoulder.

"Whoop." Hayley waved backwards, hair hanging down Kyle's back, butt in the air. "Bye."

"Drive safe," he called after them.

"You too," Kyle called back.

It took only a few minutes to get Jules's house back in perfect order. He walked through the house, locked the front door, and made his way back to Monica. Her tipsy state had her almost passed out on the sofa once again. He chuckled and held out a hand to help her onto her feet.

She took it but let it go once she was fully vertical. She stumbled, and Luca caught her by the shoulders. "Do not put me over your shoulder like..." She pointed to the front door. "That."

"I promise to leave your feet on the ground." Luca gently guided Monica through the back door and locked it. He placed the spare key back in its hiding place and the pair walked to the Jeep.

Monica was fairly quiet on the way back to her house, Luca was just hoping she didn't end up vomiting all over his Jeep's upholstery. To his relief, she seemed to be looking a little more stable once they reached her driveway and he dropped her off.

"Do you need me to come inside with you?"

Her hand rested on the door handle a moment and then she spoke, "I think I'm good."

"Goodnight, Monica."

"Night."

He waited until the front door was open and she waved back at him before he backed out of the drive.

The night sky was dark, and the roads back to the Den were almost completely deserted. It was a peaceful drive on a quiet road around the preserve. That was until a large, lifted, vehicle appeared right behind him. Headlights reflected off his rearview mirror and into his eyes. Luca squinted, he would have sworn it hadn't been there seconds ago. It looked like Kip's red, pickup truck. It was too dark outside to be sure, despite its close proximity to the Jeep's back tire.

Luca tried speeding up. The truck paced him. He tried slowing down, but it did not result in the truck going around him. Instead, he felt a surprising jolt when the truck bumper checked him, hard. Aggravated, Luca sped up again. And again, the truck driver paced him. Luca swore, knowing he had to slow as he approached a place where the forest road curved, with a steep drop on his passenger side. The truck sped up, filling the lane beside him. It flanked him, squeezing the Jeep closer to the steep drop.

Luca looked to his left. Startled when he recognized the driver. Kip was looking out his passenger window at Luca with an unreadable expression on his face.

Luca was about to give him a what the hell look when Kip grimaced and swerved, big tires slammed into the side of the Jeep. Luca countered, trying desperately to stay on the road. He was about to stomp on the brakes when Kip smashed into him again. This time, Luca lost control, swerving unavoidably. The Jeep's tires skidded off the road, hurling down the steep drop he'd been trying to avoid. Steering was useless as the Jeep careened downward. Luca saw the large boulder before the Jeep smashed into it and flipped. He had no time to react. The soft top gave easily. The weight of the Jeep came down on Luca's body with a crunch.

Consciousness waned. All he felt was pain and pressure. Blood dripped into his eyes from somewhere. He looked at the parts of his body he could see and noted there was a long gash running along his abdomen. He thought of his Little Corpse for one moment, before everything went dark.

CHAPTER NINETEEN

Night-life in the City

J ules pulled up in front of an extravagant hotel. A valet was waiting to take her car keys from her. She took the ticket, thanked the young man and walked straight to the elevators in the lobby.

Once inside, she pulled her phone from her back pocket to confirm the room number Eileen had texted her. She punched the button for level sixteen and waited. The door slid open twice before reaching her desired floor. She stepped out into the hallway and moved down the hall to the left, stopping in front of door number 1617.

She knocked and waited a few moments for one of them to answer. When Gabriel did, he looked frazzled and very concerned. "Eileen?"

"Nope." Jules moved past him into the room. She saw the splintered door was actually the one to the suite's bedroom, not the hallway like she'd expected. "Why did you think I was Eileen? Where is she?"

"I don't know. I... " His voice trailed off. "We had a fight." His head hung low, a look of pure shame on his face.

"I heard," she said, looking around the abandoned room.

"She left."

"Why didn't you go after her?" Jules was astonished. Eileen was young and untrained. There was no telling what havoc she could wreak on the city if she fell into temptation.

"Everything is falling apart Jules." Gabriel looked at the floor as he spoke. He sounded hopeless. "I lost you. Eileen left me. The media is pinning a woman's murder on me." When Gabriel raised his face there was blood dripping from his eyes and sliding down his cheeks. She didn't think she'd ever seen him cry before.

Jules walked to the side table, grabbed a tissue, and handed him the rough, thin, paper to wipe his eyes. "Stop catastrophizing." Jules placed a hand on his shoulder. "You haven't lost me. Eileen likely only left because she needed some space. But we both know she didn't leave you, she loves you. And the murder thing, we'll figure that out too. We've never seen a challenge we couldn't overcome together."

"True." He still looked crestfallen.

"So that's enough self-pity," she said sternly. "Wash off your face, grab some sunglasses and a hat, and let's go find your wife. You can tell me about the dead woman while we search."

"Sunglasses? It's dark outside. It will be for hours yet."

"Nighttime or not, your face was plastered all over the news. I recommend taking some sort of steps to obscure your identity before intentionally entering the local populace."

A sad chuckle emitted from him, but he nodded as he moved toward the bathroom to wash the blood off his face.

Nick approached Incognito with a hand still resting on Eileen's back. She was definitely a skittish one. As Nick and Eileen walked up one side of the long line, he met the bouncer's eyes and nodded silently. They were waved through without any spoken word.

"Where are we?" Eileen asked breathlessly as they breached the blood-red velvet curtains, revealing the scene within. Incognito was teaming with people. A mass of humans and vampires alike. Some dancing, some drinking; both whiskey from a glass and blood from the source. Dimmed lights set the mood, while an odd assortment of music from many eras played at random.

"A club, of the vampire variety," he said, putting an arm over her shoulders. "They exist in every major city in the world." He leaned down to whisper in her ear. "You don't have to hunt unsuspecting humans to drink blood the way real vampires should. And these people get compensated generously."

She glanced up, a look of incredulous astonishment on her face. Obviously, whoever her puritan coven leader was, had decided that by keeping this vampire in the dark about the world of which she was now of a part, they were protecting her humanity.

"You poor thing," Nick said and placed a hand on her shoulder. "You've never drank from a human before, have you?"

"Of course not! I am not a monster," Eileen said, but it lacked venom. She was listening to him.

So, he continued with a smile, "I mean, I am one due to an unfortunate genetic predisposition for addictive behavior. However, not all vampires are monsters. There are ways to live that don't include murder or abstinence. It is possible to drink from a human directly and not end their life."

Eileen again looked surprised but nodded for him to continue.

"It's a skill that takes practice, but it can be learned. Places like this provide a sort of safeguard. You see those two men over there?" He pointed towards the blood guards, standing near the black leather couches.

Eileen nodded.

"It's their job to make sure you don't drain the club's human patrons. Not even I end up draining my drink in this place."

As if on cue, the two men in black moved toward a couple along the far wall. A female was obviously drinking the blood of the middle-aged man she had in her clutches. One of the black-clad men leaned over to whisper something in the vampire's ear. When she didn't release her prey, each man clasped down on one of her arms and pulled her away from her now quite dazed looking meal. The woman sat back a little and wiped at the blood that was dripping down her chin. She then stood and was safely escorted to the other side of the club.

"I see," Eileen said after a few silent moments.

Nick smiled peevishly.

"Who's, your friend?"

Nick and Eileen turned at the question. A round vampire that Nick knew in passing was sauntering over to them with wide clomps. Here we go, Nick thought to himself.

"Carlos, old man," Nick greeted with false cheerfulness. This vampire may be twice Nick's age, but he was a pain in his dead ass.

Carlos ignored Nick like a fly on the wall and bent over Eileen's hand, kissing it. "Who, may I ask, am I addressing?"

"Eileen Prentiss," she said skeptically, yanking her hand back. "And you are?"

"Carlos my dear. I'm sure you've heard of me." A wide smile spread across his face while his nose lifted into the air.

Nick rolled his eyes and scoffed.

"Sorry, I haven't," Eileen said, taking one step closer to Nick.

"Surprising," Carlos said, reaching for her hand again. "Well come and I'll educate you." He placed one hand on her lower back, brushing her ass with a couple fingers as he did so.

Nick was about to step in when Eileen shifted out of his reach and replied. "Not interested, sorry."

"Excuse me?" Anger flashed in Carlos's eyes. He was not used to being rejected by those beneath him.

Eileen looked questioningly up at Nick. He couldn't interpret if she was unsure what to do now or if she wanted to know if this guy was for real.

"Okay Carlos," Nick said, stepping in front of her. "The lady isn't interested."

"Step aside, you insignificant worm," Carlos instructed, shoving Nick to one side. He bumped into a nearby table, knocking it, and all its contents, to the floor. One of the humans occupying it stumbled backward. Hands outstretched she slammed into the glass littering the floor. More than one vampire turned toward the miniscule cut on her hand, Nick and Eileen included. However, in a fraction of a second, one of the men wearing black, picked the woman up and whisked her away to some back room, assumedly to get her cleaned up.

"The excitement's over. Everyone go back to your drinks and dances," called Cleo, who had just immerged from the back room.

Nick turned back and balked. While he'd been knocking over a table and watching Cleo, Eileen had broken Carlos's hand and he now knelt before her. "Never touch a woman without her consent."

"Is there a problem, children?" Cleo asked the copper-skinned vampire who was kneeling at Eileen's feet.

"Not on my end Cleo," Nick said, still staring at the scene.

"This flea is my problem," Carlos told Cleo, standing and shoving Nick for no apparent reason.

"Carlos, dear one." Cleo put one hand on the older vampire's arm. "You know very well that I don't tolerate fighting within these walls."

"It's that bitch who hurt me!" He thrust his hand towards Cleo as proof. "This insolence shall not stand."

Cleo's heels clacked against the stone floor as she moved closer to Carlos, stepping right into his physical space. "You may be the second oldest thing in my bar at the moment Carlos, but you put your hands on the woman and shoved Nick here. He may not look like much..."

Nick scoffed at Cleo, who ignored him.

"But, he has very powerful friends. You don't want this fight."

"This may be your bar missy, but my age will grant me the respect I deserve," Carlos snapped.

"In the grand scheme of time, you are nothing," Cleo said, nonchalantly examining her long, neon nails. "His 'friends' are twice your age and have eyes you've only dreamt of."

Nick couldn't help it. He smirked as those eyes flashed

through his mind.

Carlos snarled, the recognition of what Cleo spoke was seeping slowly into his expression.

Nick relaxed, knowing that the situation was again under control.

Carlos looked from Nick to Cleo to Eileen, whom he looked all the way up and down. "The infant's not worth it," he finally said and then sauntered off the way he had come.

Cleo turned towards Eileen. "A drink on the house, for that little move you pulled back there." She motioned in the direction Carlos had gone. "He's a pig."

"Thank you," Eileen said. "Men like that will never learn."

Cleo nodded.

"I brought her here. Don't I get a free drink?" Nick asked.

"Nicholas, darling. You've gotten more than enough free drinks from my establishment." Cleo stood on the toes of her stilettos, placed long nails against Nick's arm, and raised one cheek towards him.

"Fair enough." He bent and kissed the woman on the side of her face, smiling at her.

"I'll have a martini," Eileen said as Cleo walked back the way she had come, lusciously round ass swaying all the way.

"She doesn't mean that kind of drink," Nick told her. His mind back on why they had come.

Jules and Gabriel walked farther and farther from their starting point. They had checked the streets and every darkened corner near the hotel, but had had no luck finding any sign of Eileen. "I thought she'd be at the pool or bar. I didn't know she was angry enough to go out on the streets alone," he mumbled for the third time.

"We'll find her," Jules assured again, feeling less confident than she sounded.

While they searched, Gabriel had told her all he knew about the Fort Miles Phantom, which wasn't very much. He looked to be in his late teens, close to Jules's human age, and yet he was at least several centuries old. Gabriel couldn't remember any distinguishing features beyond that.

"Yes. There is a place on the north side. A blood club?" Gabriel said, looking up from his phone screen and answering Jules's earlier question. "But, that's a waste of time. She doesn't even know they exist."

"But someone there might have seen her," Jules countered.

"This way." Gabriel led them down a lesser populated street. "Jules?" Her name was a question on his lips.

"Hmmm?" Jules turned toward him while still moving steadily forward.

"About the werewolf…"

"Gabriel don't," Jules said sternly. "Please," she added more softly.

"Can you just tell me why?"

"Why did you choose Eileen?" She shot back. "Yes, I know she was dying. But before that. Why did you fall for Eileen in the first place?"

"Her kindness," Gabriel said. "It was the first thing I noticed about her, after her striking looks of course." There was a sad smile on his face.

"And after you turned her, you were under no obligation to marry her. Why did you?" Jules continued.

Gabriel was silent a moment. "Life with Eileen just made sense."

"Her personality fit yours. Though you are two whole people alone, she enhanced who you are, didn't she?" Jules added.

"Are you saying that this wolf completes you?" Gabriel scowled. "But he's an animal!"

"And we are demons, if you're generalizing." Jules kept her tone level. "Not all vampires are demons, therefore, not all werewolves are animals."

"Alright," Gabriel conceded. "I won't say any more about it."

"Thank you." She knew he hadn't really heard her. But at least he was letting the fighting between them cease.

"Did you know that when you first brought Eileen back that I didn't like her?" Jules asked.

Gabriel looked at her skeptically.

"It's true." She chuckled a little. "I spent months wishing things would just go back to normal."

"But you didn't ever say anything."

"No, I didn't. You were so happy," she stated.

"It's true. I was," he said, smiling toward the sidewalk.

"And now, I love Eileen. She's part of our family."

Gabriel nodded.

"And that never would have happened if I hadn't given her a chance."

Gabriel sighed. "I don't know if I can learn to like him, Jules, but I will try to give you space to be with him." He stopped walking. Following his lead, she turned to face him. He reached his hands out, took her head between them, and brushed her forehead with his lips. "I love you. And I do want you to be happy."

"I know," Jules replied.

"Come on, we're almost there." He stepped back and continued their walk.

Nick's lips were pressed against yet another woman's neck. Her head lolled back, not in death but pleasure. He knew why most human's frequented clubs like this. Some because they liked the mental blackout that came after the bite, it gave them a kind of escape. Nick imagined some were hoping a vampire might turn them, while others simply did it for the money. All that was required was for the human to consume blood from a vampire and the change would begin. However, this occurrence was rare. Vampires generally didn't like to share, for whatever reason.

Nick's eyes fluttered as he saw a memory belonging to

the woman whose blood he was drinking. This dark-skinned beauty and another woman, happy, in love maybe. Nick fell into the trap and pulled the woman closer until he saw the tragedy of her lover's death, the event that brought her to this moment. She was seeking oblivion then. He felt for her. He also felt for himself. Her blood was rejuvenating him, exciting him. He wanted to finish her. He wanted to drain every drop of her blood and set her free from her pain permanently.

A hand clamped down on Nick's shoulder tightly. He knew this was the first warning for him to stop. He wanted to shake it off, his senses consumed by his addiction. However, he pulled back and removed his fangs from her neck. Her blood dripped down his lips onto his chin. Gently her head rested in his hand. Her dark skin was glistening where his fangs had punctured her neck. He wanted the rest of it, now. All of it. But he couldn't have it. The woman moaned pleasurably.

With difficulty, he retracted his fangs and licked off his lips. Gently he laid the beautiful woman down on the black leather couch they had both been sitting on as he stood and stepped away.

Nick turned to the pair sitting next to him. Eileen was delicately sipping from her partner's wrist. The countenance of a vampire in complete control of her own desires. A twinge of jealousy swept over him, and then it was gone. It was what it was. His father had been an alcoholic, Nick was cursed with an addictive nature, and he had to live with that. He tapped Eileen gently on the shoulder.

She pulled back easily and looked up at him, temporarily-red eyes, fangs, blood and all. "What's up?"

"If you don't want to become an addict like me, you'd better stop."

She whimpered, stuck out her lower lip for a moment, then thanked her woozy host, and wiped off her mouth. "You didn't tell me it would be like that!" Eileen almost bounced in place. "Normally I just feel peaceful, comfortable. But that was a rush! I mean, wow!"

Nick chuckled. "Come on, let's wash it down with a whiskey." He held out a hand for her, and she took it, standing.

"Why could I see his memories?" she asked as they approached the bar.

He waved his hand at Antonio. "Part of drinking from the source," he replied. "It gets pretty intense at times, but you'll learn to block it out eventually."

Antonio hurried over, but scowled when he noticed Nick was not alone.

"Two shots of your best."

Antonio raised an eyebrow and looked between Nick and Eileen.

Nick raised his back, almost in challenge.

"Coming right up." Antonio scowled and then added, "Sir," almost as an afterthought. At least Nick thought he was getting the message. Nick wasn't the dating type. The shots arrived in front of him moments later, two small shot glasses of whiskey with a drop or two of blood in each. "Drink this." He handed her one of the glasses. "Won't do anything for you, but it tastes good." Nick tossed back the shot.

Eileen copied him and then sputtered, her face contorting in disgust. "That so does not taste good."

"To each their own," he said shrugging.

"I want more blood," she blurted out just as the red in her eyes began to fade away, exposing her original color once again.

"Take it easy, tiger," he said, patting her on the arm. "Pace yourself, the next one you have to pay for. Let's dance."

Jules and Gabriel approached the unmarked building, walking to the back of a long line of humans to wait. After a few seconds, however, they were waved forward by the bouncer. Jules approached tentatively. Silently, he inspected both Gabriel's and Jules's eyes, determining their approximate age and species. Nodding low to Jules, he waved them inside the club. "That was easy," Gabriel commented.

"Age has its privileges," Jules said nonchalantly. The sights and smells hit her hard. A long bar sat to the right while to the left was a crowded dance floor. Lights flashed, loud rock music blasted over the speakers, humans and vampires surrounded them. Across the open space was a section set apart by velvet ropes. Inside it were vampires consuming fresh, human blood. Jules could smell the blood laced with vampire venom from the front of the club. Her body tensed. Her fingers twitched. Jules took a step toward that part of the club. The sight made her want to feed. Gabriel's hand on her shoulder held her in place.

"We're here for Eileen remember," he whispered sharply in her ear. This was about her coven and trying to stop an out of control vampire.

"Gabriel."

Surprised, they both turned toward Eileen's call.

"And Jules, you're here together." She approached, smiling widely at them. Jules was unnerved by the relaxed and happy expression she wore. She looked at ease in this place that was making Jules's skin crawl.

"We were looking for you," Gabriel said, sounding exasperated. But he could just be yelling to be heard over the music. Jules couldn't tell for sure.

"Well, here I am," she said, throwing out her arms. Gabriel looked her over, presumably making sure she was unhurt.

"You missed a spot," he said down his nose, pointing to a blood drop that had run down her white top.

"Oops," Eileen replied.

"Never mind all that," Jules said, stepping between Gabriel's tense expression and Eileen's jovial one. "How did you get here? Did someone bring you or..."

"Nick did." Eileen pointed nonchalantly toward the dance floor.

"Nick who?" Gabriel asked.

Eileen considered the question for a moment. "You know,

I don't know." She turned back to the dance floor and scanned it. She zeroed in on a couple grinding together to the music. The red-haired vampire's back was turned toward them.

"Nick!" Eileen shouted.

He turned at her call.

If Jules's heart had been beating it would have stopped completely.

"That's the murderer," Gabriel hissed.

Jules barely heard him. The vampire on the dance floor mirrored her frozen expression. He had her eyes, her hair, even her lips.

Gabriel stepped out in front of both women, and in a flash, punched Jules's twin brother square in his matching nose.

Nick's face jerked to the side, but he barely felt the broken nose. "Gabriel, stop!" The person Nick thought was long ago dead, shouted at the man who had just punched him in the face.

Nick barely registered Eileen running up and putting a hand on his assailant's chest, holding him back from continuing the assault. He was too focused on the tiny vampire running toward him to even address the blood gushing from his nose. Before he knew what was happening, he was holding his sister in his arms, his twin. The part of him that had been missing for centuries. His arms grasp her desperately.

After a few seconds, that felt like years and yet the briefest of moments, he set her back on her feet and looked down at her. She was just as she had been the last time he'd seen her, except she was a vampire. Four-hundred years and the memory of her face hadn't faded.

"Juliana?" he asked breathlessly, his hands in her hair, hers on the sides of his neck.

"How?" she asked him.

"Well, I'm the living dead," he teased with a wide smile. He didn't think he'd ever been this happy before. "As are you, obviously."

She punched him on the shoulder hard. He flinched but the identical smiles on their faces widened.

Red tears of joy streaked down his sister's face. "You disappeared," she said in a quieter tone.

"I came back for you. As soon as I knew that I wouldn't accidentally kill you, I came back," he said. "But they told me that Aunt Millie had been murdered. And that you..." his voice trailed off. He thought she was dead. He never would have left England if he hadn't.

"Jules, what are you doing?" The male said as he and Eileen approached the twins.
"This is the murderer!" Gabriel shouted.

"Murder?" Nick asked. Looking at the man.

"You're the Fort Miles Phantom." Jules took a step back from him, her expression one of confusion and pain.

"That's what they call me," Nick admitted easily.

Eileen looked shocked while Jules was looking at him like their parents had died for a second time.

"Julie..." The joke fell from his next comment as he put two and two together. She'd come for Eileen. If they were in the same coven, then she didn't drink from humans either. It made sense. She would be one of *those* vampires. The ones that abstained.

"Jules," she corrected, the look on her face hardening into resolve. She looked from him, toward Eileen, and then the other guy.

"Jules, let's go," the guy said, stretching out a hand for her to accept. Nick felt panic grip his un-beating heart. She couldn't leave like this. This couldn't be the end of this insanely miraculous second chance.

Jules's heart was breaking as she took Gabriel's hand and turned from the one person she'd always loved above all others. The other half of herself.

She felt a hand grasp her arm. He spun her, his grip tightening. "Don't leave me. Please, Jules." The tone of voice Nick was using meant that he felt as if his life was being ripped apart, again.

"Jules..." she heard Gabriel's voice call, but it felt far away.

Looking up into her brother's eyes, pure silver, like her own, she saw only him. His face was just as she remembered it. He still looked like an angel, or maybe he was a ghost now.

"Please..." he begged softly.

As he held her gaze, she saw all the gentleness and love she remembered so clearly. This was her twin, her blood. She loved him. Despite all of his faults, she always had. He was a murderer, but so was she. Yes, she'd found a way to control it, but could she blame him if he had not?

As she worked through the tidal wave of emotions drowning her, she heard Gabriel walk out from behind her. In the blink of an eye, he was standing threateningly in front of Nick.

"Get your hand off of her," he said firmly.

"Gabriel," she said, throwing an arm across his chest, restraining him.

"Who the hell do you think you are?" Nick spat.

"Back down. Both of you, now!" Jules ordered.

Her brothers of blood and choice took one step back each. Jules looked around them, they were drawing quite a bit of unwanted attention. A woman was approaching them, her arms crossed, looking livid.

"We can talk about all of this back at the hotel." Gabriel reached out and grabbed Jules's wrist. "The sun's coming up and we're making a scene. Let's go."

"Really Nick..." the irate looking woman began.

"Cleo, my dear." Nick turned towards the stunning woman, throwing an arm over Jules's shoulder, pulling her away from Gabriel's grasp. "Have you met my sister? As in Biologically?"

The woman stopped in front of them, tapping her long nails against her hips in irritation. "The twin that died in a fire?"

"That's the one." Nick beamed.

"Hmmm..." Cleo pressed her lips together but said nothing.

Nick rolled his eyes. "We're going, Cleo." Nick released Jules, leaned forward, and kissed the woman on her upturned cheek. "I'm sorry."

"I bet you are," she replied sarcastically, pointing to the door with one neon painted nail.

Gabriel took another step back, putting an arm over Eileen's shoulders and guiding her from the bar.

Jules's hand found its way into Nick's. The distinct feeling that if she let him go, he may just disappear into thin air, haunted her. Phantom or not, she wouldn't go through the pain of losing him for a second time.

He looked down at their hands a moment and then whispered in her ear. "Did you miss me?"

"Every day." Hand in hand, Jules left the vampire bar, her life forever altered.

CHAPTER TWENTY

Tragedy Under the Sun

L uca woke as the sun began to rise over the upturned Jeep. Though his injuries had begun healing themselves, there was blood all over his surroundings. One of his shoulders had probably been dislocated, but it had slipped back into place as his muscles began righting themselves. He reached for the seatbelt, which was still holding him upside-down. With a great yank, he freed himself. Falling onto the grass and shattered glass beneath him, Luca grunted in pain. His hands and arms were inflicted with fresh cuts as he shifted to kick what was left of the driver door clean off. He crawled out, still clutching his abdomen. Carson obviously knew about Luca's attachment to Jules.

Jules was in Fort Miles and, for the first time, he was grateful that Gabriel's dilemma had taken her far from here. However, there were others who might now be in peril. If Carson had somehow learned that Kyle and Hayley consorted with Jules as well, they could be next. He had to warn them.

With a yell of pain and a flash of light, he went from man to wolf. His paws carried him more swiftly than his feet would have, and his blood covered clothes disappeared under his fur. He climbed up the steep incline and across the road, heading straight through the heart of town.

Ricky practically jumped off the bed when he was awakened by a loud pounding on Luca's bedroom door. He'd walked up the stairs late last night to wait on him to return and had fallen asleep across the end of Luca's bed.

Ricky didn't respond to the knock, choosing instead to lay

back down and yawn. Whoever it was, was most likely looking for Luca anyway.

Just as Ricky started to drift back to sleep, Carson burst through the door, eyes blazing. He froze in the doorway for a fraction of a second and then came at the still half-asleep teen, grabbing his shirt and lifting him off the bed. Ricky wanted to scream for his mother but kept his mouth shut.

"What the..." Ricky grabbed at Carson's fist. "Let go."

"Traitors don't speak in my presence," Carson snarled.

Ricky didn't know why he was a traitor, but decided that he'd keep his mouth shut for the sake of his own preservation. Especially since the veins in Carson's neck looked as if they might explode at any moment. Ricky jerked his head toward the door when he heard his mother calling Carson's name.

"We will finish this later!" Carson said through gritted teeth just as Demetria reached the bedroom door.

"Carson!" she shrieked, running toward them.

Carson shoved Ricky back onto the bed. He bounced upon landing. Demetria ran to him, her hands hovering over her son helplessly.

He sat up, shaking himself. She hugged him around the neck, kissed his hair, and then placed herself between her lover and her child.

"In the future, Carson," Demetria's voice rose, "You will keep your hands off my child." For the first time since his father's death Ricky felt like he had his mother back.

Carson closed the space between them and struck Demetria across the face with the back of his hand. "You will never speak to me like that again!"

Demetria's hand covered her discolored cheek, but she did not move or shrink away.

Ricky stood to defend his mom, but she grabbed him by the wrist, holding him back.

"Your son is a traitor to this pack," Carson shouted, pacing menacingly in front of them but did not move toward them again.

"You are our Alpha." Demetria bowed to Carson. "But he is my son, please allow me to handle this," she begged, her head bowed submissively.

Carson glared at her and then at Ricky and back at her. Instead of responding, Carson growled and exited the room.

Ricky stepped away from his mother, dropped onto the bed and rested his elbows on his knees.

"Ricky, honey, what was Carson talking about?" Demetria asked, turning to face him.

"I don't know," Ricky said honestly. It's not like Carson had been transparent with the details of his supposed betrayal.

"What did you do?" she said, grabbing him by the arm and shaking him.

"I don't know!" he shouted yanking his arm away. Other than not censoring his actions and making friends with Luca and Jules, he really wasn't sure what he'd done.

"We have a good thing here, Son. Why are you intent on screwing it up?" she spat accusatorily.

"A good thing?" Ricky snapped, astonished. "He just hit you, Mom! Dad would never have treated us like that and you know it!"

"Not another word about your father, do you hear me?" She pointed her finger at him angrily. "Your father is dead. He is never coming back. It's time you accepted that."

Her words stung. They hadn't even spoken about his father since arriving here. She really was content to sweep Micha Harrison under the rug and never think of him again.

Leaving his mother's cold words behind, Ricky ran out of the room, down the stairs, and as far from the Den as fast as his feet would carry him.

Luca approached Kyle's apartment, shifting back into a man once again, bloody clothes and all.

He stopped when he heard raised voices coming from inside. Kyle was protesting someone's actions, and they weren't Hayley's.

"If we find out something else!" A voice shouted.

Luca walked to the open doorway and peered inside. Adam and Kyle were having a standoff while Hayley's father stood nearby, his shoulders slumped under some unseen emotional weight.

"You'll what?" Kyle spoke sharply, his hands clenched. In all the time he had known him, Luca had never seen Kyle this angry.

Hayley stepped between her husband and Adam, pushing each of them back forcefully.

"Hayley, come." Her father closed the distance between them and grabbed her by the arm. "This marriage is over. I'm taking you to Carson now!"

Luca stood his ground, although he wanted to step forward and punch Hayley's father for treating his friends this way.

She yanked her arm away as Kyle stepped up behind her. "You're not serious?" Kyle growled.

"You can't mean that," Hayley added, her voice trembling.

Her father's tone softened a little. "We must. Your Alpha still desires your hand in marriage. We must assure him of our family's loyalty."

"He'll accept no other form of proof," Adam added. "Carson wants your marriage annulled. He called this morning demanding it." Adam's tone didn't sound as impassioned as his father's, just resolute.

"I won't do it." Hayley glanced up at Kyle who slipped his arm protectively around her waist. "It's too late."

"You will do as I tell you, for once in your life!" her father yelled.

"I can't! I love Kyle. My loyalty is to him, before you, before the Alpha, before anyone."

"Your loyalty is to your Alpha first," her father said angrily. "Always."

"My Alpha is wrong," Hayley shouted back.

"That is treason!"

"Then I accept the consequences for my treachery." Hayley squared her shoulders determinately. "I am an adult Father; my choices are my own."

Adam looked from his father to Hayley, to Kyle and back to his father. "Father let's go." He stepped between his father and Hayley. He glanced over his shoulder at his younger sister. "She's right. We can't make her do this."

"Carson said..."

Adam put his hand on his father's shoulder, cutting him off. "I know what Carson said and we'll do what we must, but not this."

Hayley's father looked back at his daughter and her husband. He sighed and nodded. Both men turned toward the door and Luca bolted, tucking himself into a darkened corner as they exited the apartment.

Once they were out of sight, he crept through Kyle's door, shutting it behind him. "Holy hell!" Luca said.

Both of them jumped a little and looked toward Luca. Kyle had both arms wrapped around Hayley, who was crying softly.

"How much did you hear?" Hayley asked.

"Enough," Luca said.

"The pack is all riled up," Kyle said. "There is a lot of talk about a betrayal." Kyle looked as though he was winding up for a joke. "But, of course, everyone in this room already knows who the traitorous creature is. Don't we?"

Luca rolled his eyes, but he'd made Hayley smile. Kyle wiped a couple of tears from her face.

"So," he said, holding Hayley close again. "Why do we have the pleasure of your company, my traitorous Canadian friend... in my living room... unannounced... looking rather rough?"

Luca dropped onto the couch. He had momentarily forgotten about his bloody state. "I'm in trouble."

"Um... dude. I think we already know that. You're in love with a dead person."

"Very funny."

"Thank you."

"I mean that I was run off the road last night. I think Carson sent Kip to kill me." Luca's voice had become serious.

"Oh, that kind of trouble," Kyle said raising his eyebrows.

A phone beeped. Luca had the reaction to check his own even though he knew it was back at the wreck in teeny-tiny, unsalvageable pieces.

"Okay, so problem one hundred and two just text me," Kyle said, looking down at his phone.

Luca did not respond but smiled at his friend's sense of humor and waited for him to continue.

"Ricky says that he couldn't get ahold of you, we all know why, so I was next on his 'help me' list. Carson accused him of treason this morning."

"Considering the execution attempt I just survived, I'd say the kid is in danger for sure. Carson's lost his mind," Luca said.

"Where is he? Is he safe?" Hayley asked.

"Hold on," Kyle said and typed out the question.

After a few tense seconds, the response beeped in his hand.

"Yeah, he's okay. He's at his girlfriend's house."

"Hand me your phone," Luca said, and Kyle did so. He pulled up the number and hit send.

Ricky knew he had been very cryptic since he'd arrived at Tasha's. Probably because he knew that he shouldn't be here. What if he put her in danger? But in all honesty, he really hadn't known where else to go. Just then, his phone rang. This startled Ricky. No one actually called anymore. He glanced down and saw that it was Kyle's contact info staring back at him, so he answered.

"Ricky, are you alright?" It was Luca.

"Me. Yeah. Are you?"

"I'm alive."

"Obviously," Ricky said dryly but relief flooded through him. When Luca hadn't come back to the Den like he'd said he was going to, Ricky had worried that Carson had done something to him.

"Does Carson know where you are?" Luca asked.

"Don't think so," Ricky responded with a shrug.

"Where does your girlfriend live?"

Ricky said nothing but handed the phone to Tasha so that she could relay the address. She did so and handed the phone back to him.

"Stay there. We will come to get you soon," he heard Luca say from the other end of the line.

Ricky looked around the basement of Tasha's family home and shrugged. "Mind if I hang here a while?" he asked Tasha, who was sitting on the couch beside him.

She nodded and flashed an adorable smile his way.

"I'm good, text when you get here," he told Luca and ended the call.

"My family isn't here so of course you can stay. But you should at least tell me why you're hiding and who you're hiding from. And who is coming to rescue you." Her eyes were alight with curiosity.

"Why, is complicated. Who, is my mom's boyfriend, and who, is Luca. You remember, you met him at the bonfire." He explained the basics.

"I'm good with complicated. What happened?" Tasha said. "You know you can trust me, right?"

"I know I can... It's just..." Ricky didn't even know where to begin to explain what was happening in his life at the moment.

"Oh come on Ricky, I want to help. And I promise that I won't laugh or get scared or anything. Why are you hiding from your mom's boyfriend? He didn't hit you, did he?"

"Not exactly," Ricky admitted.

Tasha waited silently for him to continue. Ricky interpreted the determined and honest look on her face which made her even more endearing. He felt comfortable with Tasha. *I want to trust her with all of it,* even the truth of what he was.

If she freaks, what happens then? he asked himself.

He was stuck between not wanting to involve her and wanting to get her out of the dark. Deciding, he stood and took a few steps away, standing in front of Tasha.

"I really hope you're ready for this," he said aloud, but more to himself than her.

"Ready for what?" she asked, looking confused.

Ricky took a deep breath and then in a flash of bright light, released the black-haired, yellow-eyed, four-pawed beast within him.

Tasha shrieked but it was momentary. The expression on her face surprised, not scared. Deliberating, she studied him closely. After a few seconds, her mouth spread into an intrigued smile. After a fraction of a second's more hesitation, she climbed off the couch and knelt down to look into his eyes. Fingers caressed his face, stroking from furry ear to wet nose. Utter awe in her eyes.

Ricky stood very still, afraid that he would still frighten her. He may have hoped for this reaction but never, in his wildest dreams, would have believed he would get it.

Relieved, he took a few steps back and in another flash of light, from which Tasha shielded her eyes, he turned back into his human form.

"Wow!" Tasha exclaimed. "You're a werewolf! Or a lu-garu or lycan or shifter... I want to know everything!" Her eyes were wild with excitement.

"Okay," Ricky said, as they settled back onto the couch. Ricky began with his father's murder and continued until he'd told her everything: about this pack, about Jules, about the feud between vampires and werewolves, and about the fact that Carson seemed to think he betrayed him somehow.

Carson had gathered those close to him. Kip had assured him that Luca had been dealt with. Pictures of his Jeep upside down in a ditch confirmed it. All Carson had to do now was wait for the body to be discovered, and it was over. There were only two more wolves on the list that stood between him and restoring peace to his life, and safety to his subjects.

He'd sent Kip out to locate the Coopers and Max and Jed to find the boy. Neither had reported back yet.

"Are you sure he's dead?" Ben asked, the shock of Luca Cain's untimely demise still having an effect on him. Carson waited patiently for it to sink in.

"I'm afraid so," Carson nodded sadly, his mind on the tasks to come. Joe Reynolds had not assured him his daughter's marriage would be annulled yet, as Carson had demanded. If Carson had to widow the girl to claim her, then that's what he would do. He'd grown tired of Demetria's sadness. Besides, a traitor's mother was no choice for a queen. He would miss Demetria's perfect ass and glistening cunt, but the Reynolds girl could be broken and molded to fit his desires. He was sure of it. It was an ugly business, making the tough calls. But he was the Alpha, it was his call to make.

Ricky was sitting on Tasha's basement couch, one arm slung over her shoulder. "You know, I'm not entirely surprised," Tasha admitted sheepishly.

"You're not?" Ricky asked.

"Not really. I mean, I never would have voiced my observations. I never would have hoped it could be true." She spoke with an excitement Ricky couldn't understand.

"Hoped? You hoped I was a werewolf?"

"Well, yes, and do you know how exciting it is to be involved, even ever so slightly, in a forbidden romance between a werewolf and a vampire? It's a nerdy girl's ultimate fantasy!" Tasha gushed. "Of course, I always wanted to be the vampire in that scenario but getting to be a girl who has made-out with a werewolf is pretty cool, too."

Ricky started to laugh.

"What's so funny? How many girls get to make-out with a

werewolf?"

"More than you think…"

"Yes, but how many know that they have?"

"Less."

"Right, and on top of that," she said, stopping to bat her eyelashes, "how many can say they got to make out with you?"

"One." He leaned in to kiss her.

She giggled and ran her hands through his hair.

Ricky almost jumped out of his skin when the unmistakable cry of a wolf shattered the safety of his hideout.

"What was that?" Tasha asked. He released her. The howl had come from right outside the house. Ricky wasn't sure who it was. *Hard to tell.* A second howl was followed by the scraping sound of claws on glass.

"Who is that?" Tasha shouted, pointing.

Ricky followed her indication to the basement window. Through its muddy glass, he spied a standard gray wolf.

"Is it Luca?" Tasha asked.

"No," he whispered in Tasha's ear. He looked into her eyes a moment more and then, without warning, he grabbed her arm and flung her into the small basement bathroom. "Call Kyle," he said, shoving his phone in her hand.

"Ricky. Don't!" she screamed as he slammed the door shut. Ignoring her banging fists, he shoved the couch against the door so she couldn't follow him.

Glass shattered and Ricky bolted for the stairs. He could hear Tasha screaming in the bathroom but didn't turn back. The wolf who had just come through the window turned into his human self. It was Jed. He grabbed Ricky and shoved him up against the cinderblock wall before he had a chance to escape. Ricky cried out and felt it crack under his weight.

Tasha screamed again. Ricky growled and planted his elbow into Jed's side. He felt the man shudder with pain and watched as he stepped back, clutching his ribcage. Ricky bolted up the stairs. He dodged through the open door and found himself face to face with the human form of Max. He swore just before he was hit over the head from behind and everything went dark.

Luca, Kyle, and Hayley left the apartment almost immediately after Luca's conversation with Ricky. Hayley went down the stairs to see if she could get any information out of Adam. While Kyle and Luca had taken Hayley's beat up old Volkswagen Beetle and driven towards Monica's house as fast as it could sputter. As they were driving up the coastline Kyle's phone rang. "Ricky what's up?" he said, answering the call.

"It's Tasha," said a panicked voice. "They took him. They just came, and they took him!"

"Who took who? Tasha, calm down," Kyle ordered as they started in the direction of Jules's house.

"Wolves," Tasha said after a long breath. "Wolves took Ricky."

"Where are you?" Kyle asked, immediately stopping on the sand.

"Trapped in the basement at my house."

"Are you hurt?"

"No, but Ricky…"

"Can you hear them or are they gone?"

Tasha's whimpering stopped after a few moments of struggling. Silence ensued while she listened. "I can't hear anything. I think they're gone."

"Have her call Monica. If the wolves are gone she can take the girl home for safekeeping. It's unlikely that the pack would attack two human girls."

Kyle nodded and relayed the important parts of the message.

"Ricky…" Luca heard Tasha say.

"We'll find Ricky. You just get yourself out of there. And keep your head down. Understand?"

"Yes," Tasha said after a short pause.

"We got this." Kyle hung up the phone and then turned to

Luca. After only a second, the two men bolted back to the car and took off toward the place where Ricky was last seen. If they could pick up his scent they could track him easily enough.

Ricky woke, lying face down in the mud. He wanted to spit out a clump he could feel in his mouth but resisted. Instead, he played dead, laying completely still and listening to what the pack members around him were arguing about.

"Carson, what exactly is your plan?" asked a voice Ricky couldn't place.

"Should I send you away, Ben? Have your loyalties shifted as well? Should I count you among the traitors?" Carson asked. A wild, accusatory tone in his voice.

"No, no, I'm not." Ben paused, but then continued, "I only meant that even though he is a traitor, he's just a boy." Ben's voice sounded shaken.

Ricky's heart started to pound. He wouldn't put murder past Carson, but he didn't think he would do it in cold blood. *No.* First Carson would make him grovel for his life and confess. *Well, I won't do either. I'll die first.*

"I will do what I feel is necessary to protect my pack. It's my responsibility!"

Like I care, stupid tyrant can...Whoa!

Ricky was lifted off the ground with excessive force. His eyes shot open, and his nose was now inches from Carson's furious face.

"So, pup, finally come to, have you?" Carson sneered.

Ricky spat and mud splattered across the sneer in front of him. Carson's fist connected with Ricky's mouth. He felt his t-shirt rip and his lip split.

Carson stopped to listen and sniff. *Humans.* Humans were headed their way through the woods. Not only had this band of anarchists consorted with a vampire but they must have also revealed themselves to humans. Jed had confirmed that the human girl that had been with Ricky was frightened but not surprised. Humans could kill and destroy his charges if they had a hankering to. Ricky had endangered the pack twice now. The treachery could not stand.

"Carson wait. Don't!" Ben bolted toward him just as Carson brought the knife across the boy's abdomen.

Ricky cried out and clutched the cut. Carson let the boy's t-shirt go, sending Ricky down to the ground with a thud. He then turned and punched Ben square in the jaw.

He stumbled backward, a look of shock on his face.

"It is done," Carson said with a tone of finality, as he placed the silver knife back in its sheath. "Bring him," he ordered Max and Jed, gesturing toward the man he had just punched. They grabbed Ben by the arms and pulled him in the direction of the previously abandoned vehicles.

Carson didn't look back as they left the boy gushing blood into the mud beneath him.

CHAPTER TWENTY-ONE

Silver's Bane

C arson's fingers dug into Demetria's round hips. He laid on his back watching her large plump breasts bounce as she rode his cock. Two traitors were dead or dying. He bucked his hips up into her, joining her rhythm. One more to go, then he'd have his prize. His white wolf. Demetria moaned. But he envisioned the sound coming from the rare trophy that was the Reynolds girl. The thought of possessing her, of breaking her, enthused him. Demetria's long red fingernails scratched down his torso, bringing him back to the present moment.

He grabbed her around the front of her throat and pulled her body down closer to him, low enough that he could bite down on one brown nipple. Demetria cried out in the sweetest pain as he licked the trickle of blood off the peaked bud. She tried to speak but he pulled her face towards him, sliding his hand to the back of her head and plunged his tongue into her mouth, abruptly silencing whatever she'd been about to say. She whimpered when his teeth found her plump lip.

Carson groaned. Bucking his whole body this time, he rolled them over. If this was his last time inside this perfect pussy, he would maintain full control. Readjusting he slammed into her hard enough to make her whimper his name. One hand moved her thigh up his body for a deeper angle while the other found her throat again. He squeezed until her nails scratched at his hand as she began to need oxygen. Carson growled and thrusted even harder as she purpled a bit and choked out a plea.

Release, having not yet found him, he grunted, letting go

of her throat. His hard cock sprang free of her, dripping from her wet cunt. She lay limply on the bed, fully displayed for him while rubbing her throat. Grabbing both thighs, he turned her backside up.

"All fours," he demanded, satiating the animal inside him. He watched as she shifted to her hands and knees, trembling a little as she did so. "Don't turn around." He ran his hand up one brown calf, to the back of her soft thigh, to her round, perfect ass. "Don't make a sound," he instructed, then swung. She gasped as his hand slapped her soft flesh. "Bad girl." He swung again. She whimpered. "When will you learn to do as you're told?" he asked. Then reached for his belt. He may choose to keep both females for his own. His enemies were dead. Who was there to stop him now?

Luca and Kyle dumped Hayley's car about a mile from Tasha's house and continued into the woods on swift paws. Luca led the way, following his sense of direction and his nose through the trees. He stopped to sniff and, at the same moment, someone cried out. The shout sounded young and terrified. *Ricky!* Luca bolted, running as fast as he could in the direction it had come from. He started to smell blood. Werewolf blood. He could only hope that he wasn't too late.

He and Kyle broke into a small outcropping. Luca saw what he was dreading. Lying on a mess of blood-soaked leaves and grass was Ricky, bleeding from the abdomen and clutching the hand of his human girlfriend. Tasha was bending low over him, begging him to hold on while Monica stood a few steps back, clutching her side. Monica looked startled to see the wolves approaching them, while Tasha barely looked away from Ricky's face.

"Who are you?" Monica demanded, picking up a stick and stepping around the teenagers. The stick was clutched in a defensive position to strike if need be. "You better be werewolves because if you're not, I feel really stupid right now!" she shouted.

Luca nodded at Kyle and in simultaneous flashes of light, they returned to their human forms.

"You were supposed to keep the girl safe! What are you thinking taking on a wolf with a stick?" Luca snapped at Monica as he walked up and knelt beside Ricky.

"Oh, I'm so glad it's you," Monica said, taking a deep breath, completely ignoring Luca's scolding. Kyle walked over and took the stick from Monica's shaking hand.

"Let me see," Luca instructed Tasha, who was putting pressure on Ricky's abdomen with a jacket. Tasha lifted away the makeshift bandage, revealing the bleeding and blistering cut. Luca gently touched the edges of the wound with his finger and brought the substance to his nose. The foaming blood smelled of silver. The one thing that was as deadly to werewolves as the sun was to vampires.

Tasha cried out when Ricky started to cough and dig his fingers into her arm. Blood smeared his lips.

"We have to get him out of these woods," Kyle said, looking down on the scene. "Monica, can you get a car?"

Monica nodded and then took off running in the direction of her house.

"Where are you taking him?" Tasha asked.

"Jules's house. It's the only place I think the pack still doesn't know about," Luca replied.

Luca lifted Ricky off the ground. Tasha protested as Ricky shrieked in agony. "He needs a hospital," Tasha yelled.

"A hospital can't help him now." Kyle placed a hand on the girl's shoulder.

Luca could feel Ricky's blood dripping down his torso as he ran. Kyle was keeping pace with Tasha, unwilling to leave her out in the woods on her own. By the time they reached the edge of the woods, Monica had her car parked with the back and passenger doors open, waiting for them. Kyle and Luca placed Ricky down on the backseat as gently as they could. It wasn't careful enough, because he screamed out in pain. Luca started to crawl into the back seat with him as Monica climbed into the driver's seat, but Tasha grabbed his arm.

"Please, let me stay with him," she said softly, with a surprising amount of steadiness.

He said nothing, but nodded and moved away so she could hold the dying boy. She crawled in and placed Ricky's head in her lap. He groaned in pain, grabbing her arm and holding on tightly. She then placed her jacket back onto the cut and pressed down, trying to slow the bleeding.

Luca's heart twisted in pain. The bleeding would not be stopped, not when the wound was inflicted by a silver knife. Luca shut the door behind them and then turned to Kyle. "Go back to the car. Go and get Ricky's mother and meet us at Jules's house," Luca instructed in whispering tones.

"Telling Carson's lover where we are going is a risk," Kyle said.

"I know," Luca said, looking over his shoulder at the back seat. Ricky was writhing in pain while Tasha clung to him, soothing him gently. "But it's all we can do for him now," he continued, turning back to Kyle.

Kyle's eyes filled with sadness for a moment and then he nodded resolutely, stepping away from the passenger door so Luca could take that seat. They all knew Carson was an animal, but what he had just done was truly abhorrent. This Alpha had just crossed a line that couldn't be un-crossed. Carson must be stopped, no matter the consequences.

"To Jules's house," Luca instructed.

Monica pulled away as soon as the last door was closed.

"What am I missing, Luca?" Monica asked. "Don't werewolves have super-fast healing or something?"

"We do," Luca replied in a low voice, trying not to be overheard. "There is only one thing that we can't heal from."

"Silver bullets," Monica supplied.

"Silver of any kind. That cut will kill him." The gravity of the situation fell over the occupants in the front seat of the car. Death was coming for the teenage boy, and Luca was powerless to stop it. Nothing could stop silver's bane.

Carson left Demetria trembling on his rumpled sheets, ass red and welted, tear-streaked face still down in the pillows. He was feeling satiated and more relaxed than he had in years. He was going to win. Win the battle set before him. He'd be rid of the traitorous infection in his ranks. Then he would take his soon to be widowed, future queen as his own.

His heavy boots clomped down the narrow, carpeted stairs. In the kitchen he poured himself a cup of coffee Demetria had brewed that morning. Sipping the brown liquid he walked to the screen door as the distinct sound of a motorcycle approached. "Speaking of my future mate," he said aloud to himself, and the Reynolds girl screeched to a halt on her traitor husband's motorcycle. Jean covered thighs slipped off the bike. Carson leaned against the doorframe, imagining those thighs straddling him instead, her back pressed to the mattress as she screamed his name.

"Well, hello gorgeous," he crooned.

"Hello Alpha," she smiled up at him. "May I come in?"

"Of course." He stepped back. The screen door screeched open, then slammed shut behind her as she stepped inside. "I'm here to see Demetria."

"Really?" he asked. Intrigued by the both at once idea. He slid forward, forcing her to step back. The wall behind her trapping her between it and his looming frame. His arm came to rest on the wall above her head.

"Unfortunately, she's a bit indisposed at the moment." His hand slid down the wall, trailing along the side of her soft face. "Has your father spoken to you then?"

"Um…" her captivating brown eyes glanced at his fingers which had come to rest on her bronze clavicle. "No. Sorry. I haven't seen him."

"Pity," Carson crooned, hand sliding up her throat to caress her jawline, inching toward her lips.

The screen door screeched once more as Carson's thumb began to press into the girl's mouth, his body caressing her perky, full breasts.

"Married, Alpha."

A firm hand pushed against his shoulder as Kyle, her not yet dead husband, stepped between them. Eyes feral, but the anger remained restrained within them.

Carson snarled.

"Go," Kyle said squeezing the girl's hand. She slipped from behind him, running up the stairs. "You know, it's frowned upon to covet another man's wife, even if you're the Alpha." Kyle's tone was chipper. At ease as he swung the car keys in his hand around one finger. Carson could kill him right here and now and claim the girl's body as his own the next minute. Although, murder without physical evidence of wrong doing was crossing a line even he wasn't prepared to explain to the pack just yet.

Just as Carson was about to poke around for the damning evidence the two women came down the stairs. Demetria wearing some hastily thrown on sweats. The Reynolds girl scooted behind her husband to the door while Demetria walked between them. "Where are you off to?" Carson asked rotating his hand to slap her soft ass as she moved to pass him. When she didn't answer, his hand shot up and out. Gripping the woman's throat, he turned her to face him, feeling her swallow beneath his grip.

"Hayley promised to introduce me to her boss today. I forgot," Demetria mumbled. Carson noted Kyle tensing behind her.

Carson pulled the woman closer, plunging his tongue into her mouth, but making eye contact with the man standing behind her. The threat of what was to come in his gaze.

Satisfied, he released her. Demetria and then Kyle followed the human form of the white wolf out the door.

"I asked you to wait for me," Kyle called as he followed both women down the front steps.

"There was no time," his wife shot back as they swapped keys. Carson sipped his coffee as the recently childless and the soon to be widow walked to the rusty Volkswagen Beetle side by side. *Must be an important interview* thought Carson. He really didn't understand why Demetria was so determined to get a job anyway. Even after he took the Reynolds girl as his queen, he'd still let Demetria cook and clean, maybe even fuck for her continued room and board. However, if it stopped all the bitching she'd been doing lately he'd allow it.

Ricky cried out in pain as Luca lifted him from the back seat. His supernatural healing was trying to fight against the effects of the silver, but it felt like he was being burnt alive from the inside. Better if they had let him die in the woods. All this moving and jostling was making things feel even worse. "Hang on Ricky," Luca pleaded.

Ricky was carried into Jules's house and set on the soft, velvet, sofa as carefully as possible.

He looked past Luca and searched for Tasha. She ran into the room after them, clutching the jacket drenched in his blood. Her hands were stained, her clothes and face splattered, and yet, he'd never seen a more beautiful girl in his life.

Moments later, Tasha was again by his side. She was so strong and so calm considering the trauma he was putting her through. He might have even told her that he loved her if he'd been able to find the words through the pain. Just to say it. Even just once. Right now though, there was only one person he needed.

As if on cue, shouting came from the other room. His mother cursed, shoving Luca when she saw him. "Mom," Ricky choked out softly. Demetria rushed to his side, pushing Tasha away as she dropped to her knees next to him.

"It's going to be okay, baby." She stroked his hair. "I'm here."

For one moment he felt safe, like a child again. Happy that his mother was beside him now.

"I'm very sorry Mrs. Harrison," Luca said, walking up beside her.

"You beast!" Demetria exclaimed. Standing, she slapped the Beta across the cheek.

Tasha shrieked.

"You did this!" Ricky's mom shouted again, punching Luca with her fists. The Beta made no move against her. Instead, he let the grieving woman beat him in the chest and shoulders without flinching or moving away from her.

Tasha dropped back to her knees by Ricky's head.

"Leave...him...alone," Ricky managed to choke out, drawing his mother's attention back to himself.

"He didn't do this," Tasha added and once again gripped Ricky's shaking fingers. Demetria stopped and looked down at the teenagers, their clasped hands, Tasha's disheveled appearance.

"It's going to be okay, my love," Demetria whispered, leaving her attack on Luca and returning to her son's side. This time, she moved in beside Tasha, not in place of her.

"I'm right here. You're going to be okay."

Ricky nodded and took her hand. He heard the desperation to believe her own lie. But he knew. He knew she'd lose her son, just as she'd lost her husband. He knew what was happening to him and he knew without a doubt who had sentenced him to this torturously painful end.

Luca watched in a daze as Tasha and Demetria comforted Ricky. The teenage, human girl was showing an extraordinary amount of strength for one so young. Crying quietly now as she sat with the dying werewolf. Young hands clasped tightly, with all the strength the boy had left. Even so, Luca could tell Ricky was weakening. His eyes began to open less and less, and the groans of pain started to stop altogether. There was nothing to be done. It was almost over now. Hayley, Kyle, and Monica were all sitting and standing around the kitchen counter in silence. Waiting for the end.

Luca stood at the door of the living room, watching as Tasha took her fingers and brushed them against Ricky's sweat-slick forehead. Maybe as a reaction, his eyes opened once more. He held her gaze for a few seconds. Luca was struck with horror again as Ricky's eyes closed, his grip on Tasha's hand slackened, and he slipped into unconsciousness.

"Ricky?" Tasha asked but received no response.

Torturous screams escaped from Demetria's throat as she shook her son's shoulders, gripping him tightly.

"What can we do?" Monica asked quietly as she came up beside Luca.

"Nothing," Luca replied. "There is nothing we can do."

Monica placed a comforting hand on his arm. He looked down at the touch and noticed he was covered in the boy's blood. His hands, arms, shirt, and much of his jeans were soaked with the leaked life force.

Tasha began to cry softly. Monica gave Luca's arm one more squeeze and walked over, wrapping the teenager in her arms.

After another moment, and a glance back at the scene, Luca walked from the room and into Jules's bathroom. The blood-soaked shirt made a splat on the tile before he stepped into the shower. Numbly he watched as the red liquid slid over his torso, drenched his jeans, and dissolved in the stream of water that disappeared down the drain. In a surge of anger, he punched the wall. The shower tile obliterating around his fist.

The desire to kill Carson surged through him. Trying to execute him was one thing, but to brutally murder a child was another level of evil. "He's just a kid!" Luca shouted at no one. Knees giving out he slid down the wall, under the stream of water.

Luca startled when there was a hesitant knock at the bathroom door. "Are you decent?" a feminine voice asked.

"Yeah," Luca barely whispered.

Hayley opened the door slowly. He stared up at her, not having any words to say.

"I know," she said. Leaving the door wide she walked into the shower, crouched under the stream, and wrapped Luca in her arms. Kyle followed, turning off the water and joining his wife in the embrace. Luca dropped his head onto their shoulders and hugged them both tightly, finally letting out all the pain he was feeling.

Jules and Nick had settled onto the hard couch in the common area of Gabriel and Eileen's hotel suite to wait the sunny day away. They looked like complimenting bookends, each facing the other as they were.

Jules blinked, trying to keep her eyes open. Sleep was calling her, and yet, she was refusing to give into it. Wanting instead, to continue getting to know her twin once more.

Nick yawned through his last comment. Her ability to understand the babble seemed to mean their innate twin connection was still strong.

"Well, I never gave up on you." A playful glare was directed at him as she used her bent leg to kick him lightly around the knee.

"I only disappeared, didn't I? You weren't told without a doubt that I was dead." Nick paused. "They found two sets of remains Jules."

Jules raised her eyebrows at this. She'd never returned to their sleepy hometown, once Hector had gotten his clutches into her. He must have planted a second body in the ashes.

As they had caught each other up Jules had chosen to skip over the first hundred years she'd spent as a vampire. Determined to leave that part of her past in the past permanently.

Nick yawned again, obviously fighting the same call to rest that she was.

She shifted higher on the arm of the couch, looking past her knees toward Nick. He was lounging across from her, hands behind his head holding it upright and legs stretched out, taking up most of the space on the couch.

"Any epic romances worth mentioning?" Jules asked him, wondering if her brother was still the same indecisive, fluid, flirt he'd been in his human life. "Girlfriends, boyfriends, spouses?"

"Me a spouse? As if I could love with that kind of commitment." Nick laughed loudly. "You. Same question."

"I just started something new actually," Jules admitted. A blush would have colored her pale cheeks if a vampire could.

"Someone special?" Nick prodded.

"He could be," Jules replied, thinking momentarily of Luca and Aboit.

"Tell me more," Nick instructed, smiling mischievously at her.

"His name is Luca Cain and he's a werewolf," Jules said, feeling a little defensive.

Nick sat up higher. "No way! My little sister is dating a dog." He laughed loudly.

"By fifteen minutes! And don't call him that." Her arms crossed in annoyance.

Nick looked stunned. "I only meant that it's not what I expected. You know, werewolves can be dangerous."

"Not you too." Jules rolled her eyes.

"Me and who now?"

Jules nodded her head toward the closed bedroom door.

Nick made a sound that conveyed both mild dislike and annoyance for the man who had broken his nose. At least to Jules it did. "Who cares what golden boy thinks?" Nick said after just a few moments.

"I do Nicholas. Before a couple hours ago, he was the only family I had."

"Yeah, well..." Nick's next comment was cut short when her phone began to ring from the small dining table across the room.

In a fraction of a musical note, she was standing, had checked who was calling, and answered Monica's call.

"Hi Monica," she greeted.

"It's me, Jules." Luca's voice was barely audible and laced with a deep pain.

What was wrong? Why was he with Monica? And why wasn't he calling from his own phone? "Are you alright?" she asked instead of the questions flooding her mind.

He continued slow, heavy breaths into the phone but didn't speak.

"Luca?" Jules noticed from the corner of her eye that Nick had stood also. Walking to the heavy curtains, he peeled one away tentatively but dropped it back in place as soon as the bright sunlight stung his face and hand.

"I'm okay," Luca finally said. "For now."

"What do you mean for now?" Jules tried to keep her tone level, even though anxiety-spiked adrenaline pumped through her veins. "Luca, what's going on?"

"Carson knows about us."

Jules waited for him to continue, biting down on a nail. Nick gently pulled her hand away out of some form of instinct. She swatted at him lightly.

"How..." she began but trailed off when he continued to speak.

"He tried to have me killed."

"Is everyone alright? Are you?"

Nick hovered nearby, obviously sensing some distress.

"I've healed." Luca's tone was flat. Detached. There was something he wasn't saying.

"Luca, what is it?" she encouraged softly when he hesitated to continue. "Talk to me."

"It's Ricky," Luca said finally.

"What about Ricky?" she asked very tentatively but wasn't sure she wanted to know anymore.

"Carson attacked him. He's been cut by a silver blade. Jules... I," but the sound of his voice died out.

She couldn't speak either. *Cut by a silver blade.* Silver was fatal to werewolves once it had entered the bloodstream. Ricky

ASHLI T T SILVER

was not going to make it. She tried to wrap her brain around that reality.

Jules vaguely felt herself drop to one of the hardback chairs, her elbows resting on the table. "Is he...?" she couldn't finish her question.

"Not yet. But I don't think he has much time," Luca said, sounding a little steadier. "Listen, Jules. Carson is coming for us. All of us. Hayley will likely be spared, but he probably has an execution order out on Kyle by now too. I want you to stay where you are. This fight is going to get bloody, and I don't want you to get caught in the crossfire..."

"No, Luca." Jules's tone was unwavering. "This is my fight too."

"Please..."

"I am not going to hide in the shadows while people I care about are dying. You are going to need me in this fight. You know that." Her voice was as final as her decision. This was not a discussion. She was a centuries-old vampire, and she knew how to fight an enemy that was out for blood. "I'll leave at nightfall. I love you."

"I love you too," Luca said and then they both ended the call.

"So, who are we fighting?" Nick asked. Gabriel may not, but Jules knew that Nick would stand by her side.

Luca, Hayley, and Kyle stood in the kitchen. No one spoke for a long while. Luca tried to relax his body by leaning against the kitchen counter. Kyle had wrapped his arms around Hayley, who had buried her face in his chest.

"We need to kill the bastard," Kyle said quietly.

Luca had been thinking this also, he just hadn't voiced it yet. "We can't just barge into the Den and kill him, Kyle," Hayley said, looking into Kyle's eyes. "It would be suicide."

"Hayley's right. We have to be smart about this," Luca said.

Kyle absentmindedly stroked her hair.

Luca thought of Jules. He wanted her there with him. He wanted to be able to hold her. He needed her.

"If we attack Carson, we will all die too," Hayley said.

"We need more support," Kyle added. "We need allies, or this fight will be over before it even begins."

"What about Demetria?" Luca asked.

"What about her?" Hayley replied.

"Did you tell her this was Carson?"

"Not yet."

"Don't you think if she knew, she'd be on our side," Luca asked.

"Maybe," Kyle said.

"But will she believe it?" Hayley asked.

Luca didn't look up as he spoke, "she won't if she hears it from me."

"I'll tell her."

Luca's head shot up. Tasha and Monica had just entered the kitchen. Monica's arm was still around the younger girl.

"What?" Luca asked, stunned.

"I'll tell her it was Carson." Tasha fidgeted. "Ricky told me all about... everything. Who he is, who you are, who you're dating." She pointed at Luca. "And who was going to come after him if someone did."

All the wolves in the room were now looking at Tasha, astonished. "You're extremely brave to be standing here with all of us," Kyle said.

She chuckled softly. "Ricky said so too. I think it's cool." She gave them a sad half-smile. "So, I'll tell her. I think she'll believe me. I don't know any of you. I only know what Ricky told me."

"If you're willing to try to convince her..." Hayley began.

"I'll do it." Tasha paused a moment. "For Ricky, I'll do it.

CHAPTER TWENTY-TWO

Dead and Buried

L uca could hear Tasha talking to Demetria in the other room. "How would you know that?" Demetria growled. "Because Ricky told me," Tasha replied, calmly.

Luca stood just on the other side of the wall, unwilling to leave the human girl completely alone with the grieving werewolf mother. Monica and Hayley were in the kitchen talking in low whispers, while Kyle stood silently nearby, enraptured by the conversation happening in the living room as well.

"He told me Carson was coming for him," Tasha continued. "He even called Luca for help."

"How do you know it wasn't Luca? He consorted with a vampire. He's a traitor to our pack." She said the middle part in a very hushed tone like it was almost an unspeakable fact.

"If that makes him a traitor, then so is Ricky," Tasha said confidently. "He consorted with a vampire too. Jules, the vampire whose house we're in, our school librarian. He cares about her... for some reason, they're kinda friends."

"Ricky wouldn't," Demetria stated determinately. "A vampire murdered his father. He wouldn't."

"He did." Tasha's tone was firm.

Demetria was silent for many moments. "He said..." Demetria's voice trailed off a few moments more. Her breath hitched like she was having trouble filling her lungs with air. "Carson. He really did this?" Demetria's voice sounded miles away.

"I'm sorry Mrs. Harrison," Tasha replied softly.

"Excuse me. I need a moment." Demetria walked from the

living room, collided with Kyle who steadied her, and then ran out the back door without a word.

Luca watched through the open door as she dropped to her knees in the sand and began to scream like her heart was being slowly pulled from her chest. Hayley brushed past him and tentatively approached the sobbing woman.

Luca left Kyle watching them and walked to the living room to check on the young girl.

"Well, at least now she knows." Tasha wasn't talking to him, but Ricky. She sat on the floor beside Ricky's face, holding his limp hand in hers. His breaths were shallow, barely moving his chest.

"Is he going to be okay?" Tasha asked, without looking up at Luca with red rimmed eyes.

Luca walked over and sat on the floor next to her. He could lie and tell the girl he'd be fine. He could send her home and let her find out the truth in a few days, but he didn't. "No Tasha. He's not."

Tasha's eyes slammed shut for a long moment. As she looked up at Luca, new tears were forming.

"I thought not."

"The silver has made it into his bloodstream. His body is shutting down now. The harsh reality is that, he won't wake up again."

"Is he... in pain?" she asked.

"Not anymore." Luca reached out and placed one arm around her shoulders.

"I need a minute," Tasha choked out, dropped Ricky's hand, stood shakily, and walked from the room.

Luca heard a door slam.

"Tasha," Monica called after the girl, and the door slammed again. Then the crying started, coming from Jules's bedroom.

"I'm sorry buddy," Luca said, placing one hand on the dying boy's chest. Under that touch he felt two small, shuddering breaths, and then his chest stopped rising entirely. The boy was gone, and in the last moment before death, the wolf appeared. "Damn it," Luca whispered.

Nick sat, passenger princess, in the car next to his sister. Night had fallen, and they'd been on the road for at least an hour. They had been conversing sporadically. Jules sometimes falling into silence. He could feel the tension and sadness building in her as they got closer to their destination and the altercation to come. A battle that Jules's substitute brother would not fight in. Jules was determined to defend his right to choose. Nick thought Gabriel was a disloyal prat for turning his back on his coven leader, and friend, when she needed him most.

Nick jumped in his seat, startled when Jules's car began to ring all around him. The screen on the dashboard flashed the name "Monica." Jules pushed a button on the steering wheel to answer the phone call.

"Luca?" Jules asked when no one spoke.

A male voice said, "he's gone, Jules."

Jules lost control of her emotions and the vehicle all at once. Her hand slipped on the wheel, and the car swerved. "Shit!"

Nick grabbed the wheel. She would have raced into oncoming traffic if he hadn't been beside her. "Ease your foot off the gas slowly," Nick instructed as red tears slid down Jules's face.

"Jules?" the voice on the call questioned.

Nick steered the car to the shoulder and the car rolled to a stop.

"Are you alright?" The disembodied voice asked through the car speakers.

"I'm okay." Jules's voice sounded steady, while her expression was one of devastation.

"Who's in the car with you?" The male, whom Nick assumed was Jules's werewolf, asked.

"I'll explain when I see you," Jules choked out.

"How long?"

"I'm almost home."

Nick watched Jules clutching the steering wheel, desperately trying to control the pain in her tone.

"I love you," the man said softly.

"I love you, too," Jules told him. With that, she ended the call.

Nick put a hand on her shoulder and squeezed. When she turned to face him, he blotted her blood-streaked cheeks with his sleeve. "Let me drive," he suggested.

She nodded.

Jules climbed over to the passenger seat while Nick walked around the car to take her place. She mumbled directions and looked out the window. Nick stayed silent as well, letting her process this sad news in peace. She reached her fingers up to her mouth and started to bite her nails. Nick smiled silently to himself. "Still haven't kicked that anxious tick then," he said as he took her hand in his and squeezed.

"Oh." She looked at their intertwined fingers. "I didn't realize." Her gaze fell back to the passing roadside, but she didn't let go of his hand.

When they pulled up in front of a small, green house, a tall, bronze man was waiting on the driveway. "Luca," Jules whispered under her breath and was out of the car before Nick had put it in park. The werewolf held his arms open and she ran into them. He stumbled backward, losing his footing momentarily but remained upright. He bent, shoulders and back arching, to touch his lips to Jules's. Nick watched the werewolf with his sister for a moment more before he climbed out of the car and approached them both.

"Who are you?" Luca asked, noticing him for the first time.

Jules stayed in Luca's embrace while turning to look at her brother. "I'm Nicholas Bristow." Nick stuck out his hand toward Luca. "Jules's twin brother. Like from birth," he added at Luca's confused expression. Luca looked at Jules for confirmation. She nodded at him. "Surprise," Nick added with a hint of his usual sarcasm.

"Hi." Luca took Nick's hand and shook it. "But how...?"

"I'll explain later," Jules said, putting a hand on Luca's chest. One of his hands covered her own.

"What is Tai doing here?" Jules asked as Monica's ex-boyfriend pulled onto the street in front of Jules's house in his father's rusted pick-up truck.

"I'll explain later," Luca said, giving her waist a squeeze. "Do you need me to come inside with you?" he asked while waving at Tai, who waved back.

Jules could see that Luca had something to say to his friend. "No." She would face this on her own. "Talk to Tai," Jules said. "I'm okay."

Luca looked down at her for a moment, kissed her on the forehead, and then walked toward the end of the driveway.

Jules turned back to her brother, "Nick?"

"I'll be out here when you need me." Nick pointed back to her car. She knew that he was just giving her space to deal with her friends and grieve on her own. She'd always been like that, even when their parents died. He'd needed her with him, and she'd needed to face the pain alone.

She nodded her thanks and then opened her own front door. Monica came rushing toward her, hugging her tightly. Jules hadn't had a drink in a while but found she didn't care in this moment. "Tai's outside?" Jules said, looking at Monica questioningly.

"I know. Luca's going to tell him everything," Monica explained. Her eyes were red and puffy despite her somewhat cheery voice. "I should probably go outside with him. You know, in case Tai freaks out. Which he probably will." She kept her voice low so as not to disturb the others.

Jules smiled at her friend and released her.

"Where...?"

Monica pointed toward the living room. Jules could hear soft crying coming from that direction. Monica gave her hand a squeeze and then walked around her to go help Luca with Tai. Jules could see Hayley and Kyle through the back window. They were sitting on the back porch, facing the ocean, arms wrapped around each other.

She took tentative steps toward the room in which Ricky's body lay. Soundlessly, she entered. First, she saw Tasha, the source of the crying. Her back was pressed against the far wall, her face covered by her shaking hands. Then she saw the woman beside the sofa, stone-cold and still. Her features made her identity unmistakable. Ricky's mother. Under her knees, blood had soaked into the white carpet. It trailed up to where the young wolf lay, fur, four paws and all.

Jules knew when a werewolf died the last ounce of magic they possessed returned them to their animal state. The state in which they truly thrived. She'd seen it before, but never a wolf so young.

Ricky was lanky, all legs and large paws. Yesterday she'd seen the same wolf fleeing his new girlfriend's house. Thinking of their last, lively, encounter Jules felt blood tears again form in her eyes.

At that moment, she was pulled from the memory by a feral growl. Jules saw the woman stand and in one stride she slapped Jules across the face. Jules's hand rose to her stinging cheek, but she did not move away.

"It's your fault he's dead," Ricky's mother shouted.

Luca waved as he approached a very confused and frustrated looking Tai. "What am I doing here Luca?" Tai asked, looking over Luca's shoulder, seemingly worried about who might be inside the house.

"Honestly," Luca began, "I need the truck and Monica needs you."

"Monica does not..."

As if on cue, the front door opened and Monica walked out of the house and started toward them. She got half the way until she noticed the vampire lounging against Jules's car. "Who the hell are you?" she asked.

Nick sat up. "Juliana's brother."

"But you're dead," Monica stated.

"I am," Nick said. "But I am also living. I am, like Jules, living while dead."

Monica narrowed her eyes and looked over at Luca.

Luca nodded and shrugged to indicate that what Nick said was true and yes, he was confused as well.

"What's he talking about?" Tai asked, looking more confused than before. "One: Jules doesn't have a brother, does she?"

"Apparently she does," Luca told him.

"And two: what does he mean dead? Jules isn't dead? She just walked into the house. I saw her. You saw her. What's going on?" Tai stammered, looking from Monica and Nick to Luca.

"We're going to tell you everything," Luca said.

"Come on long-lost, surprise, twin brother," Monica said motioning for Nick to follow her. "We're going to need your help."

Nick hopped off the car and followed her toward them with an expression that implied that he had nothing better to do anyway.

Luca turned back to Tai. "Monica has been keeping something from you."

"I know. I'm the one who told you she was hiding something from me. What does that have to do with anything?" Tai asked defensively.

"It has to do with me. Me and Jules. She was hiding what she was hiding from you because it wasn't her secret to tell," Luca said.

"Huh?" Tai raised his eyebrows and crossed his arms.

Luca took a steadying breath and opened his mouth to

speak, but nothing happened.

"Luca, what the hell is going on? You are making absolutely no sense."

Luca sighed and tried again, but still, nothing came out.

"Let me tell him," Monica requested, placing a steadying hand on his arm.

Luca nodded. *Why not?* He wasn't having any luck.

"You know how I have a crazy obsession for all things supernatural, yes?"

Tai nodded.

"Well, part of it is because part of it is true."

"What?" Tai asked.

"I'm a werewolf," Luca said finally.

"And the reason Jules's brother here said that Jules is dead is because she's a vampire," Monica added.

"Okay," Tai began. "Very funny guys. Actually, you know what, it's not funny. It's ridiculous."

Nick looked passed Monica at Luca who'd taken four steps back. In the same moment that Luca turned from man to wolf, Nick released his fangs and hissed. Monica stood motionless, between the supernatural predators and shrugged saying, "That'll do it."

Tai jumped and cried out in shock.

"It's okay Tai." Monica reached out and took his hand, which he yanked back, glaring at her.

Luca returned to his human form while Nick and Monica shielded their eyes.

"That's impossible," Tai stammered.

"Nope. It's supernatural," Monica said with a grin and everyone but Tai chuckled.

Jules didn't know how to react. She couldn't find any words. Not of comfort. Not of guilt. Nothing.

In a matter of moments, Kyle and Hayley were between Jules and the woman who'd slapped her. "Demetria don't!" Hayley said as she put her arms out, blocking Jules from her attacker.

"She did this!" Demetria shouted, pointing toward Jules.

Kyle grabbed her as she moved to attack Jules again.

"No, she didn't," Tasha said softly.

All the supernatural beings turned toward the human girl. Tasha stood and walked past the werewolves. "Ricky would never put this on you." She addressed Jules alone. "He stood by you and Luca to the end. He chose you over his pack. Don't let her take that away from you." Tasha took Jules's hand and pulled her farther into the room.

Demetria looked stung, but without another word, she left out the back door. Hayley and Kyle follow Demetria out of the house. But Jules felt like she couldn't move as her eyes again fell on Ricky's body. "I'll give you a minute," Tasha said and left the room out the internal door.

Jules sighed deeply and fought back tears as she took in the young boy's wolf form. "I don't know how to do this," she stated aloud as she took Demetria's spot on the floor. It'd been years since someone that she cared about had been taken by death. Especially, someone so young.

She looked down at Ricky's unmoving face. Gently, she reached forward and caressed one of his velvety ears. She let her hand trail along his neck, over his shoulder, down his leg, to his front paw. She took it in her hand and kissed it. Then the tears started to flow helplessly. One dropped onto his paw. She wiped it clean almost frantically, for no reason other than grief. Her head dropped onto the blue, velvet, sofa where the blood of her tears added to the trail from the wound that had long ago dried.

"Jules it's time."

Jules looked up as Luca spoke to her. Monica had followed him into the room carrying one of Jules's blankets.

Luca crouched down in front of her. He stared at her for a moment, taking in her blood tears. She thought he might be repulsed by them until he reached up and wiped one away with his thumb. His finger trailed down her cheek. She thought she should have felt embarrassed, or ashamed by the blood streaking down her face but she didn't.

"We have to move him now," he said softly.

Jules looked back at the unmoving form of the boy; wolf. She nodded and allowed Luca to help her stand. He hugged her. She wanted his embrace to make the pain go away. It didn't, of course. But there, in his arms, she did find some comfort and peace.

With one last look at Ricky, she nodded. "Excuse me." She stepped around him, his hand falling away from her's slowly. She touched Monica's wrist. "Use the blue one." Jules spoke of a more precious piece of cloth.

"The one from Pelmoore Manor with the silver stitching?" Monica said skeptically.

Jules nodded. "For Ricky."

Monica turned and went to Jules's bedroom to retrieve the treasured quilt. Jules left the living room and entered the kitchen. She saw Tai hovering near the front door and saw Hayley's eyes go wide as she joined them.

"You got a little something on your face," Kyle said, smiling down at her.

She laughed twice sarcastically but smiled sadly up at him nonetheless.

Then Jules turned and walked back past the stunned-looking Tai. She sniffed as Luca carried the blanket-covered body out of the living room as she shut the bathroom door behind her.

Jules, Monica, and Tasha arrived at the small, hidden cemetery located deep in the forest of the preserve. It was farther than most werewolves ever bothered to travel unless they were bidding farewell to a loved one.

"I heard of this place as a child," Hayley commented quietly as a hush fell over them all.

The werewolf burial grounds were deserted. Jules had

been surprised that no one seemed worried about being attacked here. But, when she asked Kyle about it, he'd said not to worry. He explained that the burial grounds were a sacred place. That to disturb the peace in a place like this was considered treason among all werewolf packs. They all knew that they were in danger, but both he and Luca were sure that Carson could never justify an attack of any kind here.

Luca came to stand beside Jules and put an arm around her after they laid Ricky in the hole they'd dug. Jules kept her gaze above the still body, instead taking in the view around her once more.

The little group had gathered on the top of a hill. Down one side, was a peaceful stream and the other, dense trees. Fog was rising from the ground in the night air. What Jules saw was painful and beautiful. She could think of no better place to lay this young soul to rest.

Demetria stepped forward, kissed a small wooden box, and placed it in the ground beside her son. "Goodbye, my loves," she choked out almost inaudibly. Demetria stepped back and the silence stretched on as they each said a quiet goodbye.

Demetria began to cry, silent devastated tears. Hayley joined her, comforting the mother as she mourned the loss of both husband and son.

Jules closed her eyes for a moment and then let them fall on the blanket she'd had for over three hundred years. It was the last piece from her past. She felt that using it was a fitting way to honor the young soul and to say goodbye.

"I'm sorry," she said, apologizing to the boy for the part she'd played in his death. *You deserved more,* she thought but couldn't bring herself to say such a thing aloud.

Luca gave her waist a squeeze. She looked up and spied the tears running down his cheeks. Her instinct was to look away, but she didn't. Instead, she took his pain into herself and held it in her heart.

Demetria freed a shovel from the soft ground and dropped

a pile of earth onto her fallen loved ones. Silently and, to Jules's surprise, she held the shovel out to her.

CHAPTER TWENTY-THREE

Blood-Addicts Anonymous

N ick was left in Jules's house alone while the strange assortment of friends had gone to bury the boy. He wandered around the house. It felt like her. The colors she chose, the simple, chic style it was decorated in, and the books. So many books. The one thing out of place was the putrid smell of werewolf blood.

He found the source easily once he breached a room to his right. The dried blood stung his nose and eyes but didn't send him into a need-to-drink frenzy as human blood did.

"Well, somebody has to do it," he said aloud to no one and then he set to work purging the boy's blood from his sister's home. He pulled the covers off the sofa cushions and threw them in the washer, hoping he didn't damage the expensive looking fabric. On his hands and knees, he scrubbed at Jules's carpeting. There was no getting the smell out completely, but the death of a friend was hard enough without having to clean up after it.

Under the sofa, his hand hit something smooth and hard. It was a phone, covered in blood. He flicked the side button and it powered to life. The background that flickered into being was a picture of the young girl who was just here and a boy about her age. Presumably the werewolf teenager whose blood he'd been cleaning. But what struck him was the familiarity. Staring back at him was a face that had recently burned itself into Nick's subconscious. The teenage boy who'd died here, Jules's friend, was the boy that had run away as Nick had ripped the heart from the wolf-cop's chest.

The phone dropped to his side in a limp hand. Jules would

never forgive him for this. After a few moments, Nick came to his senses. The only witness was now gone. So, the only one who knew this fact was him, and Nick wasn't going to tell her. He sighed in relief. But as he looked down at the young couple staring up at him from the phone screen, he felt something. *Was it remorse?* Nick shook his head, attempting to force the thought from his mind. Of course, it wasn't. It couldn't be. Nick was who he was, and he had never questioned it. However, this feeling continued to nag at the back of his mind as he wiped the phone off with a clean corner of a towel, set it on the coffee table, and resumed his attempt to clean up.

He was just throwing the last of the towels in the washer when the front door opened and Jules and the werewolves returned. "You're back," Nick commented as he walked toward them all.

"Kyle, Hayley, this is my brother Nick," Jules introduced flatly. Nick noted the sadness that had dripped down his twin's face. His heart ached with her pain.

"Where are the humans?" Nick asked, noting their absence.

"Monica and Tai took Tasha home," Jules replied.

He nodded like that meant something to him. He was honestly relieved that they had not returned. He wasn't feeling the most in control at the moment.

Jules looked toward the living room. "I should..." Jules began.

"It's already done," Nick said, placing a hand on his sister's arm.

"Thank you," she replied.

The grief was palpable. Nick could feel it wafting off of the people who had just entered. Without a word, the werewolf couple, apparently named Kyle and Hayley, walked through the living room and out the back door. Nick assumed they might be going for a late-night stroll.

"So, Luca, tell me about yourself. Hobbies, interests, bad habits. If you're as great as my sister seems to think, I simply must know why." Nick said this with a smile on his face. If he was good for anything, it was to lighten a dark mood.

"Luca don't answer any of that." Jules elbowed Nick in the stomach as he wrapped her in a hug. "Let nosey here suffer a little longer."

"Well, that's just rude," Nick said in mock horror.

Luca smiled, grabbed Jules by the hand, and pulled her away from Nick and into his own arms.

"Oh, so that's how this is gonna be?" Nick joked. But before anyone could respond, the front door opened again. Nick's attention shot toward it. The humans were back, minus one dead werewolf's girlfriend, and looking as sad as the others had before. Nick leaned close to his sister and whispered in her ear, excusing himself from the gathering of grieving friends. He shut the front door behind him just as the human girl began to cry, falling into Jules's arms.

Too many displays of turbulent emotion, mixed with the fresh, luscious smell of human blood, was overwhelming him. So, he settled into the straight-backed, wicker chair on the front porch to wait out the grieving, and for the supposed fighting to start. He was about to contemplate going for a walk down Jules's darkened street when another vehicle pulled up in front of her house.

The people inside this one he recognized. It was Eileen and her snob of a husband. He waved to them as Eileen opened the passenger door. Standing, he met them halfway up the crushed-shell driveway.

"Jules inside?" Gabriel asked.

"Her, two humans, and three werewolves last time I checked," Nick replied. "Which was like five minutes ago." He added as an afterthought.

Eileen shrugged and took a few steps toward the house. Gabriel grabbed her wrist.

"Gabriel, I'm going in to give my condolences to our friend," she said, looking over her shoulder at him.

"There's three of them," Gabriel hissed.

"And if they were going to hurt vampires, Nick wouldn't be

sitting outside avoiding the emotionally awkward situation. He'd be inside protecting Jules from them. Isn't that right?" Eileen turned on him, looking for confirmation.

"Right. It's pretty doom and gloom," Nick said. "But I don't think there is any danger in there. More like, out there somewhere probably coming for us all." He waved his hand in some general direction away from the house.

"If you want to face the werewolves then fine, but I will not accompany you. If you decide to put yourself in that kind of danger you do so alone." The tone of Gabriel's voice implied that he thought his wife would cave to his wishes. Nick didn't think it was very likely.

A few awkward moments later, Nick's assumption was met. Eileen pulled her arm away, raised her eyebrows at him, and stood her ground.

"Fine," Gabriel said, turned, and walked back to their car. He climbed into the passenger seat and slammed the door.

Eileen watched him go but did not join him.

"Come inside with me?" Eileen asked, obviously a little more unsure than she was letting on when she'd stubbornly refused to change her mind via ultimatum.

"But, I'm uncomfortable in awkward situations with new people," Nick said, looking at her with mock seriousness.

"Yeah, right," she said with a laugh as they entered the house together.

Jules was surprised to see Eileen accompanying her brother back inside. She walked over to meet them.

"I'm sorry for your loss," Eileen whispered in Jules's ear.

Jules hugged her for a long moment. "Thank you so much for coming," Jules said. "Where is Gabriel?"

"In the car, pouting." Eileen scowled.

Jules let out an exasperated sigh and took a step toward the door. Eileen caught her by the arm. So, she turned to look at her friend.

"Just give him some time," Eileen suggested. "He won't leave me and I'm not leaving you. So, I think he will come around."

Nick looked past them both toward the rest of them. "I'm gonna go outside and pretend I care," Nick said, playfully excusing himself and walking back out the front door.

Jules rolled her eyes but made no comment. She found herself studying him as he disappeared from view. She felt like there was more that he wasn't saying. Jules let that thought leave her mind and said, "thank you for being here." She smiled and motioned for Eileen to follow her.

Carson's fury exploded from him. "Where is that insolent fool!" he yelled as he paced up and down the street in front of the Den. Jed's text had come through over an hour ago and he was impatiently awaiting his return. Demetria had not returned since leaving with the Coopers. If she betrayed him as well, her fate would be that of her son's. Only one wolf would be spared from the act of treason. And he'd take what he wanted from her whether she willingly participated or not.

The thought of the mutiny this traitorous Beta had caused made his blood boil. He had been so naive to trust the wolf on legacy alone. Never again would he make that mistake. The thought of the vampire coven that Luca had decided to align himself with made every nerve in Carson's body and mind unravel. This danger, this anarchy had lasted long enough.

Carson punched the Den's rusted, metal, mailbox in a desperate attempt to relieve some of his frustration. Leaving it bent in and unusable, he began his pacing once again just as Jed's beater car came rattling up the road.

"So?" Carson said once the shaky, gangly wolf had parked his car in front of the Den.

"I-I found th-them," Jed said, pushing his glasses up on his nose. "A-all of them."

"Great." Carson's hatred spiked. It was almost over.

"There are... c-complications," Jed stuttered.

"What?" Carson questioned impatiently, wishing the fool could just spit out what he had to say.

"There are hu-humans with them s-sir. Two."

Humans were indeed a complication, he didn't want to kill any, but he would do what he must. "Anything else?" Carson gripped the man's shirt, shoving him back against the car. "Speak damn it!"

"Lu-Luca C-Cain."

"He's dead," Carson said. Kip had assured him of this.

"No... no, sir." Jed shrunk away as he spoke. "He is the-there. Wi-with Kyle Cooper."

Luca Cain cannot be alive! This blight had to be obliterated "The Reynolds girl?" Carson asked referencing the woman he intended to bare his pups.

"Sh-she... is with th-them... sir," Jed stuttered.

Jed's words were drowned out by Carson's roar of fury. "This changes nothing." He released Jed's shirt. "Summon the pack," he commanded before walking into the Den, screen door slamming behind him.

With his jaw clenched, he tried to restrain his anger over what he had to accept. Luca was alive.

Carson could hear Jed calling each hand-picked member of the pack in turn, bringing them to their Alpha's aid. They would all be by his side soon enough.

Jules let Eileen hover close to her side as she and the werewolves discussed next steps. "I think we should let it sit for just a little while," Jules stated. She put a restraining hand on Luca's arm. It seemed he was going to violently disagree. "Not let it go, Luca. Just let it sit. Give everyone a little time."

"Let it sit?" Kyle said. "He killed a kid! He tried to kill Luca! He has to go down for this!"

"Although I'm ready to follow Jules, my coven leader and friend, to the end. I think that everyone who loved this boy should try to accept that vengeance isn't going to bring him back. Our main concern now is to stop anyone else from being unjustly slaughtered. So, we need to think before we act," Eileen said boldly.

Some faces looked at her with shock, some with pride but all seemed to know that Eileen spoke the truth.

"So, how long are you proposing we wait? Not that I'm in a rush or anything, but Carson will find us. If he hasn't already," Hayley said.

"Then we wait as long as we can," Luca answered sternly.

Kyle nodded begrudgingly, but seemed to relax a little after he'd done so.

"Can we slip away for a moment?" Luca whispered in Jules's ear.

Jules looked skeptically toward Eileen who had just entered into a conversation with Monica and Hayley.

"Yes," Jules said as soon as she was satisfied that Eileen was going to be fine on her own.

Hand-in-hand, Luca and Jules walked out to the beach behind her house. He brought their intertwined hands to his lips and kissed her's.

"Hi," she said, stopping to stand in front of him and looking up, searching his face.

"Hi." His smile was small but breathtakingly beautiful.

"So..." She put her free hand on his abdomen. "Was there something specific you wanted to talk to me about?"

He let out a long sigh and his hands came to rest on the sides of her neck. "Kyle is right," he said looking over her head instead of at her. "Carson can't live through this, Jules. Not after what he's done."

"I agree. That said, please don't go rushing in." She took a fistful of his shirt in her hand, pulling his attention down. "I won't lose you." The statement was painfully true. "I love you." Her eyes pleaded with him to be careful and think.

He nodded silently. "I love you, too." Leaning down, he lifted her by the hips. Instinctively her legs wrapped around his torso. One arm slipped under her ass while the other pulled her as close as possible. His lips met hers as her hands ran through his hair. After a minute that could have been a moment or an hour, Luca pulled back. Resting his forehead on hers he said, "we will be smart about this. I promise."

"Okay." She raised up in his hold enough to kiss him on the forehead. His head fell onto her soft breasts. He kissed her there but then grumbled. She ruffled his hair playfully.

"But I should probably find Kyle." He set her on her feet gently. "He can sometimes be a hothead, and I don't want him to do something stupid."

Jules wasn't ready to let go of this moment, but she'd left Eileen alone long enough.

Hand-in-hand, they walked back to the house. Kyle and Hayley were outside on the back porch, seemingly arguing. Or, at least having a heated discussion. Luca released Jules's hand and walked over to them. Jules passed them all and walked back into the house to check on Eileen and her human friends.

Luca walked right into the middle of a lovers' quarrel. He was still listening for the root of their issue, though he figured he could probably guess.

"Jules is right," Hayley shouted. "We have to think this through. I won't have you and Luca getting yourselves killed. What am I supposed to do if you die? Huh?"

"Oh, I don't know, live on," Kyle snapped.

"As Carson's whore…" Hayley crossed her arms angrily.

"Over my dead body!"

"That's the point!"

"Guys…" Luca began but Hayley put a hand out to respectfully halt Luca's interruption. "I won't raise this child on my own."

Both men stopped short and stared. Luca immediately felt as if he was inappropriately interrupting something, but it was too late to leave now.

"What?" Kyle asked. His eyes were wide and confused.

"I found out this morning." Hayley rested her hand on her stomach. "I wanted to tell you but there wasn't a right time." She started to laugh and cry at the same time. "We're pregnant, Kyle."

"Really!" Kyle exclaimed excitedly.

She nodded through happy tears.

Kyle scooped her up in his arms and spun them both. He kissed her, and she giggled. Luca was still frozen, watching the scene. *How can so much good be happening along with so much bad?* Despite all the pain, all the hate he was currently harboring, Luca started to laugh as well.

"I'm going to be a father." Kyle chuckled, glowing at Hayley. "I'm going to be a father," he said again looking over at Luca. He released Hayley and Luca hugged her.

"Do you really want to let some poor kid have this as a dad?" Luca joked at Kyle's expense while hugging him as well.

"I've been wondering about that," Hayley said, tapping her chin.

"Ha Ha. Sure, you have," Kyle said sarcastically and then kissed her on the hair.

"This kid will have one hell of a god-father though," she said, her gaze soft, and looking at Luca.

"What?" Luca looked from one of them to the other.

"Damn straight he will!" Kyle pulled Luca into a hug.

"Or she," Hayley said and smacked her husband.

"Or she," Kyle agreed, turning back to focus solely on the glowing Hayley.

Luca bowed out gracefully, to let them have the rest of this precious moment alone.

Jules walked out the front door with Eileen and looked toward Gabriel's car. Eileen said he was there, but the car windows were tinted so darkly that she couldn't see anyone inside. She watched as Eileen walked around the vehicle, opened the driver door, and joined him there. Jules did not follow. Instead, she stopped when she saw her brother laying across the front of her car with his hands under his head. She tapped his knee, and he sat up.

"Hey, it's me in girl form."

"Only in looks."

"True. I've always been the fun one," he joked and slid off the car.

She rolled her eyes but stared at his smiling face. She couldn't get enough of his familiar features, all of which had been fading for centuries, even though she'd fought with everything she had to remember every detail. Now that he was standing in front of her, though, she had noticed that he looked a little different than she remembered, but she was sure she did as well. *Death will do that to you,* she imagined him joking. She chuckled at herself.

"What?" he asked, watching her with the same intense gaze.

"Nothing." She smiled. "Just you."

"I know, I'm still amazing, but which of my wonderful traits has you smiling?" he asked.

Jules ignored Nick's call for compliments and answered honestly. "Actually, I was scrutinizing the changes I see in you."

"And what did you find?" he asked, crossing his arms.

Jules leaned against the car next to him. "I don't remember you being this tall," she said, noting that he towered over her.

"To you, little one, everyone is tall." He reached over and measured the height difference between them.

She elbowed him.

"Still height sensitive. Got it." Nick said. "So... to blatantly change the subject, how did you meet Luca exactly? More specifically, how did you get tangled up in a werewolf war and then fall in love with one? Or was it the other way around?" Nick said.

"It was option B," Jules replied. "Luca and I met on a blind date actually. After that, we were just kind of drawn together.

It happened so fast, but seems like it has always been this way. Loving each other just came naturally. He's the first person I've loved since…" but her voice trailed off. Hector was the last thing she wanted to be thinking about right now.

An astonished look appeared on Nick's face.

"What?" she asked.

"Since when? You were human? Are you implying that you haven't been in love in over four hundred years? That's so sad. I love falling in love!"

"No, that's not the since I was referencing." Jules laughed out loud. "But, do you remember your friend Laurence, he was my betrothed after you disappeared."

Nick laughed out loud. "Boring old Laurence…" Jules felt there was something Nick wasn't saying, but she didn't push.

"I turned into a vampire and he joined the priesthood." Jules said. "He didn't take it in stride, that's for sure."

"I'm sure he got what was coming to him," Nick said vaguely. "Albeit a couple decades late."

"Maybe," Jules said with a sigh.

"But that's just the prologue," Nick stated. "There has to be more epic love to tell me about."

There was another, but Jules wouldn't speak on her next and last romantic relationship, before Luca "What about you? Mister 'I love to fall in love'. Has there been anyone significant in your existence?"

"No…" Nick said too quickly. "I mean…no. We'll go with no."

Jules looked at him like she very much doubted the authenticity of this answer. "Liar."

"Undoubtedly." The twins laughed lightly. Each determined to keep their secrets.

Nick's return had made Jules feel lighter than she had in centuries, despite all of the bad happening around her. And yet, this being, her brother, was still a killer. How could someone who felt things so deeply, because Nick did, even if he didn't admit it, be the Fort Miles Phantom?

"What has your face all squished like that? What do you want to know?" Nick asked.

Jules chewed on her lip nervously. She didn't want to spoil the moment. "Why do you still kill like you do? Human life deserves to be protected, no matter the personal cost."

"Not you too!" He rolled his eyes, let go of her shoulder, and slumped back onto her car.

"Me and who, exactly?" she asked leaning over him.

He sighed. "Never mind. It's just an old fight I seem to have every fifty or so years."

"Nicholas. What are you…"

He cut her off. "It doesn't matter right now. I've already agreed to battle my nature and lay off the killing to stay with you. Can't that be enough for now? Will I slip up? Probably. But I feel like I have part of myself back… with you here. I felt it from the first moment I saw you. I don't want to lose you over this."

He seemed to be having a conversation with himself that she wasn't privy too. "Nick, I just found you. I'm not going anywhere. But you have to understand, I don't live like that. I can't."

He raised his eyebrows at her.

"I mean, I literally can't," she said exasperatedly.

"You're an addict too!" He smiled.

"A recovering one," she admitted. "And I won't go back, do you hear me? I love you Nicholas, but I won't be that again."

Nick placed his hand over her mouth, silencing her. "Okay. I hear you." He looked her straight in the eyes. "I'll work on it. Okay?"

She nodded.

He moved his fingers just as the front door opened and Luca walked outside.

"Hayley has something she wants to tell you," he said as he walked over to them and wrapped Jules in his arms. He placed a kiss on her forehead. Jules was surprised to see him looking rather happy.

"Okay, let's go." Jules laughed lightly, as she and Luca began to walk toward the house. But then she stopped, walked out of Luca's embrace, and grabbed Nick by the hand, pulling him with her.

Luca led the way through the house and out the back door where the rest of the group was chattering excitedly.

Eileen must have managed to convince Gabriel to join the rest of them because the two of them approached the commotion seconds later. Gabriel looked awkward and nervous, but his presence was a step in the right direction.

"Hello Mr. Prentiss," Hayley greeted.

Gabriel's eyes widened.

"Hayley Reynolds," he said stiffly, "you are part of this?"

She nodded. "Wait," Eileen said. "You took my husband's English class, didn't you?" Eileen asked with a smile.

"We all did," Tai interjected.

"Duh, he is the best teacher at Aboit High," Monica said with a smile.

Jules walked over to Gabriel, while Eileen chatted easily with Monica and Hayley. She crooked her arms around his and whispered in his ear, "I'm really glad you're here."

Gabriel shrugged, and half smiled. "I'm here for you."

"I know."

"Okay, okay, everyone listen up!" Kyle waved his hands and the chatter faded, leaving silence in its wake.

He seems happy. Jules wondered what could have possibly happened to make Kyle forget how angry he was at Carson.

"My wife has an announcement." Kyle motioned to Hayley.

Jules's confusion grew. Kyle was glowing and fidgeting with excitement.

"Hayley and I have a surprise," he said while bouncing on his heels. "Honey, you should tell them."

Hayley rolled her eyes but smiled and joined him, taking his hand in her own. "I didn't want to say anything now, but…" She paused, and Kyle squeezed her fingers. "We're going to have a baby!"

Monica squealed, Luca gave Kyle a high-five, and Jules ran to give Hayley a hug. "Congratulations."

Gabriel did not join in but stayed rooted in his spot. At first, Nick hung back as well, as if he wasn't sure if he should be involved or not, but he was soon drawn into the quiet revelry. "I don't know you but congrats," Nick said, shaking Kyle's hand. Laughing, Luca reached out to him and clapped him on the back. Gabriel even cracked a smile.

"There's more," Hayley said, her arms still wrapped around Jules. She looked over at Kyle, who nodded. "Kyle and I talked about it and Jules, would you be our baby's godmother?"

"Me?" she asked, stunned.

"Luca is the god-pops. So yeah, you," Kyle said, resting his elbow on Jules's shoulder.

"Yes, you." Hayley took Jules's hands in her own. "I've never met a stronger woman. And I trust that should you agree, our child will never be unprotected or unloved."

Jules was on the verge of tears, again.

"Jules?" Kyle asked.

"Of course I will," she said, hugging Hayley again. For a brief moment the companions had a reason to feel true joy, even if it was fleeting.

CHAPTER TWENTY-FOUR

Battle for Immortal Lives

Carson paced irritably in front of his hand-picked group of soldiers and sacrificial lambs. All of them had promptly heeded the summons, including Joe Reynolds and his eldest son. Carson fought to keep his emotions under control. Each of them looked nervous, as if they weren't sure they wanted to be there. Nonetheless, each was there, faithful to the one who ruled and provided for them.

Carson stood, cleared his throat, and addressed his subordinates. "We've found them. It's time to eliminate this threat and anarchy once and for all."

Some of their eyes brightened. Some of them shifted uncomfortably.

"Jed, what are we up against?" he asked.

"Va-ampires and we-were…" Jed began to reply.

Carson's eyes shut aggravated. He stretched his tense neck. "How many are there?" he asked through gritted teeth.

"Um…well…t-two humans, th-three traitors, and four of… of them." He meant the vampires.

"Four?" Carson questioned, his eyes opening to look at the tracker.

"Yes, th-there was ah-a fourth," he stammered and cowered.

"Fine. At least we know going into this." Carson started to calculate a strategy.

"Who are the traitors?" Ben asked.

"Luca Cain, Kyle Cooper, and Hayley Reynolds-Cooper," Carson said, staring down her family, daring them to object to his ruling of her traitor status.

More than one wolf looked at them, some with what might have been pity.

Joe Reynolds dropped his eyes, defeated, while his son looked like he wanted to speak against Carson's words. Carson silenced him with a look laced with his Alpha given authority. "However, due to her family's show of loyalty. I have decided to pardon Mrs. Cooper. She will be spared."

Her father breathed a sigh of relief, but her brother narrowed his eyes at his Alpha. He could be a problem, Carson noted to himself.

"Reynolds." He held an ultraviolet B light out to the man. "You and your son..." He blanked on the boy's name as he looked at them both.

"Adam," the boy said, taking the light in place of his father.

"You will dispose of the male vampire."

"Th-he new..."

Carson growled at Jed for interrupting.

"T-two males," Jed said, cowering.

"The blond male," Carson clarified.

They both nodded at him.

He put a firm hand on Joe Reynold's shoulder. "You have no need to go up against your daughter, leave that to another."

Adam scowled but Joe nodded. He didn't know if Joe and his son could take down the vampire but if they died in the attempt, it was no great loss.

Carson turned his attention toward another. "Max, you will handle the young female vampire," Carson instructed, handing Max a light as well. "Kip, help him out."

Kip nodded while Max bounced on his heels excitedly.

"And Ben," he held out another light.

"You will finish off whoever this new one is."

Ben took the order and the light submissively. Carson didn't know anything about this new vampire. Ben had the likeliest chance of defeating him. Besides, if he did lose, his loyalty had been shaky since Carson's sentencing and execution of the boy.

"And I will defeat the last vampire," Carson announced. "None of you will interfere. That red-headed-demon is mine," he growled. It would be a pleasure to bring her existence to its final and irrevocable end.

Two of the younger wolves were instructed to take care of the humans, while the rest were assigned to handle the rogue wolves and help against the vampires.

Carson turned toward the screech of the screen door. With a nod he greeted the newcomer. Dressed in tactical gear, the man leaned against the wall, resting the butt of a long range rifle on the toe of his combat boot.

"Wolves," he addressed the gathered pack members, "majestic ones, it is time for this threat to be eliminated. Once and for all."

Cheers and shouting erupted.

"It is time for the law of the pack to be upheld. The traitors who have thrown away the pride of their pack must answer for their betrayal. And Aboit must be freed from this vampire plague!"

More cheers rose into the air. Several of the followers threw hats and fists upward.

"Wolves, dawn approaches. The plan is set," he said. Of course, he hoped it would be a bright, sunny day. Making the vampire's demise easier. But, according to the weather report, this was unlikely. "Who's with me?" He rallied them. "Who's with me?" he said again. "Let's move!"

He stopped in front of the last man who'd entered the Den. "You ride with me. We have targets to discuss." Clapping the man on the shoulder, he stomped toward the front door. Ripping the screen off the hinges, he led the war party down a back street and toward the traitors, the demons, and their retribution.

Jules heard Gabriel calling her name. His voice was coming from down the beach where he and Eileen had left to walk earlier. She sat up from where she lay on Luca's chest in the sand. Everyone had been taking a moment to enjoy the calm before the storm. She could just barely see the two figures running towards them. Luca, who had fallen asleep, stirred in the sand beneath her. Jules could tell the sun was rising, but it was a blessedly overcast day. It even looked like it might be about to rain.

"What's going on?" Luca mumbled as she stood to her feet.

"Gabriel! Eileen!" she called as she spotted the two vampires running toward her.

Nick appeared by her side almost instantly, she didn't know where he'd come from specifically, but was again thankful he was here.

"The werewolves are coming. They are almost here," Gabriel said calmly while still at a great distance.

"And it doesn't look like they are open to negotiations," Eileen added.

Nick took a running jump, shooting off the sand to perch on the roof of her house.

"What do you see?" she asked him.

"The ocean," he said with a devilish grin.

She rolled her eyes and looked up at the roof. It would not be hard to make that jump. She took three steps back and shot into the air herself. Then, landing on the roof in a crouch, she spun to face the direction her brother was looking. With vampire sight, she saw what she was looking for. "There!" she said, pointing off in the direction of the rock caves. "I can see them. There is a large group moving toward us," she called down to Luca.

Jules jumped from her perch, landed silently in a crouch, and stood beside Luca, who was now wide awake. She turned to Gabriel. "We need you."

"Jules, I..."

"Please, Gabriel. There are too many of them, I'm not sure we can win this fight without you."

"I'm with you either way." Eileen took a step away from her

husband, chin held high.

Gabriel looked at his wife like he might be seeing her for the first time. She would stay without him. His jaw twitched, he turned to Jules, then nodded. She nodded back. "Let's go." Jules spun and led the way back inside. Luca, Gabriel, Eileen, and Nick trailed her.

"Tai!" Jules shouted.

He meandered out of the bedroom. "What is it?" he asked, his eyes droopy and his hair rumpled.

"Take Monica and get out of here!"

"Wait, what's going on?" Monica protested, appearing next to her boyfriend.

"They're coming. You need to leave," Jules said sternly. Risking Monica or Tai's human lives for this fight was not an option.

"I'm not going anywhere!" Monica stamped her foot and stormed over to where Jules stood by the back door.

"Yes, you are," Jules said, hugging her.

"Tai." Jules handed Monica off to him. "Make sure she stays away."

He nodded in compliance. Monica protested harder and started to cry.

"You have to go." Jules stretched up and kissed her friend on the forehead. "Be safe."

"You guys too," Tai said as he began to drag Monica toward the door.

"Now, what's the plan?" asked Kyle.

"Maybe we should leave, too," Hayley suggested

"Run and you can never come back. None of you could," Gabriel said.

"No. This ends here," Luca said.

Jules watched as Luca nodded at Gabriel and he nodded back.

"We fight," Gabriel stated, and Jules knew without a doubt that he was with them now.

For just a moment, no one did or said anything. Jules felt

love for everyone in the room. She looked at each of her new and old friends, feeling responsible for the lives of each and every one.

"Don't worry about us," Hayley said, walking over to Jules.

"You should leave," Kyle said to his wife. "The baby."

"I'm not going anywhere." She turned to her husband. "You know I'm not leaving you."

"If I fall," Kyle placed his hands on either side of her arms. "You run. Don't look back. He will not have you. Or our child."

Hayley kissed him. "That, I'll do."

"If we are going to do this, it has to happen here. Right now, the pack is still crossing the private beach fronts. The families that own those houses are rarely here. And definitely not at this time of year. We need to go out and meet them. We shouldn't draw unwanted attention if we can keep the fight down on the beach. The last thing I want is my neighbors seeing and police getting involved, or worse, killed."

"Jules is right, we should go now," Luca said.

"In a moment." Gabriel took Eileen's hand and led her into the kitchen. "Jules," he called her after him.

"Nick," she called over her shoulder and he followed them as well.

Gabriel opened her refrigerator where he must have stashed more blood.

"This is the last of it," he said, as Eileen pulled glasses down from the cupboard. He handed each vampire a bag of blood and Eileen handed each one a glass.

Nick stared at it. "But it's cold." He grimaced.

"Just drink it," Eileen commanded.

He shrugged, pulled a mug from the sparse cupboards, dumped the blood in, and put it in the microwave.

Jules took a deep breath, drank, and felt the red liquid course through her like instant strength. She stood in bliss for a few long seconds until Luca's voice called her back to her senses. Her eyes opened, and his widened. Instinctively, her eyelids slammed shut over her red eyes.

"Sorry, I..." She hadn't ever wanted him to see her in her most demon-like form, revealing the monster inside.

"Jules," he soothed, lifting her chin. "I love every part of you," he assured, reaching a finger to touch beside her eye. "Even this."

Jules reopened her red eyes. She let out a long sigh and closed them again as he kissed her.

Nick faked a cough and cleared his throat. This made Jules roll her eyes as she pulled back from Luca.

"We have a battle to win," Luca said, looking down at her.

"I need one more thing first." Jules walked to her bedroom and up to her closet, looking up forlornly at the long and slender box on the top shelf. Scowling, she turned to Luca. "Reach that blue box for me." Laughing, he complied.

Taking it from his hands and setting it on the bed she gingerly lifted the lid. Nestled in fine velvet sat two matching fighting knives. The steel blades gleamed up at her. She knew these weapons. She had trained with them until they felt like extensions of her own hands. Picking up one intricately designed handle she slid her finger along the blade, making a small slice. Lifting the cut to her mouth, she licked it clean of blood.

"You're a little scary sometimes," Luca commented staring down at her.

A wide smile crossed her face, all light and joy once more. "I know." The holster hadn't fared as well as the blades themselves, but she strapped it on anyway.

Once they had rejoined their companions in the living room, everyone moved toward the back door. The battle for their immortal lives was about to begin.

Kyle walked down the beach next to his family and friends. The heavens opened. Rain began to pour down, drenching them all. Anticipation and adrenaline made Kyle shift back and forth on his feet as he watched their adversaries

BANE OF HATE AND SILVER

approaching quickly.

Leading the charge was what was left of the Den members. Ben, Kip and Max, were flanking Carson. Twenty or so more wolves followed behind, some he knew and some he didn't, but he recognized all of them.

On one edge of the group, Kyle spied his father-in-law and brother-in-law. Adam was carrying one of the lights Carson had used to torture Jules in the library, not yet flicked on. He snarled in distaste.

Kyle glanced past Jules, who had come to a stop next to him, to where Hayley was positioned. She growled, her shoulders hunching over angrily. Obviously, having spotted her family as well. Participating in this fight must be part of the actions Carson was requiring so the Reynolds family could prove their loyalty to their Alpha. Apparently, in addition to delivering their eldest, already married, daughter to him as a mate. Hatred toward Carson trickled through Kyle and he growled as well, taking a step forward.

"Kyle hold your ground," Jules whispered, reaching her hand out toward him, though the distance was too great for her to actually restrain him.

He glanced at her to his right and Eileen to his left. The group stood stretched across the beach in a line, alternating vampire and werewolf. Gabriel had suggested this order. He figured they would have the best chance at staying alive if they helped each other through the battle.

Carson brought his army to a halt. Kyle nursed a glimmer of hope that he would consider negotiating, and there would be no battle. However, before this could even be suggested, Carson howled the order and the pack began to charge toward them, closing the gap quickly.

Kyle ran at his soon-to-be-attackers. He tried not to register who exactly they were. In his purview, he saw the flash of light as Hayley became the majestic white wolf. She charged the wolves in front of her. Some four-legged, some still running on human legs. Eileen and Jules sped out from either side of him.

He picked up the pace, running faster than he ever had before into the fray.

Kyle let his teeth and claws extend but didn't turn fully yet. He growled and punched a wolf-shaped nose jumping up at him in the furry face.

Gabriel balked as his former student shouted, "Dad, catch!" Adam Reynolds tossed an illuminated, manufactured, sunlight bulb past Gabriel's shoulder. He spun just as the light was jammed into his neck. The manufactured sunlight searing through him like the fire of the sun. Rage built inside him. Hatred for this species. For these beasts that were barely better than animals. Lashing out with a swift kick, the man fell to the sand with a thud. Gabriel turned on him, about to lunge for the kill when he heard a crunching sound and then a yelp. Stunned, he turned to see Hayley, who had bitten down on the lighted weapon, rendering it useless. The werewolf child that sat in his classroom not three years ago. A soon to be mother. A good person.

"Hayley are you okay?" Adam asked her as he ran to his little sister's side. This was wrong. It was all wrong. Adam had taken Gabriel's class half a decade ago. He couldn't be more than twenty-four or twenty-five years old, and he was always a good kid. A little surly and serious, but Gabriel remembered him as a good student with genuine character. As was Hayley and the rest of the Reynolds kids. This fight did not seem like something the boy he remembered would choose to be a part of. Unless he was only acting due to the orders of the Alpha. Gabriel's head cocked to the side in contemplation.

However, in the moment of distraction, the Reynolds father had gotten to his feet. Gabriel was hit hard in the gut. Rather than fall, he spun; lifting the werewolf off the ground as he went. His fangs extended, preparing to pull him in for a bite to the neck.

"Mr. Prentiss don't!" both Hayley and Adam shouted

together.

Gabriel's attention moved to Hayley, now in human form, kneeling on the sand beside her brother. He thought of Landon, in his class last year. And Amy whom he taught now.

"He's our father, please," Hayley begged.

He looked up to where the werewolf man dangled off his feet, his throat gripped in Gabriel's outstretched hand. This was war. He knew, better than many, that war meant death and sacrifice. One wolf dead would help even the battlefield.

"Please." Hayley's plea was barely a whisper. The expectant mother's eyes were wide and tearful.

After another moment, Gabriel threw the man down on the sand. "Take your father and go," Gabriel instructed Adam. "If you stay here, I will be forced to kill you both."

"Dad, get up," Hayley said, as she ran to their father's side.

"Carson's orders are for us to take on the blond, male vampire. Apparently, that's you," Adam told him. "We won't be able to resist a direct order very long."

Gabriel said nothing but nodded and placed an encouraging hand on the boy's shoulder. He flinched but didn't pull away. Just then, their father lunged at him. Both of his children grabbed him by the arms, holding him back.

"Fight it as long as you can," Hayley told them. "We may have a new Alpha soon."

"That's treason to speak of," her father grunted. It seemed as though he might be in pain.

"If fighting for what is right is treason, then I am a traitor." Breathing heavily, Hayley helped her brother drag their father away.

"You've been pardoned," the father reasoned.

"To be breeding stock to a monster. I'd rather die a traitor," Hayley said evenly, as she and her brother struggled to drag their father to the edge of the fray.

"Since when is our English teacher a vampire?" Adam asked his sister almost conversationally.

"Pretty sure the whole time," Hayley replied.

"So, vampires are not all bad then. I mean, for a teacher, Mr. Prentiss is alright," Adam said like he was trying to work something out in his mind.

Gabriel almost smiled at this but then he saw it. A wolf collided with the young werewolves. Knocking them both off their feet. Gabriel ran at them and threw the wolf-shaped werewolf at full strength. It landed back into the middle of the battle.

"Adam, get your family away from here," Gabriel shouted.

"Hayley come on!" Adam continued to fight his father. It looked as though it was taking all his strength to do it. Gabriel knew that they would be forced to try and kill him again soon, but he certainly hoped they could hold out. Though the father's resolve seemed faulty at best.

"Thank you Mr..." Hayley let out a cry as she was flung down onto the sand. Gabriel had pushed her out of the way, kicking a wolf who had charged her in the shoulder.

Hayley stood, shook herself off. "Go help your brother," Gabriel nodded toward Adam, who'd lost control of their father. Hayley nodded to Gabriel, turned and ran across the battle as a white wolf once more. Gabriel noticed that she was, in fact, stunning in wolf form.

"Gabriel look out!" Gabriel spun at Jules's shout. A wolf in human form charged forward. The gangly wolf was easily thrown backward when Gabriel kicked him. He sputtered and charged again. This time, changing into a wolf along the way. Anticipating the flash of light, Gabriel covered his eyes and took the wolf's impact square in the chest. The two fell backward but Gabriel was too strong for his opponent. With a threatening hiss, he lifted the animal up and tossed him so hard that he hit a rock cliff and landed on the sand with a thud.

Gabriel spun, ready to take on the next challenger. To his horror, he saw Eileen across the beach, cowering. A light was laying along her neck like the blade of a deadly knife. He knocked over a few charging wolves in his attempt to get to her. Leaving his assigned post, meant Jules and Hayley were exposed. This formation was his idea, but he couldn't leave Eileen to die. Before he could reach her, however, he saw Kyle shove the man off Eileen, pulling the light out of his grasp as they fell, the light landing feet from them both.

Luca, in wolf form, took the light in his mouth and bit down. The bulb shattered and flickered. Luca shook blood and glass out of his mouth.

Gabriel was knocked sideways again, and again he moved to overpower the attacker.

Carson leaned nonchalantly against a rock cliff on the edge of the fighting ground. Scowling he was forced to move aside when one of his chosen came flying at him in wolf form. He peered down at the injured wolf, or maybe it was already dead. He didn't bother to check. Instead, he zeroed in on the one he intended to take for his own. The white wolf looked radiant in her fur. She would make him strong and handsome pups. Carson began to move onto the field toward her. Carnage rained around him. Bodies dropping right and left. He saw none of it.

Kneeling, the Reynolds girl turned back into her human form as her subjugate father dropped to his knees in a bow. Reaching out Carson grabbed the back of her hair and lifted her to standing. Sniffing deeply, he ran his nose up the side of her neck and face. "Alpha, please have mercy on my daughter," Joe Reynolds begged pathetically. Her brother, on the other hand, tensed into a fighting stance.

"Turning traitor, pup?" Carson asked him. Intentions of the consequences of that action flooded the boy's mind.

"No, Alpha." His knees hit the sand next to his father's.

Growling possessively, hot air bounced off her soft cheek as he pulled her back against him. He relished in her toned curves.

"Let me go." Her voice was strong, all the more fun to break. He could command her of course but where was the fun in that?

Sliding a hand up her body, grazing her left breast, Carson's palm came to rest over the rare wolf's tanned throat. "What a queen you will make." His cock strained in his jeans at the thought and the feeling of her ass against his body.

"I will never be your queen." In the same moment she spoke, her claws extended out of her fingers and sliced into Carson's hand.

"Hayley!" Her traitor husband shouted, still at a great distance.

Releasing her with a shock of pain, he spun her and back handed her across the face. Hitting the sand hard, she covered her stomach with her palm. Most woman protected their face, except when they were with child. She was carrying a bastard offspring. He moved into kick her right over her abdomen when her brother dived in front of her, taking the kick for her and falling to the sand in a heap.

"Alpha!"

Carson stiffened at the sound of the voice who had called to him. It was a voice smooth as warm honey with the confidence of a roaring fire.

"I thought it was me you came to kill?"

Slowly, Carson spun toward the voice taunting him. The small frame that haunted his nightmares. The ancient eyes that tortured him blazed with disdain.

"Jules, don't!" The white wolf shouted. Her father shushed her, pleading with her to be quiet.

Carson pleaded with no one. The white wolf had obviously grown up in a family who neglected to teach their children to respect their betters. Once this was done, it was decided that her father would be the one to pay for her crimes. Maybe his execution for her treason would break her enough to get her in line.

Carson leaned down so that his face was close to his future bedmate's. "You will learn your place, Bitch," he said as he took a firm hold of her chin. Carson forced her eyes to meet his and let just a little of his Alpha's command force its way into her. Not enough to ruin the fun, just a promise of what was to come. Her eyes fell and he released her.

He turned his head to face his next obstacle. "After I dispose of the demon," he said as he stood to face his challenger.

Jules stood her ground as the Alpha approached. Happy to have successfully diverted his attention from Hayley and her future godchild. Circling he shouted to those nearby to stay back. One on one it was then. Spinning her daggers in both of her hands, she took a fighting stance. Feet equidistant for balance. Knees bent ever so slightly. "Come on then," she taunted.

Snarling, he mirrored her, leaving the knife at his side sheathed. The two predators began to circle each other. Sand shifting under their feet. Lethal claws extending from his fingers. "You first Bitch."

"Gladly." Jules lunged. Slashing her blades through the air with expert ease. He dodged, but she managed to slice into one beefy arm. He growled at the pain as she spun, lashing out at him again. This time slicing each side of his face. Blood dripped from the wounds, coloring his cheeks in red. "Sorry, not sorry." She said shrugging and rolling the blades over her hands once more, switching up her hold. His eyes ignited wolf yellow with hatred.

While Carson turned from evil man to monstrous beast, Jules was forced to close her eyes from the flash of light. She went down hard when the wolf form of the Alpha pounced, losing grip on one of her knives. The other swiftly cut a chunk of fuzzy ear from Caron's furry head. He bared his teeth down at her, dripping drool onto her face. One big paw pushed down on her shoulder, digging deep with thick claws. She stabbed her remaining knife into his paw and he reared back. Another flash and she was being straddled by thighs the size of tree trunks, her arm with the knife pinned. A meaty fist connected with her face. Carson raised his chin to howl in premature victory. Jules's loose hand searched the sand behind her, fingers brushing a familiar hilt.

With a loud yell she brought the knife forward, sinking it deep into one thigh. A sound of pure rage escaped him as she took the moment to turn the tide, freeing herself from his hold. Rolling herself up and moving behind him she placed one knife against his neck, the other positioned over his heart.

"You really don't want to do that little menace," Carson crooned.

"Yes, I really do!" She snarled back. "There is no mercy for killers of children."

"I kill traitors." Carson nodded toward the house next door.

She followed his line of sight to a lone wolf, perched on the rooftop. Rifle clearly lining up to take aim.

"Release me and drop your weapons or your lover dies."

Jules glanced at the barrel's aim, following it right to Luca's head, while he fought his own fight, oblivious to the imminent threat. Reluctantly Jules stood and moved away from the Alpha. "Gabriel," she called, her tone barely audible. His eyes locked with hers almost immediately. With an almost imperceptible flick of her eyes, she pointed out the shooter to him. With a minute nod, he disappeared in a blur.

Carson lumbered to his feet, favoring his injured leg. "Carson," someone shouted, tossing a death light that the Alpha caught with ease.

"Drop them," he demanded of her own weapons. "Three..."

Jules glanced at Luca.

"Two..." He flicked on the lightbulb.

With great effort she released her favored weapons, letting them fall to the sand at her sides.

Luca heard a yelp from behind him, he knew someone was dead by Nick or Eileen's hand, but he didn't have time to register who. Taking advantage of Luca's distraction, a wolf's nose and ears barreled into his ribs. Luca rolled out from under the impact and turned with a growl as he bit down. He felt fur and blood in his mouth and heard a yelp from Kip. Luca had successfully put a gash across his pretty muzzle. The two clashed again, a flurry of bared teeth and sharp claws. As he fought, he couldn't help but feel it was payback for running him off the road.

Luca bit down again and Kip stumbled backward. He took the moment to return to his human form. Kip's blood splattered the sand as Luca spit it from his mouth.

Kip growled.

"Back off," Luca barked at him.

Kip became human as well, trembling, bleeding, but still without the look of hate in his eyes. "I'm under orders," Kip fought to say.

"Carson ordered you to kill me?" Luca circled him.

"Days ago," Kip said, panting. "I, personally, have nothing against you or your hot little girlfriend. I really couldn't care less who you're banging. But you know I don't have a choice."

Luca growled audibly. Carson turned friend against friend and cared for no one but himself. He was not a true Alpha, but a power drunk maniac.

Luca stopped, breathed deep, centered himself, and gathered what power he carried inside him by his lineage and position in the pack. He felt it from his fingers to his chest, drawing on the will power of all the wolves around him. Condemned traitor or not, he still held the power of the Beta and of the Cain line. Letting out a slow breath, he searched for the hold Carson's order had in Kip. The roots were deep. He could not erase it, but maybe he could manipulate it. "You may carry out your orders after the battle has reached its conclusion. Your Alpha needs you elsewhere."

Kip stood up a little straighter, squaring his shoulders as some of the burden of the order lifted. He nodded at Luca, who nodded back.

Of course, Luca was banking on the fact that they would win. But for the time being, it had worked. Kip was free from the order's hold over him enough to subdue it.

Luca turned from Kip who limped away from the fight but did not leave. Instead, he plopped himself down on the sidelines, so he could watch how it all turned out. Luca rolled his eyes.

Luca kicked a charging wolf, unwilling to be taken by surprise again. The impact was enough to throw him backward. He flew into Nick, who had been holding his hands over his eyes and crushing a light under his boot. The two of them laughed lightly and helped each other up.

Nick turned to finish off a bleeding Ben, but Luca put a restraining hand on his shoulder. Ben had looked out for him when he'd first joined the pack. Luca looked down at him and saw that he seemed to be silently begging for his life.

"Leave that one alive," he told Nick.

"Pick and choose much," Nick said but smiled, shrugged, and turned away from the wolf lying helplessly at his feet. Ben tipped his head at Luca and flopped onto the sand with a sigh.

Luca's heartbeat lurched when he heard the scream that haunted his nightmares. Jules in pain. While he'd been distracted, it seemed that the tables had turned. Carson had a fist full of red hair while the other hand pressed an illuminated lightbulb to one of Jules's cheeks, blood and blisters were beginning to form around it.

Jules was on fire. At least, it felt like she was burning from the inside out, starting with her scolding cheek. Since her blades hit sand, she'd refused to fight. Glancing up at the shooter every time the desperation to lash out overtook her. Her eyes fluttered as her consciousness waned. "Jules!" Hayley shouted from across the sand. A blood tear dripped from her eye as she watched Hayley try to shake her brother and father off to run to her aid. "Who knew a demon could love?" Carson asked. "And, that it would be her undoing."

"You're the foulest of beasts," Jules spat back. Another glance toward the roof. Her breaths came a little faster as Gabriel engaged the shooter. Locking into hand-to-hand combat.

"You are nothing," Carson said. His tone calm, too calm. He handed the light back to the wolf hovering nearby. Every muscle tensed as he pulled his arm back and then swung forward, swiping wolf nails across her face, leaving deep slashes. Blood splattered as her body spun. She would have fallen if he hadn't grabbed a hold of her wrist. Twisting her arm, he snapped bone. Jules couldn't hold back the cry.

Her eyes blanked, retreating to a place she'd long since left behind. Pain was nothing. She knew pain intimately. He continued to beat and tear at her. She felt nothing.

Turning her face to the side she checked the roof again. Gabriel pulled his fangs free of the wolf's throat. The wolf was dead before the body hit the sand. "Jules!" Gabriel yelled, blood dripping down his chin. "Fight back!"

A new momentum washed over her and she retaliated with her good arm. Aiming for his right eye, her fingers dug into his soft flesh. He snarled trying to shake her off, but she doubled her efforts until she freed the eye from its socket with a wet pop. Kicking out at him she rolled. Standing, she tossed the blood drenched little body part at him, hitting him in the face with his own dislodged eyeball. "Who's nothing now?"

The rage in him built with every ragged breath. Jules turned, content to leave him stewing in his own misery when she felt a searing pain shoot through her back. The light laying flush against it. Stunned, momentarily, her body refused to listen to her mind's command to run.

"Give me that," Carson commanded. "No one touches her."

Carson's hand fisted in her hair. The light now pressed directly against her forehead.

Luca spun toward her when another crying hiss erupted from Jules's throat. Carson had placed an ultraviolet B light directly in the middle of her forehead. Kyle broke away from his tussle, yanking the light from Carson's hand as Gabriel, appearing practically out of nowhere, barreled into the Alpha, knocking him to the sand.

Kyle crushed the light under his bare foot.

Before Gabriel could go in for the kill, a wolf jammed a large, wooden, stake through his back.

Gabriel fell, sputtering.

Eileen screamed.

"Well, that's not very original," Luca heard Nick say from behind him as he ran with Eileen to help their fallen comrade. From the side of his vision, Luca saw Nick yank the stake free. Gabriel would live.

Jules, however, might not. Luca was almost to her when he was hit from behind. Two wolves landed on top of him, pinning him to the ground. Helplessly, he watched as werewolves of all sizes and ages gathered around the spectacle of Carson and Jules, cutting off her escape.

Hayley was kneeling on the sand, her shoulder bleeding while her brother shielded her from more attacks. Kyle had been seized by some pack members. Nick had a long gash on his face, hands up in surrender as Eileen had a death light pointed to her chest. Gabriel lay at their feet barely moving.

To Luca's great relief, Kyle broke free. He was almost on Carson when the Alpha spun and spoke to him.

With a lurch and a cry of pain, Kyle dropped to his knees on the sand. Hayley screamed, attempting to run to him, but was grabbed around the middle by her brother. She thrashed against him as Kyle bent to Carson's will. Twitching and shouting as he tried to resist the order not to interfere. Luca's heart sank as wolves moved in to restrain Kyle and Carson's full attention was again on Jules.

Jules's escape route was completely blocked. Her spin back was slow and unsteady. She had been severely weakened by the light's effects. There was no choice but to face Carson alone and not at full strength. A wolf near the inside of the gathering circle lashed out. With sharp claws on a human hand, she dragged her nails across Jules's back. Out of surprise and pain, Jules lurched forward, losing her footing.

"Touch her again and you die. She's mine!" Carson growled. As Jules returned to standing. Rain beat down on her, red hair dripping. Eyes blazing with fury. Carson moved the same moment Jules did. In horror Luca watched as a silver blade sunk deep into her stomach. Jules gasped. Carson lunged, grabbing Jules by the hair and forcing her face up to look at him. He was taunting her, but her eyes searched the crowd for something, someone. Their eyes locked. "I..." she began to speak but twitched as the blade was twisted inside her abdomen. Then stumbled back as it was pulled from her flesh. Seconds later, Luca saw Carson's arm swing forward and he stabbed her again.

With a great heave, Luca freed himself from his captors. Slipping on the sand he ran toward them. Someone bit down on his leg while another couple converged on him.

"Jules!" Luca yelled.

A glimmer of hope hit Luca as he saw Nick break the light threatening Eileen and lunge towards Jules. If he couldn't save her, maybe her twin could. Nick only made it about a half dozen feet before wolves converged on him. It took six wolves to take him down to the sand. Luca's hope evaporated when Nick was successfully restrained.

He watched in horror as Carson grabbed the disoriented Jules by the neck and threw her on the sand below. Luca lashed out at the attacking wolves as he tried once again to reach her. He had to save her. His future was nothing without her.

Carson looked over at him and sneered as he brought his blood spattered boot down on the side of Jules's head.

Jules clutched her bloody abdomen and took the impact of Carson's boot on the side of the head. Her skull cracked under the pressure. Involuntary shivers wracked her body, but she wasn't cold. "Die, little demon."

This couldn't be her end. Not now. She'd just found Luca. She'd just found Nick. Hayley, Kyle, Monica, Eileen, Gabriel. Now was not the time to die.

Jules's eyes shot open. In a surprisingly swift move, she rolled. Taking Carson's legs out with her she knocked him to the ground while propelling herself to her feet. Fangs extended, blood dripping from everywhere. Rain washing her clean. She glared down at the large bloodied man. Smiling at the gashes and scratches she'd left on him. His missing ear and eyeball. Carson's remaining eye flared with hatred, but her fury was just as strong. It was her or him this time. This was the fight she couldn't afford to lose. He got back on his feet but didn't move toward her. "What's the matter, big bad wolf isn't bad enough to beat one tiny demon?"

From the corner of her eye, Jules saw a wolf from the circle begin to move toward her.

"I said leave her!" Carson shouted at the boy. "She's mine!"

"I belong to no one." She began to circle him like a predator stalking its prey.

"You'll die by my hand regardless," he growled, charging her.

She managed to flip his large body over her back then spun. As he attempted to get to his feet, she kicked out. Her foot connected with his face with a satisfying crunch. Carson collapsed back onto the sand.

"Not yet." Jules leaned down to finish him off when he pulled the silver knife out from behind his back and sunk it deep into her chest. The blade slipped between her ribs. If she had needed a beating heart to live, this blow would have killed her instantly. Her vision blurred as she fell to her knees. Carson stood and punched her hard in the face. She flew back, her head hitting the sand hard. Before she could move, Carson was again straddling her. His knees pinning her arms. He pulled the knife from her bloody chest and dropped it on the sand beside them. Leaning over her, he sneered down with a maniacal smile.

"You're a feisty one." He leered over her as she sputtered, coughing blood onto his face. "Fucked my Beta stupid, didn't you?" Jules followed his gaze through the crowd to Luca, thrashing against those holding him. Looking murderous and desperate at the same time. His name floated from her lips as Carson leaned back and brought his fist down onto her face with every ounce of momentum he had left.

Somewhere between consciousness and unconsciousness, she realized that he was right, she was going to die.

"That's right, little menace. Your time is up."

"Jules!" She heard Luca's desperate call but couldn't respond. Her long existence was coming to an end, and no one could stop it.

CHAPTER TWENTY-FIVE

R.I.P.

Demetria sat on the edge of Carson's bed. This was not her bed. This was not her room. Not her home. This place was a waystation of death and pain. She'd fled here when Micha died in hopes Carson had changed. That he'd see the truth laid before him. She'd run back to the past she'd run away from, in hopes of protecting her son's future. Allowing her past abuser to possess her, violate her, in hopes that both her son and she would be protected should the vampire try to find and murder them.

Instead of granting that protection, Carson slaughtered her son; sentencing carried out without a trial. Guilt considered proven to only one. Demetria relived the last moment she'd seen Micha alive as she did every time Carson had been inside her. Her husband had kissed her on the hair and told her he'd be back soon with their son. But he'd never returned. Her last moments with her son had been clouded under an argument. Carson had taken every last shred that was left of her and murdered that too. Ricky was dead. Micha was dead. And either she or Carson was going to join them now.

Demetria stood on determined legs. With a great howl her wolf form broke free from inside her human one. Out of the room, down the stairs, and through where the screen door should have been, she ran.

Her need for vengeance drove her through the edge of town toward the vampire's house. There was no justice strong enough to be served. But revenge, revenge she could have. Carson had gone out to the coast to meet the traitors in battle, but they would not be his doom.

As she neared the beach, she swerved around a cop car with flashing red lights. Carson had stationed wolves, pretending to be cops, or maybe they were cops, at every access road to the area. At least there were precautions in place to stop avoidable human casualties. Demetria didn't take any notice of anyone, werewolf or human alike.

Once she arrived, sand shifted under every paw fall as the sounds of growling and cheering grew louder. Still at a distance she returned to human form. It took only a few moments for Demetria's steady stride to place her in the midst of the jeering pack.

A few wolves turned toward the new arrival, but most remained transfixed on the small, red-haired, vampire pinned as Carson's large fists connected with her face repeatedly. The vampire was weak, no longer resisting. He could kill her, but instead, he continued to extend her pain.

Ben noticed Demetria. "This ends now." Her voice was barely audible but Ben nodded. He knew then, confirming once again who'd murdered her child. Silently, he and the big attractive Den member parted the sea of bystanders so Demetria had a clear path to the Alpha.

Carson's back was too her, he lifted his shoulders out of a hunch, pointed his face upward, and howled; a wolf's cry of victory. Others followed their Alpha's lead, a great roar penetrating the sounds of the stormy sea.

Demetria's gaze fell on something else. The essence of power harmlessly lying beside Carson's right knee. The large silver knife. The one Carson kept by his bedside. The one weapon that held the power to kill if only it was wielded.

Using the chorus of victory howls as a distraction Demetria approached, lifting the blade off the sand. She acted faster than anyone could react.

In the space of a small breath, the curved blade plunged into Carson's back, right between his shoulder blades. He roared in agony, attempting to dislodge his attacker but

Demetria's grip on the knife was firm. She wrenched the blade free and placed it across his neck.

Carson froze and sniffed the rain thick air. "Demetria? Why?"

"I know what you did," she snarled, digging the blade into his flesh enough to cause a thin necklace of blood to form. She leaned down close to his ear. "And now you will die for it."

Carson began to shake, the silver beginning to enter his blood stream from the wound on his back. "The boy?" he choked out as he weakened.

Demetria ignored his words, not caring what came out of the murderer's mouth. "But you didn't know. You are too blind to see..."

"Whore," he sputtered and made to reach behind him in a feeble attempt to dislodge her. In response she shoved at the back of his head, forcing the blade to cut deeper into his throat.

"It's ironic really," Demetria crooned. "For one so obsessed with legacy to have murdered his own."

"What?" Carson forced out as his body began to give way to the poison. Silver poison eroding him from the inside, like it had done to her child.

"He was your son." Her tone was lethally calm. She lifted the knife from Carson's neck and he looked up, his eyes meeting hers. The surprise there confirming that he had understood her. Without another word she brought the knife down in a swift movement, plunging it into his chest, right into his barely beating heart. She left the blade lodged there, injecting silver straight into it, killing him instantly. She shoved the body sideways as it fell, keeping it from crushing the mostly dead vampire. Her son's death was not the vampire's fault. Carson's blood drenched body dropped to the sand with a thud.

Moments later, the beast was gone. Only the body of an unremarkable grey wolf remained. "Any who mourn him are fools," she spat. The wolves parted as she moved away from her vengeance. Abuser. Monster. Murderer. Dead.

With a pained howl, Demetria returned to her natural state; lost forever inside her grief and fur. She would finish her journey on this earth with four paws.

The rain stopped.

Luca broke away from the wolves who had been keeping him from Jules's side as they stared at their dead Alpha. The pack seemed stunned and confused.

"Jules," he shouted as he skidded to a stop next to where she lay on the sand. "Jules?" He knelt, cradling the top half of her limp body on his lap. She lay unmoving, not even a flutter of eyelids when he begged her to wake. The sand beneath them continued to drench with her blood.

"Wake up?" he said, brushing sand and blood off her face. "Please wake up." Tears started to well up in his eyes as he stared down at her unmoving, badly beaten, body.

Luca barely registered as Jules's twin brother dropped to the sand next to them. "She needs blood. Now," Nick said, placing a hand on her unmoving chest and looking up at Gabriel expectantly.

"We don't have any more." Gabriel's head hung low.

Luca stared at her, panicked. He knew she needed human blood; wolf blood would do nothing. He could do nothing to save her. He pressed his face to hers, willing her to wake regardless.

"Then we find some. There has to be a human around here somewhere," Nick snapped standing to his feet.

"I have blood."

All eyes turned toward the strong feminine voice that had spoken. Towards the two humans approaching them from the direction of Jules's house. Looking up with tear obstructed vision, Luca saw Monica and Tai. When they had arrived on the beach, he couldn't guess.

"She wouldn't want that, Monica," Gabriel told her, placing a hand on the young woman's shoulder, while staring down at

Jules.

"I don't care what she wants," Monica said, yanking her shoulder free. With only the slightest moment of apprehension, Monica bent over the dead wolf. Reaching down with trembling fingers, she pulled the large silver knife from the beast's chest with a sickening squelch. "That's... gross." She cringed but closed the distance between them while Tai retched behind her.

"Monica wait." Tai ran after her, but before anyone could interfere, she sliced her arm above the wrist. Crying out in pain, she dropped the knife, and held her shaking arm.

In the blink of an eye Nick was lunging for the bleeding human. Kyle tackled him to the sand and was able to restrain him with the help of Adam and Kip who'd been standing nearby. "Not again." Luca heard him say.

Gabriel, seemingly in complete control of himself, had wrapped his arms around his wife, who thrashed against him.

Despite the danger, Monica walked forward, blood dripping down her arm, and knelt in Nick's vacated spot by Jules's side.

Luca threw out his hand, grabbing Monica by the wrist. "Are you sure about this?"

"Not at all," Monica replied. "But she's worth the risk." Luca was stunned by Monica's show of courage as she leaned over Jules and let her blood trickle between Jules's lips.

"Drink, Jules," she pleaded quietly.

After a few moments of no response, Luca's heartbeat started to quicken. It couldn't be too late. He couldn't lose her now.

One moment, Jules's tongue peaked out from between her lips to lick the blood. The next, Monica's arm was clamped by Jules's hands. Her fangs sinking deep into Monica's flesh as she drank. Monica winced but didn't pull away.

Jules saw a familiar face, but it was different, the

perspective was off. The face more angular, the hair brighter, the iridescent silver eyes alluring. Ageless. She hadn't seen that face since she'd become a vampire. Her face, but not her face. This was her vampire face through the eyes of one that loved her. Jules heard Monica's vibrant laugh accompany her own musical one.

The image of Jules faded, and Ethan became the focus of Monica's next memory. "You can't have a crush on my best friend. It's creepy. Get over it!" Monica yelled at the beautiful, blue-eyed boy. Jules could feel the irritation Monica felt but also the love.

"I don't have a crush," he whimpered, a red flush betraying him. "And I'm not creepy."

Next Monica's blood led Jules to Tai and then her parents. There was so much love in this human's life. "We have to go back Tai," Monica pleaded.

"We can't. Jules said..." Tai began to protest.

"Jules is wrong!" Monica shouted. "You know we have to go back."

The look on Tai's face betrayed him. "Fine, but we stay out of the way. You can't rush into a super human battle!"

Monica jumped forward and kissed him on the cheek. "Fine, can we go please!"

Jules continued down this path, consuming the blood and memories of her most precious human friend. She couldn't stop. She didn't want to. She could feel her wounds healing as the opulent blood entered her body, saving her from the brink of a finite death. Somewhere far away, Jules gripped Monica's arm tighter.

And then she saw it. The face of the girl reflected in the mirror at her bathroom sink. Her soft brown skin was blotchy. Warm brown eyes red and puffy. She'd been crying, mourning. The loss of what, Jules wasn't sure.

"Jules stop, you're killing her," someone said softly. Someone Jules wanted to listen to. Her eyelids fluttered open, revealing the same face that had been reflected in the mirror only moments ago. Those same brown eyes were no longer puffy but clear, searching the face of the one who was killing her.

"Red eyes. Blood eyes. Red Jules," Monica commented, but she sounded strained like she was running out of breath.

Jules's eyes focused in on the face before her. It was Monica. She loved Monica. If she didn't stop, Monica would die. She had to stop.

Jules closed her eyes and forced all of her focus on removing her fangs from the source of the blood. Trembling and one by one she peeled her fingers off her friend's arm. Never before had she found the will to stop before a body was drained of every ounce of blood. But this human meant more than her addiction. With cracked lips, she smiled up at her friend. "Yes, they are red when I drink blood."

Jules had just consumed a great portion of her blood, nearly killed her, and Monica simply smiled back. Monica rocked on her knees. She was obviously feeling the effects of the vampire venom. Tai ran to her and caught her in his arms. He looked at Jules with panic in his eyes, but she smiled at him.

"She will be fine Tai. I promise," Jules said with a thankful sigh. "She's just a little high right now."

Tai nodded but still looked a bit uncertain as Monica moaned and curled her body around his. Jules saw him inspecting the wounds on Monica's arm. He took off his shirt and began to wrap it around the punctures and cut. The smell of fresh blood was deluded with her venom.

Jules was about to explain that the effects would wear off soon when Luca touched her lightly on the cheek, pulling her focus to him.

"Hey there," he whispered.

Moving into her field of vision was the tear-streaked face of the werewolf she loved. His warm strong arms cradled her gently. "Thought I lost you there for a minute."

"Nah," she replied. "I'm harder to kill than that," she joked through cracked lips and an equally broken voice.

"Yes, you are, my love." Luca lowered his face to hers and kissed her with a feather's touch.

"Ouch." She sucked in a deep breath.

"I'm sorry." He pulled back but still stared down at her.

Jules registered that she didn't know the fate of her friends and family. She had no idea who else made it through the battle. "Nick? Hayley? Gabriel?" Looking around desperately, she searched for them.

"Here," Gabriel's soft voice said. Jules saw him nearby, arms wrapped around Eileen.

"We're okay," Hayley said leaning over Luca's shoulder to look down at her. "We're all okay." Her hand came to rest on her not yet showing belly.

"I'm not!" Her brother's muffled voice shouted. Luca helped her sit up while she searched for him. Finding him face down in the sand under three big werewolves.

"Sorry, but not actually sorry, Jules's bro. We couldn't let you kill our badass human," Kyle quipped, climbing off the vampire and motioning for the others to do so as well. "Not our fault you're one, strong mother fucker."

"I'm a badass human," Monica proclaimed happily. Jules and a few others chuckled.

"So degrading." Nick spat sand out of his mouth as he stood. "Being taken down by a pack of dogs. Twice!" Nick's tone was light, and he was smiling as he brushed sand off his face and clothes.

"Drama queen," Jules mumbled more to herself than her twin. "Carson?" she asked, realizing the fight was really over. Even the wolves that had come with their Alpha were now standing docilely around them.

Luca indicated a direction. Her gaze followed his to the limp body of a smaller than the average werewolf.

"How? Who?"

"Demetria," he explained simply.

Jules swallowed but made no comment. Content that the woman who had lost her child and likely suffered untold horrors at Carson's hand had gotten the justice she more than deserved. The battle was over. The people she loved were safe. They were all safe.

Feeling a little steadier, Jules leaned off Luca taking her own weight. Turning her neck, she stretched up, brushing the side of his face with her fingers. For a moment, the only being in existence was him as their eyes locked on each other. As he bent toward her, all she felt were his warm lips on hers and his strong arms wrapping back around her.

"I love you," he said lips still brushing against hers as he spoke.

"I love you, too." She smiled. No one would try to stop them now. They could be together. No one would ever try to keep them apart again. Jules felt light in Luca's arms as he stood and lifted her off the sand. She leaned her head against his shoulder but winced when her cheek touched his skin.

"You okay?" he asked, seeming panicky.

"I'll heal soon," she assured him. "I'll be alright."

Luca slowly set Jules on her feet. She swayed too much for his comfort. He tucked the unsteady vampire protectively under his arm.

"Luca," Ben called as he approached them both tentatively, head bowed in a form of submission. "Carson's dead."

Luca cocked his head wondering why that needed to be stated verbally. Everyone could see the proof of it.

"You know what that means, don't you?" Ben seemed to be fishing for something.

Reality hit him like a speeding truck. He was never officially removed as this pack's Beta. Thus, according to werewolf protocol, he was Carson's successor. "I'm the Alpha."

"Kneel before your Alpha!" Ben shouted, throwing Luca's arm into the air.

One by one the wolves around him began to bend the knee or bow, depending on which form they currently existed in.

Kyle wolf-whistled as he and Hayley followed the rest of the pack.

Luca felt a great weight press against his shoulders. A sort of heaviness came with this responsibility. There was power but also the weight of the lives he held in his hands. Instead of settling into his new role he began to itch. It felt unnatural. He'd never wanted to be Alpha to a pack other than his father's. Taking the Beta position under Carson had been only for formality's sake.

Scanning the faces of a tiny portion of his new subjects made him want to run for the hills of his home in Canada and never look back. *However,* a plan began to formulate in his mind. He looked down at Jules, nodded to himself, and then searched the crowd.

"My first order as the Aboit pack's Alpha is this; this pack will no longer give in to prejudice and hate. These last weeks have taught me that, like any other species on this earth, all vampires cannot be judged by the actions of a few. Protect Aboit always, but do not condemn the innocent. We will never again cast judgment on an individual without proof of wrongdoing, solely based on who or what they are."

Luca paused to ensure that the pack members around him were offering submissive nods of understanding. "Spread that order to all."

Only once he was satisfied there would be complete compliance, did he continue. "Kyle Cooper. Stand." He bounced up from the center of the pack. "With me." Luca called, motioning to the spot next to him. Ben took a rather reluctant sidestep, allowing for Kyle's place. Kyle's body almost buzzed with excitement as he took the place indicated. "My Beta, and successor." Kyle dropped into a bow, but Luca reached out, lifting him back to standing. "Do you accept?"

"Duh?" Kyle said smiling.

"Hayley, come, join your husband," Luca instructed. Once she had joined them Luca turned towards the crowd once more.

"As my last act as Alpha. I step down." He squeezed Jules's side as she stiffened. "It's what I want," he assured, looking down at her. "You're the Alpha now." Luca bowed his head to the new Alpha and stepped back.

All eyes turned to Kyle. The wolves wore a mix of expressions on their faces. It was evident some didn't care about the change, but others looked downright frightened.

"Oh." Luca stood and stepped forward again. "And I name Hayley Reynolds-Cooper as the rightful Queen and Beta." Kyle beamed at his wife who narrowed her eyes at him. Luca heard several audible sighs of relief.

Kyle turned toward his new subordinates, a look of mischief and glee on his face. "Sit," Kyle commanded the few who were still in wolf form. He chuckled and jumped up and down when they obeyed. "Lay down." The wolves did as he asked, and he turned to grin widely at Luca.

Hayley rolled her eyes and started to yell. "Kyle Cooper you are an Alpha now, grow up and act like it!" They would do fine.

Luca chuckled. He'd left the pack in good hands.

Kyle was shaken to his core, but genuinely happy to accept the responsibility given to him. He understood Luca's choice. He had other priorities now. Kyle and Hayley had grown up in this pack. Aboit was their entire world. Luca had Jules to think about. His pack originated far from these shores.

"Kyle, they've suffered enough!" Hayley snapped from beside him, smacking his bare arm.

"Yes, jeez!" he said, dramatically rubbing the red mark that appeared on his stinging flesh. "All right, all right. I've been overruled. Take care of Carson's body, can't have it just lying there forever. Take it up to the burial grounds. He may have been a power-hungry wretch, but he was still a werewolf. Then you are dismissed. Spread Luca's decrees. See you all at the next full moon."

A few wolves started to move toward Carson's body.

"You really have to take this seriously. It's a big responsibility and…"

Kyle put a finger to Hayley's lips. "I know, honey, I know. I am," he assured her.

"There's one of yours over there by the rock cliff," Gabriel told Kyle.

"And another down by the water," Nick added with an ashamed grimace.

"You four, with me," he called to Adam, Kip and two others. "I'll be right back," Kyle said to Hayley. He placed a hand over hers, resting on her stomach, and kissed her on the hair. "The rest of you, go home to your families. Nurse your wounds and kiss your loved ones. This fight is over." The remaining wolves nodded their compliance and dispersed.

Kyle turned away from his wife, took a deep breath, and walked toward the fallen werewolves. He sighed deeply, not wanting to know who had lost their lives in this fight. However, it was his responsibility now. Luca had trusted him with it; he was not going to let anyone down.

Jules stepped out of her bedroom once the back door opened. Luca, soaked and sandy, came walking in from the beach. "Is the pack settled?"

"As settled as we can get them in one day. Kyle's first full moon gathering is going to be…" He paused, thinking while he pulled off dirty converse. "Interesting."

"Are you okay? Leaving the pack in his hands?" Jules approached Luca, wrapping her arms around his torso.

"I had the birthright to a pack's rule once. This one was never mine." Luca brushed her hair behind her ear. "Besides, he'll be fine." He rested his hands on the sides of her still healing neck. "He has Hayley."

"True." Without indication Luca slid his hands under Jules's backside, lifting her up to his level.

Jules let out a little shriek and then chuckled.

"Everyone gone home?" Luca asked.

"Well..."

"Except me. Everyone has gone home, except me," Nick said walking from where he'd made himself comfortable in the living room, to the kitchen where they'd stashed a resupply of blood sent by Nick's bar owner friend Cleo.

"Yeah," Jules began looking back at Luca. "About that..."

Luca laughed. "He's your brother. I'll get used to him."

Jules could hear Nick heating up yet another mug of blood in her microwave. Luca bent his neck enough to touch his lips to Jules's neck, right under her ear.

"You have a blood problem," she said as Nick reappeared. Luca laughed into her skin.

"Yes, I have a blood problem. And a sex problem. And commitment issues..."

"Well," Jules was responding to her brother but looking deep into the eyes of the werewolf who held her. "I think I'm about to have a sex problem." Luca growled and pulled her closer to him. Rotating her head sideways as he kissed down her neck to the top of her breasts. "So you should probably take your blood to-go for the moment."

"Oh hell no." With less than a moment's hesitation Nick was gone, out the front door and probably three streets over.

Together, Jules and Luca laughed while he carried her back into the bedroom. The French doors were open, the sound of rain and waves crashing into the room rhythmically. Luca set Jules down slowly. Pulling off his socks and jeans, kicking them aside, he dropped to his knees in front of her. Peeling his wet shirt off, it joined the rest of his clothes. Luca reached out, pulling her towards him by cupping the back of her thighs. He kissed her on her stomach over her shirt and then lifted the fabric so his lips could touch her skin. She pulled it off, revealing yet another of her lacey bras and multiple healing stab wounds. Her hands found his hair, tugging on it slightly, she pulled his gaze up to her. His chin nestled between her breasts. "Hi." She smiled down at him.

"Hi." He smiled back and then pulled his gaze away. "Tell

me if anything hurts," he said as he slid the loose sweatpants and panties down her body, tossing them aside. "Or if you aren't comfortable with something." His fingers trailed up the back of her thighs and over her ass, while she pulled her bra over her head.

Moving back a little, she leaned down and placed her lips on his. "I will," she whispered into his opening mouth. Their tongues wound together while his fingers glided between her legs from the back, to caress her center. She moaned. He growled. Already wet and aching for him she deepened the kiss, craving every connection with him she could get.

Luca backed out of the kiss, pulled Jules's body toward him, and sucked a hard nipple into his mouth. Jules moaned at the sensation, leaning heavily into him. Head dropping back. Trembling legs barely kept her standing as he slid one finger inside her, while another continued to massage her just where she craved. When a second finger joined the first inside, her body erupted into orgasm. Trembling, her knees buckled.

Catching her with his other arm he smiled a gratified grin. "You good, Baby?" he asked her as he lifted her off her feet and onto the bed.

She mumbled an incoherent response as she felt all contact evaporate. Moments later he was back, hovering over her, fully nude and ready. Opening her legs, she beckoned him up the bed. Instead of verbal consent she reached down and placed his large shaft at her entrance herself. He groaned as she slid him inside. Stroke by stroke he went deeper.

There was no thought of the past. No thought of pain. Or feelings of lacking control. With Luca she knew he didn't want power, he didn't need to dominate her to find release. He wanted pleasure with her. He wanted to be one with her desires and needs. And she found she wanted the same for him. They fit in a way no other had.

One of Luca's hands glided up her body, pinched her nipple, and then found her hand. Intertwining their fingers above her head. Her other reached up to push against her headboard so she could meet him in every thrust.

Together they found release. Together they panted, boneless, and satiated.

Luca dropped down on the bed next to Jules. She turned on her side, watching the waves from the open doors. Unwilling to let her go just yet he reached forward, pulling her hips back into him. Arms wrapped tightly around her, he moaned contently in her ear. Her fingers intertwined his as she tucked his arm close to her heart.

After a few quiet moments she spoke. Softly, tentatively, she said, "Nick and I were talking earlier, and we started reminiscing about England. Would you consider..."

"You want to leave Aboit?" He cut her off, propping himself up on his elbow to gaze down at her.

"Not right this second, and only if you'd want to," she told him, twisting to look at him. The look in her eyes told him she wanted to go, but, that she'd be willing to compromise if he wanted to stay.

"But we're safe now. There's no threat. Why leave?"

She reached up and brushed his lips with her fingers. "I said only if you wanted to. And I don't mean forever. But with everything that's happened," she paused and sighed, "I just feel like maybe I need a change."

He considered this. "Kyle does have the pack now, and Hayley, and the new baby on its way. But I can't leave until after his first full moon. Maybe two."

"No. I know that. It's just that Gabriel and Eileen have already decided they are leaving. They are leaving the country for a while, because people still think he's the Phantom. Tai's finishing up his general education classes. So, he and Monica will be going off to some prestigious university soon. And if I'm being honest, Nick will get restless at some point. I don't know how long he'll be willing to hang around here." There was desperation in her tone and expression.

Silence stretched between them for a few moments as they studied each other.

Luca smiled. "With every end, there is also a beginning." His life with the Aboit pack might be coming to a close, but his life with Jules, the love of it, was just beginning.

Luca watched Jules laying there, looking up at him with a gaze full of love. His eyes drifted to her mouth and he leaned in. She lifted her head ever so slightly to meet him in a kiss.

It was always as if time stopped. Nothing in the world mattered to him but her. They were two bodies with one heartbeat. Hers would never beat again, and right now his beat fast enough for them both. Where they were didn't matter. How they chose to fill their hours didn't matter. That they were completely and inescapably in love was the only thing that mattered now.

EPILOGUE

Several Months After That

The stunning specimen of a human woman beneath him screamed, out of fear or pleasure, was no concern of his. Regardless, he pounded his cock into her and drained blood from her carotid artery simultaneously. The high of blood and sex mixed with the thrill of the kill, as her life drained before his eyes.

A meek knock on the ornate wooden door pounded in his ears. Who dared disturb him without an invitation?

Ignoring the attempt at an intrusion he continued his rhythm. His body coiling tighter with every ounce of her blood and thrust of his hips. As the screaming weakened his pace quickened. Perfecting the practice over the last thousand years had this act down to a flawless euphoria. He drank the last drop in tandem with the release that crashed over him.

He gripped her red hair in his hand and twisted her neck, to ensure there would be no rising from the dead. Her nose was too big anyway. The knock came again. A little harder this time. Scowling, he rose, unstrapped the dead woman from her restraints, and pulled a velvet robe over his sleek, chiseled, body.

Walking to his ornate drink cart, he poured himself a glass of a perfect vintage bourbon. Vintage to the world. Vintage to him was nonexistent. "Yes," he called to the knocker as he sat in one of his ridged armchairs. Giving the person on the other side of the door permission to enter but not necessarily permission to leave.

"My Lord," said a loyal werewolf slave named Jameson as he opened the door tentatively. Werewolves generally didn't enter his place of rest, unless it was to clean his fireplace or make his bed.

"My Lord, she is back..."

"Who?" He was annoyed.

"The one you instructed us to watch for," Jameson added. He could almost feel his dead heart beating with excitement.

"Are you sure it's her?" he asked, rising to stand threateningly over the man before him.

"Yes, My Lord. I saw Lady Juliana myself." The wolf trembled.

"Thank you, Jameson." He placed his hands on either side of the wolf's neck. "Does anyone else know of this?"

"No... no, My Lord." Jameson shook slightly.

"Good." He kissed the man's forehead and then twisted harshly. The body slumped to the ground, his neck broken.

"Damn," he said aloud to himself as he walked over to his desk and slid open a drawer. He'd forgotten to ask Jameson if he had acquired the scotch that he'd been sent out for. "Oh well," he said, pulling out the gun he kept stashed there for moments like these. Aiming at the back of Jameson's head, he squeezed the trigger. The wound smoked where the silver bullet penetrated his brain.

"Juliana Bristow. Come back home, have you?" He turned the image of the girl who got away over in his mind. Her soft auburn hair and delicate frame had eluded him long enough. The dead woman on his bed was a pour substitute. They all were. "You *will* be mine once more," Hector declared and then walked from the room to find someone to dispose of the bodies.

www.ingramcontent.com/pod-product-compliance
Lightning Source LLC
Chambersburg PA
CBHW030551260626
47157CB00006B/2276